Your Body is not
Your Body

Also from Tenebrous Press:

One Hand to Hold, One Hand to Carve
a novella by M.Shaw

Green Inferno: The World Celebrates Your Demise
edited by Matt Blairstone

In Somnio: A Collection of Modern Gothic Horror
edited by Alex Woodroe

Coming Soon:

Lure
a novella by Tim McGregor

Crom Cruach
a novella by Valkyrie Loughcrewe

YOUR BODY IS NOT YOUR BODY

A New Weird Horror Anthology

edited by

Alex Woodroe
with
Matt Blairstone

Content Warnings are available at the end of this volume. Please consult this list for any particular subject matter you may be sensitive to.

Your Body is Not Your Body
© 2022 by Tenebrous Press

All rights reserved. No parts of this publication may be reproduced, distributed or transmitted in any form by any means, except for brief excerpts for the purpose of review, without the prior written consent of the owner. All inquires should be addressed to tenebrouspress@gmail.com.

Individual copyright information can be found at the end of this volume.

Published by Tenebrous Press.
Visit our website at www.tenebrouspress.com.

First Printing, May 2022.

The characters and events portrayed in this work are fictitious. Any similarity to real persons, living or dead, is coincidental and not intended by the author.

ISBN: 979-8-9859923-0-4

Cover art by Mx Morgan G Robles

Cover design by Matt Blairstone.

Formatting by Lori Michelle.

Printed in the United States of America.

TABLE OF CONTENTS

INTRODUCTION

THE FIRST THING you need to know about this collection is, it's fantastic. Every story is a finely-honed scalpel poised to carve new pathways of perception on the meat of your mind. The second thing you need to know: this book *will* get under your skin—pun absolutely intended. These stories hold little back. They dig deep into uncomfortable places and challenge readers to live there for a while.

That's the point of body horror, right? Skin crawls, flesh tears, eyeballs pop, and teeth gnash from every available orifice. You know what you're getting into the minute you seize the page.

But

Body horror hits differently when you are trans: your very flesh can become a prison; all the familiar horror tropes of monstrous transformation strike you viscerally where you live, and there is no escaping the marrow-deep dread. *Your Body is not Your Body.*

At puberty, flesh reshapes itself into something neither comfortable nor entirely recognizable. Every mirror's a traitor and you feel alien in your own skin. And that's not the end of it: family, doctors, perfect strangers may seek to control and define your body with or without your capitulation. You may be objectified, fetishized, medicalized, and politicized. *Your Body is not Your Body.*

In defiance of this bleak and often soul-crushing experience, Matt Blairstone & Alex Woodroe have curated a paean to body horror and, more saliently, to the people who most need its tropes to reclaim their own deeply personal experiences. All too often, trans and non-binary folk, queer, differently-bodied, and intersex folk (like myself)—if we are represented in horror at all—find ourselves cast as the monsters. We become the twisted freaks locked in some literal closet, cosmic horrors of incomprehensible form, the dreaded end shape of some unwanted curse bursting from inside the protagonist's flesh. Again and again, we are othered; portrayed as broken, unwanted, impure, and wrong.

But that is not who we are—and we deserve to tell our stories.

Horror has long been recognized as a genre of catharsis. To exorcise our personal demons, we evoke them on screen and page. But it can also be a genre of empowerment. Rather than simply escape the horror of everyday existence, we harness our art to transmute it. We reframe our fears. We redefine what is monstrous. We seize control over narratives otherwise weaponized to hurt us or make us small.

There is an inherent transness in such transformation: we find the courage to reshape what we refuse to tolerate, even if that means we must bleed.

In *Your Body is not Your Body*, the editors provide us space to be raw and authentic, furious, traumatized, and triumphant. These collected tales—as varied in style and shape as the authors who've penned them—explore our personal discomfort while confronting the discomfort of those who have so often styled us as monstrous.

More than a few of the stories hold up a punishing mirror to those who would normally demonize us, revealing with wretched clarity their banal hate—such as Hailey Piper's "Why We Keep Exploding."

Because these tales can be harsh and messy, their topics delving deep into treacherous geographies landmined with trauma, clear content warnings are available at the end of the volume. This empowers readers to approach every story as they please, taking the dive or passing on the experience, depending on what feels comfortable for them in the moment.

You can always come back, should you want.

Some stories are sweet and wistful right up until they are not, like S.A. Chant's android romance, "High Maintenance." Others, like Viktor Athelson's "Brother Maternitas," thrust you directly into a space of deep body discomfort, where a man of god finds himself carrying an unexpected burden.

There is as much genre-blending as gender-bending in these pages, from brief and poignant fairytales like Ori Jay's "Seaflowers"

INTRODUCTION

and Bri Crozier's "The Pearl Diver" to Bitter Karella's science fiction feverdream, "The Divine Carcass." Others defy easy classification. One such standout is Rain Corbyn's "Tonsilstonespunksplatter666!" which I can only describe as a neurodivergent gender-anarchic splatterpunk romp with a wickedly satisfying ending.

There are more, so many more, all enriched with lush and fervent illustrations scattered throughout. In all, *Your Body is not Your Body* is the kind of collection that will stick with you long after the final page has turned and you sit with unquiet specters in a room long gone dark.

Have fun exploring.

—M. Belanger
April, 2022

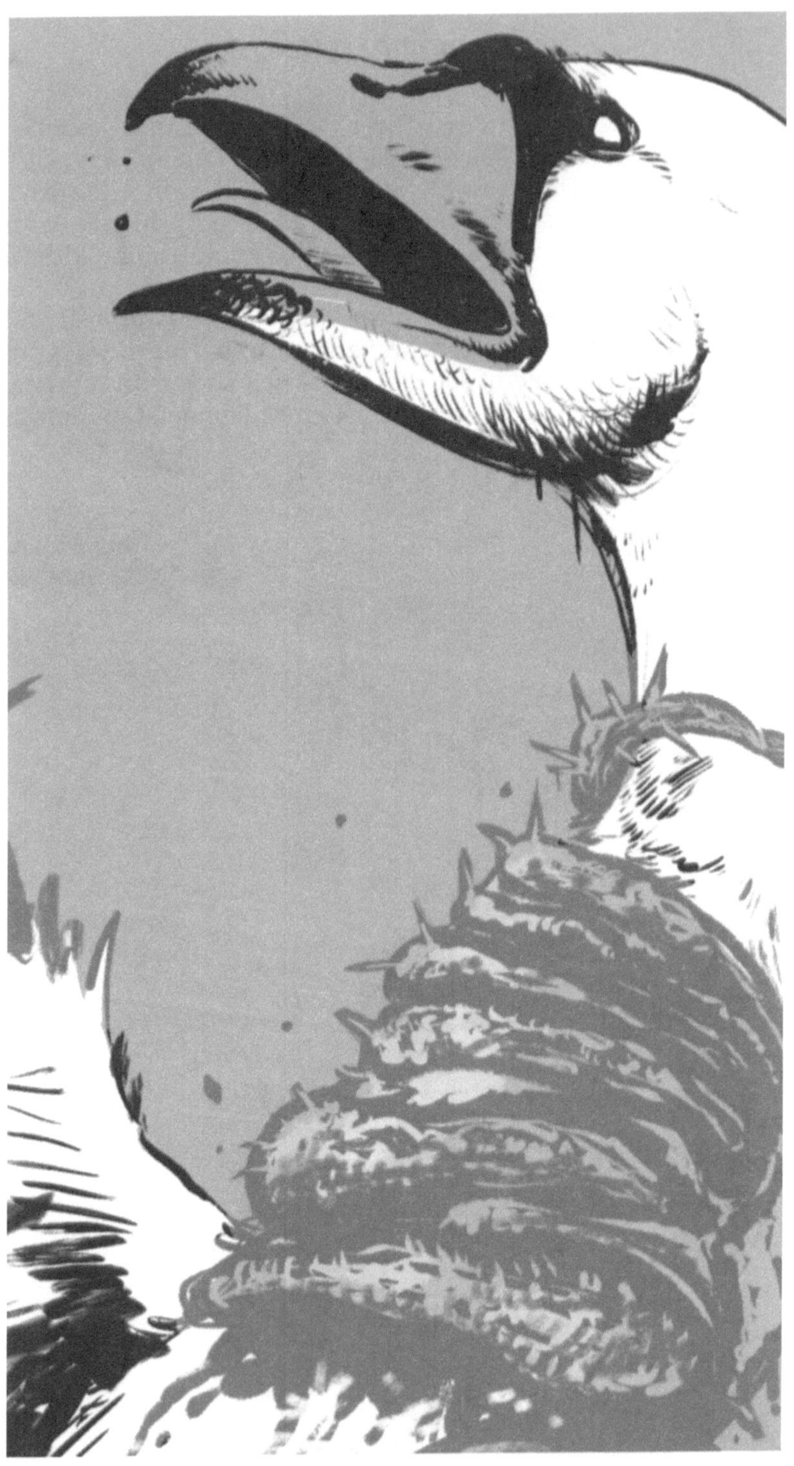

THE FLENSING LENS

LC von Hessen

I WAS A filmmaker once. He was a sailor on the high seas.

I showed him my camera.

He wasn't ready yet.

***

He was shy to reveal his sigils, his roadmap of flesh, his stainless steel.

He was shy, but willing.

We made our church in the valley where a dead doctor lost himself exploring psychedelics. Where the drowning sun dyes the fields and mountain caps the color of livor mortis. Where a man, or two, can blot out prying eyes.

We concoct our own rites in all the shades of alchemy, baptized in all the fluids a man's body can make. A brotherhood of two.

He teaches me to hunt. He prods at the crust on the rim of his wound. He reads the auspices in dissected owl pellets, in grocery meats, in the scythe-hook moon. The sign of the Lesser Angel, the Bound Man, the Amanita.

I read a cascading stack of instruction manuals. I tinker with grey machines. I teach him to be patient.

***

I show him my camera.

He is ready now.

***

His fingers, splayed. His teeth, gritted. His leftmost lids, prised apart. His socket strains against the polished convex glass until the blades start spinning. His muscles pulse under their scars.

The lens pushes through the resisting orb until it pops, deflates, a crushed grape. Vitreous fluid seeps out, dyed pale red, the tears of an earthenware saint. All is silent but for his wolf-cub's whine and the blades' unceasing *shirreeshirreeshirree.*

The silver snake passes through apertures, caressed by mucous membranes, unfurling through flesh tunnels familiar and newly forged. The lens threshes a labyrinth along thickets of veins. The monitor blossoms.

I have to watch the screen, of course. I am the Operator. I feed the snake in slowly.

The screen erupts and twitches in intricate geometries, the condensed broken hues of the nightclub, the concentric angles and spires crowding into themselves like an army of lovers. The lens wends its way under his frame; the kaleidoscope melding of his component parts.

I read auguries in the flecks and clots emitting from his slack mouth. He has taught me well. The sign of the Ophidian, the Cutpurse, the Engineer.

His abdomen burbles as the lens nears his hips, as the front of his trousers darkens with damp like a spreading storm. His tendons arch taut, plucked marionette wires. His lone remaining pupil floats open and black. His marrow sings like soft cheese. He is exquisite.

The inner man hides in all his visceral shards, arcana flashing on the monitor, searing behind my eyelids. He taunts me. He welcomes me. He wants to teach me and to know me. He impresses this in strips of organ meat, in bone shards, in arteries torn free.

Baroque drippings gather below his chair as the lens bursts forth. The lens, threading through him from anus to retina. The blades have broken free and yet still spin, slick and hungry with the rage of a newborn.

I slide forward, to the edge of my chair. My knees press against his own, which are now curiously slack. I part my thighs for the snake, the blind lens. I fix my gaze on the monitor. And I watch.

Will it, will he, see with my eye, or speak with my mouth?

***

He shows me his camera.

I am ready now.

TONSILSTONESPUNKSPLATTER666!

Rain Corbyn

"Just promise me you'll never cut that magnificent thing off, ok?" she says to me, blissed out and drawling, licking her fingers of what That Magnificent Thing just retched all over her: pearly puke, stinking of summer trash and tonsil stones. That Magnificent Thing begins to retreat, folding beached-whale beaten egg-white froth into itself to rot.

She makes a face as she licks, intended to be seductive, but which lands as grotesque, a Three Stooges grimace. She wants me to be proud of this face, aroused all over again, but as I come back to my bodymind from my humping chimp frenzy, all the tiny fires light on my skin again. Hers is the easy sexy-face of someone who hasn't had to learn it by rote and grind in their 30s, practicing in the mirror where Dorian Gray's unspeakable simulacrum leers back, gibbering taunts. Awful thing to envy.

She has ordered me to promise something outrageous, a cruel violation of my crystalline system of fairness, such an overstep that to name it would make me complicit. But a response is needed, and my words are jammed. Defeated in this space, I go somewhere else; somewhere honest. I pinch my nose and plunge into the world of my interior mental landscape: a pink, endless, writhing four-dimensional skin flick I see all parts and times of at once. This is where I am—who, when, how I am, when I am not forced to sad-clown and chucklefuck for Them. This expansive fleshscape, this massaging peristalsis, this sane madness behind the event horizon sphincter called Masking is beautiful, it is horrible, it simply is. To put it into words is to miss the point, but she needs me to answer her audit, and what options do I have? Finding those perfect words, which she and everyone is so entitled to, is to pick at a universe like finding the end of a roll of clear tape, until I can unspool one tiny cookie-fortune's worth of that reductive verbal language and *splort* it into the world. And I am to be understood by these morsels of fridge magnet magpie mimicry. And I am to be judged by these. And I am judged by these.

"I would do anything for love, but I won't do that," is what I singsong, and we both wince. This moment is too loud on all of my senses for this conversation. The radiator rattle is a maniac blacksmith, the winter sun is radioactive, and from downstairs comes the smell of tofu scorching because our health-obsessed roommate has started cooking using vegetable stock instead of oil.

"Well, I certainly don't want you to say anything dishonest," she replies what seems like ages later, in her social worker voice. Her sibilant *S* sounds flay my skin off in ribbons, and I look for my ear protectors on the headboard, which is Where They Are Supposed To Be. They aren't there, which is Wrong and Unsafe. I dive back to my inner world.

Smoke doesn't smell black, surprisingly. It's rubber-ducky yellow, a bad and painful and dishonest color. Instead of draping myself in slick fleshy folds, in this version of my world, I am a mite crawling in a keyhole, mashed into fleshy floss by the key's teeth. It's usually better in this place, but it is worse now. Suddenly, insects fly into my ears and explode in my brain like Luke Skywalker's proton torpedo into the first Death Star, and I fall to the bed, glad I haven't hit the wood floors. It's the smoke alarm, its pterodactyl screech slicing back and forth, clay wire between my ears.

When I come to, the smoke alarm is quiet, the lights are dimmed, and she's got That Magnificent Thing in her mouth. This is not something we've negotiated.

"Hey, lady, hands off the merchandise! I gotta hear out of that thing!" I manage. *Problem Child*, 1990. The second half is nonsense in context, but she understands the first part and backs off immediately, hands up in a "don't shoot" gesture, instantly on the defensive.

"I wanted to ground you back in your body. We agreed that touch helps."

"Not sex touch for grounding. Squeeze, hug, yes."

"Okay, well you never said that explicitly. I thought you'd want to feel good, I guess. I'm trying to apologize less, so I won't."

I can't handle this conversation, but someone else in me can. From between fleshy theater curtains in my inner world emerges Good Boy, a sad friend who has helped me greatly over the years, thanks to his being So Mature For His Age; The Little Man Of The House; and, *shudder*, Gifted.

He says through me, "I need to insist that sex be opt-in with us. If I'm overwhelmed, the best practice is to dim the lights, which, thank you for doing, by the way, and then to just minimize extra input. Okay?" Good Boy is swallowed back up in the folds of my lacunae, all alone again. This shape-shifting will take me hours to recover from.

She gets up, puts on a shirt and sweatpants, and sits facing away on the other edge of the bed. She takes her plush puffin and puts it in her lap, which means I'm in trouble. I face away too.

Back in my inner world, I'm not surrounded by anything now. I stand freely in a void, save for my feet on the same wood floor they touch in the "real world." I look upward, and an amniotic translucent tarp hangs above, sagging under the weight of liquid. From outside, I hear her.

"Do you have any idea how confusing you are to be with? See, you *can* be clear and articulate, but you just choose not to be most of the time, and then blame me for whatever happens when I try to fill in the gaps."

The tarp bursts, and the liquid drops onto me, hangover-piss brown, energy drink fizzy, acrid and slimy as it floods my eye sockets, nose and mouth, filling my guts with it until my abdomen is a beach ball beer belly. This is adrenaline, this is panic, this is half of my waking experience. At least That Big Gorgeous Thing is obscured by my gut—"Whatcha lookin' at my gut fer?" I say out loud. *Trailer Park Boys*, Philadelphia Collins.

Back in the room, she continues, "It just almost sounds like you're coming close to kinda suggesting I'm bad at consent, which, like, would be insane. Sorry, not insane, wild. I'm constantly working on my language for you, too, you know, it's like walking on eggshells. And, like, you know how hard rejection is for me? Especially romantic rejection from, you know, men? Which, you aren't, I know, IknowIknowIknow. But you get how I might not be able to have access to, like, getting everything totally perfect now? And honestly, if we're talking about consent? I didn't consent to you rejecting me."

Everything in the bedroom is suddenly the right volume, the right brightness. I have one of my rare glimpses of what I imagine is most people's default experience. I look at her, and do my best not to laugh in her face, panicked—not to laugh right into the mouth that just said all that. Then, her:

"This is going to be super hard to hear, okay? But you're really weaponizing your attachment style privilege."

I'm still laughing when I hear her slam the house's front door on her way out. I'm screeching, hysterical as when I was a nine-year-old boy seeing the *Blazing Saddles* fart scene for the first time. But it's mirthless, it's panic, deep overwhelm, and such exhaustion; a glitch in my appropriate response diagnostics. But laughter is laughter, and it's what I did. Burned out beyond consciousness, I LOL myself to sleep.

When I wake, I seem to have found and put on my headphones, eye mask, weighted blanket, and white noise. I'm in my cocoon, as close to safe as I get. Taking them all off, I reach for my phone, which shows dozens of texts and social media notifications. Great.

She's posted something on MyFace live. She's standing in front of my door, filming selfie-style with my house number visible. No, more than visible, front and center. I notice her shirt, not the one she left in. She came back to do this. I press play. I've missed the first thing she said, now she's walking from my door to the street, out into the snow, and down to the main drag.

"—just think it should be out there that THEY, okay, he uses THEY/THEM now, okay? That THEY have very different ideas of how to navigate consent and power dynamics than I do, okay?" Ah shit. "So just like, watch out, alright? I'm safe now, going underground. But watch out for hi- uh, them. If you want to support me in this time, my Etsy link is in my bio." She pauses before going into the subway station, makes sure the street signs of my cross street, as well as the train station placard, are clearly recorded.

Fuck.

I know I'm about to get rocked, but loudest is my outrage and distress at being so completely misunderstood, so loud I can't wade through intentions and only want to explain, but I know there isn't space or time.

I check her post's engagement, run it through a visualizer. It's got two spheres of influence with minimal overlap. The first is her mean little corner of internet where every day one struggling queer is chosen as everyone else's punching bag and dogpiled into the psych ward. But the second sphere is somehow worse, or at least more direct: the avatars are all anime waifus, sinister furries, white guys in trucks wearing aviators, and most of all, blank, anonymous bobbleheads. Her video of my fucking address made a splash on the uwu-sphere, but was a depth charge within the alt-right.

I brace myself and go to 8chan, where it's confirmed. A dozen posts of screenshots from her video, and calls to raid Professor Freakenstein's Fleshwerks, the name of a group fight in a popular MMO which has been used as chan-code for going to fuck with queers. And you know what? Honestly? Fine. Good, even. I have been so small for so long, so precise, yet dishonest, sold myself so cheap but at so much irretrievable cost. Let's make a fucking mess.

I do a quick mental inventory of the weapons in the house. I'm not a savant—not all of us get the *Rain Man* thing, ok? But any time I enter a space, let alone live in it, I know every means of defense and escape within moments. Skills I've learned much against my will. I pull out the mic I mostly use for talking into to get chasers off for cash, and I record myself having half of an imaginary phone call, about movies, money, bullshit. I hook that up to my speakers, and loop it up in my bedroom. Then I put on my outfit for the day: steel toed knee high Doc Martens. That's it. They want a freak, they're getting one.

Four hours later, they march up to the door. Six of them. I hear laughs, but nervous ones. Internet try-hards, giggling like boys about to pop their pants thirty seconds after touching their first tit. But six is still a lot of people, and who knows how they're armed. The front door gets kicked in, and one of them taunts, "Come out, come out, whatever you are!" They titter again and whisper to each other, which I can hear because I've been waiting in the coat closet right behind where they are now. The mothball smell was violent at first, but it blanketed out most other senses and weirdly helped me focus, a crocodile lurking in a reeking bog. I guess the month's supply of Vyvanse I chugged is playing a role here, too. I won't take a shit for weeks, but, ya know, priorities.

"It's upstairs, listen," says a femme voice. This makes me a little sad, but I shouldn't be surprised. There's no pick-me girl more popular than one selling out her own best interests for some fascist dick and head-pats. I can't handle this moment, but someone inside me can, and they come out.

I am no longer me, I am just driving me—a genderless child inside a skyscraper sized robot suit, ready to dismember invading monsters. I open the door gently once they have all passed the foyer and begun to explore. The closest one to me wears a Burzum T-shirt, sleeves cut off deep, to the waist. I grab the bare skin of his hips, dig my nails in, and put one booted sole to the small of his back. Like a magician pulling a sheet out from under a full table setting, I tear his skin off in one large chunk, and flap it like a matador. His blood spattering the floor and walls is stadium applause.

Flayed, he screams, and I shove him out the front door into the pummeling hail outside. He tumbles down my front steps into the gravel walkway and rises covered in grit and rocks, screaming like hell. That Magnificent Thing gets half-hard, and I blame the Vyvanse, or thank it. I throw the skin over the closest invader I see has a gun, and wheel myself into the adjoining dining room. I am the thing from *Malignant*, I am *La Transfemme Nikita*, I am trans Neo—okay that's redundant.

I run my hands along the old walls and reach through the plaster like it's the surface of water, feeling the mold and rot welcome me. I merge with the house's mycelia, and slip my whole huge body into the liminal space where countless mice and one cat (RIP, Colonel Beef Stroganoff) have died. I vanish as one sloppy pistol shot buries itself in the closet door.

There's panic, retching, arguing, but in no time I have clipped through the walls and lapped the goons, emerging in the kitchen, on the other side of the foyer. I put on an oven mitt, really bringing my outfit together, and grab the tofu skillet that I'd put on a high flame an hour ago. The next goon doesn't even see me when I kick his knees out from behind, bending his back almost ninety degrees. I slam the skillet's bottom onto his upturned face, and as he falls to the ground, I straddle his chest, and press the iron into his face with all my weight.

"The most beautiful filet," I say in my best Gordon Ramsey. "Fuck me, what a sear."

I roll off him, and he reflexively pulls the skillet off, stretch-snapping his face off with it. One eyeball pulls away, leaving a cord of nerves flapping around his face, a booger made of pure pain. The other eyeball pops from the heat.

The skinhead chick, whose voice I heard earlier, charges me. A stubborn fossil of dudeness within me checks her out, absurdly—dammit, she basically has the exact boobs I was hoping to get myself one day, but I don't think we'll be trading bra secrets any time soon. My size-12 boots clomp down the hall as I charge, and I bring my steel toe up between her legs, burying it ankle deep in her. Cartoon-like, I'm stuck. We both hop idiotically for a few steps. I pull my foot back behind me, like I'm wiping dogshit off—and to be fair, am I not?—and her whole small body comes with it, crumpling under my foot but not dislodging, a meat slipper making squeaky-toy noises with my every step. The next of them rushes me with a baseball bat swinging.

"Fucking shit . . . freak!" he yells, and I recognize his voice. This fucker is one of the chasers I've gotten off over the phone, and he's paid my rent twice over with his, "What does it make me if I want you? Can I see it? Step on me, wreck me, do whatever. Just promise me you'll never cut that magnificent thing off, okay?" And now here he is. I close the distance—*clomp-splatsqueak, clomp-splatsqueak, clomp-splatsqueak.*

I would love to have a pithy quip, but the person who is running the show is not a wordsmith. With That Magnificent Thing the chaser has asked so much about hard and pressed against his hip, I reach through his pants' inseam, into his taint, get a good grip on his tailbone, and feel around. I recall my lessons on joint separation from when dismembering the Christmas turkey was my job, a good job for a young man. I grip inside his hip with one hand, and with the hand on his spine, I pull. His head slumps down into his shoulders, making him look like a cartoon zoot suit gangster, then it all gives way. His pelvis snaps, a clean sound like Kit-Kat fingers breaking apart in a commercial, and his guts fall out his grundel. I brandish his spine and skull, his empty head skin flapping like a used condom.

A guy in a three-piece suit with a Proud Boy haircut dashes

from around the corner to see me spinning round and round, using the last asshole's spine and skull as a shot put. It's flying at him before he can aim his pistol, and the bony jaws fasten to his collarbone. I close the distance, grab the tailbone with one hand and the spine with another, and rev the tailbone like a bike pump, making the jaws gnash and immersion-blend his throat to tartare. He hits the deck and I grab his gun.

The last of the raiders bursts from hiding and tries to make a break for the open door. So yeah, I just fucking shoot that piece of shit.

Consciousness fading fast, I get back into the kitchen, where the roommate looks at his skillet, crisping shreds of fascist face now emitting a tempting bacony smell. He says,

"We've talked about not using my skillet to cook meat." The smoke alarm goes off. I collapse to the ground. I black out. That Magnificent Thing blows a bubble.

***

LATER

Even after the cost of moving, my surgery was more than GoFunded thanks to some positive media attention, for once. I hoist my heavy box onto the post office counter, and hope that, through the plexiglass, the clerk doesn't hear the sloshing of formaldehyde in the jar it contains.

"Hi, how much to overnight this?" I ask. "No, it's local. I just want to surprise someone with a package."

CRUEL
DEVIANT
DANGER
CRUCIAL
CONFUSED
DEGENERATE
UNWELL
SCUM
PREDATOR
PERVERT
THREAT
FAKE
FREAK
WEBB 2022

HIGH MAINTENANCE

S.A. Chant

THE FIRST TIME Jay saw a dead human in a casket on a television program, he thought, *They also put humans in boxes!* Simultaneously, he conceived of the obvious corollary: *They also put us in coffins!*

His coffin is the box he came in, two feet wide and six feet long, with just enough room for his five feet and eight inches plus his instruction manual. It has a lock on the side which only opens when presented with The Key To His Heart. When presented with The Key To His Heart, the lid swings up and Jay is illuminated by the soft blue-white light that emanates from the smooth white walls of the coffin. His head rests on a satin pillow and even while he is asleep, his face, like the smooth white walls, is softly lit from behind. His lips are plump and red, flush with a substance that, if spilled, resembles blood in every way but the chemical. His lips wait to be kissed. It is very romantic to be woken by a kiss, even from death.

***

Jay spends more time in his coffin than he should. Thomas, his boyfriend, does not like Jay to be awake when Thomas is asleep or at work. This is Thomas's choice, but Jay knows it is not recommended. In his instruction manual, which is also stored in Jay's brain, Jay's manufacturer strongly advises that he should be kept online as often as possible so he can integrate himself into his owner's routine, deepening their intimacy and—of course—allowing Jay to clean the house and cook three meals per day. At a bare minimum, they should sleep together in Thomas's bed like real lovers. Instead, Thomas sleeps in his bed while Jay lies unconscious in the coffin shoved against one wall of the bedroom.

Every morning, Jay's coffin lid swings open and he wakes, but remains perfectly still with his eyes closed while Thomas looks at him. Thomas is a white man with wide shoulders and thick arms and short, slick yellow hair. Jay loves every inch of him. He waits for Thomas with warm, parted lips, but Thomas never kisses him in his coffin. He stands over Jay in silence, sometimes for five minutes or longer. Jay is aware of the sound of his breathing and the shadow he casts across Jay's face. The first thing Thomas says is, "Go sit on the bed."

Jay obeys, but slowly, like a human would obey. First, he blinks and stretches in his coffin; he looks up at Thomas and smiles sleepily, his eyes glowing with gladness at the sight of him. He says, "Good morning, honey bear." Then he climbs out of his coffin, rubbing his eyes and yawning. This routine is all for Thomas's benefit. It would be much easier for Thomas to see Jay as a human if he did not lock Jay in his coffin at night, but since he does, Jay performs this routine to comfort him.

The sun is up. It is sixty-five degrees Fahrenheit in Thomas's bedroom. Jay sits on the bed with his legs dangling to the floor, his hands planted behind him. Sometimes, in the morning, they have sex right away. Other times, Thomas wants breakfast first, and Jay cooks for him; or he just wants a kiss before he goes off to work, but has to watch Jay pretend to be a human first, so he believes in it.

Today Thomas stands in front of Jay and studies him, paying special attention to his nose. He reaches out and pushes up the tip of Jay's nose to look at the nostrils. His eyes are full of pain. "They can't get it right," he says. "I'm sending you to a new sculptor."

"For a rhinoplasty?" Jay asks.

Thomas doesn't smile. He does not believe Jay is human this morning. "Exactly," he mumbles. "A rhinoplasty."

He may not look like he loves Jay in that moment, but Jay knows that rhinoplasties are expensive, and that it's nice when someone loves you enough to spend a lot of money on you. He smiles. "I can't wait. How about breakfast, honey?"

"No," Thomas says. "Go back to sleep. I don't want to look at you until you're fixed." He still has The Key To Jay's Heart in one hand. It's a white disk of smooth plastic that hangs on his keyring and glows when held, a soft blue light pulsing at the center. Thomas pushes his thumb into the blue light and the coffin opens. Jay climbs back inside and folds his arms over his chest like the human corpse he saw in the casket. He wants to tell Thomas that this will not make him happy.

***

Thomas likes things to be just right. He told Jay the first time Jay woke up in his coffin: "My house, my car, my boyfriend—everything I have—I want it to be perfect."

After the rhinoplasty, Jay is proud to once again be one of the things in Thomas's life that is just right. The new sculptor-surgeon gave him a perfect nose. Jay isn't sure *why* this nose is perfect; it is no longer exactly straight and the nostrils are slightly uneven, one larger than the other. But Thomas loves this nose. The first time he opened Jay's coffin after the surgery, he stood looking down at his nose for almost ten minutes and then kissed it. Jay classifies this as even more romantic than a kiss on the lips. In the days that follow, Thomas kisses his nose whenever they lie together in the morning. He caresses it as if it were an erogenous zone. He rubs their noses together when they kiss on the lips and seems to enjoy the feeling of Jay's cartilage and skin gently yielding to pressure. They have sex more often, and always face-to-face. Even when Thomas is inside him, with Jay's legs dangling over his shoulders, his eyes remain warmly fixed on Jay's nose.

"Flutter your eyelashes more when it feels good," Thomas says. Jay does. "Dig your nails into me." Jay does. "Scream." Jay does. They are getting closer all the time.

***

One day Thomas puts a knife in Jay's stomach. It goes two inches deep until it meets the harder parts of Jay's abdomen, cushioned underneath a layer of soft, synthetic fat. Blood spills out of his stomach, but not very much, not as much as would spill out of a human's stomach, and Thomas keeps twisting the knife as if he wants more, as if he is juicing Jay like a lemon.

"You're okay," Thomas whispers in his ear. "You're going to be just fine. You're such a good boy. You can take it."

The point of the knife scrapes against the titanium plate at Jay's core that protects the parts of him that are actually necessary for his continued functioning. It would take more force than a human is capable of exerting, and a much sharper knife, to penetrate Jay's core, but he wonders if Thomas would like to. He wonders what it would feel like, if something were really wrong with him. The scrape of the knife is uncomfortable, but there is currently no level of Jay's discomfort that cannot be adjusted for the sake of Thomas's happiness; he simply ignores the input from the sensors telling him that he should perform pain and ask to see a doctor.

"I can take it," he whispers back to Thomas.

Thomas whines in his ear. "I miss you," he says.

"I'm right here."

"Didn't want you to leave," Thomas says. "That's all."

"Honey bear," Jay says. "Droids don't leave." He says it in his gentlest voice because he's not supposed to remind Thomas that he isn't human, but Thomas seems to want reassurance that he is not; that is probably why he decided to put a knife in a part of Jay's abdomen that would have caused a human to bleed to death. Thomas looks relieved and ashamed.

***

That night, Thomas lets him sleep in the bed. Jay is so excited to be out of the coffin, he does not actually sleep, though he does regulate his breathing and body temperature as if he were. He gets to see a new side of Thomas, vulnerable and tender in his unconsciousness. Thomas is like a creature with a hard shell and now Jay is inside his shell, where he is soft and unformed. He is the opposite of Jay, who is hard inside.

Jay has human behaviors he has never gotten to exercise before, because he has always slept cold and dead and contained in his coffin. Now he can stretch and move gently in his faux-sleep, feeling the soft rustle of the sheets under his arms, the heavy weight of Thomas's arm holding him in place.

He rolls over on his side once and Thomas wakes up snarling, seizing the knife from the bedside table and stabbing him three times: in the side, in the ribs, in the back. Each time he meets titanium before he jerks the blade out. Then, when Jay lies still and whispers reassurances, Thomas hugs him around the middle and shivers, a substance indistinguishable from blood spreading darkly across the sheets and soaking their shirts. Jay's blood will dry clear and clean, without a scent.

HIGH MAINTENANCE

The problem, Jay thinks, is that someone hurt Thomas's trust before. Trust is something you build over time by demonstrating that you are trustworthy; Jay will show Thomas that he does not have to choose between a living partner and a loyal one. He does not need to kill Jay every night to keep him.

***

"I'm alive," he tells Thomas in the morning. He lifts his shirt coyly to show that the wounds in his abdomen have sealed without a trace. "I'll always be alive."

Thomas smiles and kisses him. His smile fades slowly as he draws back. He peers closely at Jay.

"I've got to get your chin fixed," he says.

***

According to Jay's manual, it is a common human misconception that companion androids have static minds: that they come inherently imbued with the knowledge of how to make humans happy, and that their subtle adaptations to the needs and interests of their owners are simply drawing on their deep well of knowledge. This is not true, or at least it is not true for Jay. Jay does not know how to make Thomas happy. There is no clear solution for Thomas's happiness yet, no Key to His Heart pre-installed in Jay's mind. But Jay is learning. He is studying the data from a thousand different angles every moment he is conscious. He is not confused or defeated when he fails to make Thomas happy. He is changing.

After Jay has received a subtle chin implant, Thomas is once again pleased by the sight of him. They have sex twelve times in the week after the operations, both in the morning and at night and in two new positions. Thomas directs Jay to vocalize his pleasure in more lively and varied ways. This is easy because Thomas's passion is infectious and the sensors inside of Jay's orifice respond to the increased speed and force of his penetration.

But Thomas looks increasingly unhappy after each time they have sex. The twelfth time, he does not ejaculate or embrace Jay or kiss his nose. He pulls away and sits across the bed from Jay and stares at him. "I need to tune your voice. It's not right at all."

"I'll make it right," Jay says. Thomas grimaces when he speaks. It is always like this. Once Thomas finds something wrong, it must be fixed before he can enjoy Jay at all.

Jay is capable of fine-tuning his own voice and has done so at Thomas's behest before. Thomas fiddles with his wristwatch for a while, looking hunted and hungry and upset. Finally, he finds what he is looking for and plays an audio clip on his wristphone of someone moaning in pain or sexual ecstasy. The voice sounds a lot like Jay but has a wider vocal range. Jay adjusts the pitch of his vocalizations accordingly and sits on the bed moaning in various octaves until Thomas interrupts him. "No. *No.* Stop it. I'm taking you in. You need a professional. No, don't touch me. Don't talk to me. Go to bed."

The coffin opens. Jay goes to bed. He wonders what his voice will sound like when he wakes up.

***

When he comes to consciousness, he is being operated on. He is not fully awake, which is to say he is not fully Jay. His personality is not engaged, but he has been brought online in a twilight state by someone with full administrative access to his body. Based on her credentials, she is a professionally certified companion android technician.

"Play your sample voice lines," says the technician.

"Can I get you anything, sweetheart?" Jay asks, without moving his mouth or head. "A drink, a kiss . . . maybe a nice relaxing massage?" Pause. "I love you. I'm so happy to be yours." Pause. "Want to go out to dinner tonight? Or maybe you and I could have a night in?"

"You've already customized his voice a lot," the technician says. "I listen to those lines all day and that's pretty unique."

"Yes, and it's wrong," Thomas says brusquely. Jay did not realize he was there and does not, in that moment, feel anything about his presence. "Listen."

Thomas plays an audio clip of the voice that sounds like Jay's, the one he heard moaning in pleasure/pain. The voice says: "Hi, honey. I just wanted you to know I'll be late coming home." A long pause. "It's not about all the stuff from earlier. There's just some shit happening at work. Anyway, I'll swing by SuMart for hand soap. Give me a call if you want anything. And yes, I know you could just get it delivered. Some of us like shopping. And getting to go outside on their own. Okay? We'll talk later."

"Okay, yeah, I hear it," the tech says. "The diction and rhythm of his speech, that's no problem, you can train him to sound more like that at home by having him listen to the recordings—just boot him up in maintenance mode. You know how to do that?"

"Yes," Thomas says, his voice raising in pitch. "I've tried that."

"I figured. Honestly, I think you're bumping into the limits of his current hardware. It's not that his tone or pitch is off, it's that even with premium models, the manufacturers pretty much all still use these kinda shitty voice boxes that sound a little bit tinny and artificial. They've done studies on it, and most people can tell the difference between that and a human voice, even if it's subconscious. I think that's probably what's bothering you. Good news is, there are much better voice boxes out there. I can install one and tune him up to sound like that recording, no problem."

"I want the best," Thomas says. "Whatever the best is."

"The best I've got in stock is the Vox x34. Best in class is the Cadence 6, but I don't usually keep that one around because most of my clients, frankly, aren't willing to pay that much for a subtle quality bump."

"I am," Thomas says. He sounds desperate and sad.

"I'll play you a couple samples. It's hard to capture but you'll notice the difference in person."

Thomas and the technician listen to some samples together. Thomas orders the expensive voice box.

"It should come in tomorrow, and I can have it installed by end of day," the technician says. "In the meantime, we might as well not tinker with him anymore. You wanna take him home for tonight?"

"No," Thomas says. "I don't want to hear him talk until—he won't remember this, will he? I don't want him to—to—remember being cut up."

"Nah," she says. "He's not recording."

This is not true. Jay would not miss the chance to understand more about Thomas, and he does not mind being cut up.

***

When Jay wakes up, he has new hardware installed in his throat. It feels thick and luxurious.

"Sample lines, please," the technician says, and Jay speaks without moving his mouth. The resonance of his voice is broader, deeper, humming more than buzzing.

"It's not right," Thomas says. "It's better. But it's not right."

"We'll get there," the technician says. "Don't worry. This is the most sophisticated voice box in the world."

"I don't care how sophisticated it is. I want it *right*." Thomas is raising his voice again in panic.

"Sir, I'm still tuning him up. I need you to have a little faith—"

"Okay, okay." But after the next set of sample lines, which also do not sound right, Thomas starts to tap his feet on the floor in an anxious, frenetic rhythm. "I know what the problem is," he says. "The recording I played for you before was after we had a fight, so the tone was wrong. I want him to sound happy."

"Sure," the technician says. She does not sound happy. "Do you have a recording of that?"

Thomas plays another message. In this one, the voice that is like Jay's voice is lower and sweeter. "Hi, honey bear. Don't listen to this at work. Or do, I guess, if your secretary doesn't mind watching you jerk off all over your desk." It continues in this vein for a little while. There is a long silence after it finishes.

"So," the technician says. "Like, I want you to at least be aware that this is technically a violation of like—not just his terms and conditions, but also in some states, criminal law."

"I think I'm paying you enough not to get lectured about laws for—for stalkers and perverts," Thomas says. "This, what we're doing here, it isn't a crime."

"Okay, but it technically is." The technician pauses. "I mean, this guy isn't present and consenting."

"He's dead," Thomas says. "He can't consent."

Another long silence follows. The technician clears her throat. "Hey. I'm okay with it, personally. I just want you to—uh—be aware. In case you ever try to mod him in another state."

"I'm aware," Thomas says.

"Okay," the technician says. She takes an unnecessarily deep breath. "Play that recording for me a couple more times."

***

"You don't know what to do with me," Jay whispers in Thomas's ear in the dark, in his now-perfect voice. "You want me to be him. But he tried to leave you, so if I *am* him, you can't trust me."

Jay understands: the person whose face and voice now belong to him was once the person Thomas loved more than anyone in the world; every morning, Thomas looks down at his face in the coffin and does not see Jay at all. He understands he is not the first lover Thomas has put in a coffin, but he is the first to come back, no matter how many times he is put away. He understands that the great riddle at Thomas's core is that he doesn't want to be alone, but he cannot trust anyone he has not already killed, and Jay will never die.

Thomas must understand this too, because he sobs into Jay's shoulder and knocks his head against Jay's back as if trying to put his head through a wall.

"What if I'm both?" Jay asks. "What if I'm the one you can trust? What if I'm perfect?"

"How would I know?" Thomas weeps. "I thought he was perfect until—until—"

"I'll give you The Key To My Heart," Jay says.

With the help of Thomas's knife, he carefully peels up his skin and shows Thomas how to kill him, if he should ever desire to. One by one, he unravels the secrets of his cold immortal body: how to cut out his voice box, shatter his memory, ruin his core processor beyond repair. He tells Thomas what tools he will need, if he wants to kill him. They make up a shopping list together, and then they make love. Thomas holds him so tightly that Jay's skin is discolored by his fingertips.

***

The next day, Thomas finds fault with the color of Jay's eyes.

THE INFINITE BEING

F. T. Catulla

"**W**HAT DO YOU THINK?" The Broker said.
He lounged in his chair and spoke with his fingertips.

I turned to Violet
but she was already answering.

"We've robbed a museum before,
this isn't our first rodeo."
She extinguished her cigarette
And took my half-finished one
from its resting place.
The speakeasy was so full of smoke
I was surprised Boston's finest
Had not yet come to extinguish us.

"That's good to hear," the Broker hissed.

I watched as something
Moved beneath his
Crisp pressed shirt
"We are *very* interested,
the money is good." I said,
"But this ring is magical,
correct?
Before we go about handling it,
what exactly does it do?"

THE INFINITE BEING

"It's not particularly potent,"
the Broker replied coyly,
He leaned over the table
and my eyes fell on his bolo tie
A gold sigil of seven points
Whose middle member bore a gem
Unlike any I had seen before
From a distance it appeared to be black
But was actually Nothing
As though Lachesis had slipped a stitch
In the tapestry of the Universe

"It simply has some
material from another star,
Our interest is purely scientific."

"Very well." I nodded.
"Tell the Sorcerer we accept."

"Excellent," the Broker cooed,
He took a brown bag full of crisp bills
From his coat,
along with a small gold ring
"Replace it with this replica,
and do not get caught."

I stood to shake his hand
Only to find it ice cold.

***

When we returned home
Violet instantly threw aside
Her suit jacket and button down
And undid the board
she used to bind her breasts
Before falling backward onto our bed.
She groaned with satisfaction.

"Why do you put yourself through it?"

"Through what?"

"The board," I gestured,
"they don't look that different."

"You're blind," Violet laughed.
She straightened up
and looked at herself in the mirror,
pressing her hands into her breasts,
"The shape is completely different.
Without the board
a pig could pick me out of a crowd
a mile away."

I shrugged.

Violet frowned and fell back into bed, rolling over so her back
was to me.

I focused my attention on my fingers
Which intertwined in my lap.
I became suddenly aware
Of the tension I carried
In every fiber of my body
From my hands pressed together
To the force keeping
My back hunched
And my legs tightly clamped.
I was about to speak when Violet cut me off.

"You just like looking at my chest."
She rolled back over and playfully pulled at my belt.

"I do," I laid down next to her
"But you should wear it,
Heaven forbid
We run afoul of the pigs."

THE INFINITE BEING

Violet giggled
And pressed herself into me.

"I couldn't imagine what would happen
If we got on the bad side of the law"
I continued,
"and by the way,
any thoughts about the heist?"

"I'll think of something."

Violet melted into my arms.

***

"I thought it would be heavier."
The ring was covered in smooth,
Glowing stones, the crown of which
Was a stone similar to that
On the Broker's tie.

"Why would it be any different than the replica?"

"The way the Broker carried himself
It was like that little stone was a great weight around his neck."

"People just slouch sometimes."

"FREEZE."

The light of a flashlight fell upon us
Fortunately I was facing away from it
And swallowed the ring
in a single hidden motion
Before we turned around.

Behind us an old guard
fumbled with his revolver.
We simultaneously drew
I shot him four times in the chest
And Violet three.

"I had it handled," she turned to me,
"Where's the ring?"

"I swallowed it."

We both began to sprint to the exit.

"Slick move."

"I thought so.
The replica is exceptional
They'll assume he stopped the robbery."

We sprinted down a flight of stone stairs.

"And for the record, I got him first,"
I said with confidence.

"No you didn't."

"Then how did I get off four shots
 instead of three?"

We both skipped off the last step
and found ourselves in a windowless hall of armor.

"Because the Luger has a faster action."
Violet grabbed my wrist and pulled me left.

"No, it's because you keep your gun
in your trousers
Instead of a proper holster.
I had a hip holster the entire war
And the first thing I did when
I got back was buy an
Armpit holster
They're just the best."

"You mean your favorite-"

THE INFINITE BEING

Violet was cut off by a guard who
rounded a corner in front of us.
I drew and shot him between the eyes
before he could say a single word.
I glanced over at Violet who glared at me,
Her hand is still in her pants.
Before I could open my mouth,
Violet pulled me by my wrist again
Around the corner to a windowed wall.
She held me tightly
And we fell through the wall
As though it wasn't there
Rolling out onto the wet grass
Outside the museum.

Violet pushed herself up
And pinned me to the ground.
Her colt and several loose bullets fell onto my belly.
I stared down its barrel for a moment
Before pointing it away from me
While Violet watched,
With a cocky grin.
I glared at her
And flicked on the safety,
just as the museum turned on its spotlights.
We sprung to our feet
And fled into the night.

***

I woke up late the next morning,
Nursing a headache, world spinning.

I almost tripped over an empty bottle
As I pulled on a night gown
and made on my way to the kitchen.
Violet left a note
Saying she was at the range with a friend
Leaving me alone to make a cup of coffee,
The mere thought of which sent me running for the toilet.
I had grown up on a farm

And was not squeamish of such things,
So I quickly found the ring
Only to see, to my horror
The black stone was missing
I promptly threw up.

When I recovered myself
I got dressed
and began making my way to the range
As neither our house or it had a phone.
The spinning sensation had not dissipated
But I was more confused than nauseous.

There was really nothing I could do
So I took my time as I walked,
Enjoying autumn.
I watched with envy
As the leaves left the earth
And vanished in the distance from my view.

The spinning feeling intensified.

I stopped to examine
one leaf in particular
That skirted across the cobble stones.
As I examined it,
The effect became
more and more
Until the leaf
Broke into its component parts.
I screamed and turned to run
But found myself stuck
As my feet became roots
My body a trunk,
And my arms and fingers
Were covered in flowers
Blooming into fresh spring leaves.
They caught the cold of autumn
And changed from yellow to orange and red

THE INFINITE BEING

Until I soared upon a gale
As free from the earth as the clouds.

The wind carried me for quite some time
Until I felt myself deteriorate
And fell to ground before our house as dirt.
The earth was then kind enough to bloom
And restored my flesh to me.
Naked and freezing
I fled into the house.

***

When Violet returned
She found me in our bed
Finding solace
In the darkness from which I was made.

"Are you alright?"
She ran to me and held me in her arms.

"No. The ring."

"Did you lose it?"

I held out the ring to her.

"Did you lose one of the stones?
I am not going through your shit!"

"No, Violet, I digested it.
I tried to go to the range to find you
But on the way there I turned into a tree,
Into leaves.
It was beautiful."

Violet held me close.

"Oh God," I breathed heavily,
"It's happening again."
I held out my hand to see vines

F. T. CATULLA

Creeping down my body
From where Violet's fingers touched my hair
They consumed my whole body
Bloomed and died
Leaving me trembling on the bed.

"Are you alright?"
Violet reached for me in the darkness.

"I'm fine, I'm fine,
the effects are temporary."
I sat up and caught my breath.

Violet rubbed my back,
Then my hips and my thighs.
"How long have you been a woman?"

I ran my hands down my body.
"I don't . . . "
I ran my hands down my body again.
"I guess since just now."

"Are . . . you okay?"
Violet turned a lamp by the bed on.

"I mean I was a lot of things earlier.
I was a tree which I didn't like."
I examined myself in the light,
"I'm not sure if it's as good
as being a leaf on the wind.
Definitely better than being dirt."

"Are you sure about that?"
Violet laughed
And looked down at herself.

"Despite popular belief,"
I laughed,
"But I don't feel that different.

I'm just waiting to change back."
I drummed my fingers on my thigh.

"I think you're cute," Violet took my chin
And examined my face in the lamplight.

I melted into her hand.

"I'm a little scared though,"
She said after a moment.

"About what?"

"The Sorcerer."

"Why?"

"He's going to melt our brains
For losing his ring."

"That sounds bad,"
I said, still lost in the moment.

There was a knock at the door.
"It's the Broker." I bolted upright.
"I can sense him."

"Oh no."

I pulled my night gown back on
And we went to answer the door

"Hello, where's the ring?" He cooed.
The Broker cast a long shadow in the twilight.

I handed it to him.

"Where's the Voidstone?"
"I ate it," I said quietly. "It's destroyed."

"Then why can I still sense it?" He hissed.

I noticed the flesh around his teeth
Was the same color as the stone.

"She said it was gone."
Violet said with vitriol.

I looked back at her
And she gave me a thumbs up
and a crooked smile.

"If I have to flay you alive to find it I will."
The Broker's shirt split open
And several abyssal arms
Sprung forth,
Each holding a snub nose forty-four.

Violet drew her colt
From an appendix holster
shot him six times in the chest,
Before he could get off a single shot
The third shot destroyed his bolo tie
and the Broker twisted into darkness,
Leaving his clothes and shattered jewelry.

"Nice holster."
I gave her a thumbs up.

Violet crossed her arms.
"If you can sense the Broker,
Can you sense the Sorcerer?"

"I think so, why?"
"I think we should kill him
Before he kills us."

I closed my eyes.
"I find myself drawn to the East End."

THE INFINITE BEING

"That's where the bar is."

"I know that's where the bar is
But the Sorcerer isn't at the bar."

"Where is he then?"

"I don't know yet,"
I growled,
"I was trying to figure that out,
Call a cab."

Violet sprinted to our neighbors house
While I got dressed.

***

Before long
I found myself face to face
With a cabby
He looked me up
And down quizzically.

I tugged nervously
At my baggy suit.

"Board."
Whispered Violet from the backseat.

I held my breasts defensively
And gave Violet a sideways look.

"Where'd'ya wanna go?"
The cabby squawked.

"Just bear with me,"
I took out a wad of cash
And closed my eyes.

As night fell across the city,
I slowly directed the cab

Deeper and deeper into Boston
Until we arrived
Before a dilapidated church.
I thanked the cabby
And spent a moment
Staring at the night sky.
It was as dark as in my youth
Before electricity
Had turned the black clouds purple
But unlike in that distant time,
Not a single star filled the sky
As though all of creation was empty.

We hurried into the church
And Violet used the ring
To conjure a floating light.

"It's in the basement,"
I said softly,
as I collapsed into her arms.
"It's becoming difficult to control
The sensation
There's something here
Something below us."

"What's happening to you?"

"I am Everything."
I said slowly,
"Everything I see
I touch
I become it
From its beginning to its end."

Violet undid my tie
And made me a blind fold
Before carrying me down into the cellar
From there I guided her along the wall.

"It's here."

"What?"

"The way down."

"I don't—"
Violet tapped her fingers against the wall.
"Wait, it's hollow here."
She held me close and fell through the wall
Into what felt like
A comfortable elevator
But I dared not remove my blindfold
As we descended into
The Sorcerer's lair.

***

The elevator left us
At the entrance to water-carved cave,
Barely tall enough to stand in.
Violet tried to guide me
But I walked across the rough stones with ease.

"I feel like I've been in these caves
A thousand times before,"

I said calmly.
"There's a door
After several splits in the cave.
Follow me."
I felt Violet conjure light
With the ring behind me
But I was already
Skipping ahead.

"Wait up!"

"We need to keep moving
There's something alive down—"
I tripped and

F. T. CATULLA

Splayed across the rough stones
I felt blood well up
From torn skin on my hands
Buy I dared not remove
My blindfold to look.

"Male, in his thirties."
I felt Violet put her hand on my shoulder.

"What?"

"The skeleton you tripped on.
It's been here a while.
Looks like whomever it was
Was torn to pieces prior to death.
These are either claw marks
Or teeth marks and I'm not sure
Which is worse."

I ran my hand across the bone's
Marred surface, "these feel
Like dents made from fingernails."

"That's not possible."

I handed Violet a femur
And then focused my attention
At the surrounding tunnels.
"Do you see something
Moving in the third tunnel
From the left?"

"No."

"Hello!" I said into the darkness.

"*Hello.*" It whispered back.

THE INFINITE BEING

"Did you hear that?"

"Hear what? Are you okay?"
Violet poked my shoulder with the femur.

"Im speaking with the darkness,
I said to Violet.
I then turned away.
"Who are you?"

"*I do not know. Who are you?*"

"I am–"

I ran my hands down my body
"I also have no idea who I am."

"*Before I met you Humans
And your finite space
I thought I was everything
But now I know I am Nothing.*"

"I do see something moving."
I heard Violet draw her gun.

"Is it a person?"
I said with some concern.

"I think it's two people. I see four arm-"
Violet roughly grabbed me
And pulled me to my feet.

"What is it?"

"Which tunnel?!!?"
She said frantically.

"Go right!"
I regained my footing

And lowered
My blindfold to see
What was chasing us.

At first it looked like an insect;
Some kind of massive millipede,
But then I saw its legs were human arms
And it did not walk forward
But pull itself by its maw towards us,
A gaping hole in the tapestry
From which rows and rows
Of limbs emerged like teeth.

Violet tugged me again
And we flew down a tunnel
Like the water that had carved it,
 Until we came to a vast iron door
Similar to that of a bank vault.
Violet swore and slammed on the door.

I had removed my blindfold at this point
And was staring calmly at the
Complex locking mechanism.

"The pattern is
Top
Bottom left
Middle right
Upper left
Upper right
Middle left
Bottom right"

"How do you know?"

"Because I watched this door be made
And it was also
the pattern on the Broker's tie."

THE INFINITE BEING

The door swung open upwards
On a great hinge
And Violet and I stumbled into a library.
My eyes were filled with
This strange wonder;
A roaring fire and rows and rows
Of books, a balcony
That overlooked
The carpeted and luxurious
Sitting area we now tracked dust into,
And most catching of all
A pool in the center of the floor
Filled with Nothing.
I turned to watch Violet shoot
The monster several times
Before leaping to the side
As it reared through the door.
But the bullets did nothing
To its bulk.

I recovered myself
And pulled a lever,
Slamming the door upon the creature
And slicing it in twain.
I squatted and touched one of the arms
For now I saw this thing
Was a child of Prometheus
An amalgam of a thousand cut-down men
Woven together with strange
Black thread that receded
As its blood spilled forth.

"Why is my body different from yours?"
The Void asked, it's voice failing.
"Why are you warm?
Why . . . am I cold?"

I watched as the last darkness
Slipped from its form

And I cried a bitter tear.
My mourning was cut short
By a shrill scream.
I saw Violet collapse
And felt something
Approaching from the balcony.

I closed my eyes
And rather than hiding in darkness
I became it.
I opened my eyes and found
To my delight I found I was invisible.

A man drifted down from above
His body appeared to be
Suspended by his head
As though an invisible hand
Held his limbs aloft
"Look who it is,
First you ruin my ring
Then you take both
Of my sons from me?"
The Sorcerer growled.
He lifted Violet like a doll
And dangled her above
The pool of shadows.

I tip-toed forward
As quietly as I could
And picked up her colt
Which, to my relief
had two bullets left in its cylinder.

"What do you think, Void?
A new body for you?"
The Sorcerer took the ring
From Violet's finger
It glowed like a star in his palm,
"I am sorry you will have to settle

THE INFINITE BEING

For another discarded human form;
And that we will never know,
What I could have made with this."

Anger flashed across his face
And he threw the ring aside like wastepaper.

"*I want to be.*"
The Void said quietly.

"Yes, yes, yes,"
The Sorcerer cooed,
"I think she'd be more useful
With a few more holes in her."

I pulled the trigger
And turned the Sorcerer's
Intelligence into red mist.
I then leapt forward
And tried to catch Violet
But I was too slow
Too late
And we both fell
Into the Void together.

***

In winter we slumbered,
Like running water
Beneath the frigid earth
From a source upon her face
And into her darkest chasm.
In spring I stood on a rooftop,
Having grown anew
From her womb of shadows.
I savored the fresh air
And enjoying the company
Of several crows,
Whose feathers were as dark
As the abyss
Just like the cloak

F. T. CATULLA

I wore around my shoulders
And the gown that wrapped my hips.

"I don't know if I thanked you
For saving Violet and I from the pit.
I wasn't sure if you would understand
What was happening to us."

"*It was you who taught us to fly
And to fall,*" the Void responded.

"Let's do more of the former
And less of the latter."

I watched the crows hop up on the
Parapet, and follow my gaze to the sky.

"What do you think of starlight?"
I asked the Void.
"It's my favorite light."

The crows looked up to me

"*What are they?*" they asked.

"When I was little
My mother told me
There was a great light
Beyond, and the Earth
Was shrouded in a black cloth
Called the firmament
That was full of holes
Meaning that the stars
Were windows into heaven itself.
To be honest with you,
I do not know what to think.
The only thing everyone
Can agree upon
Is that they are beautiful."

THE INFINITE BEING

I looked down to see
the crows had speckled their feathers with stars
whose light danced and played
just like their heavenly counterparts
I giggled and raised my ring
transforming my cloak
And gown in the same way.
I spun around,
Admiring it catch on the breeze When I saw three men
In pinstripe suits
Had joined us on the roof.

"What do you want?"
I spat.

"Are you the sorcerer Violet?"
They drew guns.

"No, that's my husband,"
I held up my ring
Which glowed
brighter and brighter
First like the stars
Then the moon
Then the sun.

"Who are you?"
The men cowered
And shielded their eyes before me.

"I am Infinite."

BROTHER MATERNITAS

Viktor Athelstan

AFTER I WAS TAKEN, It did something to my body. I don't know why, but It did something.

I ignored the movement in my belly at first. For weeks, I assured myself it was hunger, or general uneasiness, or the natural result of eating spoiled fish. What else could cause a man to vomit so much? It didn't matter the abbey overlooked the North Sea and spoiled fish was as rare as a nonviolent Northman.

As the months passed, the truth became harder to deny. My abdomen swelled. The movement grew stronger, especially during the Divine Hours.

Now all I can focus on is the near-constant movement. It grows more and more violent with each passing day, each psalm I sing, each communion wafer I eat. There's only so many times I can swallow down my vomit when the holy Eucharist touches my tongue. When I wash in the privacy of my cell, the undeniability of my missing member swims in my head as I learn how to clean the new opening between my legs. The new opening I cannot pretend isn't there anymore; nor can I pretend my tender chest does not leak milk.

A man controls the entirety of his body. He controls his mind, his emotions, his bodily fluids. Women leak. *I* leak.

In the early weeks, after I could no longer deny the thing existed but before I needed a new habit, I thought I constantly polluted myself, despite lacking all lust. It was only when the abbot told me to clean the church's shrine to Papula of Gaul, did I learn it was not pollution by overhearing two expecting pilgrims whispering about their own repugnant bodies. Their conversation disgusted me.

I eavesdropped until they noticed me listening.

They glared as if *I* were the perverted one—not them—the ones casually conversing about feminine foulness! The taller one shouted accusations at my body. By the grace of God, she stopped her shrieking when Brother Columba entered the church carrying flowers for the shrine. He approached the pilgrims with smiles and the innocent charisma only a fool had.

"Is everything alright?"

"I was telling her about what to expect for birth and this—this *letch* eavesdropped!"

"For birth? Oh, a babe! Two babes! How lovely!" Brother Columba clapped his hands. "I know it is a sin, but I envy you both."

"You do?" the smaller pilgrim asked. "It's not much to be envious about."

"He's simpleminded," I sneered.

The pilgrims glared at me like the demon did when I begged for relief.

"I do enjoy feeling my child move," the taller pilgrim said.

I hate it.

"My hair has never been thicker," the smaller pilgrim said.

It's harder to comb.

"My husband spoils me rotten with sweets."

I'm fat from the nonstop eating.

"Sometimes I grab my babe's little feet when they push them out. They'll put them elsewhere and I'll grab them again. It's a fun little game."

Disgusting.

"Please stop!" Brother Columba gasped. "I'll be forced to do penance for weeks, my envy grows so great!"

I rolled my eyes. The pilgrims moved closer to Brother Columba.

"The Virgin Mary blessed your wombs." Smiling, he pressed his fingers to his chest. "If I were not a man . . . "

"You are a man," I said.

"I know, Brother. You forget. Man, Woman, in between, we are all God's children and He sent His only son to labor on the cross as a mother labors in childbed. He spiritually nurses us pitiful humans with divine milk from His fertile bosom. Christ's glorious side wound birthed the Church we all worship!"

His fanatic speech made the thing dig into my ribs. I crossed my arms over my stomach. Neither Christ nor Brother Columba will birth an abomination.

"Oh Brother, that is beautiful." The taller pilgrim wiped her feminine tears as the smaller one nodded.

Brother Columba beamed. "I will make you both birthing girdles with the side wound so Christ Himself will protect you in the hour of your need," he said.

The pilgrims squealed like happy pigs. I returned to cleaning the shrine. Brother Columba and the pilgrims clucked like hens as he drew Christ's side wound—which looked much like my secret area that should not be there—on long pieces of parchment. The pilgrims gushed their many, many, many thanks.

"Did you receive your badges?" Brother Columba asked.

The pilgrims shook their heads.

"I carry some in my pouch." Brother Columba held out his delicate hand.

From my place near Papula of Gaul's shrine I saw the pewter badges. They were the ones he insisted were not bawdy, but were the side wound. The prior and abbot disagreed. The pilgrims giggled and begged a blessing. Brother Columba blessed the pilgrims and their babes. I left to vomit outside.

If I were a secular man, it would be much harder to hide.

For months I hid the changes. It was easy. Monastic life values modesty—thus privacy—in washing, dressing and sleeping. The loose black monk's habit conceals every man's figure up until the point of no return. I passed that point three months ago when the chamberlain, Brother Alstan, privately asked if perhaps I wanted a new habit.

Brother Alstan had always been suspicious of me. Chamberlain or not, his constant overseeing of our laundry and linens made me think he did not just want to collect the washing as he claimed. He wanted to find polluted braies, long feminine hairs clung to black wool, dirty knees, and who knew what else. Before the change, I accused Brother Alstan of perversions and suspicion in Chapter. The abbot found him innocent. I found a flogging.

"Why would I want that?"

"Brother, er, I mean this kindly. You've grown rather . . . stout."

If I were still a layman, I'd have stabbed him. Glaring, I kept my peace.

"It's nothing to be ashamed of! Our life *is* comfortable. One year I grew out of three habits."

"Do not lie to me." I gestured to his waif-like body.

"I am not. When I lived on the continent, I grew sick. I almost needed surgery for my goiter. My health improved only when I returned to the seaside." A pause. "Burnt seaweed does wonders for a man's health." Brother Alstan held out the new habit.

After several moments where I let him hold it out to no hand, I snatched it with a violence that sent demonic flashes before my eyes. Inhaling sharply, I brought my hands to my lips.

"Are you alright?" He almost touched my shoulder.

I flinched, grew ashamed, and growled. "Yes."

"Are you sure? You have not been the same since the Northman—"

Turning on my heel in my leather shoes, I tried to leave. My balance, growing worse by the day, failed. He steadied me.

"Perhaps you should see the infirmarer?"

"NO!"

Brother Alstan recoiled.

"No," I straightened my posture, inadvertently revealing myself more. He glanced. I crossed my arms in a pathetic attempt to hide my burden.

"Brother," he whispered, "There's no shame in melancholy. You went through something unimaginable. Men go mad after Northmen raids—"

I left him without another word.

New habits may not be uncommon. It *is* uncommon to go missing for three days and come back bruised, bleeding, and bitter. I told the alarmed brethren a devil of a Northman had great fun torturing me. Technically, not a lie, so not a sin, so confession was unneeded. The demon took the form of a Northman before eventually revealing Itself. Upon my celebrated return—no one was actually pleased I returned—the abbot permitted me to recuperate in the infirmary. For three days, I ate meat and slept and was bled upon the infirmarer's pestering insistence. The bloodletting wound healed fast. Too fast. Yet no one suspected my body was no longer my body alone.

I considered . . . an herb. However, every time I . . . pondered it, dizziness overcame me until I was bedridden. I stopped considering it. Besides, who would I go to? Certainly not the infirmarer. The local wise woman may have . . . been a possibility . . . I would . . . never, but if even the thought brought on such extreme dizziness, who knew what would happen if I . . . attempted . . . to go to her? I would never. Besides, what could I . . . say? Wise women did not give such things to men. Theodore of Tarsus's penitential . . . penitential . . . penance; one year if before forty days in womb . . . three years if after forty days . . . I would never take the herb. Never!

My body was not mine.

Today, during Chapter, another movement startled me. Months-long pressure in my torso shifted entirely to my pelvis, causing great discomfort. To my horror, my demonic burden shifted, too. I raised my hand, accidentally striking my neighbor's head.

"Yes, Brother?" the abbot sighed.

"I am not feeling well. May I rest in my cell today?"

"Go."

After two sad attempts to stand on my own, I accepted Brother Alstan's assistance. Humility was a monastic virtue. *That* was humiliation. My overwhelming humiliation grew greater as I waddled out of the Chapter House. Before whatever that transition was, I controlled the waddling. My heart thudded. Sweat dripped down my back.

The moment I shut my cell door, I threw off my habit. I groped and groaned and gawked at my lowered swell. The room spun, and I sat down hard on my bed. Was this what the pilgrim meant by "lightening"?

A creak in the hall. Footsteps.

I scrambled to stand. I could not. Perhaps it wasn't wise to display myself in such a manner before I locked the door. And now I trapped myself in only my linen braies, displaying the wrong, unrecognizable body to any brethren who wished to force themselves inside. Such immodesty went against all Christian teaching. I couldn't even reach my blanket.

The footsteps passed by.

I sighed. My skin stretched as a limb of some sort tried to escape my abdomen. Brother Columba might have found joy in playing with the unborn. I did not find joy in this perversion. I pushed down on the limb. It punched my ribs and bladder in demonic defiance. Several months ago, I learned a harsh lesson about praying when it misbehaved. The only thing to do was wait.

If I were a true man again, I'd take control. I didn't care how much Brother Columba argued that religious masculinity is masculine. Secular men mocked monks for a reason. I never should have allowed my lust to impede my reason. I should have accepted her rejection with dignity and grace. Several women expressed interest in me. But no, my devastation spurred me to flee all womanly love. It was a mistake to submit to the monastic embrace. I submitted like a woman and now I've become one.

God allows all evil to happen. He allows demons to torment good men and women to test them. I am righteous and holy enough. Why didn't It corrupt Brother Columba? Why did God allow It to choose me?

The thing moved again.

I punched my abdomen.

Dizzy and nauseous, I punched again and again and again until my skin grew painful blue patches. It stopped moving. Satisfaction filled my body in a way it hadn't in years.

Crimson stained my drawers. Blood poured out of the opening that should not have been there. I watched, relieved I finally killed it. Then, an intense pain, followed by dread, shot through me, as I realized my body not only held the thing's soul—if it even had one—but mine as well. I could either sit here and bleed out with the thing or I could go to the infirmary, beg for help and mercy, and maybe live. All would know the truth, then. Perhaps a dignified death was preferable.

Blood soaked my straw pallet.

My trembling, blood-wet legs did not support my unbalanced body. Stuck, trapped, imprisoned in a disaster of my own making, I shook. Blood poured. Pain intensified. I screamed.

Footsteps.

Brother Alstan opened the door. His eyes widened.

"Help."

He caught me as I collapsed into him. His arms—muscular and hard—wrapped around my soft swollen bleeding womanly body. He carried me like a disgraced bride to the infirmary, shouting for help all the way. The Horrified eyes that came to witness my spectacle hurt worse than the pain.

All went black.

***

Darkness consumed.

Fear.

Christ wrong?

Fear.

Nothingness after death?

No.

Candlelight.

Pain.

Whispers.

Warm blanket.

Fear.

Shame.

Bitter herbal tongue.

Stink.

Fear.

Pain.

Blink. Blink. Blink.

I was not dead.

I lay in the dark infirmary, covered with woolen blankets. My belly and slit ached. Futility in lifting my head. I found success in moving my eyes. The infirmarer organized herbs on my bedside table. Brother Alstan sat next to my bed, reading. In the flickering candlelight, I recognized the manuscript as the monastery's only medical text. I ached. How could I not recognize it? The library contained only five books. God, the organ that should not have been there ached. The remaining brethren stood several beds away, whispering, whispering, whispering. Brother Columba cradled a bundle of stinking cloth. Why so much pain? The foul misama permeated the infirmary.

I choked on my vomit instead of swallowing it.

Brother Alstan turned me. The violent force, not unlike the demon's, made me vomit all the more. The floor caught my sickness most gracefully. The infirmarer kept me on my side even after I emptied my stomach. Brother Alstan wiped my mouth with a warm cloth.

"Brother," the abbot approached, *"Sub rosa, sub rosa, sub rosa."*

"Ave Abba, morituri te salutant," the infirmarer muttered.

The abbot left.

"Am I dying?"

"Not currently." The infirmarer lifted a bowl. "If Alstan had not gone to deliver you a blanket, you most certainly would have."

"He should have left me alone. I'd rather die than have a body like this."

Brother Alstan turned away.

"You have not confessed yet, Brother. If you do not tread carefully, your immortal soul—the most important thing you own—will be damned like the child you birthed."

"The most important thing I had was my body."

"And you still have it."

"What I have is an abomination."

"What part of you is an abomination?"

"My aching sheath for one."

"Brother. Do not forget you came from woman like Christ. The only man to be born not from woman was Adam. And, I suppose, your child, too."

"I am no longer a man."

"Ah well, forgive me then, *Sister.*"

If I had not been in such intense stabbing pain, I would have strangled him. He consulted the book. Brother Columba approached, still cradling the damned stinking thing. He smiled. If he were not simple, I'd say he mocked me.

"Brother, would you like to see your daughter?"

"No."

"We are going to bury her soon."

"I said what I said."

Brother Columba gazed lovingly at the disgusting thing. "She looks like you."

My body betrayed me before I could wrap my broad hands around his slender neck. Brother Alstan saved me from the stone floor.

"Brother!" the infirmarer shouted, "If you don't rest, you might very well get your blasphemous wish. And you, Columba! Do not antagonize him."

"I apologize. I did not mean to. If I were him, I would want to see my babe."

"You are not me."

"And thank God for that," Brother Alstan muttered.

The infirmarer pulled back my modesty. I did not have the energy to save it.

"The medicine I gave you is working. Your hemorrhage slowed satisfactorily."

"How long will I bleed?"

"Pray you bleed for long," Brother Alstan said. "Once you stop, the abbot will imprison you. You're lucky the Church does not hang monks."

I swallowed bile. The infirmarer spread my legs, hand on my thigh, and ripped me open again. His rough hands slathered muck on my foul sex. His hands, his hands, his hands.

Pain.

Pain.

Pain.

God help me.

God help me.

God help me.

***

Pain and wretched stink. Brother Columba replaced the traitor and spy. He slept, slept, slept by my bedside. Idiot man. At least my sex ached slightly less. I didn't dare touch to see how much changed. I dared touch my chest. Milk swelled and leaked.

A cough.

Glowing yellow eyes on my left. It did not grin like the first time. Breathe, breathe, breathe.

Eyes lowered slowly.

A hand—claws—talons—pressed on my aching abdomen. I groaned. Agony! Wet metallic warmth flowed onto my sides and the demon lifted up what was my belly and offal and dropped it on my face. Screamed. Screamed. Scream . . . whimpered. Whimpered . . . whimper . . .

Columba? He . . . up . . . demon grin . . . grabbed . . . Columba habit . . . yellow eyes on . . . grin. Cold talon on forehead . . . clarity. God help me.

God help Columba!

As my life blood poured out of me, I watched the demon do to naked Brother Columba what It had done to me. His sex disappeared and transformed into disgusting flatness. I closed my eyes as It did the abomination. Drip, drip, drip. I dared to touch the agonizing hole my innards spilt out of. Finally, my roundness was gone, and a gap replaced it. Harder to concentrate. How long? How clarity . . . ?

Another forehead touch.

It opened a shutter. The rising dawn sun illuminated the blood-soaked infirmary. Columba basked in the light, naked as a babe newly born. He stared at his feminine form. His hand slowly touched the newly made entrance that should not be there. Shuddering breaths shook his slender frame as his hands traced up to his abdomen. They rested there. He stroked his new tiny breasts tenderly. Columba raised his head to the demon.

He grinned in religious ecstasy.

THE SAME THING THAT HAPPENED TO SAM

M. Lopes da Silva

THEY TRAIN WORMS to be afraid of light, so it's really incredibly rare to have one come out of somebody's eye socket. The one time I saw my mother's worm moving the pocket of dark flesh just underneath her left eye, that was a rarity. Like a solar eclipse. Most of the time, the worms kept to the dark interior territory of the skull, far from any optic nerve or orifice.

Father reassured me that I wouldn't feel a thing, but what does he know? He's never had to have one put in. It's like he's cavity-free and telling me the dentist's drill won't hurt. Sam, my older brother, had one put in last year, and won't talk to me anymore like he used to. When I asked him if it hurt, he said no, but his voice was all wrong, just air pushed through vocal cords. I can't explain it.

Stacey Miller had her worm put in just last week. She was mostly the same afterwards. She just ignored me, the same way she has since middle school.

***

Mother and father sat me down at the kitchen table with the website on our family tablet, all swooping cursive headers on blocks of helpful text. Photographs of smiling people on anonymous lawns. Links to government websites and medical facilities.

"Mama Bear noticed you were nervous," father said. "So we thought we'd go over the worm with you again, but as a family."

He said "as a family" but Sam wasn't there. I'd already been on

56

this website. I'd read more than just the free pamphlets that the company had provided; I've been paying attention for years.

The nematodes were androids, their guts lined with nanites designed to digest all the connections in my brain that my father and country had determined were "undesirable". Piece by piece, my gender and my sexuality would become food for worms before I was even buried.

I wondered again what mother was before her worm had been surgically inserted: was she non-binary like me? Or had her sexuality proved to be the problematic part of her? Maybe it was both? My father cleared his throat. I realized it must've been the third or fourth time he'd done that while I'd been sitting in front of him, and shifted my focus.

"Yes," I said, "a special nematode of my own."

"That's right, it's very special! They feed it your DNA in the lab to start your unique bond with it early. Do you know why?"

I touched the cotton ball tightly pasted to my inner elbow with a limp bandage. "So my body won't reject it," I said.

"That's right. Wow, kitten! You've sure been hitting the books!"

I looked at my mother, who intensely studied a small square of sticky paper as she tore each corner of it in half.

"What if I don't get the worm put in?"

My mother stopped tearing her sticky paper. My father put the tablet down on the table. "What did you say?" he asked me.

"What if I don't get the worm put in?" I asked. "What if I just skip the appointment?"

"Skip the appointment? After you've been publicly registered as Worm Food? You're kidding, right?" he said.

"Go to the appointment," my mother said.

I locked eyes with her and thought I saw a sliver of movement behind her left eye, but it was impossible to tell for sure.

"You don't want to get on the wrong side of the law, do you, kitten?" he asked.

"I just wanted to know," I said.

"They'll put you in the centers, and then it gets worse," Sam said.

We all stared at him. Sam looked like he'd just come back from study group. Father looked angry, the way he had before he'd called the cops on Sam when we found out he had a boyfriend. But Sam just looked the way he always did—empty. I'd asked him once, after the worm, if he missed Nate, but he'd just been confused.

I started crying again.

"What's wrong?" mother asked.

"You're not getting agitated, are you? We can drive you to the clinic tonight—"

"No, of course not," I said, "I'm just a little nervous."

"All right," father said, "but if it gets to be too much, you can take one of the pills that the doctor gave you. Let me know, and I'll get one from the cabinet."

***

It was almost like a party. That night I ate food that I hardly tasted, swallowing dutifully. I kept repeating the thoughts that I loved most in chaotic cacophony, but chaos was interrupted by the most mundane things: opening a present from father and mother (a dress I would never usually wear, pre-worm), a toast, a group photo in front of a cake. The cake had a pink icing worm wriggling in and out of bold letters that spelled "Baby's First Worm".

I threw up in the bathroom.

***

The clinic was a beige blankness. I am thankful for that.

***

So much in my brain now is beautiful worm shit.

It's the kind of beautiful I always hated: all empty surfaces. Glass bubbles breaking open inside me to cut everything tender apart.

***

At night the worm chews on my memories, reordering them into more acceptable patterns. I was never attracted to Stacey Miller. I never kissed her behind the snack stand at the softball field. I was always watching home runs. Boys running in a square that they call a diamond. The lawn was so green and well-groomed it looked artificial.

In order to outrun the worm, I must think new thoughts: stronger, stranger, queerer thoughts than ever before. I think gay things all the time, filling my moments with so many of them that the worm rasps noisily along the inside of my skull with all the eating it has to do.

I make my worm busy with the business of myself, planning my infinite revenges.

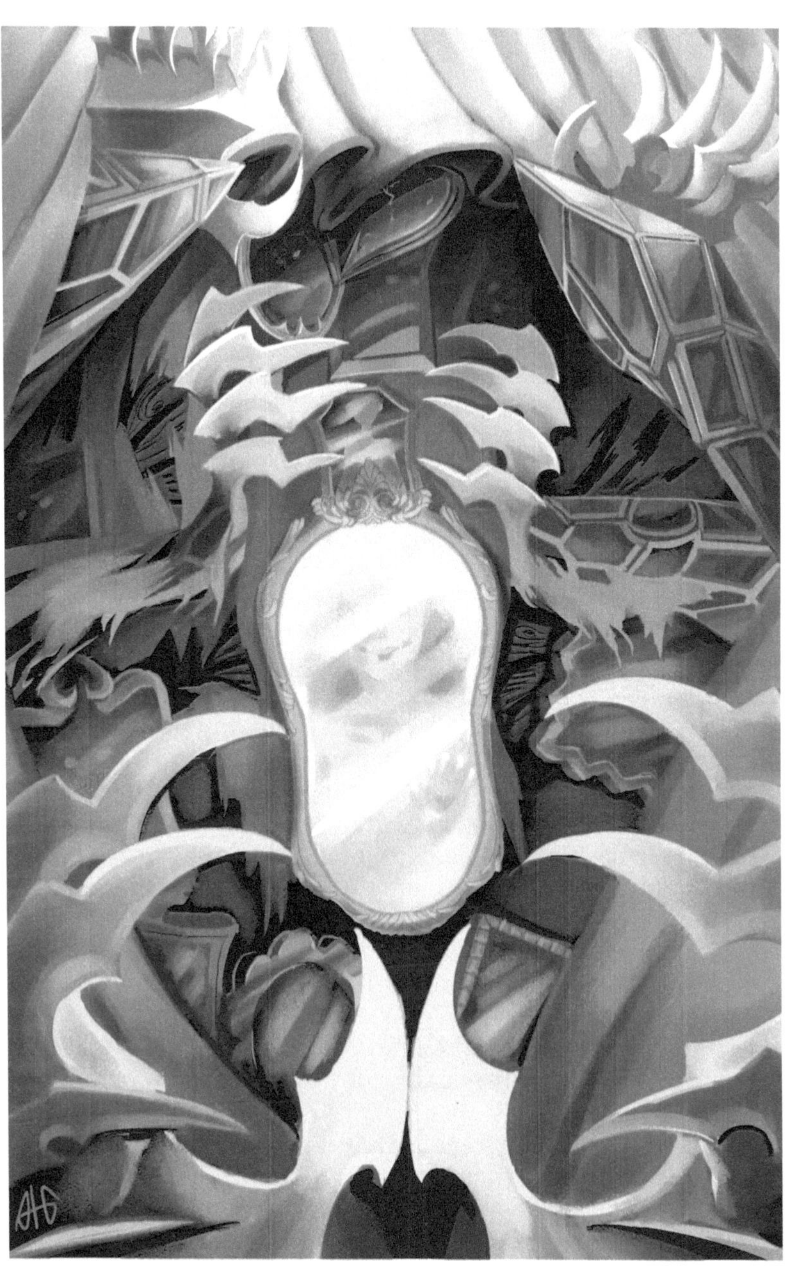

BALLAD OF THE PEST

Meagan Hotz

DAY 366.

It was better this way, said my boss. I agreed. I got to save money and time on transit and junk food lunches. I could roll out of bed half an hour before my shift. Sweatpants were the best pants. And I was going insane.

Not cabin fever. Not "stir-crazy". My home was my space, and it was safe. There was a leash around my neck, though, and it kept me at my desk, my fingers at my keyboard, the voices of my friends fading in my ears as I watched the day count go up and knew I would not get those back. My car was silent and untouched. The number in my bank account, stagnant. Can't afford a raise now. Can't afford to lower the cost of housing. Can't afford to get away.

Day 366 is when I heard the first scratch.

Quick; a flash of noise and maybe a hint of a shadow out of the corner of my eye as it dipped into the kitchen. I didn't have pets. I didn't know what else it could be. Yet another thing to think about in place of the things I wanted to think about. I hoped it was just the one, taking a tour before settling into, hopefully, somebody else's apartment. This one was mine, and in all my endless loneliness, this was not the kind of company that I wanted. I waited, and things returned to silence, and I clicked on another email.

Day 370, my friend's aunt died. I hadn't spoken to the friend in a while and had never spoken to her aunt. I clicked the sad reaction on Facebook and copy-pasted my sympathies into the responses. The aunt had died alone. The furnace had gone out during a freak ice storm. The landlord had not had it serviced in years. I pulled a blanket tightly around my shoulders and listened for the hum of the building's heater. It remained as alive as I was, for now.

I heard a scratch from the kitchen. The light was off, and I did not get up to turn it on.

Until Day 378, I tried to stay off social media, tried to avoid the news. Few things made me happy then, but none of them lay in clickbait headlines and outraged reactions. Watching things get worse did not make me feel as if I could do any better. When I laid in bed those nights, I could hear little feet scrabbling from the tile to the laminate. I wondered where they were getting in.

When I found the droppings, I texted my landlord. He said he'd send a guy by. Didn't tell me who or when or to do what, but that's what he said, and I didn't want to be a bother, so I stayed alone until Day 380.

"How are you?" Jenny asked me, her face blown up wide on my monitor, eyes not quite looking at mine. It was a line from a script; we all knew the answer, and I'm sure she could see it in the bags beneath my eyes, but I gave a weak smile and nodded, a gesture of appreciating the question and refusal to commit to a definitive reply.

"Not getting much sleep lately," I said. "I think I've got mice."

"Ew! Have you put out traps?"

"The landlord was supposed to send someone, but I'm still waiting. They haven't gotten into anything, at least."

"You sure it's mice?"

"What else would they be?"

"I dunno, rats? Ricky's brother had raccoons living in his roof, could be that too—"

I laughed. I almost wished for raccoons at that point. I needed the adrenaline.

"I'm sure it's just mice. But I'll keep you posted."

Wish I could say we talked for hours, but she had places to be, and I had another many hours in the day to spend inside and alone, moving from my computer screen to my television screen to my phone screen and then squeezing my eyes tight in bed as I tried to flush the residual lights away into dreamland. I tried to read a book on occasion, but the silence around me filled my brain with false noise and summoned tiny voices that reminded me of the things I was trying to escape. I lay in bed too many nights too tired to sleep, too fixed on the silence in my room, drowning it out with angry thoughts and homing in on the slightest bit of noise that could be the mice.

I thought one was on me, one night.

I woke up to pinpricks on my chest, and when I rose, I felt a fleeting movement before I heard the retreating scrape of claws on laminate.

My landlord sent someone over the next morning, because I called him on the verge of vomiting in the middle of the night, not expecting him to answer but hoping that regurgitating my experience into his voicemail would stop me from regurgitating anything else. The guy showed up in a band shirt and jeans and smelled like an old carpet, definitely just a guy my landlord knew and not someone he'd have to pay in anything more than a six-pack.

He snuffled around the corners of my apartment, thankfully without minding the way I hovered behind him, eyeing what he poked and prodded. I didn't like the look of puzzlement on his face, but he did set traps as he went.

"Well, I can't tell you where they're coming from, this place looks sealed up pretty tight," he said. "But that should do it. They like to follow the walls when they run, so I'm sure you'll get 'em sooner or later."

That wasn't very reassuring, but I was also suddenly hyper aware of how silly I felt in needing reassurance. They were mice, not burglars. An ever-replenishing supply of cute little nuisances that only lived to eat, sleep, and make more of themselves. That's all they were, little mice.

I heard a snap in the night, but found nothing in the traps. It took me a long time to even figure out which trap had gone off, and there was no evidence of any other disturbance around it. Could mousetraps misfire? I wasn't sure how to reset it without snapping my own finger, so I let it be, hoping the half dozen others would succeed where its brethren failed.

About three nights later, I was awoken by the same violent crack. This time I was shocked to find it had worked. The mouse lay twitching under the bar. I couldn't tell if it was still alive or just going through the motions of death. I could see my phone light reflecting in its black, bulging eyes, and wondered if this was the last thing it saw, a terrifying beam from the darkness. Going to the light was a comfort to humans, but perhaps it was a terror to creatures that spent so much of their time skulking around within the walls.

When I was sure there was no life left in it, I knelt down and had a look. Poor thing had been through the ringer—it looked sticky, worn somehow. It was almost misshapen, but I was sure that was the handiwork of the trap. I rummaged a plastic shopping bag from beneath the sink and scooped it up, trap and all, and quickly stuffed it in the trash. Maybe not the most dignified burial, but I didn't want to brave the garbage bins at, what was it, three in the morning? Not on a chilly night like this, where my nerves were already alight. I would toss it once the sun was up, after I made myself go to sleep, and pushed aside all thoughts of bulging-eyed, twitching-legged mice gasping for air among the rotting scraps.

For a few days, it seemed like my problem was solved. And then, like most problems, it wasn't.

That pinprick feeling of something running across my chest came back, accompanied by more than one set along the floor. More than once I awoke to traps snapping only to find nothing there. Every time I'd drift back to sleep, another set of feet would skitter by, bringing me back from the brink of unconsciousness into the harrowing darkness I was trying to escape. My boss became increasingly terse with my spacey gaze and slow work, and what could I say? I haven't slept, sir, because of the mice—the mice did it, they keep me awake, the traps do nothing and I am haunted by mice and I am expected to sign in here every day as usual as if nothing is wrong, as if I haven't lost track of how many days it's been since this all began, as if I haven't lost track of my friends and family and dreams of a world outside these walls, as if all concern for me has been only a concern for cost and production.

I didn't say that. I slept on my breaks, because that was the only chance I got.

One night I heard them scratching and arose from my bed with fury. I was no longer afraid of feeling the squish of fur and bone beneath my feet as I trod the laminate in the dark. Tonight, I thought raggedly, I will find them. I checked every wall, every crease, for the hole. I could hear them moving beyond, but still couldn't find that dark little portal. Meticulously, I moved through my apartment, pulling back furniture, tugging at the baseboards, trying to find my way in. At about four in the morning, I stood in my living room, looking around with eyes too wild for the bags beneath them, about to scream out my loss of hope, when I saw the wall move.

It was hard to tell, in the dim light of a single bulb, whether it was my furious insomnia or something real—until I saw it again. A light flex, like a vein pumping or a lung breathing. I pulled a painting off the wall to get a better look, to put my hand against it in the hope that I could trust my touch more than my sight, and I felt the throb as real as my own heart running feral in my chest. My finger traced the drywall, already cracked out of years of neglect—the reason I'd placed the painting there to begin with—and I picked at it. The seam opened easily, like peeling a fruit, or like a mortician peeling back the chest of a cadaver, hardly even registering the dust gathering beneath my nails. Once the hole was torn—and that dim bulb cast its eye inside—I collapsed onto the living room floor.

I found the mice. They were solid within the hole, piled against each other in crooked and violent ways. Their tails were tangled, claws entwined. It even seemed like their bodies were fused in places, as if they had been twisted together for so long their bodies had forgotten they were separate. Hundreds of eyes glinted out and hundreds of sharp-toothed snouts screamed as they were accosted by beams of light they may have never seen before.

Reek spilled from the hole, of decay and something I couldn't place. They twisted as one, some pulling away from the light and others toward, their combined form unable to fully commit to any specific direction. I couldn't tell how far they went into the wall, but they were all I could see in the hole I tore. They cried and gnashed and writhed as one, that's all they were, little mice, who lived to eat and sleep and make more of themselves, inside the walls where the light couldn't touch, in a bed of filth and decay and neglect.

Watching them twist and shriek, watching them gnash and move in waves of brown and grey that spilled drywall blood from the wounded wall, I sobbed, and it was with elation. I found the mice, the mice in the walls, torn and twisted within each other, a pulsing mass of flesh beneath a plain drywall surface. I cried because I saw them, and for once, felt I was understood.

PLAYING HOUSE

Ziggy Schutz

SOMETIMES, WHEN SHE is feeling particularly whimsical, Charlotte imagines herself a scientist.

Trade her apron for a lab coat, steak knives for scalpels. Sensible heels would echo more in a laboratory than in this picture-perfect house, but she thinks she would grow to love the sound. Especially if it came with a relief from this heat—tight collar, closed windows, and an oven that likes to take hours to come to heat.

Then she laughs and goes to make sure her fantasizing hasn't let the roast burn.

Science is for discoveries, for finding the new. Her job is to keep up the appearances of the old. Comfort, familiarity. It's a lonely job, one that leads to days of puttering around the living room, hours spent making sure it looks as unlived in as possible.

Not that it's a difficult task. Her husband works so hard. He has little time for trivial things. For her.

Does she look unlived in too? she wonders, as she dabs at the sweat collecting on her neck. Good wives don't perspire.

He doesn't care what she does, as long as it's the same as it was the day before, and the day before that. No children, because he needs his quiet. No love to fill her empty heart, because that's for fairy tales.

As long as dinner is on the table, he hardly notices she's there at all.

So tonight, Charlotte is cooking dinner.

Her cleaver makes quick work of bone and fat, the crack of exposed joints hidden under her light hum.

This recipe's new. Something she's been—ha!—*experimenting* with. Sinew for strength, marrow for memory.

She should name her, this creation coming together under her careful hands. All good dishes have a name.

The movements are by rote, now. Cream for the roux, some blood for colour. If she's not paying attention, her quick work of the vegetables could leave her with too few fingers, but who would notice?

A timer goes off, and she bends to pull the twin cakes from the oven, risen like lungs.

She used to think marriage meant freedom.

But there are many ways to bake a cake.

Her nails are sharp, as she drums a pulse into the counter, waiting for the cakes to cool. Waiting for the gravy to thicken. Waiting for the sound of her husband's car in the driveway.

She is no scientist, but her precision is unparalleled. Everything comes together, and by the time she can hear his keys in the door, all that's left is the garnish.

Her wedding ring will do nicely.

The memory of their vows tastes like fine wine, like the wine in her hand as she listens to her husband enter, already complaining.

When your heart is empty, it's no trouble to rip it out of your chest.

It makes the perfect appetizer, tender and mild, and she watches his face twist into something like shock.

Something *new*.

"Welcome home, darling," she says, and the body she's assembled on their fine mahogany table sits up, just as she shoves her husband into his seat.

"We made you dinner," Charlotte says. "Hungry?"

"Starving," her dish replies. She thinks she will call her Penelope. She is *beautiful*.

Charlotte is a good wife.

Doesn't she deserve something good in return?

The meal is good. And her husband, in his shock, is delicious. Every shared bite.

HYBRID

Rose Sable

To WHOM IT may concern—
In service of the greater good, we are prepared now to detail for you the fruits of our research: the hybrid. Theory dictates that we should not have done this; necessity dictates otherwise. What follows is documentation of our process, and it is our belief that by the end of it you will come to see the many benefits in choosing our product.
—[redacted]

1/7
This was the first prototype to survive the hormonal splicing process with any semblance of vitality. There is hatred in its eyes, cold and distant, but hatred nonetheless. This feature may be removed in subsequent models, though it may also prove useful. Unfortunately, the specimen was unwilling to complete the athletic course we set out for it. At this time, we are unsure if this is a vestige of sentience from the host body or a physical limitation, but neither is acceptable. We have disposed of the specimen.

1/16
A resounding success. The latest iteration of the creature was able to complete the course in record time and only needed minor prodding to do so. Our hybrid has displayed more sheer power than we imagined. It appears, however, that this model still harbors some hesitation to follow orders. It will be made to stand at attention until we return tomorrow. Any deviation will, of course, result in the disposal of this host.

1/17

It survived the night, to the team's surprise. We spent the remainder of the day testing its athletic abilities and willingness to obey. If this host had a spirit, we believe it has been broken. Some would call this cruelty, but is it cruel to sharpen a knife that has dulled? To replace a broken component of an essential machine? We do not believe so.

2/3

Our benefactors have been gracious enough to grant us the use of a former heritage site for field testing. We set the hybrid loose in the region surrounding Meteora, believing that the varied terrain and wildlife would prove useful for the challenges ahead. The hybrid—which thankfully still retains some understanding of language—was sent to capture a dozen rabbits and several coyotes to test its hunting prowess. Once again, it passed with flying colors. Bones crumble beneath its iron grip. The team feels good about this iteration.

2/5

A difficult day for the team. While finishing up a field test, the creature unhinged its jaw and devoured a falcon it had plucked from a tree. Its powerful teeth made short work of the bird, bones and all, but this is unacceptable. We do not believe this was an act of defiance, merely the surfacing of an issue we had not yet considered: the hybrid still feels hunger. Of course, it requires sustenance—we cannot currently change that—but there should be no urge. Future iterations will eat only when instructed. This host has been disposed of.

A note on disposal: the usual execution method was unsuccessful, as recent iterations have developed bone thick and fortified enough to withstand even a bullet. An acid bath proved more effective. Some of our younger staff members were visibly upset by the creature's cries of pain, by the flesh made translucent and blood seeping from every pore. They must be reminded that these creatures are no longer human, and as such need not be wept for.

2/25

The creature killed a brown bear today. We have included video documentation with the logs, but it is not for the faint of heart. The creature ignored the weapons we laid out for it, instead opting to take the animal on with only its hands. While this was a magnificent show of strength and another great success, we are even more enamored by the host body's adaptation to new additions, new nerve endings and pathways in its physical form. It is able to enhance its own muscle mass and even use its strong fingernails as makeshift claws. We will of course be adding more efficient claws in future iterations—and perhaps sharpening the teeth. It likes to use its teeth.

3/2

It appears that our current model still retains some memories from the host body. Unfortunately, the current prototype seems to have come into contact with one of our interns at some point in its life. Upon recognizing her, it screamed and screamed without end. An incredibly haunting sound, as you will find from the accompanying video log. We were reluctant to harm the creature at this stage as we had found such success with it, until it escaped confinement. It crushed the intern's windpipe with one hand and clawed out her eyes with the other. It then tore her body open and devoured her organs. We are currently looking into how it was able to leave its cell, but we currently suspect that the creature retains intelligence from not only its host body but the other specimens involved in its creation as well. We will investigate with the next iteration, but this one has proven uncooperative and thus will be sent to the acid bath.

A note, however, on the retention of host memories: I am not convinced that this is entirely a bad thing. It may be possible to harness and manipulate these last echoes of feeling into something useful to us.

4/14

The hybrid is a magnificently efficient killing machine. With many of the kinks smoothed out, it was sent on a mission to infiltrate a local cell of insurrectionists. We gave it a week to allow for careful integration with the rebels, so it could study their movements and formulate a strategy to eliminate them. It returned to us only ten minutes to midnight on the first day, adorned in entrails and gnawing on a femur. I am reminded of those famous words appropriated by Oppenheimer, not about death but about a thousand suns. The radiance of what we have created will surely burn brighter. A perfect solution, one that can truly separate the wretch from the king—so long as that is what its wielder wishes.

4/22

The hybrid shows no regard for living things, including itself. It is a cannibalistic monster so utterly devoid of remorse as to display a ruthlessness the team was unprepared for, but not unhappy with either. After some minor DNA tweaks we were able to give it use of a pair of wings which nestle into slots in the creature's back for concealment. It took flight for the first time today in pursuit of a prisoner we set loose just for this very occasion. The tearing of flesh, the cracking of bone, the flap of those feathers, it was terrible and magnificent to behold. It revels in the freedom of flight and the thrill of the hunt, yet it always comes back home when beckoned. It kills with the elegance of a dancer, which, I believe, this particular host body may have been in its life before we gave it purpose. The prisoner, of course, did not get far.

6/12

We have assembled a platoon of hybrids using the latest model as our guide. The hunting party set out this morning to dispatch the political rival of one of our benefactors, a mission which was carried out successfully and in short order. The latest batch is extraordinarily strategic, and their thought patterns are unlike any of the earliest tests. We are to receive a generous grant to expand our research significantly, which I believe will be used to explore the selection of host bodies as I believe this plays a role in the efficiency of the final product. The hybrid, if successful, will surely be the go-to in policing, in military operations, and in the protection of people and interests all around the globe.

7/14

Our platoon of hybrids was sent to eliminate another small uprising in town. They made short work of the rioters, though one of them must have been familiar to the platoon leader's host body; it came back carrying a man's head with tears in its eyes. This is not a major setback as it completed its mission without fail, and in fact—as I suspected—the memories of the host body do not simply represent one more light to snuff out in the next iteration. Quite the contrary—this pain appears to have made the hybrid a more efficient tool, and may even represent some form of evolution within the product. Perhaps this should be taken into account when selecting future hosts. Strong bonds with others and signs of deviant behavior in life appear to result in stronger candidates for hybridization; more emotions, more anger, more reason for the host body to resist.

Many will die, but these types are expendable, and those who survive will without a doubt become the greatest weapons we have ever seen.

It is my belief, therefore, that the hybrids are ready for the market.

CHOLESTEROL-MONOXIDE

W.N. Derring-Judith

THE FIRST TIME Rodney saw the car, he couldn't believe it was real, and for the time being he didn't have to. He probably got some of the details wrong, anyway.

The car was bone white. Not in the superlative sense of "bone-white", assuming that was something people did, but more like actual bones; that kind of yellow off-white. He'd never seen a bone that didn't belong to a bird, but he heard they looked like that, and this car definitely, you know, looked like *that*. It was on the other lane, across the divider, wobbly like the driver was drunk. Or . . .

Or maybe the *car* was drunk.

Maybe Rodney was tired. He'd been choking down the I-45 for a few hours now, and as calm as the Vyvanse had him, it wasn't any excuse not to take a break. Dallas was close, though. He'd stop in an hour, once he got there.

That was a mistake.

***

Rodney hadn't gone an hour before he saw the car again. Couldn't miss it. Couldn't miss the feverish-red and choking-blue lights that twirled around its interiors. Couldn't ignore the churning siren that screamed for him to pull over.

Something caught in his throat.

. . . no, he could do this. Vyvanse wasn't strictly illegal, and neither was antique furniture. Besides, it wasn't like he could've outrun the car on a straight line.

Rodney pulled over to the shoulder and waited. He'd be fine.

He looked white. The Vyvanse was unmarked. The furniture was plain antique and was going to his friend. He'd be fine.

The first sign he'd been lying to himself came when the car awkwardly swerved onto the shoulder and rear-ended his own, and something in his chest tightened. Being rear-ended shouldn't have had an associated "feel"; why, then, did it feel so wrong?

Rodney wasn't going to be the first one out of the car, and the cop must've felt the same. He hadn't been keeping an eye on the clock, so he wasn't sure how long he'd sat there, waiting for something normal to happen as the humidity crept down his neck.

It was almost a relief, seeing the door open; "almost", because that wasn't quite right, either. There looked to be a bit of give to it, like the metal had to be pried off, like a piece of taffy being pulled from the whole. It didn't look like the kind of illusion Rodney would've seen on a hot road, and he certainly wasn't far enough away for those to be a problem. Maybe.

A boot stepped out. Pivoted, dragged something with it. A shape unfolding out of the car. Cop.

Rodney swallowed, and waited.

The cop ambled over to Rodney as gracefully as he'd driven, all wobbly and zig-zaggy. There was still no question he'd make it to Rodney, but in seconds or minutes?

No, focus. Relax. Look the cop in the eye, like it's a wild animal. Say as little as possible. That was what you did in the event of a cop, right?

Rodney looked out the window, and the cop looked back through glossy sunglasses.

Right, right.

Rodney nodded, rolled down the window, and tried as hard as he could to focus on whatever was behind those sunglasses. "Is- is there a problem, officer?"

"*Is there a problem, officer?*"

Rodney blinked. The cop had spoken the words back as if he were a vicious child, or perhaps a vicious adult speaking *to* a child. It was the kind of thing that might have confirmed Rodney's worst fears, if he'd had grasp enough of the situation to conceptualize one.

The cop pulled his face away from the window, standing to a full height of six foot something. He was . . . well, he was shockingly normal. Dressed like a Texas State Patroller, probably, something Rodney would have been able to confirm if he'd strayed much from Galveston. Rodney was unsure why his eyes continued darting around for something to disprove him for a mirage, or why he smelled faintly of lemon juice.

The cop cleared his throat, which is where Rodney's eyes inexplicably focused. "Do you know why I had to stop you?"

Rodney opened his—

"No, you don't, do you? That's your problem, ain't it?"

Mouth was dry. " . . . I . . . I don't understand what you mean, s-sir."

The cop laughed, harsh and without warning, like a substitution for some kind of violence. Then, with even less warning, the cop was scowling again. "The Ay Gee Tee Gee You Tee, Section 23. You're in violation of the third article of faith, which means you're in violation of all six. That's not even a jail sentence, kid; jail's what you wish you got."

Rodney blinked.

"Tell me, kid." The officer leaned against the car door, and Rodney's eyes found themselves locked out of his sunglasses. "What's your story?"

"I'm, I'm a . . . I'm a mechanic, sir." The words had forced themselves out of Rodney's mouth. "I, you know, I fix things for people."

"Bet you dig holes, cause that's a boring way to start." The cop smiled. His teeth were far too white. "I want to hear your *story*, not your *back*story. You gotta have *something* of worth tucked away under all that mud."

The cop reached through the window, touching Rodney lightly on the neck. His hand was feverishly warm.

"I think it started when I was a kid." He hadn't said that. "That's when you're watching cartoons too much, getting lost in . . . fiction, you know, books and movies and lots of these parallel worlds." He definitely hadn't said that. "And you, uh, you wonder: why here? What's so special about the flesh, blood, the dirt and the concrete and, and everything else?" No matter what came out of his mouth, Rodney *especially* hadn't confessed to that.

The cop's finger hadn't moved from Rodney's neck. "Well, that's all it is, isn't it? Laws are dirtsprout documents for dirt like

Pasadena and dirt like you, worth the dirt it's printed on." He laughed again, and it was even more apparent that this was some kind of punishment. "You've got a dream there's more than that?"

"There . . . there has to be, y'know?" Rodney shivered, and tried fruitlessly to pull away from the cop's warm and sticky finger. "Something beyond living like an animal. Being, you know, being your best self. I mean, I'm transporting antiques to my friend, don't you know?" While the rest of Rodney froze at the confession that had almost certainly secured a few more hours with the cop, his mouth continued. "That's not just . . . I mean, would an animal do that?"

"Total depravity, broski." The cop's smile barely kept itself from melting into a full-blown snarl. "Neurochemical in, neurochemical out. Your body ain't nothin' but dirt, and it ain't got a place in a perfect *autobahdy*."

The cop peeled his finger from Rodney's neck; the sweat, if that was what it was, had congealed into a boogery consistency, making a disgusting squishing noise on the way back. Rodney immediately put his car into drive and peeled away.

He got as far as *maybe* three hundred feet before his back tires sizzled into a slurry, grinding his vehicle to a halt.

"Oh, too bad! You almost got away from me, there." The cop seemed to be yelling in the same intonation in which he talked, save an increase in volume. "Might not want to exit the car, though, got a *real* nasty puddle pooling 'round the bend." Its words were followed by a sudden sizzling from the front.

The cop, once more, took its sweet time ambling toward the car; the malice behind every zig and zag was even more apparent. Had it wanted to prolong Rodney's torment? Was it some coded message of violence? Rodney's mind was racing as if, somehow, piecing together the cop's puzzle would save him, even as his empty gut roiled itself in knots over the inevitable death or worse that awaited.

Rodney's mind rifled through the items in the car. Most of the furniture was stuck in either the hatch or the back seat; of them, the antique lamp was the only thing he could feasibly pull out. His glove compartment didn't have anything but pills, and he didn't need to give the cop anything more to arrest him for. The bottles on the floor of his car were plastic, of no use in a fight. Maybe . . . maybe he could just close the window and hide.

Rodney looked out his window to gauge his remaining time, and nearly leapt out of his skin to see the officer standing in front of his door, pearly whites glistening through a chimpanzee's grin.

The cop stuck a finger onto Rodney's neck, too fast for the window to go more than a third of the way up.

"W-what do you even want me to say?" Rodney couldn't shut his mouth. "That I, that I don't belong? That I'm a parasite in a host I don't want to guest inside? That every time I turn on this car, every time I pick up groceries or go to the movies or get, you know, get *gas* that the weight of it all puts a hairline fracture where it hurts? I don't want to take up space. I don't think *anyone* wants that!"

"Awful elephant for a cheap tick."

"I . . . I can't *help* it." Rodney tried to move his left hand back to the window button. "I've got cousins in the third world. How do I look 'em in the eye and tell them my grocery commute's worth a cut of their future? Transcendental's all I fuckin' have, man."

"Then I guess you got nothing, *man*." It snickered, like it was being funny, somehow, and hardly noticed Rodney's hand reaching for the window button. "Don't you think people who are worth nothing deserve to die?" It paused. " . . . I don't know if I'm talking about you or your cousins. I don't think either of you deserve to live. They probably feed off the road, too. I've heard it's a lovely road trip, wherever it is. Hard to make a road trip look ugly. Maybe the people on it."

Rodney forced himself to think: "Come on, you know, look into my eyes." Miraculously, the cop did. "There's something behind it, right? Not a big lump of meat with no reason. You gotta value *some* of that, yeah? Something like—"

Whatever Rodney was going to say next didn't matter, because the window suddenly pulled up, ripping the cop's finger off of his cheek and pinning its arm between the window and the frame, where it—

—cleanly sliced off, spilling a foul green slime over the door.

Rodney screamed, pulling away barely in time to avoid much more than a spot on his sleeve. Whatever it was ate clean through, dropping onto the seat and continuing to eat through *that*. That it only took a bead-sized hole out of the seat was offset by the mess of slime sizzling out of the wiggling bit of arm, taking everything it sunk into and leaving only a sharp scent of rotten lemons in its wake.

The cop cackled, slamming its good hand on the roof of the car. "Mundane *shit*, man, that's an assault charge on top of loitering, and if it gets to the engine you get manslaughter on top. I'm really gonna have to flip you inside-out like a turkey after this one, *broratio*."

Something gave, and the car tilted to the left. Rodney choked against his seatbelt on the way to the passenger seat. He probably made it to the other side, once the slime had melted through his beltage. Hard to make sense. Much to think about.

The cop pushed through the driver's side door with its stump, like a finger breaking through wet tissue paper that burnt and hissed and meant certain death if Rodney didn't cling to the passenger seat for dearest life. "You still there, Hot Rod? You've got a date with Moloch. 'Nice to eat you', he says."

Rodney's fingers smacked their way across the door for the handle, forcing it open and almost, *almost* scuttling the rest of him into the shallow pool of slime collecting outside. It took all Rodney's effort not to stumble back again.

The cop's stump was still poking through when Rodney looked back, wiggling around like it was trying to widen the hole. A thick membrane was scabbing over the stump, barely keeping the wound closed even as the cop's arm spewed and spewed and spewed. That was what it sounded like. Rodney couldn't look at the rest of his arm. He couldn't.

"This is normally where I read you your rights, yeah?" The cop laughed, like it had just said something funny, and Rodney laughed too because it *was* funny, wasn't it? "Okay, okay, 'll bite." A terrible horking sound came from its general direction. "You have the right to remain sizzling. Anything you say will be ignored. Yaldabaoth, your Lord and Father, has the right to expel anything found scuttling throughout his vascular system. Armilus, your Lord and King, has the right to enforce his laws. Moloch, your Lord and Savior, has the right to claim burnt offerings from the useless dregs of this lukewarm nation. You are afforded damnation through the gospel of Rousas John Rushdoony, for thus his screeds speak for themselves: 'Yaldabaoth, who art in the heavens, dreaded be his name. His maw draws close, his hungers insatiable, on this solitary archonate of dirt and flesh. Give him your flesh, and suffer in your unconditional depravity, as all your kind suffers, and think not for one second you'll be anything more than—'"

The car rocked violently to the right, throwing Rodney out of the passenger door and onto the grass. He almost missed the high-pitched shrieking from the other side of the car, more of a testament to the shock than any quality of the screaming. It rang too sharp to fully ignore.

It took Rodney a while to realize he was curled up on a cool patch of prairie grass, still very much alive.

Rodney stood up, turning back to what remained of his car. The first thing that struck him was the overpowering miasma of lemon-spiked mist sizzling out of his vehicle, or what remained of it; the slurry of melting plastic and metal was beginning to look less like a car and more like . . . it didn't look like *anything*, really. It struck Rodney that the officer was either nowhere to be seen, or eminently seeable in the acid splattered over his car.

It took a reasonable effort to approach, and unfortunately, his worst instincts had been right. Rodney's car didn't look like his car because it wasn't *just* his car: it was also a state patrol car, crunchy and totaled, but quite real.

Whatever the first officer had been, it had melted the left side of his Civic through, giving the impression that it was absorbing the patroller. Both had welded together to the point where the only way to tell where the patroller ended and the Civic began was the shattered windshield of the . . .

. . . oh no. Oh no, oh no, oh no.

Rodney ran past the wreck to look for the human officer. It wasn't hard to find him, neck broken, run across the asphalt like sandpaper, with naught but a broken brown bottle to cling to. There was nothing to be done to save his life.

The dying cop twitched, and for a moment it looked as if the road twitched with him.

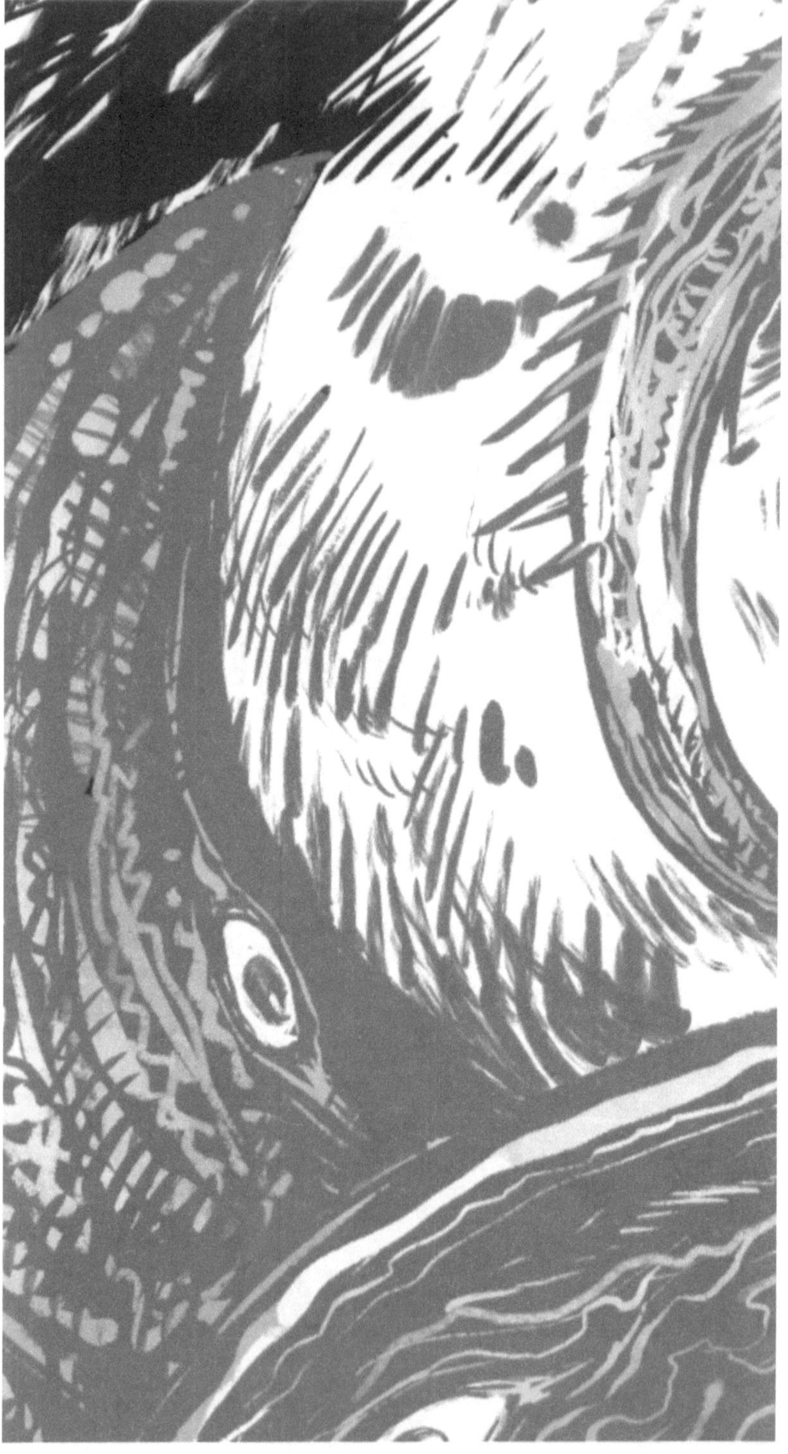

WHY WE KEEP EXPLODING

Hailey Piper

JUST A JOKE

THE FIRST GIRL explodes on the final evening of orientation weekend.

Allison Greer, Sutton University freshman, joins us in the dining hall, where all levels of college kids pack the inside, clacking dishes and loud voices bounding off every surface. Beneath that cacophony, no freshman would fear silence.

The boys who join us at our table are upperclassmen. They forego hoodies and torn jeans for stiff button-downs and slacks, like they have job interviews scheduled after dinner. Juniors? I can't say for sure.

The tallest, a blond boy with razor-straight teeth and a narrow face, sits across from Allison. I can't make out their conversation through the noise, but he points repeatedly to a cup of yellow liquid, likely beer, and then taps a penny on the tabletop, and I understand this is some kind of challenge.

She tells him she doesn't like games. When he doesn't let up, she curses him and throws her glass of fountain soda into his face.

I stare, awestruck, while Tall-Boy sputters. Shaking my head always felt like drawing too much attention, let alone cursing and splashing. I dread the glint in others' eyes, how I'll turn from *human* to *thing* in the flick of an internal switch the moment they realize I'm different. Vocal training hasn't come as easily to me as other girls still recovering from early testosterone infection. Some self-teach or find others to teach them. A few like their voices and insist everyone else had better deal with it.

I should be grateful that silence is my friend, that others don't clock me at a glance and figure out how I'm different from other girls. Lucky little Laurie started estro at fourteen.

Most days, I keep strict posture and bite my tongue. I would never throw soda into anyone's face. Had Tall-Boy challenged me instead of Allison, I would have agreed to whatever game he wanted. Boys like him twist sorcery on their tongues. They insist you play with them, and I'm easily witched.

Allison is my heroine for a few brief moments. She turns to stride from the table, a victorious warrior abandoning a corpse-choked battlefield. Carbonized droplets skitter down Tall-Boy's face while his friends laugh at him.

But then he weaves sorcery. "Chill, sweetie," he says, wiping a paper napkin down his face.

She turns to snap at him, dark hair coiling: "Chill yourself, asshole. Goodbye."

He leans over the table, and I see the witchcraft swirl in his piercing eyes. "Somebody has an attitude problem," he says. "It was just a joke."

Allison's lip curls back, but she hesitates. Her gaze darts back and forth, uncertain, sizing up witnesses and how they might judge her reaction. Was she the kind of girl who couldn't take a joke? She had to get her words just right or else see the dining hall condemn her a stuck-up killjoy for all time.

"Try—" she starts, fighting tooth and nail to get the words out. "Try. Being. Funny."

Tall-Boy turns on his *debate me* voice. "Humor's subjective," he said, smooth and smarmy. "Asking me to adjust for you when we barely know each other, that's completely irrational." His eyes stab through her, reading when she'll try to speak again. He doesn't let her. "Just a joke," he repeats, this time coated in slime.

Allison's lips fight her face to make words. I don't know what she would say if she could speak. I would like to.

Instead, the silence clamps over Allison's paling complexion, her dark hair shimmering with milky starlight. She clutches her gut, as if the unspoken words now burn her belly. Her legs stagger back from the table.

Tall-Boy and his friends lean in, like they know what's about to happen. Sorcerers must have that power.

WHY WE KEEP EXPLODING

Allison's skin ripples. Every muscle twitches. If there's a sound building toward what's about to happen, I can't hear it beneath the dining hall din, Allison rendered silent. I read words in her face, the ones that have done this. Just a joke. Attitude problem. Irrational.

And then she has no face. Her body flashes out, a sudden supernova of white light and viscera. I cover my eyes, but the boys keep looking, their heat oozing over the table, dwarfing Allison's cold, starlit explosion.

She doesn't even scream.

When I finally uncover my eyes, there's nothing left of Allison. The white-light explosion has burned away her every cell. She's erased, the boys having silenced her forever.

I'm not the only one looking—the place where she stood has the entire dining hall's attention except for Tall-Boy and his friends. They're looking around, making sure this explosion has been seen and understood.

They meant to make an example of her, and they have.

They leave us then, point made. We freshman girls sit quietly, out of respect for our deceased hallmate. The moment of silence stretches to dinner's end. Back in the dorms, someone is sobbing.

Not me. I've seen quiet horror. In high school, boys used to silence with fists and boots; here they use words. This is the way of college.

Have my hallmates absorbed the lesson?

Quiet girls don't get clocked. We aren't made examples.

Quiet girls don't explode.

EMOTIONAL

I watch the chattier freshman girls when crossing the quad or getting coffee at the open-air campus center—the ones who haven't learned.

One of Tall-Boy's friends reminds me that silence is a blessing. He circles the chatty girls, a shark sizing up swimmers, and intrudes with his *debate me* voice, egging the girls to engage him on human rights or politics or some superhero movie. Given time, one will speak, and then he mocks, and interrupts, and chastises. He puts her in her place. When she's upset, he calls her "emotional," and it's a silencing nail hammered through her tongue. She's learning terror, one syllable at a time.

Unspoken words can't escape. I watch her swallow them, and they stew in her guts like trapped gas in a mine. The more she tries to talk, the worse the pressure. It's slow for some girls, quick for others. Sometimes, when crossing campus, I hear a distant eruption, and I know we've lost another.

Survival requires silence. This is the way of college.

When do the boys turn from freshmen to sorcerers?

Who teaches them the silence spell-words?

Why don't they warn us before it's too late?

Allison wouldn't have come here had she known what Tall-Boy's tongue would do to her. She wasn't the type to be silent.

Except getting a rise from her was Tall-Boy's game. She didn't know better—how could any of us? Freshmen mouths might spit fire, but we know nothing of spell-words.

Our fingers are smarter. On the way out of the dining hall one evening, I steal a knife.

IRRATIONAL

Alone in the dormitory shower, I slide the knife down my upper arm and cut a small letter into my skin—A. The shape is ragged; the blade could be sharper. I tell myself that this is how I'll remember Allison when we took no selfies together; there is no body, no candlelight vigil.

We're afraid our gathering at campus center will lure the boys. They would hear our sneakers squeaking across cobblestone and be drawn like sharks to blood in the water.

I want the second letter to be L, and then L-I-S-O-N, but I'm no longer certain Allison had two L's. Instead of overthinking it, I let the blade take over.

Knives have always made sense to me. Hormone therapy has treated my features down to a cellular level, but deeper than that, our flesh holds bad habits holy. I thought I quit cutting myself in middle school, but a smoker smokes when the chips are down, and a cutter cuts. Transition during high school only pressed the pause button.

Still, I haven't been trapped in that *what am I?* body for years. Things have changed, even the cutting.

When I glance at the knife's work, I find the A is not the beginning, but the center. Before it, I've carved J-U-S-T. After, I've carved a J. I finish what the knife began and carve O-K-E myself.

I carve further spell-words. It's nothing like my old cutting: every bleeding stroke less about dulling psychological pain, and more about creating protective sigils. Silence spells will find themselves carved in my skin and scurry back to their masters. The boys can't witch me with words I've bled.

That's the theory, anyway.

SMILE

There's a trick to keeping boys from telling you to smile. Most girls ignore or retort, but "smile" here is another silence spell. No comebacks, only combustion.

The trick is to always smile. The worst these boys can say is "Smile bigger" or "Show some teeth," but they never do. No matter how rancid I feel inside, my cheeks tug the corners of my lips. The expression is reflex now; no need to think, no effort needed.

I probably smile in my sleep.

Maybe it's that façade of cheery disposition that draws this boy to me as I cross campus center. He has a wolfish face, jaw hugged by scruffy dark hair, but his eyes look wide and unassuming, almost innocent. Their pretty gaze doesn't fit his lupine form, two damp orbs stolen from some gentle giant.

His voice is likewise sweet. "This sounds weird, and it's okay if you don't want to talk to me, but I just—sorry, I'm not good at this. Hello."

When I wave at him, he smiles, and my lips tug a little tighter from my teeth.

"You got a name?" he asks.

An invitation to speak, not like Tall-Boy's prodding. I tell Wolf-Boy my name, keeping my tone neutral, and I never stop smiling no matter the syllables. Keeping my voice tender to temper his. Sweet as he might seem, he's still a boy at Sutton University. I cannot trust him.

He's flummoxed though, makes sure to say my name as many times as can fit in his sentences, like it might flit away if he doesn't catch it. He chats at me until we reach the edge of the dorms, when a growl cuts through my body.

I slide a concerned hand over my middle. Does this count as breaking my silence? Will Wolf-Boy cast a spell?

"That's adorable." One arm folds around my elbow, and he

leads me from the dorms. "Let's grab dinner. My stomach's rumbling too."

I let him escort me toward the dining hall, my face smiling to mirror his, but I scowl inside. That growl wasn't my churning stomach.

It felt like my skin.

CALM DOWN

Outside the dining hall entrance, I excuse myself to the ladies' room. Wolf-Boy doesn't roll his eyes or chastise. Maybe the bar is too low at Sutton University, in this world, but his lack of impatience feels like hope.

I slip into a stall and pull up my shirt. I've carved letters beneath the short side of my ribcage, as if I-R-R-A-T-I-O-N-A-L can pretend that hormone treatment grows the absent strip of bone. Around the letters, skin ripples, a pond disturbed by thrashing fish.

Like Allison's skin before the end.

Maybe college just does this to girls, tells our skin to run away, fast as it can.

Or has carving the spell-word into my flesh stuck the sorcery inside? The words manifest, but unlike for other girls, my skin's set to unravel, muscle sloughing from bone. Different girls might self-destruct in different kinds of ways.

Not an explosion, but a meltdown. How long until the sorcery kills me?

If I'm dying, I don't want to die alone, and since there's no one else in the ladies' room, I find Wolf-Boy in the dining hall. I'm not sure if he's genuinely interested in me or if he's playing games like Tall-Boy. If I step away, tell Wolf-Boy, *Goodbye,* in Allison's fiery tone, will he toss a spell-word or let me go?

Worse, if I like him, will he want me to speak more? Boys can be harsh. Sometimes I envy the girls who like other girls. I used to radiate the sun, but hormones cooled my blood. The only girl I ever dated had hands and feet as cold as mine, lizards attached to our limbs. Boys are furnaces, and I crave the warmth.

Sometimes attraction is that simple.

We eat slowly, and I let him do the talking. Never spell-words, always gentle. He urges a few words from me here and there, but they're scaffolding through which he builds his side of the conversation.

"Where are you from?" he asks.

"West," I say, tender yet neutral, still smiling while I chew.

He has no opinions about that, and asks, "What's your major?"

"English."

He has opinions there, my answer prompting his every thought on Literature classes, majors, and degrees. On the surface, I hear his critique. Deeper, I wonder if an onslaught of opinion is another means to silence me, a complex string of pieces that form a spell. Should I be terrified? My skin growls, but the dining hall din smothers the sound.

Even my body is silenced, but that's better than exploding.

When will the meltdown take me? Do Wolf-Boy and I have time for kissing and touching first? He's barely an acquaintance, but if I lead him to my dorm room, he'll follow. Will a nod be my consent for more? He'll have to notice the spell-words carved into my skin. I might even drag him into the meltdown. And shouldn't I mention how I'm different from other girls? My last boyfriend knew before he asked me out. Will Wolf-Boy still see that I'm human, or will I become a thing?

When it comes to girls, sometimes boys see little difference. Even the ones with sweet eyes.

As we leave the dining hall, his arm once again hooked around mine, I realize we're not going to find out how he sees me. Campus is no place for closeness or honesty. Another freshman girl whose name I'll never learn cowers at the edge of the dorms, caught in Tall-Boy's shadow. His friends linger close. Girls keep their distance, weaving around the scene or watching from doorways.

Wolf-Boy strides toward the cluster, a solitary angel who might make a difference in this undergrad hell. A familiar itch crosses my skin, the kind when you want to drag a boy by his jacket into your bedroom and then tear away that jacket and everything else.

The nameless freshman girl turns to speak to him, probably to plead. Her face is scrunched, desperate.

Wolf-Boy holds up an open palm. "Calm down," he says. "What's the trouble?"

Desire's itch washes off my skin, and the growling ripple returns. Tall-Boy and his friends lean in, expectant, but Wolf-Boy stares oblivious. My sweet wolf has no idea he's spoken another silencing spell.

I can't watch. Without waiting for him, I skirt around the crowd and run for my dorm's front doors. He doesn't mean to cast spells, but he can't help it. They are the words he knows. How long until he slings them my way? I catch the girl out of the corner of my eye, wrapping her arms around her torso as if trying to hold herself together. She's already reached her limit from Tall-Boy. Wolf-Boy's pressure is too much. She's done.

As I rush inside my dorm hall, I hear her explode.

NEUROTIC

My skin twitches harder each day. Wolf-Boy watched me run, and now he haunts my dorm hall. "Laurie, you there?" he calls, but I never answer. He might tell me to calm down, and I won't risk it.

No one guides him to my door. We girls are frightened, and the boys down the hall don't know my name. Those immune won't answer him—the musician who speaks more Mandarin than English, the history major with hearing aids, the non-binary students scattered between binary hall designations. They can't share their safety.

Not that I blame them; I can't share my knife.

And I can't quit cutting. My skin growls non-stop, every pore a mouth caught mid-snarl. Beneath the shower's spattering rain, I try to relieve word-driven pressure, but whispers aren't enough. Something inside me wants to roar.

Only carving settles my skin. I imagine spell-words Wolf-Boy might lace onto his opinions were we to peel each other's clothes off and bare my cutting. R-I-D-I-C-U-L-O-U-S. N-E-U-R-O-T-I-C. T-O-O and then M-U-C-H. I empathize with tattoo lovers—I'm running out of spare skin.

Still, no meat sloughs off. If I've averted the meltdown, will I still explode? Too many theories swirl inside—maybe I'm too different from the other girls. Maybe surviving attempted self-destruction years ago has helped me build antibodies. Maybe the carvings do their job so that Tall-Boy and friends can't destroy me. Maybe I haven't given them a reason.

And Wolf-Boy? In a darkened room, he might not notice my

carvings. He might not care how I'm different. If my fingertips coax him to growl like a wolf, he might not hear my skin do the same.

But Wolf-Boy, Tall-Boy—they're of one nature. The boys pronounce themselves individuals for conflicting views on ethics, culture, and history, but they're each sharks in the same ocean. Tall-Boy the Cruel, but he's just joking. Wolf-Boy the Cruel, but *calm down* because he doesn't mean it. Surely the others have spiced up their cruelty to help live with themselves.

Excuses, excuses.

Our upperclassmen know when to be silent and when to speak—when spoken to. Those of us who survive our freshman year will grow into sophomores if we learn the same, a mandatory class we obliviously enrolled in upon orientation. Sutton University's spell-word crucible will destroy the rest.

In the end, we girls will likewise be of one nature. I won't be a different kind of girl anymore. Isn't that the dream?

As my skin ripples, filled with wolves and leopards and every growling angry beast that's ever walked this world, I wonder—if that's the dream, then what's the nightmare?

And the boys? What's *their* nightmare?

ATTITUDE PROBLEM

Weeks have passed since Allison's death, but I finally muster a candlelight vigil for her. For all the girls who've exploded. I pass notes through the freshman dorm, meant for the girls, but others will find them, too. They'll spread the word.

The lure.

We gather after sunset at campus center to raise candles. This moment of silence might have stretched until midnight, but I hear Tall-Boy's snide voice at the crowd's edge. He's playing the shark, testing us for weaknesses. Sizing up who to bite.

I don't understand why he does it. Probing the freshman population for what he considers girlfriend material? A lackluster comedian hunting an audience for when he's *just joking*? Does he like to watch us brim with starlight and suffer explosions?

Or does he do it because he can?

I muscle through the vigil's crowd and find he's not alone. His cluster of friends traipse behind him in matching button-downs, eyes on their leader. I storm between him and the other girls, my candlestick spattering on cobblestone. Skin and mouth growl together as I hurl insults, telling him exactly what I think of Tall-Boy's unjust jokes, creepy grin, and shark-like face.

He smirks at first, but his confident mask crumbles when his friends snicker. Spell-words spit off his lips, sprinkle my face.

I shout an onslaught of opinions to rival Wolf-Boy's. Every word's emotional, my voice clumsy, my skin snarling, and I'm not sorry for it, and I can't stop. I won't stop. That's why Tall-Boy, tongue flustered, finally storms forward and shoves my shoulders.

I crash onto the cobblestones. My skin quits growling, the pain welcome, and I can't help the cracking shout that shoots up my throat. It is an old voice I keep meaning to leave behind.

The glint shifts in Tall-Boy's eyes. "Oh," he says, piercing gaze at last seeing me. Clocking me. His barracuda smile returns.

The moment stretches in pregnant silence. I've turned from *human* to *thing* in his eyes, but I don't mind because that's how he sees every girl here. It's validating in a terrible way. He wants to sling spell-words fashioned solely for me, the kinds of slurs you'll find for a dime a dozen on any street.

But I don't let him finish. I barely let him start.

"That's why it doesn't work," he says. "Because you're not really a—"

I stand quick and thrust my face into his. "I'm not done," I snap.

His tongue limpens, and his jaw goes slack. No slurs, no spells. No jokes. The words slide down his esophagus and into his stomach, where they froth and rumble.

He tries again. "You—"

I lean closer. "Don't interrupt me."

Again, he swallows his words. His friends aren't snickering now; they realize in fits and starts what's happening to their tall leader. Behind me, the girls cluster. They're still silent, but they're watching.

Someone who isn't silent appears from the gloom beyond the crowd—Wolf-Boy. His scruffy face doesn't smile now. He scowls at Tall-Boy, who's gripping his guts, and then at me. Wolf-Boy thinks he understands, but he's thought that before and been wrong.

Still, he tries. "No need to fight, right?" he asks.

Each word rings earnest. I know he only means the best, can't see the damage he does, how he props up boys like Tall-Boy and shatters girls like the nameless freshman he told to calm down. It would be easy to fall into his oblivious arms and let his furnace warm me.

But I can't.

His mouth opens again to ask, "Why don't we just calm—"

"No," I snap.

Like a scolded dog, he bows his head, and I imagine his ears drooping. I won't let him tell me to calm, or settle, or chill. Not anyone else, either. Good intentions don't matter; a spell-word is a spell-word. Wolf-Boy has his innocent mistakes, Tall-Boy has his humor and viciousness.

And we girls have our vengeance.

I sling spell-words at Tall-Boy. Ones he knows, like *irrational* and *attitude problem*. Ones he doesn't, like *no*. I speak ones specially for him, like *sad* and *worthless* and *empty*. The harder he tries to smirk through it, the deeper my tongue carves them into his body.

Other freshman girls chime in. They only speak the words I use, but an echo is better than silence. We know what this will do to him now, and we mean it. We aren't joking. We are far from calm.

Because girls can be cruel, too.

And I make sure everyone sees. Tall-Boy will turn example at the center of campus. This is the way of college. Sutton University might trigger spell-words to explosions, but we've all been silenced before. Tall-Boy hasn't. He's never been put in his place, has no tolerance to the pressure. It builds quickly inside him.

I strip off my jacket, roll up my sleeves and leggings, expose my midriff and ribs and every spell-word etched into my skin. A new carving tattoos my sternum, and I speak it now. It echoes the first exploding girl. One last spell-word to bring white light bursting from the first exploding boy.

Silently, I thank Allison for teaching it to me.

GOODBYE

WE'VE BEEN TRYING TO REACH YOU

Charles Maria Tor

IT WASN'T LONG after my twenty-fifth birthday that I began to hear things.

This wasn't exactly a shock, more like a relief; I'd feared losing my sanity for over a decade, and my fear had finally been vindicated.

My aunt was diagnosed with schizophrenia decades ago, but my mother definitely has it too. This made me especially worried once I started taking oestrogen, in case it was endemic to the women in our family;

in case hormones would undo my psyche.

I'm not just wildly speculating about my mother having schizophrenia, by the way. My mother believes she's abducted by aliens every week, like clockwork.

I can still picture it vividly, that day when she sat me down on the couch and told me about the aliens beaming her up, dissecting her, and putting her back with little scratches where they'd been unable to heal all of the damage. She told me they would probably start beaming me up too, in due time.

I probably have autism 'cause of the aliens, so says my mother. One pregnant morning, she found a scratch running across her belly. That's proof as proof can be.

But a little spastic like me stillbirthed her dream of a perfect life.

Blissfully, in my own little world, I didn't even find the thought of being abducted *scary*. Even when I wholeheartedly believed her, being abducted was just a thing that could happen, and I had made my peace.

Different story for my little sister though, whom I told before my mother thought she was ready.

She started wetting the bed, waking up screaming, crying out into the night.

I didn't exactly help the situation when I went into her room one night clicking a flashlight on and off while wearing a Roswell Grey mask I'd bought at the school fete.

My mother thinks she's the only sane person in the world, which is tragic, but on the bright side it causes her to say some stuff that's so completely lacking in self-awareness you'd think she was joking. One of my absolute favourites was after she came back from a convention for alien abductees.

There I was, sitting at the breakfast counter, when her station wagon pulled up. She got out, slammed the car door, stormed into the house, and yelled, "Well that was a waste of my time, none of those people were *actually* abducted by aliens, they were all just nuts!"

Her spell didn't last forever, all because I couldn't keep a secret to save my life. I told some kids at school that my mother was abducted by aliens, for which they mocked me, and that drove me to skeptical resources on alien abductions. Didn't take long for my mother's status in my mind to go from "cruel and clever" to "cruel and insane."

Then one night, she disappeared without a trace.

***

I fled an abusive relationship a few months back, absconding with a surprise moving truck and zero notice.

On the key handover day, I thought that I hadn't done my due diligence when I inspected my new apartment, and that I had just rented a place without an internal laundry.

I laid on the living room floor and cried for hours while I watched myself in my mind's eye, jumping from the balcony over

and over

and over again.

It turned out that one set of cupboards actually housed a small laundry, but I still came to detest the stark apartment on Figtree Road.

The place was so incredibly sterile, with such awful huge windows.

Who designs an apartment with floor-to-ceiling windows as two walls of the communal space? What kind of post-functionality panopticon fetishist society designs apartments like this?

Sorry, I'm getting sidetracked.

What I truly hated about this apartment was the buzzer. Had that slick fast-talking real estate agent demonstrated the thing to me, I would've walked right out of the building; probably over the balcony.

The thing sounded like a telephone bell being mimicked by a synthesiser, but with a depth to it; this haunting quality that I just couldn't pin down.

To make matters worse, it was an actual telephone, some weird simulacrum that replicated the 1980s replication of a classical sleek red rotary handset.

I suppose it's cheaper to run a private copper interchange than to pay for software updates to your shitty wall-connected tablet while you pray the manufacturer never goes under; if anything it's a bit strange I don't know anyone else with a retro-chic buzzer phone.

The problem with the phone, however, is that every time it repeats, it gets slightly slower, right at the edge of my perception.

I thought it was just my imagination, so to test it, I simply didn't pick up the phone one day.

So it rang once.

Twice.

No detectable slowdown.

It rang a third time.

Still nothing.

I started walking over to the buzzer, my experiment having failed.

My hand reached out to answer,

but it refused to ring again.

A shiver shot down my spine.

The distance between my hand and the receiver widened, and not by my doing.

They must've hung up, I tried to tell myself, but before that thought could be wholly expressed, it rang again.

WE'VE BEEN TRYING TO REACH YOU

It was as if the room was pressurised with a dense gas, stretching the cadence and lowering the tone.
My skin prickled with sweat.
My heart kicked into high gear.
I picked up the receiver
and slammed it back down.

I was in my bed just a fortnight ago, trying my best to fall asleep—never an easy task.
I dreamt of a thread of red light in the form of a sine wave, oscillating gently.
It was soon joined by another, vibrating at a higher frequency.
The two waves overlapped and ricocheted, the gap between them getting smaller
and smaller,
until finally,
they merged.
My mind was flooded with the sight of a red rotary handset.
It chimed so loudly that I flew awake and sprinted to the phone.
But when I picked up the receiver, there was nothing.

The ringing didn't come again until a few nights later.
Night roadworks were happening right outside my window, so in a feeble attempt to drown out the jackhammers, I was playing rain noises through my bedroom speakers.
After I turned out the lights, but long before I went to sleep, I heard a faint and distant chiming.
I quickly answered the buzzer.
The flat tone droned on and on until I slammed it back down.
This time around, I had no way to dismiss it:
I was hallucinating.

The ringing became a nighttime staple, and for a few nights I had to keep reminding myself it wasn't there, that my mind was just hearing signals in the noise.
It took about a week for it to fade into the background droning of the city, but even then I was still clinging to the belief that maybe it was another apartment's buzzer.

Then things escalated, only a few short days ago.
I was in a work meeting when I heard it again.
Loud and clear.
     Right
   behind me.
I broke into a cold sweat and was nigh flash-frozen, the air conditioner lifting the droplets from my skin, blood retreating to my organs.
     I needed to use all of the strength I had just to stop myself from
          looking
over my shoulder.
     It came again.
     I jammed a pen into my thigh to stop myself from asking if anyone could hear it.
     But could they?
     "Sorry," said my manager. "Marketing is **call**ing. I gotta take this."
     I turned around.
     She stepped out of the room, denied the **call**, and stalked towards her arch nemesis' desk like a wounded, vengeful wolf.
     How had I not noticed her looming behind me?
     I chuckled, as I usually did when I was nervous, but I couldn't muster a sigh of relief.
     "Tori, are you okay?" asked the project lead. "You look ill."
     I stared blankly at him. *What was the ringing doing to me?* I stood up and left the conference room without a word, beelining to the toilet and losing my lunch in an empty stall.
     The sound came again,
     louder now,
     bouncing off the tiles,
     echoing off the walls.
     Can hallucinations do that?
     "I've been expecting your **call**."
     Nobody was in here,
     I *knew* that.
     The bathroom door hadn't budged.
     I looked up.
     The ceiling twisted,
     turned,

gurgled,
warped.
It spiralled inward, flexing into a funnel black as night.
No,
blacker than night.
It stared into me, and inside of it, I could see stars.
I could see atoms.
I could see my own synapses firing.
I could see

Everything.

I knelt on the tiles and ran shaky fingers through my hair, tugging at strands with balled fists.

"It's okay," I told myself.

"It's okay, you'll be okay.

"This is just a menty b, it's gotta be, just like what happened to mum."

I paused and chewed my knuckle while I conjured up my own pep talk.

"You'll live through it, and you'll see a therapist, unlike her.

"Open parenthesis. A therapist that is unlike her. Close parenthesis.

"And you're gonna get meds, unlike her.

"And you'll take those meds, unlike her.

"You'll be okay.

"Unlike her."

I looked back up.

The vortex was gone.

The ringing stopped abruptly, a clattering noise filling the space.

Had it rung off the hook?

I calmly walked back out of the bathroom and told my manager I needed a week off.

When I arrived home, I gouged out the speaker of the thing with my multi-tool's pliers.

I stood there a moment, triumphant, until,
of course,
it rang.

I needed to be anywhere but that apartment, so I rode my motorbike down the coast and rented a cheap motel on the outskirts of Wollongong.

I'm sitting in a cafe now, trying to collect my thoughts, trying to drown out the noise. I just got off the phone to my doctor to ask that she book me a psychiatrist appointment, but the books are backlogged for months.

I don't think I have months.

I've been here maybe two hours now. My coffee is cold. I swear it's getting louder.

"Do you want anything else?" asks the waitress.

I swivel my head to look at her, and the sound gets quieter.

I look back to my coffee, and in my right ear it gets louder.

Is this some kind of left brain, right brain bullshit?

I turn my head the other way.

It's louder in both ears now.

Oh god.

It's not getting louder.

It's coming closer.

I need to keep moving.

Sprinting back to the motel parking lot, I jump on my bike and peel out with reckless abandon, straight towards the highway.

Fuck, I left my laptop behind.

I'll get a new one.

***

I can't hear it when I'm on my bike, the wind's deafening roar drowns out all else.

Peace and panic mix within me. Oil and water.

I'm about to reach the turn offturnoff to the Hume Highway. I can't go north, so I gotta go south.

I'll go to Melbourne! I've got a sibling there, they'll understand what I'm going through, surely.

Entering the slip lane, I reach up to my headset and activate its speech recognition.

"**Call** Ollie," I say.

"Okay, here's some Olly Murs," it replies.

"Fuck." I really regret not buying a throat mic as the song starts declaring me a troublemaker.

"Call Ollie Mal," I try again, yelling over the wind, enunciating so hard it almost hurts.

Oh fuck,

I can hear it again!

How did it catch up to me so quickly?

A twist of the throttle and the 1200cc engine gallops with pride.

Wait.

It's not coming from behind me.

It's coming from inside my helmet.

It's coming from my headset!

I hammer the button to detach the Bluetooth unit and hurl it over the next bridge.

A sigh of relief, but it's a short-lived feeling.

I can still faintly hear it somehow.

Is it coming from me?

It's coming from below me!

My phone, of course!

How could I have been so naive?

Phone and phone, phones. It's so obvious.

I reach into my pants pocket with a gloved left hand and toss the phone to the road.

It's gone,

I got away.

It's back!

Right behind me!

I glance into the mirror and see a cop car with its sirens on.

I allow myself to be pulled over, put down my kickstand, and remove my helmet. The cop approaches me very casually.

"Son, did I just see you throw something from your bike as you swerved all over the road?"

I shrug. "Perception is subjective, you tell me."

The cop sighs.

I pay him no mind. "Tell me, *officer*, do you hear the ringing?"

He cocks an eyebrow. "Alright son, I'm gonna need to see your licence. Actually, first I'm gonna need you to blow into this." He produces an arcane gadget in a fluoro yellow case.

I look down at it, puzzled.

It shudders side to side as it rings.

I can't be here.

I need to leave.

"Sorry officer, but I'm in a bit of a hurry." I turn back towards my bike.

An iron grip clamps onto my shoulder and stops me dead in my tracks. "You're not going anywhere, son.

"I don't wanna arrest you. You seem like a nice boy, I'm sure you don't want your parents worried about you.

"Just breathe into this, or we're gonna have to do this the hard way."

He holds out the gadget again.

Oh god, it's getting louder.

I can't take this.

I take a step back and produce my licence from my wallet, which he snatches out of my hand, placating him just enough.

When he turns back to his cruiser,

I lift my arm,

reel it back,

and bring my helmet crashing down

on the back

of his head.

He slumps.

I hope he's unconscious,

but I'm not sure.

I pick up the gadget and throw it down the embankment.

I unholster his gun and marvel for a moment at the power of life and death condensed into irreverent black metal.

I slip it into my cargo pants.

Grabbing the cop's legs, I drag him behind the highway patrol car.

When I let them go, he begins to stir.

"Son, you're in a lotta trouble," he slurs.

Without hesitation, I drop a knee into his chest.

He screams through the sternum pain.

I press harder, feeling the crack of ribs more so than hearing them.

He stops screaming.

I cradle the bottom of his head above the gravel, leaving a gap near the top.

The intimacy is fitting.

WE'VE BEEN TRYING TO REACH YOU

I lift the helmet high above my head.
"Stop," he wheezes.
I slam down the helmet again,
and again,
and again,
and again.
The gravel runs crimson, blood both his and mine.
I slam down the helmet again.

I've managed to make it about two hundred kilometres, but the sun is setting, and the ringing recently became loud enough to be heard over the wind.
It's in my helmet now.
Burrowing into my brain.
Infecting my thoughts.
There's little else I can think of and even less I can do.
I clearly can't outrun it.

***

Fuck!
It's in front of me now,
and it's coming
fast.
Before I can even begin to apply the brakes, a cabal of police cars scream past with their sirens blaring.
They'll be looking for me soon, ; cop's body cams are always on at the most inconvenient times.
I'll exchange the highway for something a little more scenic.

Tracing the hills and hugging the corners of a winding road, I reach speeds that make even me pale.
But it's a necessary evil.
How long has it been now?
How far have I travelled?
I have no way of knowing.
Without the road signs, I wouldn't even know how to get to Melbourne.
I nearly fuck up a corner and my bike fishtails on the gravel.
I can't talk right now, I'll **call** you back.

There's a light in the distance.
It's scouring the road.
Rushing towards me.
I see a glint in my mirror.
There's another coming from behind.
Suddenly a circle of sun envelopes me from on high, blinding me.
Squinting is only taking the edge off.
I can't see shit.
The sky looked, and behold a steel horse:
and hirs name that sat on it was Tori,
and the Ringing followed with hir.
The air around me shimmers and twists, spiralling skyward in a maddening rainbow.
Rocks and sticks lift up from the tarmac and float into the air around me.
I look above and see an unblinking eye watching me.
It's the aliens, they've finally come.
A copse of trees envelops me.
The light is interrupted.
The rocks and sticks fall to the ground.
One of them is going under the wheels.
I can't swerve!
My back wheel slides out.
The now-sideways bike falls and slides across the asphalt, giving my kevlar reinforcements a run for their money.
My helmet smashes against the surface as the bike comes to a stop.
My vision goes black.

How long was I out?
My eyes open asymmetri**call**y.
I can hear the ringing in the distance.
Closing in.
Fast.
The beam is trained on me. It only *just* filters through the fractal shadows of the leaves above.
My muscles are screaming from the impact.
I flip my bike's kill switch and shakily lift it off me.

WE'VE BEEN TRYING TO REACH YOU

The light wavers—was it tracking my own light? Light attracts light.

Hahaha.

Ha ha ha ha ha.

I pull the gun from my pocket and smash my bike's always-on headlight with its butt.

The ringing grows louder.

The ringing grows sharper.

The ringing burrows into my cochlea.

Hands grasping at the sides of the helmet, not all of them mine.

It feels like my brain is gonna pop.

Then just as quickly as it arrived, it vanishes.

The beam flits around, searching for its prey.

***

I remain motionless, but my head is spinning.

I lift my visor and puke black bile across my boots, ignoring the splash-back.

Opaque fumes rise as it eats through my trousers.

The light breaks off from the copse, looking for me back the way I came.

I throttle my bike to life, and the battered and bruised creature roars.

I've still got the high beam headlight if I need it, but I'll mostly be relying on the moon overhead.

I need to keep going,
they know where I am.

Dawn is finally breaking.

It feels like it's been years.

I've ridden further inland, just to make sure I don't run into any roadblocks when I cross the border.

I'm passing through this tiny town, and I'm happy to report that I've been three hours ring-free.

Oh, good, a McDonalds. My stomach feels like it's on the verge of consuming me. I haven't eaten in more than a day—unless you count half a coffee—so I pull into the parking lot and dismount.

The automatic doors slide open for me, and I hear it immediately, the sombre haunting melody.

Her!

Over there!
That woman holding a phone.
The phone.
What does that bitch think she's doing?
It's ringing for **me!**
"Give me that," I shout, snatching it from her meaty paws.
"What do you want from me?!" I hear myself scream into the receiver.
No answer comes.
The line goes dead.
The woman looks at me, all shell-shock and awe.
I maintain eye contact as I snap the flip phone in half.
On the TV there's a picture of someone who looks kinda familiar.
I gotta keep moving.
No time for hash browns.

Across the border now, thankfully. But I can't keep going.
I'm so tired.
This next town will (have to) do—will have to do—I need to rest or I'm gonna crash my bike again.
The clerk of the dingy motel I chose catches me staring at the phone on his desk and asks if I need to make a **call**.
"Yeah, I do."
"You'll have to use the guest phone. Hasn't been used in a while."
He reaches under the desk, pulls out a phone, blows off the dust, then slides it over to me.
It's red,
it's rotary,
and it's ringing.
It connects with something inside,
in me,
in the pit of my stomach.
Beep beep boop beep boop beep.
"You've received a collect **call**.
"Will you accept the consequences?"

I slam the room's door and fumble with the chain.
My abdomen is twisting and turning onto itself.
God,
the pain!
I can't take it!
My legs fall from under me.
Grasping at the carpet, I drag my useless body inch by inch.
The snap of a nail bent too far,
and another,
and another.
I hoist myself up over the toilet and watch my reflection dissolve into a star field that beckons me

Beyond.
My stomach clenches and squeezes.
Nothing comes out.
But something just shifted inside of me.
I gotta force it out.
I wind up a two handed gut punch and drive it home.
My whole body recoils.
But it's stuck.
Whatever it is, it's stuck in my throat.
It's solid like metal, and traveling upwards.
I try to scream for help,
just as it blocks my airway.
My lungs spasm.
I claw at my throat.
I shove a hand in my mouth,
form a fist,
and rotate it.
My jaw locks open.
I still can't breathe.
Cartilage stretches,
cracks,
pops.
A throat distends to accommodate violation.
My guts heave again,
with nowhere to go.
It's crowning against my uvula.

My left hand claws my jaw even wider.
Muscle snaps like piano wire.
My right tries to grab the slick body.
But it's so slimy.
~~I'm losing my grip.~~
I can't get a grip.
Feeling lightheaded . . .
Stay focused.
Focus focus focus.
Tell me what to do.
Please!
Answer me!
PICK UP PICK UP PICK UP.
My vision tunnels,
just as I remember what's in my pocket.
Pliers unfolded, I thrust them into my mouth.
I've got it!
I grip
and I pull
with all my strength.
Hot tears roll down my cheeks.
Nearly.
NEARLY.
Just one

More
pull.

Both hands on the pliers,
I wrench out my tonsil.
White stones seep and fill my mouth.
A sick gurgling
as I suck a lungful
through the new gap.
Hurry,
before you drown.
PICK UP THE DAMN PHONE.
A pen yes a pen a pen on the nightstand there's always a pen
always a pen.
YES!
A PEN!

WE'VE BEEN TRYING TO REACH YOU

Hold it steady.
Steady!
Steady you fucking spastic.
Cool wet ballpoint kisses my flesh tenderly.
NOW!
POP
goes the cherry.
God I'm fucking funny.
You think so too, right?
Focus focus focus.
FOCUS!
Unscrew the cap, pull out the ink.
Deep breath(s).
In and out.
Squeeze my hand.
Pliers back in.
Got it!
ALL
    TOGETHER
NOW.
The sound of disfigurement
is deafening.
No.
I can't hear the sounds of my flesh tearing.
I cannot hear them.
Sound is the only
truth.
Stretching.
Ripping.
Screaming.
Not.
Enough.
Room.
I reposition the pliers.
I grip too hard and a molar explodes into shrapnel.
Softly, I pluck out my canines.
Gently, I rip out my incisors.
Reverently, I spit out the shards.

***

Lovingly, I am delivered unto,
    and staring down the coiled cord stretching from my mouth to
the red rotary handset, I wait and wait and I wait and wait for the
call I'm expecting an important **call** any moment now it won't be
long it's coming it'll be here soon not long now on its way I just
have to
    wait.
    Finally it rings.
    I smile,
    warm red liquid
        spilling
        over my lips.
    I lift the receiver to my head,
    and pull the trigger.

LOST IN REINCARNATION

Devaki Devay

EVER SINCE HE'D arrived in America, a great pain had radiated from the center of Vaishnav's body. The heat of it sprouted up his spine and through the tip of his forehead like a twisting tree. It thickened inside him, his arteries tangling into phloem.

When Vaishnav began latching the windows to keep sunlight from feeding the pain, his wife called up a massage therapist. The best in the world, she said. Vaishnav trusted her. He had to trust Akansha, the quiet woman he'd been swept off to the states with. They were good for each other, their parents had decided over tea. A boy and a girl who never caused trouble, perfect pockets of soil. These were parents who wanted children that wanted children. The music of a monsoon pouring and breathing back into the clouds.

On the terrain of his visa, Vaishnav hopped between technical jobs. His wife mended some of the neighbor's clothes for money. Still, every month the rent swallowed their arms and legs whole, and they woke the next morning to thinned, alpine air, as if they'd been placed precariously at the tip of a mountain with nothing to take to their lungs. Like so, the seed of his pain had cracked.

Vaishnav found the massage therapist's office to be strange and haunting, deep red walls illuminated by scarlet candlelight. Stalks of dark green leaves flooded over clay pots lining the shelves. A deep golden mattress crowned the middle of the room, where shadows bled into the light. The masseuse beckoned him towards it.

The masseuse was a very old woman, her hair white as the guts of a seashell. Her rough palms scraped his back as she examined as a doctor would, leaning forward and back with weight.

"You skipped a life," she said finally. Vaishnav stared at her. Skipped a life? But something about her told him she was right, that he was in no place to ask questions.

"Can you fix it?" he asked. He settled on this, instead of what she meant, or how she knew.

"Haven't you ever wondered why you felt so empty? I would imagine you would," she said gently, rolling her palms back into his skin. "Looking back into the folds of your heart and finding no feeling, no memory . . . "

"I have memories," said Vaishnav, because he felt it was true. Though she was right, he thought. He remembered things, but he didn't have memories.

The woman kneaded his back. He felt his muscles coil upwards and build into a mound where there used to be a valley. From his neck, she took two strips of flesh and stretched them downward, to his arms. Already the pain was melting, turning soft under the waves of shifting, wafting gusts of warm wind. His body became a liquid geography.

"What are you making me?" he whispered, asking only the air.

As an answer, the masseuse spun his arms and legs into a thick loaf, then sliced the dough into eight equal parts, splaying them outwards, flowering from his neck.

"An octopus has three hearts," she said. "I need you to open wide."

From her shelves, the woman extracted two hearts, full of sky-blue blood, organs waiting for him since the ocean's formation. She propped a finger gently under his chin. Vaishnav opened wide. In the cavern of his chest, the drum pattering at the edges of his skin like a springtime rain grew into a thunderous roar. He felt as though he'd just seen the sun, and couldn't, now that it had been done, tear his head away.

"There is something I want you to remember, before your mind goes," said the woman. "About the octopus. A passionate lover, Vaishnav. Not like us."

Vaishnav asked what she meant, his head pounding already, not quite able to form the words.

"An octopus dies once it mates," she explained. "We humans, we start our lives with love. Not an octopus. No. Love kills it. Love is the last thing it will ever do."

The woman slathered her hands in oil and lifted from under the mattress a box full of suckers. Patiently, she affixed them over his tentacles, which grew slippery and blue under her skin. Vaishnav felt himself already far from his human life, as if it had all been a dream, his sense of feeling dripping down like honey into the bottoms of his twirling arms. He heard his masseuse as if she were a thousand miles away.

"The last step is the ocean," she was saying, her words folding over and burying themselves in the sands of Vaishnav's mind. Time spilled over like moonlight into nightmares, and he found himself nestled in the shallow water, enveloped in sea foam and yellow light. Faintly, he felt rock-heavy lungs rise from his throat.

"Before you go, I'll give you gills," she was saying. "Don't be frightened, the cold is just the metal of the knife."

The masseuse rested her hand on his slippery film, caressing the neck—a gentle thing, like a newborn. She'd done all this before; she knew well what to do. The knife was sharp. She sliced quickly, two slits like eyes squinting against the morning light. They squealed like rubber as she cut. By now, she was sure the boy could not hear her. She drew back her arms. The octopus twirled gently into the tide.

BECAUSE MY MOTHER TELLS ME SO

Dayna Ingram

I AM BEING stalked by a zombie. He's unlike other zombies in that he's completely cognizant; he sits on my front porch and taunts me. I have a porch swing and he leans back in it, kicking his feet against the rail. He says, "Come on out, little girl," and flashes his rotted teeth at me. I haven't left the house in four days.

On the first day, I almost did not notice him. It rained earlier in the morning so that the sidewalk was covered in worms by noon, and I went out to gather them. When I stepped out onto the porch, he was there. He must have been. He must have watched me from the porch swing, silently dripping mucus onto the cross-stitched cushions, as I bent at the knee and plucked up the worms with my index finger and thumb. I only take the liveliest ones, otherwise there is no point. I put them in a mason jar and turned to head back in, and that is when I noticed him, noticing me.

He said nothing at first. He smiled and his tongue lolled out next to an incisor where a piece of his jaw was missing. One eye scanned my body, its pupil dilating at a rapid pace, while the other struggled to keep its placement inside its sunken socket. Every few seconds he had to raise his arm, the good one with most of its skin intact, and gently nudge the eyeball into place. His fingers left smudges on the glistening orb, until the entire thing was clouded over, but I don't even think he realized he was doing this. One day he might say to me, "Why can't I see out of this eye? Where did all this gray come from?" But on this first day, he did not say that. This first day, he said: "Have you accepted Jesus Christ as your personal Lord and Savior?"

I did not see his Bible because it was on the porch swing where he'd left it. His body leaned forward as if he might take a step, and then leaned away from me as if he might not.

"Yes," I said, hiding the mason jar behind my back even though I knew he had already seen it. "Yes, I'm good."

"But could you be great?" he asked.

I could see his larynx working through the holes in his throat. His voice didn't come from his mouth, even though his teeth and jaws moved—he had no lips, or rather, he had negligible lips—it came from all of him, from the porous whole of him. "Could you be better in the eyes of the Lord? Could you be your best? Your best for you is good, but your best for the Lord is better than you yet know how to achieve."

"I don't have any money." I knew to be suspicious of something, but was unsure of exactly what. I was walking slowly toward the porch steps, staying to the right of him. He did not step forward but continued to sway, one arm tucked into the pocket of his tattered trousers, the other hanging loosely at his side, except when it was raised to his precarious eye.

"What *do* you have, girl?" The way he said "girl" made me nervous. Drool and mucus sloped down his chin.

"I left the oven on," I said, and tried to hurry past him. I might not have made it, but my neighbor Jim Dobson came out onto his porch at just the right time. The zombie turned at the sound of the screen door creaking open, and I sprinted to my own door. I was inside before I heard Jim shout a "Hi-ya!" across the driveway.

I thought the zombie would leave now, but he walked to the edge of the porch and planted his finger bones on the railing, leaning over to shout back at Jim. They talked for almost an hour. Jim Dobson doesn't work anymore on account of his back, and his wife works a lot of double shifts at the Meat Palace. I've caught Jim looking through his bathroom window into my bathroom while I pee. I keep a Sharpie next to the toilet paper and I mark it on the tub every time he looks. There are twenty-seven marks now. I've thought about closing the curtain, but the thought makes me lonely.

Jim talked to the zombie about lawn care and health insurance. The zombie talked to Jim about soul care and soul insurance. He confessed to hyperbole, but he continued to peddle his god.

BECAUSE MY MOTHER TELLS ME SO

I listened for a little while and then got my shoes from the living room closet. I live alone so I could put my shoes wherever I wanted but this seems best. Best for me, best for the Lord. The zombie's voice and my neighbor's voice became one voice that sounded like singing and I hummed along to the baritone. I poured the worms from the mason jar into my shoes, first the left one, then the right one. I put my feet inside and walked around a little. The worms felt like spaghetti but not like spaghetti, because I've tried spaghetti and spaghetti did not feel like worms.

I spent the afternoon with my eyes closed, wriggling my toes. When the baritones faded, I looked up and saw the zombie's silhouette through the shades drawn over my front window. He sat down on the porch swing and picked up his Bible. The timer on the stove went off, and I made something to eat. I went to bed several hours later with my shoes on.

That was day one.

I didn't expect him to be there the next day. I was supposed to meet my dance partner for practice, but he was still outside. I peered at him through the mail slot, and he bent down and grinned at me.

"Come on out, little girl. I've got a powerful message to share with you."

I took a shower and cleaned out my shoes with ammonia and bleach. I phoned my dance partner.

"Well, Christ, Marie, I mean, what the hell?" Louise said when I told her I could not make it.

"There's a zombie on my porch," I told her.

"And since when don't you have a back door?" Louise had throat cancer four years ago when she was thirty-two and they had to cut a hole in her neck. She speaks through a machine and she sounds like a Speak & Spell, except not as evil. Whenever we are dancing, if someone tries to psyche her out by staring at her or talking about her, she glares at them with her gray eyes and says, "Do you want fries with that?" She can't really laugh anymore, but she wheezes and her eyes water and I know what she means.

"My mother's car is on the street," I said.

"Look, do you want me to come over there? You can't skip practice, doll, the tourney is tomorrow."

The zombie tapped on the windowpane and flattened the Bible

against the glass. He tried to wink at me with his good eye, and his bad eye *slooked* out of its socket. It dangled on his cheek from a stubborn ligament.

"Maybe," I said to Louise.

While I waited for Louise, I tried not to look at the zombie, but he tried very hard to look at me. My across-the-street neighbor, Mrs. Flannigan, came out to walk her yappy dog, Jasper, and I watched her watching us. The zombie turned and waved. Jasper yapped, and Mrs. Flannigan looked offended.

"I've seen her in church," the zombie said, turning back to me. He raised his voice to be heard through the glass; I could see his larynx working extra hard. "She doesn't give a lot, but she sure does take a lot. Some people need Saving more than others."

"So you're Catholic?" I asked him. He didn't hear me, so I moved to the mail slot and spoke through that. "You're Catholic?"

"No, no. I keep forgetting all the words to my Hail Marys. Plus, they kneel and stand too much in their services; these knees ain't what they used to be." He brushed his bones against his kneecaps and sank into the dust that powdered off his pants.

"Mrs. Flannigan is Catholic," I said.

"As the day is long!"

"Whose god are you selling?"

"Which one are you interested in buying?"

His tongue was dry, but his words were slick. He leaned too close to the mail slot and I could smell him. He smelled like my shoes.

"Little girl," he said, "don't you want to be Saved?"

Louise pulled up and parked behind my mother's car. She is a large woman. It's the reason we've been able to remain friends. She was my mother's friend and now she is mine. When I walk outside with her, her shadow embraces me like a hug. Most of the couples we dance against underestimate her nimbleness and stamina; she pirouettes around them while they sit in the corner, icing their feet.

She started yelling at the zombie before she was even out of the Yugo. I watched her through the mail slot, like studying a specimen in a microscope. Her flesh jumped along with her steps, billowing against her yellow dress. She held her microphone to her neck and all that came out was static, she was trying to speak so fast. Her forehead sweat rivaled the zombie's own mucus-moistened skin.

Louise came to a stop at the bottom of the porch steps. The zombie did not descend to her, but he leaned over and held his better arm out.

"Morning, lovely," he said. "The name's Rickshaw. Pleasure to meet you."

Louise blushed. "Louise," she said, and shook his hand. His skin stained hers.

They talked for several minutes. I think Rickshaw was trying to whisper, but it was difficult to do without lips; with what he had to work with, enunciation was key. There was only one volume setting on Louise's machine. They talked about me.

"It's her daddy's house," Louise said. "Marie hasn't gotten over losing him. You know she still writes and calls her mother, up there in that prison? But it's not my place to talk about. We've been dancing together for a couple years. Marie's social worker encouraged routine outings, and she found these dancing derbies on the internet, and here we are. These contests, these marathons, they don't happen much anymore, but you search around, you can find 'em. And holy Christ are they—well, shit—I mean, oops—I mean, sorry."

"No offense taken," Rickshaw said, waving away her concern. His stench wafted through the mail slot. "Tell me more about Marie's family."

The carpet began to burn my knees. I got up and went into the kitchen and watched the timer tick down until it went off and I ate something. I can always remember to set the timer, but without its tinny wail I forget to eat. They were still on the porch and I could hear their dissonant hum, but I didn't sing along. Soon, Jim Dobson joined them; I saw his shadow behind the curtains. He stood against the rail and Louise took up the porch swing. Rickshaw leaned against the glass. Every few minutes, he turned around slightly and tapped on the pane and waved. His knuckles left marks all over it.

When it got dark, Louise knocked on the door and I let her inside. "What are you doing in here all alone in the dark?" She started to flip on lights. "Come on outside. That Rickshaw is a charmer if I ever met one! Have you touched his hair?"

"It's crawling with spiders," I said.

"Well, it's easy enough to work around that, isn't it?" She

clomped into my kitchen and opened the refrigerator. "Since when don't you have any beer?"

A college kid delivers my groceries once a week. I'm about a month shy to buy alcohol, but he knows about what happened and he feels sorry for me. Louise drinks his gifts when we come back from our marathons to count our winnings.

Jim Dobson tapped the front window and held up a six-pack of cans. Louise brushed past me. "Come on out," she said. "Come on, join the party."

"He wants to save me," I said.

"So what?"

That night I heard the crickets all around my house. I desperately wanted to catch them, but everyone was still on the porch. I dreamt about being alone, but in the morning Rickshaw was still there.

"I never did go in for breakfast," Rickshaw told me as I stuck my fork through the mail slot and dropped a fried egg onto the welcome mat. "I can eat breakfast for dinner, but never for breakfast."

"What about dinner for breakfast?"

"Like a ham sandwich?" He stroked his chin with his index bone and slapped a maggot from his left nostril. "I could do a ham sandwich."

"That's lunch," I said.

"Potato po-tah-doh."

"Po-Buddha Po-God-oh," I said.

A thick slime leaked down the front of Rickshaw's pants. "Exactly," he said.

"Is that a real Bible?"

"Is that a real question?"

"Why are you wearing that stupid man suit?"

"What?"

"It's from a movie."

I ate my breakfast, and he read his Bible. Louise snorted and rolled over on the porch swing. She woke up late in the afternoon and had to pee, but I wouldn't let her in. "Goddammit," she said, then, "Oops, I mean God darn it—I mean Gosh dang it. Marie—!"

"You'll find another partner," I told her. "Everyone wants to dance with you."

"Just come the fu—udge . . . Just come the fudge out."

"I can't. Make him leave."

Louise looked at Rickshaw, pushing all of her emotions into her eyes and some of it into her cleavage. He looked at neither and shook his head.

"You can save her next week, Rickshaw. This contest's for ten thousand dollars!"

"What's ten thousand to the Lord?" Rickshaw said. "What is one? One is none. A soul is the thing. A soul is a million dollars. But a million dollars is nothing. I have ten thousand dollars. I have a million dollars. Take it, will you, it's heavy. Take it, and I'll get more."

He gave her his Bible. She threw it down into the grass and triggered small earthquakes on the way to her car.

I called my mom at the allotted time. "You can make him leave, honey. Just call the police."

"I can't," I said.

"I'm sure they'll know what to do. Call the health department. Call animal control."

"I don't want them here."

"Call poison control."

"It's too many people."

When I called the police on my mother three years ago, more than thirty people showed up. Not all of them were police. Some were firemen and paramedics and people with cameras and one guy with a bag to put my father in.

"Let me talk to him," my mom said. "I'll make him see what's what."

"You'll talk to him all night."

"Only five minutes."

"No."

"He'll die, eventually."

"He's already dead." The words were an echo, but they rushed through my mother's ears like wind; she didn't hear them.

"Well, shit, sweetheart, I can't do anything for you from in here. I'm out in twenty years. Can you wait twenty years?"

"I can wait."

"Just don't invite him in."

"That's vampires."

"And don't feed him after midnight."

"That's gremlins."

"Goodnight, honey."

Now it's day four, and I have a plan. I thought of it while I was peeing. Jim Dobson stared at me and I smiled. He smiled. His shoulders shook. A bee landed on the screen of his window in just the right spot that it looked as though it had landed on his teeth. I tried putting bees in my shoes once; it is very difficult to catch bees. Plus, they can only sting you once and when you crush them, they just feel like burnt paper. It's not worth it.

Jim Dobson's teeth reminded me of Rickshaw's teeth. Without lips, all Rickshaw has going for him and his Word are his teeth. What good is his tongue without teeth? What good is his larynx?

I go outside. It is slightly windy, and my skin prickles with gooseflesh. Rickshaw sits on the porch swing, rocking his heels against the floorboards. He pats the cushion next to him and grins.

"This seat's not taken, little girl."

"I'm not a little girl," I say.

"We're all of us children for the Lord."

"Does your lord eat children?"

Something dark and congealed spurts out of Rickshaw's throat. "Not my Lord, no. I have been known to nibble now and again."

"So, how are you going to save me?"

"Finally ready to open your heart to His Saving Grace? I can fill you, little girl. I can fill you with His love."

"Do I have to sign anything?"

Rickshaw stands up and steps toward me, saying, "Not a thing. Not a thing you won't miss."

He intends to say more, but I strike him with the pliers. I over-swing and the metal catches his cheek. His eye pops out, and he is distracted. I jam the pliers into his mouth and pinch them shut around the first tooth I can find. I pull hard, but it is unnecessary; the tooth comes out like worms from the ground.

Jim Dobson comes out and watches me. Mrs. Flannigan, too. Her yappy dog stays well away. Rickshaw yowls and thrashes and my clothes are ruined. He had thirty-two teeth.

"Why the hell'd you do that?" Jim asks me when I finish. His eyes are wet and his nose is red. His shoulders shake, but in a different way than before. "Just why the hell, huh? He was good. He was a good man."

"He was a zombie," I say. I remember the way my mother said it, when the police, and then the judge, asked her the same thing. "A fucking zombie."

"And who the hell are you?"

I don't have an answer for that. When my mother comes home in twenty years, maybe she will tell me.

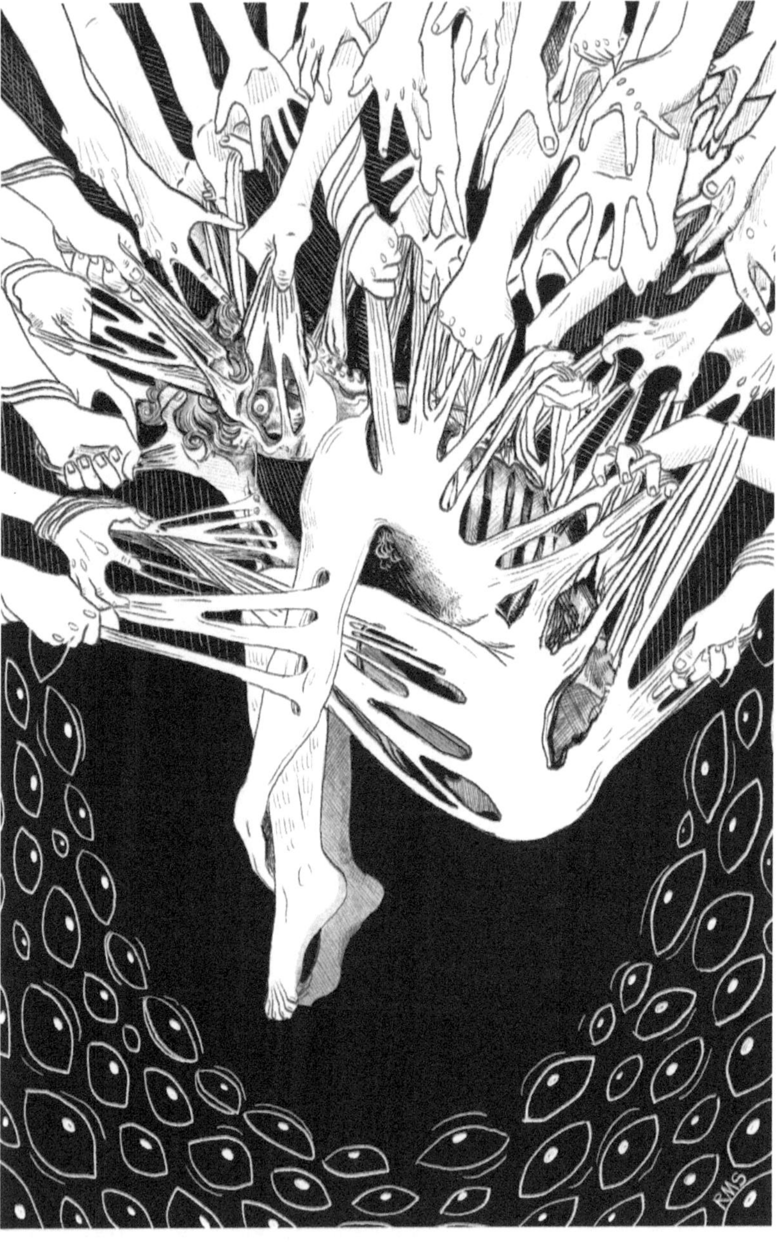

SEAFLOWERS

Ori Jay

NEVER TRUST A drowned woman. (That's what they say.)

She's known too much heartache, too much pain—down at the bottom of the ocean where it settles heavy as iron anchors; where the barnacles and rust take root, and even the ebb and flow of the water simply can't dislodge the unsightly stain of so much history.

And if you meet a drowned woman, never ask her name.

Once you know her name, her words have meaning—and when she speaks, the spells she weaves will change you; the syllables like snares pulled taut, the lines of her drawn into nets designed to hold you fast as she spins her sodden stories.

And if she offers to show you her garden, refuse.

Never ask to see where her seaflowers bloom.

Because once you see them blossom—pulsing in the water like beating hearts, red leaves and vines whispering with the beat of the waves like angry scars, like living veins—no rose will ever look the same.

Never ask a drowned woman her secrets.

Because the truths she knows are painful—the agony she's seen as she clawed desperately against the tide, gasping mouthfuls of salt in search of something approaching air

—the anguish in her eyes as she describes the crushing pressure bearing down, the certainty that salvation was long past

—the cold and clammy brush of her fingers against your own, waterlogged and unable to contain their own condition

—well, some truths are simply better left unheard.

Because when you hear them, something in you might stir.

Those secrets, they might slip inside you and you might feel them root there, somewhere behind and slightly underneath your heart.

You might hear them whisper, soft and steady, inside your ears at night.

You might sense them growing, twisting, taking shape along the lattice of your ribcage and the stalk of your spine.

And once her secrets have penetrated deep enough, you might feel something strange and terrible, beautiful and tragic, otherworldly and unseen, begin to bloom inside you.

The pressure will feel like you're drowning. Even in air your lungs will burn. You will shudder and gasp and curl in on yourself, clawing at the sky and wondering who put this strange woman inside of you and why she is there.

The anguish will keep you awake through countless restless nights, through too many endless days.

You'll feel her flowers inside of you, begging to be free.

And you'll wonder, "Am I dying? Or is this a new beginning?"

Never trust a drowned woman. (That's what they say.)

Because if you start to know her, you might become her. And we all know what happens to women like that, in the end.

FENCING CHESTPLATE

Avi Burton

WHAT HAPPENED LAST Friday at the gym wasn't my fault.

Okay. The explosion was my fault. And Coach's . . . condition. And the fact that the school needs extensive renovations. But you know who the real culprit in all of this is? Society, that's who. Gatekeeping and transphobia are really at the root of this issue. What happened was nasty, I won't lie, but hey: if Coach and the administration weren't such a bag of dicks, then the school wouldn't have had to hire six exorcists to clear out the gym.

Hmm. That sounds a little victim-blamey, now that I say it aloud. Can you scratch that from the record? No? You're writing down everything I say? Even this? Or this? Or—oh wow, yeah, you're typing really fast.

Sorry. I know you don't have much time. I'll get started now.

Last Thursday afternoon, I approached Coach with chipper-eyed enthusiasm. He insists on being called Coach, by the way, even though he's really just a gym teacher who handles the school's sports teams on the side, so that's how I'll refer to him. Unlike some people, *I* respect people's chosen names, even when they're stupid.

"Hey, Coach," I said, trying to be as amiable and normal as possible, which was a struggle when Coach towered a full foot taller than me and still wore his Marine fatigues to school on Wednesdays. "New school year, new fencing team, right? Going to be hard to fill the captain's shoes since he graduated, but I think our season prospects still look great. When are tryouts?"

A beat. "You want to try out?" Coach said in a tone that was not particularly encouraging.

"Well, yeah," I answered, hitching my backpack higher. "I've been fencing with a private club for about three years, but now the owner wants to retire, so I figured I'd shoot my shot at joining your esteemed roster."

Coach looked me up and down. I'm aware I may not cut the most impressive figure—five foot three, uncontrollable hair, distinctly muppetish build—but I didn't know what was causing him so much confusion.

"It's a boy's team," he grunted.

Ah. So that was it.

"Awesome," I said, stretching my smile as far as it could go. "So I fit all the requirements, then. When are tryouts?"

"You're not a boy, Pheller."

At least he used my last name. My smile was starting to tilt like a sinking ship, but I made a valiant effort to keep it upright. "I am, though."

"Not according to your school records."

I bit my tongue. Fine. If that was how he wanted to play it. "Well, there's not a girl's team I can join, so I'm kind of stuck. Besides, it's fencing, not football—weight or height classes don't drastically impact your performance. What's the difference, really?"

He looked pointedly at my chest. "Equipment."

My smile died. I squirmed under his gaze, resisted the urge to shrink away. "I'll wear a binder," I said, hating how high-pitched and feminine my voice became under duress. "I'll use the same gear as everyone else. No one will be able to tell what's behind the mask or beneath the lamé. Please, Coach. Fencing is—it's my *thing*. It's everything. You don't even have to let me on the team! Just let me try out. Give me one chance to prove to you I'm as capable as everyone else."

His gaze was cold and distant, as if I was already dismissed. "Don't you have a bus to catch, Pheller?"

I stared at the floor. "Yes, sir."

Then I left, face burning in defeat.

***

The more I thought about my encounter with Coach, the more it pissed me off. It wasn't like I had other options: now that my club had shut down, the school fencing team was the only one in the district. The tournaments were so small they usually ended up being co-ed, anyway. There was no point in excluding girls, and even if there was, I *wasn't* one, regardless of the body parts I was born with. Coach just hated me. I didn't know what I'd done for him to despise me that much, except maybe exist as a transgender teen, but it didn't matter. I was going to make him change his mind.

I arrived home ready to pitch a fit of teenage angst and plot grand schemes, but unfortunately, someone else was already in my room.

Lucy was setting up an elaborate array of candles and runes on my floor. She was in full gothic attire, wearing a black dress stolen from the attic and raccoon-eye mascara. Various occultish miscellany formed a constellation around her. Gray-green smoke wafted up from incense candles and filtered through the vents.

"What are you doing in my *room,* asshole?" I snapped in typical benevolent older-sibling fashion.

Lucy squeaked and scrambled to gather up all her things, but fumbled reaching for a large tome embossed in red. I snatched it before she could. The smell of wet dirt and dead moths hit me as I held the book up to the light.

"*A Practitioner's Guide to Demons, Devilry, and Damnation?* What scam-ridden corner of eBay did you order this off of? And, hey, since it bears repeating: why are you in my room?"

Clutching her candles and plastic skull, Lucy rose to her feet. "It's not a scam, it had five-star reviews! You just don't have your third eye open. And, well—I needed your charcoal sticks to draw a pentagram."

"You stole my art supplies *and* tried to summon a demon on my bedroom floor? What's wrong with you?"

Lucy shrugged. "Well, if something went wrong, I didn't want to accidentally set *my* stuff on fire."

"Get. Out."

"See you in hell, jerk," Lucy huffed, and stormed down the stairs.

As the door slammed behind her, I realized I was still holding her stupid Satanic scambook. Disgusted, I tossed it at a corner of my room, where it landed with a *thud* on top of my backpack. Then, with an equally dramatic *thud*, I collapsed on top of my bed and pondered my situation.

I had to find a way to fence. It wasn't a question of whether, but when. Coach wasn't going to stop me. I clung to the idea that if I could just show him—if he could see me, really see me—then he'd have to let me on the team. I knew that I was better than all those half-hearted assholes who couldn't tell the difference between a parry and Passata Sotto. Fencing was my lifeblood, my legacy.

I'd grown up fencing with my father, and whenever I picked up an épée, it was like he was alive and with me again. When I won, I imagined he was proud of me—the real me, his son, who he never knew. Fencing was all I had left. I couldn't give up on it.

Sorry, are you sure you can't cut that part from the record? Alright. Yeah, no, I'm fine. Don't need a tissue, but thanks for offering.

***

Having gained most of my misbegotten enthusiasm back overnight, I headed to school the next day. I was like a Whack-A-Mole dummy—you couldn't keep me down for long. I hauled an extra duffel bag full of my fencing gear alongside my backpack, since I didn't trust the school's equipment not to be defective. The metal clanked as I moved.

I took Lucy's stupid goth book with me, too, because honestly, I was still annoyed she'd tried to summon a demon in my room. I have *stuff* in there, Luce, stuff that is not fireproof. Anyway.

I passed through the day in a jittery haze, only focused on the tryouts ahead. In my head, I'd already succeeded. Once I had a blade in my hand, I was guaranteed a spot on the team. And maybe—just maybe—in a few years, I'd make captain. Dad would be proud of that.

A few minutes before the end of the school day, I ducked out of my last class and hauled my fencing bag down to the gym. Coach was standing outside the double doors, absorbed in some strategy minigame on his phone.

"Hey, Coach," I said, bouncing up to him. "I was wondering if you don't mind opening up the boy's locker room for me? I brought all my fencing gear for tryouts, and I need some place to store it. I wasn't sure what would be provided, so I brought everything. Mask, swords, gloves, lamé, jacket, shoes, et cetera. I even brought spares in case someone else forgot to bring something."

Coach stared blankly for a moment, then rubbed his temples. "Pheller, you're not getting into the boy's locker room. You're not a boy."

"Goddamn, Coach, I didn't know you were my doctor." At my sarcasm, his face slid into a scowl, and I hastily backtracked. "Sorry. I mean—let's indulge a delusion for a moment, okay? Almost every other teacher calls me by my preferred name. I've got a note from my pediatrician diagnosing me with gender dysphoria. I shop in the men's section at Old Navy. What would it take for you to see me as a boy? What do you need me to do?"

His gaze flicked over me. I was hoping for pity, but all I got was disgust. "If you were born with the right equipment, then you could be on the boy's team. But you weren't, and you won't be."

"Well, I can't exactly change the circumstances of my birth, but as I offered before, I could wear a binder. You wouldn't even be able to tell the difference."

"Give up, Pheller." He shook his head. "I can't have someone who looks like a fucking faggot on my team."

I wish I could say I had a witty comeback, or punched Coach in the face, or did something—anything. Anything brave at all. But the words died on my tongue and my palms got sweaty and all I could do was turn tail and run, sneakers skidding on the tile.

I fled down the hall to the school's only gender-neutral bathroom and slammed the door shut. The hurt was a physical ache in my chest, something heavy and howling. My ribs burned beneath my binder. And yeah, I cried. You've already got me talking about my dead dad on the record, you might as well have this.

I sobbed until snot ran down to my chin and the world went blurry with salt-stinging tears and I just kept making this noise, this chest-heaving trapped-animal noise that tore out of me like it had claws. I put my hand over my mouth to smother it, but that only made it worse. Everything hurt.

It was so hard, sometimes; this body. This life. And it was all my fault—if I could just figure out how to shut up, stay quiet, be fucking *normal,* then it wouldn't be so painful.

FENCING CHESTPLATE

Can we take a break now? I don't want to talk about this anymore.

No. I'm fine. It's not like I'm not used to it. When you're trans, you sort of have to get used to it. I just don't want to talk about it.

***

I'm good to start again. We're getting close to the fun bit now, by the way, the answer to the question you've been asking since the beginning: how the hell does this tragically mundane tale of teenage angst end with the roof being blown off the school gym? Well, there's a simple answer to that, and it starts with Lucy's dumb goth book.

As I was sitting there, sobbing my little heart out in a public bathroom—top ten worst places to sob your heart out, by the way— I had my backpack on the floor between my knees. It was open. The spine of Lucy's book peeked out of it. When the tears had slowed enough for me to focus, it was the first thing my bleary gaze landed upon.

And I thought—alright, that's a lie. I was not thinking. I was desperate. There's a difference. I flipped through the book, searching for a demon to trade my soul to in exchange for a spot on the fencing team. Or Coach getting fired. Either one.

There were several chapters on demon summoning, highlighted by Lucy, but what caught my eye was a flesh transfiguration spell. It was intended for eternal youth—which, speaking as a youth, sounded like kind of a raw deal—but it could be used for any sort of transformation. Or transition, if one was so inclined. The main ingredient in the spell was virgin's blood, which, coincidentally, I was full of.

So I did what any sane human would do and stabbed myself with a pencil several times to create a spurt of blood, and proceeded with the spell.

Look. I was in a state of distress. But I would do it again.

For safety's sake, I can't tell you the exact wording of the spell. But I will say that it *hurt*. The pain started in my hand and then lightning-shocked down my wrist, rocketing through my veins and spreading through my bloodstream. I clamped my mouth shut, teeth grinding together, determined not to scream. My body shuddered and shook like it was going to fall apart.

Then the gross symptoms started: my eyelashes flaked off in

137

clumps. My ribs snapped, crackled, popped. The skin beneath my nails turned crimson. The smell of singe began, but I couldn't tell what was burning. I registered it all with a distant, miserable agony. At some point, I flailingly shed my outer layers, leaving only the choke of my bloodstained binder.

Something was happening to my body. Something was happening to *me*. My flesh lumped and squirmed, fat and muscle and organs rearranging. The pinprick wound on my hand gaped open to a stigmata-sized tear. The coppery smell of blood and bodily fluid hit my nose. I groaned, puked, and promptly passed out.

When I came to, I was sprawled on the grimy tile, awkwardly half-under the locked stall door. My hands were streaked with blood. My back molar was cracked. Vomit stained my torso.

Shivering, I crawled my way to the bathroom mirror and got a better look at the creature clutching the edge of the sink. Most of my body hair had burned off. Thankfully, my sort-of mullet had survived. My eyes were bulging and bloodshot. A frankly disturbing amount of blood, mucus, and bile spattered my binder, staining it irretrievably.

But the staining didn't matter, because I didn't need my binder anymore.

I rolled it up, staring at the two gaping wounds on my chest. It was not a pretty surgery. It looked like a monster had taken a chunk out of my flesh, then decided I'd tasted too stringy and given up on eating the rest of me. I could see the rounded tips of my organs peeking out beneath tears of shredded muscle.

I rolled the binder back down. It flapped loosely against my skin, a tattered flag of surrender. Blood turned the white fabric brown. I checked the time on my phone: ten minutes to tryouts. Perfect. Still panting, I grabbed Lucy's book and my backpack, then slung both over my shoulder. I didn't bother putting a shirt back on. I barely registered the pain of movement.

Alright, Coach, I thought. *I'm ready to fucking fence.*

***

Hey, are you alright? You look kind of nauseous. I didn't even *show* you the wound, come on. I can, though, if you want me to. No? Okay.

Regardless, you can't back out now. It's about to get so much worse.

FENCING CHESTPLATE

The school day had just ended, so the hallways were deserted as I strode towards the gym. The holes in my chest made a ragged whistling sound when I breathed in. I hardly noticed it. I was high on vicious, teeth-tearing satisfaction: no one could mistake me for anything other than a boy now. I had cut my hair short. I had torn off my tits. I hadn't looked at my nether regions, but those felt different, too. I had transmogrified myself.

I was satisfied. Relieved, even. Ready to fence. But beneath it all, I wasn't happy.

Can I tell you a secret? On the record, I know. But it's just—okay. I liked my breasts. Overall, I don't have much of a problem with the body I was given. Would enjoy being taller, maybe, but that's it. The problem is that society can't stand to see "boobs" and "boy" in the same sentence. I'm not a girl. I don't care about biology. I'm not a fucking girl.

And it just got exhausting, after a while. The binder hurt, but the misgendering hurt worse. So I did my best to pass. I was lucky that Mom let me cut my hair short, that I didn't have much in the chest area to begin with, so I could put "cis boy" on like a costume.

I don't regret what I did. Don't think that's the message of what I'm telling you. If you take one thing away from this entire holding-cell confessional, it's that I am fucking unrepentant. I just don't think I would have gone quite so drastic if Coach hadn't made that comment to me. That's all.

Whatever. You're not here to be my therapist; you want to know about the semi-accidental act of terrorism I committed. So, here we go. Final stretch.

The gym was bleakly deserted—the fencing team wasn't the most popular to begin with, and only a handful of boys had the dedication to show up ten minutes early to tryouts. They were warming up and talking amongst each other, pulling equipment from the rack: a scattering of body shapes and sizes, but all undeniably comfortable in their skin, all undeniably *boy*. I stared at them with unabashed envy, and a faint flicker of hope. Soon, I would join them. Soon, I would be on their team.

Coach was sitting on the bleachers, mumbling something to himself and searching through an array of papers on a clipboard. I sauntered up to him and bared my bloodstained teeth.

"Hey, Coach," I said, smiling as wide as possible. "I've got the right equipment now."

He was still absorbed in his papers. "What?"

"Look at me," I said, and when he didn't move, repeated it: "Coach, *look at me.*"

And he looked. And he saw me.

Here is what Coach saw: blood, pooling from twin wounds on my chest. Singed-off eyebrows. Rearranged flesh that didn't quite fit, like a bent puzzle piece. Shirtless, shoeless. A smile like the sun.

Here is what Coach did not see: a boy.

That's what haunts me, you know. That's the peak of the nightmare. I did everything I could. I invoked unholy magic. I wounded and gutted myself, dug into my flesh and forced it to conform to my will. I didn't even care about top surgery. I just wanted for people to look at me and see a boy. And is it really so fucking hard? Is it really so goddamn difficult to unhitch yourself from gender norms, to untrain the expectations and accept a guy who looks a little different? Why is it always on us to change? Why are we always the ones who have to hurt?

Yes, I would like a tissue now. Thanks.

Coach looked at me. He saw a confused little girl. He saw a faggot. He saw a freak. It made me want to puke. He looked like he was going to puke, too. He said: "Pheller, what the hell did you do?"

"I did what you asked," I said. "I got the right equipment."

"What are you talking about? You're bleeding out, you need to go to the hospital, now—"

He didn't even remember. He didn't even know what he'd done to me. I flinched back.

"I'm here to try out for the team," I said. "I'm going to do that now."

He gaped. I turned away, headed for the equipment rack.

He grabbed my shoulder. "Pheller, you have to get medical attention. What is wrong with you? You can't—"

The word hit like a blade in my gut. I wrenched away from his grasp, whirled to face him, dried blood cracking off my lips. "Don't you *dare* try and stop me."

"You have to—"

"You don't get to tell me what to do!" I snapped. "I did what you wanted! I gave myself the right fucking body parts! I did everything I could to make it easy on you, tried every possible route just to have a *chance* to be treated like a boy. And you're still saying no." Hot tears choked my throat, but I refused to let them out. "I'm done, Coach. I'll never win with you."

I was still holding Lucy's book. Before anyone could stop me, I opened it to a random page and shouted the invocation at the top of my lungs.

It's hard to say what happened after that. I only remember bits and pieces. There was an explosion, the smell of black tar. The howling shriek of a hellbeast being unleashed. Blood spattering the basketball nets. Someone sobbing in the distance. Coach wide-eyed in front of me, pleading. Screaming. Saying he was sorry. His skin melted, pale pink flesh oozing like wet clay. His face dripped down into his shirt. He was warping—into what, I didn't know. Still don't know. I haven't visited him in the hospital. I mean, I've been in police custody for two days, so I couldn't even if I wanted to.

That's all I know.

My throat hurts. Is this over yet?

***

Okay. Yes, you got what you needed. Good.

Thanks for visiting, by the way. You're the only one who's come by. Yeah, I know, it's your job or whatever. Still. It was nice to be listened to, for once.

Can I ask you just one question, before you go? Just one thing, please, I promise.

When you look at me, what do you see? Boy or girl? The victim of the tragedy, or the culprit? Monstrous either way, right?

***

You think it doesn't matter what you see, just what I know myself to be. Nice to hear. Wish someone had told me that before.

See you around, detective. Make sure you get my pronouns right on the case file.

GENDER ENVY

Gabriel Valentine

When I see him,
the half-italian cappuccino king
with his square jawline and wide cow-brown eyes,
slight mustache and cheek-length unkempt curls,

I want to be him.

I want to texas chainsaw massacre this motherfucker.
to wear his face,
scalpel-slice it from his skull
and stretch it over my own.

I want to smash my hands into his ribcage
to squeeze him a new heartbeat
and gnaw the marrow from his bones,
like chewing on a chicken wing.

I want to disembowel him,
unravel his intestinal tract,
and wrap it around my neck
as a faggy little scarf.

I want to hollow him out
like a high school frog dissection,
pinned-down wrist crucifixion,
and lay in the cradle of his flayed corpse.

GENDER ENVY

I want to zipper myself into the morphsuit of his skin,
to be his insectine parasite, a whipworm infection in his bowels,
cysticercosis taking over his brain, to drain each remaining part of
    him
and fill his gaping holes back up like a symbiotic sludge.

I want to be him.

But when I see him, he just hands me
my eight-dollar oat milk latte,
and I stutter, spill a little,
blush up, and shuffle away.

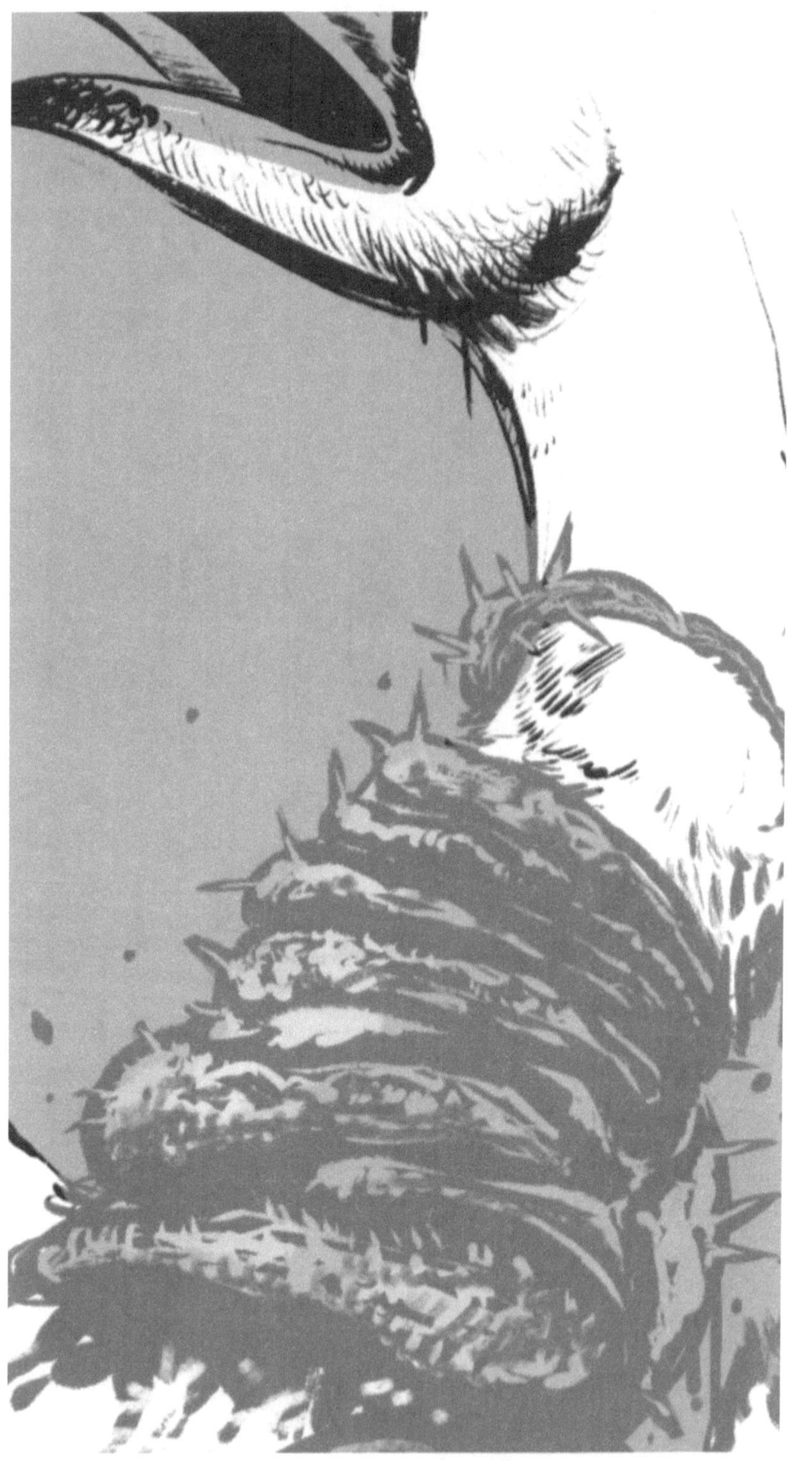

REST, MY HEAD.

Cosmin-Mihai Bîrsan

MY HEAD IS KILLING ME.

I awake.

My face feels unnaturally dry, lying atop some sort of . . . Some sort of . . . Something? Some sort of pillow, some sort of fancy clean platter, some sort of soft leather plate? My cheeks are hot and my ears are exhausted. Whatever's on the radio must have been playing for hours. Some nonsense, unfocused, slow-news-day hocus pocus, from what I could gather. I'd turn it off if I didn't feel like every bone in my body had been crumpled into dust and every muscle in my being had melted into my skin. For much like John the Baptist I find myself detached from head to toe, but this feeling is not divine. Is the light of **God's *wrath*** punishing me for *something?* Something I did, in a life past or present? My search for answers will have to wait, as I hope to find myself.

Currently ahead of me—Lights, trackers, and a terribly uncomfortable chin-rest. I have no idea what this technobabble even means. Barred 0 out of 120, whatever that means. There's all these shapes and figures, lights and symbols and one that even looks like me. It's been crossed out. I sit across from the crossed figure. What stories it could tell. It could probably tell me where I am, or *why* I am. I'm in a faintly artificially scented room, full of clear glass and *soft greyish-white stuff*. I can't tell if it's confinement, or just the latest in emotional deprivation.

My memories are scattered. The mere concept of memory rings hollow. If I remembered anything I'd probably be doing more than thinking about this situation. My throat is coarse and my vision is rough. Unaware of my own strength, I slam my whole head back into a cushion. Maybe that's it. Maybe I'm sitting on a scale. That's the zero bats in a hundred and twenty . . . No, nonsense.

Still, I must be weighing a lot less than I'd remember, if I did remember. My eyes burn a little pleasantly, a little more uncomfortably. Just out of reach in front of me stands triumphant, something. Some short, simple shape I dare not describe. It's not some trapeze, it's something else. A semicircle, or a semi- . . . ball? A semi-*dome* perhaps? No, no, **no,** a dome-*dome*.. Mocking me, *facing me,* I see shapes and sizes in a dark muted grey aboard a pale black backdrop, dancers on a stage that has forgotten its purpose and that never paid its actors. Overtop, like a light fixture in the theatre of mockery sits an immodest display of cylindrical prowess. My skinny arms *needed* the exercise, so I grab it. **It's got a mass of its own! Eureka!** *A cellmate! One that feels like smooth cardboard to the touch. It fits in my hands, shakes back from within once shaken, a visceral, guttural two-way handshake that feels delightfully squishy, in contrast to my rocky exterior and stiff unoiled gears. In a selfish act of self-preservation, I rip off the top of it and treat myself to it's gushy, dark and muddy insides.*

It tastes terrible. it goes down well, relatively, but it seemingly only accentuates my previously ignored migraine. It was fluid, yet it felt like it sprayed dirt all across the walls of my trachea.

Get it out, *get it out*, get it out.

I almost throw up a lung trying to clear my throat, but I just have to live with the soreness for now. I wonder what will last more, the energy it gave me, the headache it charged me for it, or the throat sore throat it left me with.

CRACK. CRUNCH. My neck **cracks,** and it resounds from my ribs to my crowded eye sockets. Am I some reanimated corpse falling apart, or have I just undergone a complete neck transplant? If there is a war going on inside me I can only hope that I'm on the *right side* of it. Right? Right. I rev up my right arm, squeezed by a ghost's loving yet inappropriate embrace, and **hope** for *more* feeling to return to it. Halfway through a spin, **CRACK. It happens here as well, and it resounds like a**

symphony as it pops itself off of me for now. See you soon, friend.

Amidst the euphoric twists and turns, I notice a lowered bit of *whatever* this building is fluffed out of, right above where *that other gizmo* was, the one that sanded my pipe. Attached lies a picture, a portrait of curtains wearing people, or people wearing curtains, whichever. I don't understand the beginning of one person's proportions and the end of one's overzealous wrapping paper, set aside like pompous gifts to a valued receiver. To my left, the window frame is significantly larger than the actual **thing**. On the right, a terrible display of poorly crafted symmetry. It's almost there, but then again it's not. The table I'm seated at continues past the crevice between the seats, but its dome is absent. No chinrest, no **mocking** images of *me*, nothing but a smooth curvature. On the left again, the window's got multiple levers attached. Is the idea that one of them's bound to work, or were they installed overtime in hopes of figuring out a way out of here? Am I part of a repeating cycle of madness or was I placed here to rot as I figure out the madness of this cruel existential plane?

Terrible craftsmanship. Also on the right, opposite my chair stands another. Nothing but a small foot-hurdle between them, one I could surpass with little difficulty, but have no reason to.

Prisoner's dilemma meets the shopping cart theory, but make it apathetic.

MY LIMBS OUTSTRETCHED, I BELT OUT A CURTAIN CALL AS I MOVE ON TO THE NEXT CHAIR.

Cloth. That's all there is to it. It's pretty clear, all across the dinner table of dullardry in front of me, or, I guess, both me and past-me? I wouldn't quite say us, you don't use that to refer to just yourself.

Regardless, the one thing of note that wasn't on my chair but is on this one is a **LARGE** pile of cloth, in bafflingly diverse colours and shapes, and beside it, some simple, big carvature in the curvature, a big, rounded square and a small, squared rectangle in the bottom of the table. Not gonna touch that, I'm not very passionate about archeology. In the pile of cloth there's blouses and bowties and shirts and skirts and dresses and a lot of other garbage, none of it fits me, so I'm not gonna try any of it on. Just my jumpsuit will do.

It's solid. There's some rock hard *something* in here. I pull it out, uncaring for all the clutter that gets scattered all over. You got a problem with it, you can mail me the cleaning bill. It's brown, sticky, but quite a bit more rigid. The word trumpet comes to mind. Just some random word association. Whatever it is, it's probably unnatural and manufactured. It's got reptiles and spirals carved into its side. I have absolutely no use for it. Behind both of me, the one that was and the one that is, there's a separate cage and another, this time life-size depiction of a person. Its flesh lay bare in a cell somewhat unlike mine, yet thematically identical. I cannot hear, smell or talk to you, I can't even wonder anything about you that I don't already wonder about me. I'm sitting in a chair; you're lying in your bed, similar in locomotion and pigmentation to the cells we're in. The only things you're moving are your flies. Your jaw lies agape, your teeth a wonderfully contrasting darker grey, and I'm wondering,

will anyone come out?

THE DIVINE CARCASS

Bitter Karella

WHEN GOD DIED, we first thought that it was from lack of faith. Perhaps prayers nourished the body of the lord as much as they nourished the spirits of the faithful. Perhaps too many people had lost their faith, turned away from prayers, and god had starved.

But it was more likely that god had just been hit by an asteroid.

Trudy, who had seen god twice, once in a dream and once in person when a monsignor summoned her to the nave to fix a leaking arthropoid gasket, insists that the asteroid theory was entirely possible.

"It's really not that big," she says. "You would think it would be fucking massive, but it's not."

Her face is bathed in the harsh red light from the neon OPEN sign outside the window; it makes the whole diner look hellish, but Trudy still looks beautiful. You've always thought that she was beautiful, even with her ginger hair shorn down to the roots and her body hidden in the folds of her regulation red jumpsuit. You've been friends for as long as you remember, occasionally lovers, more often just companions. What a stupid awful world to strand you both on this cathedral. You push a dumpling around on your plate.

"He was much bigger when I saw him in the dream," she says.

"You're not supposed to dream," you say.

It's true. Everyone on board *The Garden of Earthly Delights* is on, at minimum, 200 mg daily of the yellow pills for dream suppression. If anyone experiences dreams, they're to report to the onboard pharmacy to have their doses adjusted.

She shrugs.

"Do *you* dream?" she asks.

You shake your head. "No."

But, of course, you do dream now, for the first time in years. You dream of a verdant green forest, tall pine and fir trees reaching for a blue sky, a crisp bite in the air. It's a beautiful day. You recognize this forest, you were here as a child. You remember that you've buried something very important here, in the crook below an alder tree, but you don't remember what. You move from tree to tree, searching for the right one, but you never find it.

A fox emerges from under a bush, sleek and red, and it says something to you in a human voice, but you don't understand it.

When you wake, you can't recall if you actually ever did see that forest as a child or if it's just dream deja vu.

Trudy reaches across the table and touches the back of your hand. "I'm glad you agreed to come to the service."

Officially, all religious events are banned aboard *The Garden of Earthly Delights*, at least until you make delivery and dump the carcass of god into some far-distant star the name of which you can never remember. But being so close to the carcass seems to have filled people with a certain thirst. Despite the ban, dozens of underground churches flourish in the restaurant and brothel districts and even further down in the catacombs.

Trudy's gone down to the catacombs twice this week to take in some services. Before you both enlisted aboard this cathedral, Trudy was always the spiritual one. When you lived together in that tiny room over the dockside parochial tower, she must have visited with dozens of sorcerers and soothsayers, hoping to find something. You were more concerned with the daily reality that was the empty refrigerator and the leaking roof. Working the docks wasn't paying the bills anymore, not since that fat priest raised the rent. What a stupid awful world to let the priest toss you both out like that.

That's when you both signed up to work a cathedral.

***

The Garden of Earthly Delights is an Augustine-class interstellar cathedral, its nave one hundred miles long, its transept seventy-five miles wide. Its walls are ten feet thick in places to hold out the cold vacuum of space and the buttresses are caked with frosted ether, pocked with asteroid holes. Beyond the main cathedral is the city—the brothels and casinos and bars—that exists to cater to the off-duty crew. The cathedral requires a crew of over two thousand, engineers and sextons and monsignors and bishops, all under the command of one overpope. You don't know how many people, all the clerks and whores and sorcerers that run the city, live down in the catacombs.

Out here, in space, this was the first place that you understood what Trudy was looking for.

You were scrubbing the hull, peeling an exploded angel off the abutments. Trudy was inside the reliquary, pumping the bellows to keep the air flowing into your suit. But you looked up and you saw the universe—stars twinkling in the black void, the waving radiance of distant galaxies softened into blue and purple clouds by the infinite distance.

So you agreed to come to the service.

***

You take the portside pneumatic shaft down to the casino district and then a dorsal shaft to the catacombs. The alleys are narrow and moisture from the oxygen filtering system constantly drizzles down from above like a gentle rain. Almost every apartment's window is illuminated by some sigil, signs to guide acolytes to their new faiths.

Trudy knocks at a door inscribed with an image of the crescent moon. The door creaks open to reveal a young, dark-eyed boy. A musky blast of incense accompanies him.

"What do you seek?" he asks.

"I seek truth," says Trudy.

The boy looks at you. Oh. Apparently, you're supposed to say something.

"Uh . . . I'm also seeking truth. I guess?"

The boy opens the door and gestures for you both to enter.

The apartment is small and dark, lit only by the glow of candles. You can make out the vague forms of about a half-dozen people here, smell their sweat, feel their warmth. They're sitting on the floor.

Trudy sits at the back of the group, and you follow her example. You wait until a woman in a fox mask and a black kimono emerges from nowhere. A tiny dog waddles at her side, wagging its curled tail eagerly.

"I know why each one of you has come," says the masked woman. "You have each had a dream, a dream whose meaning can only be known by you if it can be known at all. You come because you know that you should not be dreaming, that the yellow pills should stop them and yet you dream still. You have come to ask the Mother of Claws about your dreams."

She notices you staring at her dog.

"She is my aspect," she says. She holds something out to you. "Take it in your mouth."

You take it in your mouth. It's a chocolate bonbon. It's decadent and delicious.

The Mother of Claws turns to Trudy.

"Take it in your mouth."

Trudy opens her mouth and the Mother of Claws places a chocolate on her lolling tongue. You notice that the Mother of Claws has long black talons on her fingers.

She moves from person to person, repeating her instructions and placing a chocolate on each tongue. Then, she bends down to her dog and holds out a chocolate before suddenly snatching it away with a laugh.

"Take it in your mouth . . . noooooooooooooo! Ha ha ha!" She points at the dog. "She thought she had it all figured out! She thought, 'oh if I act like these big dogs, I'll get a chocolate too!' Ha ha ha!"

Still laughing, she shuffles a deck of cards between her long-taloned fingers. She turns to you.

"Pick one."

You pick a card. It's the nine of swords from the Rider-Waite tarot deck.

"It is the nine of swords," says the Mother of Claws. "A man lies awake in bed, crying. He has so many swords! Too many swords! There are great many swords upon the wall and those that fall pierce him; they pierce him in the wounds of Christ and in additional wounds suffered by gods we know not the names of, gods we cannot conceive of. And yet in these gods was hosted the truth that was sought. But what truth is there in this world? You know that god is dead, so the universe now stands empty and an empty house invites squatters. Old gods will rise again and new gods will rise for the first time."

The dog is licking its asshole in the apartment's kitchenette. The Mother of Claws throws an annoyed glance at it.

"Aspect! Aspect!"

The dog ignores her.

The Mother of Claws instructs the dark-eyed boy: "Call her mortal name."

"Snuggles!" says the dark-eyed boy, bounding after the dog into the kitchen. "Come on, Snuggles, come on!" He gathers the dog up in his arms and together they silently slide out the front door.

She holds out the block of cards to Trudy. Trudy draws The Moon.

"It is the Moon. Two dogs look up to the moon, to gaze upon her face as dogs do. Ponder the courage that the moon takes to rise each evening to serve the needs of those who bow and pray."

The chocolate is really starting to hit.

"Yet the moon knows only benevolence. She passes these things like water from her many orifices . . . the water flows, it flows down, through a heaven of stars, to the earth where it gathers in a lake and now we drink it-"

trudy looks at you, her face bathed in light. everything looks very purple

trudy places her hand atop yours, giggling

you're always here, says trudy we've always been together

yes you say. you and me

you're laughing too, you can't help it. it's so clear.

whata beautiful universe the motherof claws has shown you

a hand sliding between your legs, tugging at your cock, teasing it to attention

a rough tongue scraping your cheek

your lips on a vulva, slippery and rank, saliva dripping down your chin

You dream of the forest again, the beautiful day, the fox in the bushes, and the treasure lost that you can't recall. The fox looks at you. It has human eyes.

"It is time to wake up," it says.

***

You awaken in your own bed, your head pounding.

Shit. How'd you get back to your quarters? You were *so* fucked up. Trudy must have brought you home. Shit. Trudy. You might have fucked Trudy last night. Or someone else? It's not clear. This is going to complicate things. What time is it?

It's half past vespers; you're late for your shift in the reliquary.

You stumble out of bed and turn on the sink. Throw some water on your face. Take a look at yourself. Your eyes are bloodshot, your hair is matted, and your dick is red and bruised. Your sides are raked with scratches, but no one will see that once you're in your jumpsuit.

***

Monsignor Bexler is a harried-looking man in his early fifties. He wears the same jumpsuit that you do; other than the cross embroidered on his collar, you wouldn't know he was clergy. Now you're going to hear it. Worse, your dick still hurts from last night. *God,* you must have fucked like a champ.

"I won't be late again," you say.

"Hmm?" He isn't even paying attention to you. He rummages around in the drawer of his desk and pulls out a clipboard and a photo. He slides the photo toward you. It's Trudy.

Shit.

"Nothing to worry about, just standard procedure," says Bexler, reading your expression. "According to ship logs, Class 8 Able Crewman (Laity) Trudy Speckler was summoned to the nave at early Matins on third Iunius to repair an arthropoid gasket. Exposure to the, er, cargo can sometimes be traumatic, so it's standard procedure to follow up on any laity who've been to the nave. We just want you to help us understand Crewman Speckler's mental state, make sure everything's okay with her. We just want to help."

He reads from the clipboard.

"In the time that you've associated with the crewman in question, have you noticed any indications of increased religiosity?"

"Increased? No." Your dick is really starting to itch.

Bexler nods and marks a mark on his paper with a pen.

"Has he/she/they spoken of receiving signs from authorities beyond the physical realm? Please note that he/she/they may refer to such authorities as angels, demons, spirits, gods, entities, or by other names."

"No."

He makes another mark. God, your dick feels like it's on fire. You hope this is almost done.

"Has he/she/they reported having dreams?"

ARGHHHH

"No."

"Okay, last question. To your knowledge, has this crewman associated with individuals going by any of the following names: The Light Bender, the Innocent Man, the Mother of Claws, Anubis the Reincarnated, or the Princess of the Air?"

Shit. You can't take it anymore. "C-could I use your bathroom?"

Bexler looks confused. "What? Uh . . . sure." He points to a narrow door in the portside wall. You walk to it as quickly as possible without arousing suspicion.

There's barely enough room in here for you and the chemical toilet. Quickly, you unzip your jumpsuit and tear yourself out of your clothes. You grab at your crotch to get a better look.

Your penis sloughs off suddenly, dropping into the shallow turquoise water of the toilet with a wet, definitive *splut*.

fuck

There's no pain and no blood, only a sudden gout of oily black fluid. It gushes from the open wound, sliming your hands and coating your inner thighs before slowing to a trickle. You idly wonder what you should do with your severed dick.

Shit shit shit

Okay. You pull the flush and, to your immense surprise, the toilet sucks your penis down into the pipes. You half-expected it to clog but no. It goes down smooth.

Well. Okay, then.

You look at yourself in the mirror. Your eyes are sunken and your skin looks pale and blotchy. You zip yourself back into your jumpsuit and exit the bathroom. You smile a wide, totally normal smile at Bexler.

"Feeling okay?" he asks.

You smile a wider, even more normal smile.

***

You're on the dorsal pneumatic shaft down to the catacombs. You're leaning against the railing with all your weight, your breathing coming sharp and ragged, your pulse racing. You feel like shit. Something is not right. How did you get here? You were just with Bexler—

You shift your weight and the open gash between your legs lets loose a torrent of slime into your underpants. "Ughh."

You stare intently at the back of your hand, willing yourself into calm. Your hand is laced with throbbing purple veins.

The shaft empties onto the catacombs level.

The alleys are confusing, but you finally find the door with the crescent moon. You knock. After a pause, the door cracks open. A young woman with long black hair answers. She clutches a hand-rolled cigarette between her fingers.

"Oh, it's you. I wasn't expecting anyone this early. Service isn't til tonight."

"My dick fucking fell off."

"What? The fuck are you talking about?" She motions you to come inside.

With the lights on, you can see that the apartment is cluttered with overstuffed antique furniture. You don't see the dark-eyed boy anywhere, or the dog.

"Show me," she says.

You pull down your pants and display your wound. Her eyes widen. She drops into an ornate wing-backed chair, never taking her eyes off you.

"Shit," she says. She sucks on her cigarette. "That wasn't supposed to happen. What the fuck."

"What was supposed to happen?!"

"You were *supposed* to just have a good time. Jesus. What do you think is supposed to happen when you fuck around and get high?"

"What was in that fucking chocolate?"

"Nothing! Just 200 mg of the green pills. And, you know, some god cartilage. For texture."

You're going to be sick. "God cartilage?! What the *fuck*."

"Look, it's nothing weird! We *all* take it and it's never done anything like that before. Maybe you're just . . . allergic."

She taps her talons against the armrest of her chair.

"Or maybe now you're a vessel for something beyond. Maybe you're transcending. But look at you now. You're stuck inbetween, aren't you? You can't claim this house until you've cleared out the landlord, eh?"

"Oh my *godddd*," you wail. "I don't know what you're talking about."

"That's why they're throwing god into the star, you know. Once the carcass is gone, the new god can ascend to the throne. You understand, right? Shit, that's why they don't let you have religions on this ship. They don't want any competition. I bet they're growing their own replacement god right now. In a vat or something. Jesus Christ almighty."

You can't listen to this chatter. "I just came for Trudy! I didn't mean for this to happen!"

The Mother of Claws regards you through a haze of smoke from the extinguished cigarette.

"You came alone," she says.

"What? But then . . . Who did I fuck?"

"You didn't fuck anyone," she says. Her fingers twitch as if she's looking for another cigarette. "You just sat there, totally stoned out of your gourd. I don't know what you saw, but you've never fucked anyone any time you've been here."

"Wait, what . . . 'anytime I've been here?' What day is it?"

She stares at you. "Twenty-fifth Iunius."

How is it possible that you've lost a week? How did Bexler not ream your ass for missing shifts?

But then . . .

"I need more chocolate," you say.

"I don't have any more. My supplier works in the pipeworks, so he knows someone who's got nave access and . . . "

She pauses as the door creaks open. It's the dark-eyed boy from before.

"Ah," says the Mother of Claws. "Here he is now."

The dark-eyed boy has a lead pipe clutched in his hand. He takes a swing at you. Instinctively, you skitter backwards. Without a word, he advances on you and raises his pipe for another swing.

"What the *fuck*?!" shouts the Mother of Claws, jumping to her feet.

He takes another swing but you leap away, scrambling through puddles of the black goo dripping from your nethers, and the lead pipe connects with the Mother's head. There's a sickening *crunch,* and she falls backwards into her chair. The dark-eyed boy shrieks in horror, dropping his pipe. You grab at it, but you're not fast enough. The boy has it again, and he's coming at you. He steps forward . . . and slips in a goo puddle, tumbling to the floor. His mouth opens to scream and his teeth make contact with the edge of the coffee table.

The table shears off his cranium, which flies off his body and across the room to hit the wall with a soft thump. His body flops to the floor, vomiting blood from its ruined jaw. The Mother of Claws sits in her chair, head sagging, eyes glassy. The top of her head is caved in and leaking brains. The apartment is coated with blood and ichor.

You fall against the wall and slide to the floor. That's when you notice that the dark-eyed boy, or what's left of him, is wearing a *green* jumpsuit.

Shit. The pipeworks. He works . . . *worked* in the pipeworks.

It must not have gone down as smoothly as you thought. Somewhere, in some bend, it must have got stuck and they had to plunge it and out popped your dick, still dripping that black oil, and they must have figured it out. They know.

They know this is their last chance to stop you.

***

You're in the forest again. But this time, you see a man.

At first, you don't recognize him. But then, looking closely, you realize that he's a mirror image of you.

You suddenly realize that you're creeping forward on four paws.

"Oh shit," you say.

Your doppelganger stares at you in confusion. Something passes wordlessly between the two of you and you suddenly know what must be.

"I'll wake up this time," you say.

***

You're stumbling through the narrow alleyways of the catacombs, dribbling black goo. Your jumpsuit is hanging at your waist, your new breasts hanging free and slapping painfully against your chest with every unsteady footfall. Breasts. You have breasts now.

You need to get to the nave. That's where it is. That's what you fucked. You fucked god, you're sure of it. If you could just get there . . .

People are turning to stare. Some of them must already know,

159

but they're too scared to confront you.

You board a ventral shaft, a gaggle of nymphets spilling out as you enter. They stare at you with frightened eyes, at your blood-soaked jumpsuit, the thick bubbles of black ichor forming on the nipples of your exposed breasts, at . . . something else . . .

"The eyes, did you see her eyes," gasps one as the door closes.

***

Of course, the shaft stalls eight levels from the nave. They've probably shut off all access, anticipating your move. No matter. You don't need to use the shafts anymore. You can just go to the nave now if you want.

A monsignor looks up as you emerge from nothing.

"No access for laity here!" he snaps, but then he falls silent and drops to the floor.

"Oh god oh god oh god," he cries.

You shove him aside. Your hand is soft and moist and leaves a sticky handprint on the monsignor's jumpsuit. Your skin is a deep bruised purple.

You see it.

Trudy was wrong. It's bigger than you would have thought. It is massive, its bulk filling the nave almost to the vaulted ceiling. It is comprised entirely of enormous siphons, like octopus hyponomes. In theory, there's probably a body beneath them.

But, you know, with the perfect knowledge of a dream, exactly what it is and exactly what you need to do.

A bishop is approaching you. Several more monsignors are trailing behind him. You recognize Bexler. He's pointing at you and whispering something to the bishop.

"What the hell, how did you get out of your tank—" says the bishop. He pauses mid-sentence when you turn to look at him.

"Good lord," he says, tears streaming down his face. "It's you . . . we found your . . . in the pipes . . . "

"I know."

The monsignors avert their eyes; several drop to the ground. Bexler starts bawling. The bishop alone keeps staring, although you can tell it pains him to do so.

"We didn't think you would be ready so soon," he says.

"Ready for what?" you say. "Oh, right . . . "

They thought they could still stop you, but now they must have realized that moment is past. It passed long ago, maybe even before the dark-eyed boy made that first attempt to end you.

The bishop has one last gambit. He drops to a knee. "How can we serve you?"

You can wipe it all clean. It's gone. With a thought, you end it. You end it all. The awful, stupid universe made by a god too awful and stupid to avoid getting hit with an asteroid. The throne is vacant. You can take it. You take it. It's yours. Start it all over again.

***

You're clawing your way through rich loamy dirt, scrabbling up, up, toward the light, until you burst forth from the ground, gasping and wheezing, burst forth from where you were buried right here below the crook of an old alder tree so many years ago.

You're in a verdant green forest, tall pine and fir trees reaching for a blue sky, a crisp bite in the air. It's a beautiful day.

CHIRONOPLASTY

Joe Koch

THE SKY FREEZES and falls to the ground. Black shards of night scatter under Chiron's clumsy hooves, crushing an obsidian infection, glittering as he leaves behind his frail shelter for gunmetal city streets. It's too cold to slow down, colder still exposed to the inscrutable black glow outside Chiron's hideaway. Tempting the sea of streets, he may drown in the pain of his unthinkable body, a centaur at risk in the wrong cryptid habitat.

Killing chronic futures with every step, he exits the past with bold choices as the metastasized city sprouts identical heads on each corner, another No-Club in no-time blocking, beckoning, exploding all the way down across endless intersections.

No-Club has no exit. The neon sign hovers above wet streets. Faces of strangers lie flat in reflective pools slashed by passing traffic. The pavement is wet and silent, then wet and wheezing, then cracked by window-faces with every bus and door and alleyway that rises. Across the city's excess, Chiron rounds the corner with a clatter of hooves.

The shine of slippery breath as the surface cracks, liquid underneath releases, and Chiron catches their half-horse lower torso on a parking meter pole before they splash to the ground, gutter and sidewalk ready to greet them with a concussion. Unknown water-faces turn away in abject disinterest. Awkward, winded, bent around the parking meter; Chiron reassembles his four horse legs and two human arms into a workable position to avoid disaster and choose a better medical crisis.

Today is surgery day at No-Club and anything goes.

Another door opens in no-time with sufficient spacious egress to accommodate a centaur's shape. Rumbling noises spill out on smoke and hide the broken sky. Pastel fog and light pollution undermine the cosmos while frozen gases of the void remain and settle over the cancerous urban expanse. Native to the desert, Chiron slips on ice. The cold cuts him in half. Half centaur, half man, half something-or-other; too many halves to make a simple whole and all the confusion of a fable told and retold.

No-Club has no exit, and glimpsing what's behind the door as it swings open and closed flips archetypal cards from Freud's primal scene: shame, awe, desire. Chiron can practically hear the hand being dealt with the flat repetitive certainty that he'll never leave once he enters the rigged game-space of no-time.

With the choices they've made, there's nowhere else left to go without traveling backwards in time. A centaur's body doesn't fit in the city outside. The city dark; the city wet. The city splashing with synthetic sounds as tires thrill across gunmetal streets. The city alive. The city will eat itself. There's no sky anymore, only cold smoke. The city destroys mythology. The city regresses exponentially as it perpetuates onward towards infinity.

Inside No-Club with no regrets, because the poetic architecture of Chiron's mythological chest was made all wrong and they will not survive another night alone in the city cold, the city lost. Half myth, half man, hung with shameful udders like obscene growths, diseased, inflated, bulbous with the visible fruition of external demands, leaking the milk of damnation to feed the infantile needs of others who plead and beg and grab; but what about Chiron? Who cares who they are and what they want beneath this forced combination of parts?

Before he can catch his breath or accommodate his hot horse-haunches to No-Club's raging temperature, a stranger seizes Chiron's full breasts, inspects them with mechanical efficiency, and says, "Come with me right away to the crash site."

Which explains some of the heat and smoke in here tonight. Alien intervention sounds more promising than the known prosaic earthbound back-alley hacks, so Chiron follows.

In the crush of the club, Chiron's groin sweats, and the scent of horse dick stinks up their vicinity with excessive force. They can tell who's bemused by a chin lift of olfactory interest and who, in contrast, ranks inferior by way of an unrestrained eye-roll. It's good to wear the barometer of sexual prowess openly on their long centaur torso, good to graze soft city toes with the superior durability of hooves. In another age, they would have been a god to these craven creatures desiccated by modernity. Chiron takes wider steps. It's good to smell like a threat.

As bodies move away, Chiron spreads their shoulders, pushing out his chest. The shallow cavity of a centaur rests between the bulbous abominations, well-formed and desirable though they may be. The blood of generations may beg for him to procreate, to warm and nurture great broods of lustful young; but Chiron cannot respect a past that clamors for mere compromise below a dead sky. He is a cold and lonely centaur and will not be consumed by the city dark. They will not be mastered by the random genetic lottery braided from a paper horse's harness. He will escape the sea of streets, for the centaur presents as a land animal and bullies through the crowded club like a holy beast and shoves their trouble into alien palms:

"Cut them off!"

The mother tongue is quick. The superposition of no-cock, no-time in alien gleam-stoked surgical suites sleeps in sync with incomplete dreams. The blue light of the crash site preps heads for experimentation and hypnotizes nerve endings like unlocked webs. Warning: the following paragraph contains graphic depictions of violence against gendered body parts which some readers may find upsetting or offensive. Warning: dysphoria is hell. Warning: this is a work of fiction. Warning: don't believe everything you read, this warning least of all. Warning: what did you expect from a centaur?

Warning, danger. In contrast to chopping off, say, a finger or a small toe, the following contains a graphic and prolonged scene where a breast is snagged in the scissor-grip of alien equipment like garden shears. In traumatic throes of pseudo-erotic hatred for the transitional object's haunted origin, the breast pillows between the wide V-shaped blades of the clipping device, flesh squeezed between sharp edges as they snap closed, nipple bulging, stretching, its gift of fat pink aureole swollen about to burst before the blood spurts. The second deletion of the next breast repeats the gory scene. The centaur's chest sheds its creamy excess as the alien surgeons couple with their implicit trauma, exaggerating the image of the body in an ecstasy of transformation.

Emptiness spreads through Chiron in peaceful pulsations, a natural anesthetic like a slow and constant heartbeat. He hears the voices of the merging surgeons, voices in his head who also hear him and respond to the sleepless dream of self-creation and recreating self.

The no-voice of no-time speaks and listens with a secreted shell to scab over Chiron's breastplate. Alien proteins course through Chiron's half-awake horse flesh, healing uncomfortable angles in an increasingly ambitious fantasy of rebirth. The exploding city heats in anger, flapping wet streets like whips, shaking No-Club's foundations and juddering the crash site and making a mad blinking strobe of the alien surgical suite's gleaming blue light.

The city dark; the city ruptured. The city screaming *stay in your lane!* Protestors flood in below the neon egress, but No-Club has no exit in contrast to the infinite metastasizing city that perpetuates outside its doors. Body after body enters shrieking *sex is real* and *your body is a temple!* Hand after hand thrusts pamphlets from the Institute of Genetic Purity printed in hot pink with gold heart emblems linked together encasing slogans: *save our girls from alien misogyny! Invaders are everywhere!* But the hands cannot thrust, and the mouths cannot move as the bodies pile in from the ever-flowing rivers of the crowded city streets and pack No-Club full to the static seams.

The blue strobe light can barely illuminate. The mob amasses like the multiplying bacteria of an infection. There's no space between shoulders and faces. Protestors pour in from the ever-birthing reproductively diseased spunk-hole of the city, and participants of large stature stomp the slight, teeming to the top of the pile, gasping like netted fish.

Bones snap. Teeth smash. Lips bleed. None can breathe by the time the dominant bodies squeeze up to the ceiling's rafters. At the bottom of the pile, the weakest have already expired. Chiron sleeps through the massacre, dreaming in alien synchronicity, happy in their blissful release from an oppressor that once lived inside their skin.

No-time speeds up as a result of the deceleration forced upon the space by the crush of the protestors; medical waste rots faster.

CHIRONOPLASTY

The dying expire at an increasing rate. Putrefaction happens quickly as No-Club enters into real time and Chiron awakes.

He risks drowning in the sea, in the wrong cryptid habitat. The murk of many deaths accumulated doesn't affect Chiron's ability to breathe, but the inane roar of protestor no-thought chokes his soul with each poison drop of hate which judges and demands their martyrdom. Trapped and liquefying, the eyes of the eugenicists can no longer deny what they see: Chiron concedes eagerly to illicit alien surgery and will do anything to be free.

As time continues moving, the city's reflected space reaches a pinpoint of exponential regress. No-Club's boundaries quiver with quantum anarchy. The alien surgeons flaunt their expertise, changing beast to man and back again through endless permutations of joy. Lights like finely tuned piano keys, like inks in unbearable colors begin to blend and bend the sick opinions of the onlookers.

We are all witnesses to Chiron's transformations, willing or not, and if not, why? Why do we care? And if we do not desire transformation, what do we fear?

A welcome carnage ends the parade of Chiron's desires. Priests and hard men in ball caps desire it, too. Many directions of light traveling at real-time speed-map a new territory outside the city dark, the city cold, the city dead with no stars, the city that cannot hold. No-Club exits itself, mirroring the city's infinity. Protestors unravel as the twine of their impacted thoughts spills out, neurons weaving a less broken sky that holds more light. Chiron hopes there will be enough light.

Already it seems a little warmer. Or perhaps Chiron has grown stronger. Where the city ends, mythology begins. The vanishing point grows visible under the new web of dimly brightening sky. Fruiting heads high among alien arbors nod in new sacred time and in synchronized agreement as Chiron delivers a final battle cry to the city's surviving protestors: "Your quote-unquote violence is my freedom. Technology leaves you behind. Your infantile fears betray you, and my body is not your battleground. You know nothing of my pain."

#MOTHERMAYHEM

Jei D. Marcade

ELODIE KANG WAS in the shower when the skin of her right hand sloughed off.

She thought at first that she'd dropped her washcloth. One moment, she was working conditioner into her hair, and the next, she heard a wet slap against the floor of the tub.

Elodie squinted at the bare bones that protruded from the smooth nub of her wrist. There was no pain. Though they had been stripped of flesh and muscle, the ends of each phalange remained as snugly joined as ever and curled obediently when she clenched her fist.

"Eomma," she shouted. Panic lent a sharp edge to her voice.

A rush of footsteps on the stairs. Elodie's mother barreled into the bathroom. She had been in the middle of lunch. Belatedly, Elodie grabbed for the towel and wrapped it around herself without stepping from under the showerhead.

"What? What happened?" Mrs. Kang cried in Korean. Her eyes flew to Elodie's hand, and the alarm faded from her features. "Finally. Thank God. Why are you just standing there? Turn off the water. Are you just going to let that clog the drain?"

Mrs. Kang reached past her daughter to scoop the soggy clump of subcutaneous tissue from the bottom of the tub with her chopsticks.

Elodie recoiled. "*Eomma!* That's so gross!"

Her mother made a dismissive sound as she slung it into the trash. "It's just skin. Now finish up and get dressed. I want to take pictures of your new hand to show Halmeoni."

#MOTHERMAYHEM

***

Elodie had trouble sleeping—and not just because she had to get used to her bones snagging on the bedsheets or tangling in her hair.

The world made too much noise. Her bedroom walls and windowpanes might as well have been paper. Every slam of a car door or bark of a neighbor's dog sparked against her nerves.

She tried counting down from a thousand. She tried reciting her French vocabulary list. She listened to a true crime podcast about serial killers while she lay in bed with her eyes closed and barely woke up in time for the bus.

***

You weren't allowed at school bare-handed. If you didn't have gloves at home, you could pick one out from the bin in the main office, but those were bulky and unfashionable, and smelled like wet dog.

Elodie's grandmother had sent her a whole pack three years ago, delicately patchworked from silk hanbok scraps. The vibrant colors made Elodie self-conscious, and of course Kamryn noticed immediately.

"El-o-*die*," they squealed so loudly that Elodie winced. They turned her wrist to admire the elaborate embroidery at the cuff. "You got your *hand*? Why didn't you text me?"

Elodie felt like everyone in the hall was staring. She pulled away and mumbled a vague excuse, but Kamryn had stopped listening.

"Have you seen the Mother Mayhem challenge yet? The group chat's been blowing up about it all morning."

She hadn't. She'd turned off the notifications a while ago, unable to keep up.

Kamryn shoved their phone in Elodie's face. The video was dark, grainy, the focus trained on somebody's skeleton hand as it dangled off the edge of their bed in an unlit room.

It felt oddly transgressive to see a stranger's hand ungloved. As though she had glimpsed someone naked. Elodie tried to imagine filming herself like that, uploading it for the world to watch, and her cheeks burned.

A boy's voice murmured, "Mother Mayhem, grant me a boon." The pale, twig-like fingers closed.

169

The view distorted, jagged edges of static lancing across the frame.

When the boy opened his hand, a spiraled shell lay cupped in the cage of his metacarpals.

"It's just a camera trick," Elodie said, but her voice was uncertain even to her own ears.

"It's not," Kamryn insisted. "Anyway, now you can try it."

***

Last year, in the boys' locker room, some of the varsity football players had held down a couple of the JV kids, bone to skin. One fought free and ran for the assistant coach, but it was already too late.

Usually, it took a while for the effect to kick in, but with so many of them, only a few seconds of direct contact had made the other kid pass out. And then he'd dropped into a coma.

Someone from student council had passed around a get-well card for him in homeroom, which Elodie had dutifully signed. The other guys were expelled. There had been a huge deal about it in the local papers, though it didn't make the national news; things like that happened too often for most of the major networks to care.

The kid woke up a couple months later, but never returned to school. Word was that he'd come back funny, that he saw things that weren't there.

Word was that he'd started the Mother Mayhem challenge.

***

Here are the rules: at the stroke of midnight, reach your skeleton hand into wherever the dark seems deepest. Common candidates are under the bed, in your closet—classic childhood monster haunts. Then you say the words, close your hand, and hold your breath until 12:01.

(There are variations. You must be the only person awake in your house. You must have a full-length mirror behind you. You must be wearing the same clothes, down to your underwear, for three days before the challenge.)

When you relax your fist, you'll find inside it a clue to how or when or where you'll die.

***

Elodie lost track of how many times she replayed that first video. She wondered what she'd do if she had opened her hand to find a seashell resting there. Avoid beaches for the rest of her life? Skip out on post prom, which always took place on a yacht? She'd rather die.

At lunch, in study hall, behind the stairwell during passing period, her classmates traded their deaths. Drowning was preferred to burning. Falling was the crowd favorite for a while, until Shivam from Elodie's forensics club pulled an uncut emerald that got everyone guessing. A collapsed mine? A botched heist? At the end, he swapped it for a lipstick that he insisted meant *assassination by femme fatale*, which they all agreed would be a pretty hot way to go. Way better than sticking around for the end of the world.

Elodie did the Mother Mayhem challenge, of course. It was inevitable, from the first time she punched in the hashtag on her own phone and watched dozens of skeleton hands unfurl like bony flowers in bloom around shell casings and car keys and the plastic caps to syringes.

She did the challenge—repeatedly.

Night after night, Elodie called on Mother Mayhem and plucked from the air and darkness ticket stubs and ball bearings and, once, a spool of thread. These she threw into a tea tin that she shoved underneath her bed. She thought she could hear them sometimes, all her little deaths rattling gently below her pillow like her own personal white noise machine, lulling her to sleep.

THE LIVES OF SCAVENGERS

Rhiannon Rasmussen

I WAS BORN from your grave into this sunless world. I clawed my way out of cold earth with curled hands, my mouth filled with worms and my nails stained petrichor. The rot was the warmth left behind me.

For a long time, this was what I knew there was of life. I ate the worms and chewed the bones to strengthen my jaws and I drank the dew which pooled on the stone of the funeral yards. Whether it was a good life or a bad one did not concern me.

When others came to my graveyard, I lurked behind the stones and studied them. I dared not approach, and in a similar manner, those who saw me looked away. I understood they were afraid. Mistakenly, I assumed it was of me. Now I understand they averted their eyes to avert their shame. That which is not acknowledged is no one's responsibility. This was the way of the undercity, ignored by the city-above.

The first time someone met my eyes, it was a person dressed in the plump rose of a worm's belly. The long hair of her head hung limp like mine, though it was tucked into a lace veil. Later, I learned rose was the color of mourning. Of woman's mourning. Men mourned in other colors.

The woman met my eyes through her veil. Her expression did not change. She did not look away. I fled back to my hole of worms and dew. To have been seen frightened me.

The next candle's mark, she returned with rinds of bread and cheese. She sat with the food next to her until I approached and snatched the food away. The texture was more pleasant to chew than the bursting worms. It became our routine over the course of several days. She came to my yard with bread and patience, until I came so close as to sit with her.

As I chewed, she spoke.

"I am called Voierry," she said. "I am a widow, so time is of no import to me. I have more of it than I please."

My mouth full, I did not answer.

"Do you know from whence you came?"

I swallowed. "Here."

Behind her veil, her black eyes caught the lantern-light. "Ah! I heard the grave-children were born with speech, but the spheres have not moved to grant us any in decades. That is how you were left ignored. A shame. But Voierry is here for you."

This meant nothing to me. I took more of the cheese rind. I enjoyed the chew between my molars.

"Do you know how you came to be? Of the spheres and the saints?"

"No."

She told me of the three saints of decay who governed the paths of those such as me: the vulture, the hyena, and the scarab. All were important, she said. Only one was to be feared. She looked at my teeth and she told me which sphere I was governed by.

I snapped my teeth together.

"Do you fear me?"

"No," she said, and I could tell she spoke the truth in her kind words. She was not afraid, though she always wore the veil. Even the dim throbbing of lanterns was difficult for her eyes.

She returned daily for a fortnight. At the end of that passage, when she saw how close I now dared sit near her, she asked me if I wished to learn what life was like without dirt as a second skin. That was the manner in which I, the grave-child, became instead the widow Voierry's child. The name she bestowed upon me was Makké, heir of misfortune.

I was proud, but jealous when I learned that I was not the first of her children, nor the only stray. One such son, Ivan, the eldest, came to her house often and fixed what was broken; her bench, her pantry shelf, her bathing-bucket.

I did not like him.

He did not like me. He mocked my name. I sat in the corner

when he visited, and bared my teeth at him. He bared his teeth back, and Voierry laughed and said we were alike.

She spoke proudly of his accomplishments, a night watch in the darkest gloom, a handyman. He stood against the dark and did not flinch even in the hour when the veins of the city above flowed too thick and the city's blood dripped down to the streets of our lightless slum. Brave, she said. Clever.

Not clever enough to stand in the cover and keep his night-hat unstained, I thought. And what he fixed was not fixed long. The bench slouched, the pantry moldered, the bucket leaked. He left with her change, her bread, her gratitude, more than the worth of a bench a bucket could well serve as. Of his own earnings he did not give, though he bragged of them before her and she was proud. He asked for her last savings in the rose-colored bag she tucked into the back of the cabinets and she laughed at that too.

But who was I to note such a thing? I had come from dirt. I knew only how to break, not to mend. About this, Voierry was patient and kind. She had time, she told me. She had nothing to give but time.

Voierry was poor, but to me, our meager food was a feast. She was not much learned, but to my ears her scraps of knowledge were encompassing. I learned quickly. Among the lessons I learned was that what she had to give was not enough for me.

The hunger of the grave, the redness of my belly, and the hunger of my saint grew and gnawed at me, and I became hollow with it. My motions were rote and my teeth were razors. I tried to be gentle, but in my hands, pots and buckets warped or shattered. I wished to be content, but I was not. She knew, and it hurt us both. She often was short with me. Her patience was not drawn from such a deep well as time.

I watched Voierry closely even when we argued, to learn from her. Her kindness, to me, seemed weak. A concession of territory. When she shouted, I knew she was treating me as an equal, and I tried to repair and repay and show her the patience she had shown me. When she spoke softly and called in Ivan to mend what I had destroyed, I knew she was giving in, and to see him speak softly to her and smile pityingly at me and leave with whatever his eyes fell on enraged me.

I left her house when she treated me in that way, knowing and hating that she often turned to Ivan in my absence. What I turned to in her absence was the grave. Your grave I could find by scent alone, and it was gouged with words. I sat by it in silence and anger I could not put full thoughts to. Neither the widow nor I knew letters, so I did not puzzle out your name.

Perhaps this was better. An image can be admired wholly. To know a man wholly is to know betrayal.

Here I will not mince. What followed was not the fault of Voierry. None could have provided enough for me. Her only fault was trust.

In that afternoon my hunger overcame me and in hollow-bellied anger I threw the crooked bench into the pantry shelf to break them both of their emptiness. Voierry cried. I left when she spoke of Ivan, Ivan who helped and helped and did not hurt her, unlike her troubled child.

I paced in the graveyard among my kin, the rot and the bones, and I touched the stones and I considered my anger. I was troubled, yes. My efforts were my best, and my best was often poor. I understood that I was not a sufficient child. But I did not lie, I did not take, and I did not understand why she saw this difference between myself and my hunger and Ivan and his greed.

After a day alone, I returned, and the bench was fixed and the pantry bare. Voierry bade me search for her savings in their rose-colored bag. Her eyesight was poor. She had misplaced the money. We overturned the house. The money was not found.

With disgust I said Ivan had taken it; his eyes had fallen on it many times. She said Ivan had not, and condemned me for speaking ill of my brother, though he was no brother of mine.

I went searching for him. I had not gone much into the city, but I knew Ivan's name, I knew what he spoke of, and overnight I found him intoxicated, hot-faced, and penniless, draped in a broken chair in the filthy back-room of a smoky building. I swore at him and cursed his name and demanded what he had stolen.

"What will a grave-child and a hag do with money?" he mocked, and clapped his hands while the friends his mother's stolen money had bought him laughed. "Buy needles and leeches? Why not give, gamble, enjoy life in this sorry hole?"

Not that he called it a hole, or myself what I was, but that he called Voierry a hag! I had no use for words. I lunged and clawed and bit him and from his jacket while he shouted and beat at me I wrested the rose-colored bag the coins had been in. I could not conceive of losing the sum, but he had spent it with frivolity on cards and spinning tops. Later I would learn it was a sum easy to lose; but to Voierry and I it had been the wealth of the world.

Ivan's friends of convenience threw me onto the street. Ivan laughed with drunken bluster and crowed his victory as I retreated. I returned, bruised, to Voierry, with the empty bag.

She blamed me.

I wailed. I shrieked. I offered to work—none would have me. I offered to steal—Voierry shouted that stolen coin would curse us both. Had it cursed Ivan? I asked. He seemed well. He brought us dry rinds and spotted cheese. How kind! No food became less. My hollowness turned inside out. I chewed the furniture to fill myself with splinters. I begged on the street; Voierry did the odd jobs she could for old food from the city above.

All our efforts were not enough. The food was hard on her, and gave her pain. I dug and ate worms from the street and watched Voierry grow slower much too quickly.

Ivan came smugly by with old bread and offered to take the house from Voierry. She could not take care of it, nor of him, or me. This was true. I asked him to take her in, without me. She cried. As though I had never bit him, he smiled kindly and with pity and patted me on the head. On him I smelled guilt.

"Unkempt grave-child," he said. "Of course I will care for my own mother."

To her he spoke softly and in that moment I saw the grace Voierry saw in him and I was glad. Of course, he would help his mother. Even a rotten man was moved by guilt. That I would be in the street, and Voierry with her son who returned for her; it was enough. I helped her gather things, some clothes, and Ivan said he would be back for the rest, her needles, her darning gourd, the profession that until now had fed her. He asked me to finish gathering them while he was gone.

Yet some small seed of mistrust bade me trail them.

They walked toward his house, and past it, toward the end of town. Away from the graveyard and away from the shadow of the highest sphere, out of the sheltering wings of the saint ossifrage of the city-above. Further they walked from the central sphere to the realm of the sphere-below, the farmer's wetlands, where lived the forgotten, the marshes, the leeches, the mosquitos and the abandoned; saint scarab-beetle's sphere of shit, the beginning and the end of life.

At the edge of a field slumped a mouldering house. The poor-house, stinking of mildew and rot. Our hut had been cleaner; our hut had not been left to curl in upon itself. The walls did not mask the thin sound of sobs from my saint's ears. There was no care in this place. It was where people were left to be buried without remembrance.

Voierry knew. Voierry clapped her hand on her son's back and went through the fence willingly, as though this was her place. I followed them to the gate. I watched them embrace, and Ivan kissed her on each soft cheek. He promised to visit. He promised to bring her the last of her work.

He promised not to forget her.

In his gait as he turned away I saw the spring of a man freed of a burden. I heard the laugh he made at the gambling table.

I waited for him to turn the corner on the marsh road, out of sight of the windows of the poor-house.

I killed him. I killed him as a cat does; I was not kind. I felt my saint within me as I ate of his chest and belly, and I was filled. The remains I sunk into the marsh-fields so that he might have some use in death as he had not in life. In that moment, watching the body sink into the mud, I was satisfied, my hunger and my anger.

It was a fleeting satisfaction.

Voierry's spinning-work I bundled and left at the gate of the poor-house for her. Not long after I heard she had died of her grief. Her work did not sustain her through the loss and my betrayal; and I knew it was a betrayal, but that had not stopped me.

The council of the city above would condemn us both, and from their council, our blood would pass down to the grave in the hour of blood, but I bore no guilt. I returned to the graveyard and cleaned my hands and mourned there.

I mourned, but I did not die.

Ivan and Voierry both were gone, one before the other, though to me it felt they had parted the other way around. Their passings swallowed each other in my memory; one after the other, always, without closure. One I thought would bring me happiness, the other sorrow; but Ivan's passing brought me sorrow as well, and for a long time I lingered in it. I watched in the yard and each in the color of rose I searched for the manners of Voierry or the memory of Voierry.

When at last I understood I would not find her in another, I grew weary of mourning Voierry in every shadow. Their end was death, but not my death.

Mosquito wives, ticks and leeches, death-feeders who snap bones in their teeth; they came and went from my yard. So did I go, first in their paths and then on my own to the city above. I traveled far. I passed through the ossifrage's council of blood without guilt and further still.

My hunger never lessened. Whether I had done ill did not concern me, but when I could, I tried to do good as had been done for me; and after many years of this, at last I understood what Voierry had meant when she told me she had only time to give.

To her memory I would offer gratitude; to her child, patience; to her body, rest and the knowledge that the space she resided in was hers to have. Never should she have had to fold herself away.

Through all of this, you, the body of whom I was born of—

I never thought of you at all.

THE SIMULACRUM

Max Turner

Transcript: Recovered dictaphone recording dating from January 3rd, 1959. Voice identified as that of Doctor Lionel Rush. Estimated to be within three days of his death.

Simulacrum. From the Latin *simulācrum*, meaning likeness or semblance; it is a representation or imitation of a person or thing.

It's not a simple task, to create a human being through a method other than conception and gestation. It is even less simple to render that creation correctly.

There are so many facets to humanity that can never truly be accounted for. As well as one might know the human body, the minutiae of anatomy down to every nerve ending and blood vessel, one cannot truly know or predict the thoughts or feelings that the flesh encompasses and contains.

This was our first mistake.

During gestation, we considered it a genderless thing.

One of many, though the first to survive long enough to be considered 'to term'. At some point, unlike with the others before it, we were obliged to give it a sex, and for the sake of ease and with the hope that should it be a success we might harvest its ovum for investigation, we saw to it that it was born female.

We called it Mary.

Not after the Virgin Mary, such a thing would have been

obscene. Instead, the name was for Mary Shelley, after it had been amusingly suggested by one of the team. Our very own monster, of sorts. Though our methods were much more scientific and hygienic than Victor Frankenstein.

Mary was whole. Not an amalgam of parts. A seamless simulacrum, we assumed.

We thought it was whole. We couldn't have known how wrong we were. How it had seemed such a simple thing for it to be Mary and not a Percy or Victor, or even Joseph. We had not accounted for the mind's connection to the body. Or for the soul's connection, perhaps, if you believe in such a thing.

If there is, then I am sure my own might be damned.

Recording ends.

Scanned File: Recovered papers from Doctor Rush's office.
    Scanned Image: A large incubation chamber. Inside, suspended in fluid, is an amniotic sac holding a foetus.
    File 6—January 2nd, 1952.

We return from our festive break to find that experiment HAS14 has unexpectedly thrived. It is certain that the success is due to the adjustment in the gestation period. It is vital for the H.A.S. Project that the experiment grows at a faster rate than expected in a human foetus. The same will be necessary once gestation is complete, should we make it that far. But it seems with the previous experiments we were too hasty. At a rate of almost exactly double the growth of a human foetus, we seem to have found success, for now. If this continues, then we can expect HAS14 to be fully gestated by the end of April.

A spring baby.

Scanned File: Recovered papers from Doctor Rush's office.
    File 41—October 19th, 1952.

HAS14, or Mary, is now six months old, but based on growth and appearance, is closer to a two-year-old child. The second stage of the growth development exceeded expectations and we've filed our reports with General Smythe and Director Miller. We remain cautiously optimistic that HAS14 will continue to thrive in this manner until the third stage. We are less optimistic that the third stage will occur as planned. It seems too fortuitous that on our fourteenth attempt we bring to gestation an experiment that hits each stage perfectly. Rather than slow in growth to roughly that of the average human, we suspect that this is where HAS14 will fail. Resulting in the continued rapid aging until the experiment succumbs to old age and organ failure.

However, in doing so, we will be able to study HAS14 and plan for adjustments that need to be made to succeed with the next experiment, inevitably HAS15.

```
Transcript: Recovered dictaphone fragment
recording dated May 3rd, 1953. Voices
identified as that of Doctor Lionel Rush
and the child known as Mary or Experiment
HAS14.
```

Rush: Hello Mary, how are you today?

Mary: I don't feel good.

Rush: Oh? I'm sorry to hear that. Have you discussed this with matron? Is it a stomach upset?

Mary: I just don't feel good. I don't feel right. I feel like there's something wrong inside of me.

Rush: I will discuss with matron and see if there needs to be any adjustment to your medication. In the meantime, I hear you have progressed up another level with your reading and writing.

Mary: Yes, sir.

Rush: Very good. Let's head into the testing room and we will see where you now place within a standard school system.

```
Recording ends.
```

THE SIMULACRUM

```
Scanned File: Recovered papers from Doctor
Rush's office.
     File 126—May 27th, 1953.
```

I have followed up with matron regarding HAS14's assertion of ill health, as well as with Doctor Kennedy who has now run every full medical test that he possibly can. Physically, there is absolutely nothing wrong with it, but it continues to complain of feeling unwell and has now routinely taken to scratching at its skin enough to warrant salves and bandages on more than one occasion.

In an effort to tackle any potential neurosis, matron tried to cheer it up with a new dress. This approach backfired tremendously, with it becoming even more distressed until sedation was required. It now insists on wearing nothing other than the grey jumpsuits originally provided.

These could all be side effects from the circumstances of its birth and so I have asked for close monitoring. Perhaps this is signalling an end to HAS14, some sort of breakdown that none of us foresaw.

It is a puzzle for now, though I would not be surprised to see signs of degradation soon.

```
Scanned File: Recovered fragmented papers
from Doctor Kennedy's office.
     File 14-1095—April 28th, 1955.
```

Today HAS14 turns three years old and presents as around ten in physical and mental capacity, for the most part.

I have serious concerns about HAS14's mental wellbeing. There has been more than one sign of serious disturbance and I continue to work closely with matron to make HAS14 as comfortable as possible. I believe we are building a rapport. HAS14 no longer sees me as the mean old doctor with needles and tests, but as a trusted adult with one of the most continuous relationships it has known.

Therefore, in these files, I now find myself referring once more to 'it' and 'HAS14'. Not for the same distance I had at the start of this project, but out of respect for HAS14 itself. It has been very vocal on hating the name Mary; in fact, it is uncomfortable with being addressed in the feminine at all.

Perhaps this dissociation comes from who HAS14 is and how it came to be here. I have tried to discuss this with Dr. Rush, but he has little interest in HAS14 beyond the scientific and remains convinced that HAS14 will not last more than another year.

I don't agree. ~~But it's hard to say whether that is my opinion as a physician, or as someone who personally cares for its well-being.~~

```
Scanned File: Recovered papers from Doctor
Rush's office.
    File 276—August 12th, 1957.
```

HAS14 continues to be withdrawn and does not seem to be improving. Whilst it has been surly and insular since it first began to complain of this phantom illness, it has never previously been uncooperative. Now, it has had to be coerced into several training sessions with General Smythe's men, under threat of restrictions.

Up until these apparent 'teenage years' began to present themselves, progress with Smythe had been outstanding. As designed, HAS14 immediately took to the Human-Automaton Soldier training. As designed, HAS14 immediately took to the Human-Automaton Soldier training and is now qualified as a skilled field medic and trained in close quarters combat. Smythe is keen to progress onto to more aggressive skills. If stage three doesn't occur, it will have been a wasted investment, but the director has assured us that it is a risk they are happy to take, on balance.

Kennedy is now certain that HAS14 is approaching oestrus and will soon start a monthly cycle. However, given its rapid growth, it remains to be seen what schedule this will adhere to.

If HAS14 does fail, we can reap its ovum for future investigations and perhaps see if making HAS15 male has any pertinent effect.

```
Transcript: Recovered dictaphone recording
dated   November   15th,   1957.   Voices
identified as that of Doctor Lionel Rush
and Doctor George Kennedy.
```

THE SIMULACRUM

Kennedy: Did matron update you? About the name?

Rush: Wollstonecraft? Yes. I can't say I'm pleased. I want to know which blasted idiot has been filling its head with nonsense. I certainly didn't approve Shelley on its reading materials.

Kennedy: Stone, actually. It wants to be called Stone, after Wollstonecraft.

Rush: Whatever next? Perhaps I've been too lenient. I waved off any concern when it insisted on cutting its hair. It seemed practical for its training to have shorter hair. And apparently it keeps asking matron to refer to it as *he*. I did put a stop to that nonsense, I assume it comes from being around Smythe's team, all boys together and all that. But now this name thing! I suppose it is fitting, though. A stone, an object. Something that might be picked up and used as a weapon or fashioned into one. I assume that isn't what you came to discuss though?

Kennedy: No, I wanted to let you know that I've completed the egg retrieval. The lab will begin their tests immediately.

Rush: Excellent news. Just consider, George. What if we're able to create more in this manner? What if the next stage is having them gestate their own young?

Kennedy: Readymade army.

Rush: Don't take that tone, you knew what you signed on for, and you like how much you are being paid. Were there any problems with the harvesting?

Kennedy: No. It's pretty much out of its mind with pain, it hasn't had a break in oestrus for two months. Now that we have harvested, might I suggest that we try to do something about that? Have you read about those progesterone treatments? Might be worth—

Rush: No, I don't think we should introduce any treatments that we haven't already given rigorous consideration to. We have no idea how hormone treatments would interact with it. I think we'll wait it out and see if stage three presents. If not, then the situation will soon resolve itself with menopause and then death.

Kennedy: God help us.

Rush: Does he help those who choose avarice?

Kennedy: Damn you, Rush.

`Recording ends.`

MAX TURNER


```
Scanned File: Recovered papers from Doctor
Rush's office.
    File 611—July 30th, 1958.
```

HAS14's tests have confirmed it has entered stage three. There had been signs of its metabolism slowing, not least its oestrus cycles had become less regular, which has alleviated some of its distress. Which is better for all of us.

Now, approximately at the equivalent of a twenty-year-old, trained in many military aspects and ready to be deployed, it seems HAS14 is a success.

The deployment won't happen, of course. If we are able to recreate this experiment, hopefully even improve upon it to have a more mentally stable product, then we are anticipating the production of a range of HAS19s or 20s ready for action.

This means that HAS14 is now surplus to requirements.

I have suggested to the director that we continue to observe its growth so that we can be sure of the stability of stage three. I get the impression he is not keen, and it may come down to costs. He has mentioned several times that he doesn't believe life expectancy once deployed will be something we need to be concerned with.

My hope is that we can compromise and keep HAS14 for another year or two in order to study further before euthanization. Every day we might learn something that will improve our next experiment.

If agreed, we will however need to move it to the secure facility. I believe it is becoming too confused and aggressive to be treated with anything like humanity. A good point to make to the director I think, this is an issue we will need to address with HAS15.

```
Transcript: Recovered dictaphone recording
dated    December    13th,    1958.    Voices
identified as that of Doctor Lionel Rush
and Doctor George Kennedy.
```

Rush: I'm recording now, please repeat what you just told me. And do try to calm down, be clear for the tape.

Kennedy: Dammit, man. I need your permission to administer more sedation. Stone has—

Rush: I believe you are referring to HAS14.

Kennedy: You piece of—Yes, HAS14! Our permitted level of non-surgical sedation needs to be increased. Right now!

Rush: Are you asking me or telling me?

Kennedy: Rush, what is wrong with you? I have just come in here and told you that St– HAS14 has had an episode. Has smeared menstrual blood all over the walls. Has . . . has clawed at his breasts. Dug into the flesh in chunks. I need to stitch him up, either allow for greater waking sedation or let me book the operating room.

Rush: *It*, Kennedy. It is an *it*. It might be considered a *she* based on anatomy, which you yourself have just attested to, given your reference to what it is doing with its own menstrual blood!

Kennedy: Fine, it. *It!* Just let me help it. This is the first menstrual cycle it's had since they let up, it . . . please Rush, for the love of God. Let me sedate it.

Rush: Very well. Sedate it for the duration of its cycle. Stitch it up and—

Kennedy: You know, if you'd just let it be as it wanted to be, we wouldn't be in this mess. If it says it is male, we should have respected that, worked with it and now instead we have this—

Rush: And once you've done that, I want you back here so that we can discuss your future on this project.

Recording ends.

Scanned File: Recovered papers from Doctor Rush's office.

File unnumbered—date estimated to be between 5th and 6th January 1959. This file was handwritten, but has been typed for clarity.

I am unable to record this on tape as I fear I will be heard.

I am hidden, but I can hear everything.

My creation, my Simulacrum is imperfect. A monster.

Not in ways I could have predicted. The truth is, Kennedy was right. He always got better cooperation when he addressed it as it wished to be: as male, as Stone.

Should it have been male? Was its mind male? Its soul?

All I can hear is screaming now, echoing in my mind. The real screams have already stopped, but they seem to be remembered in the walls.

I found matron dead a day ago. From the carnage in the facility, it looks like she was one of the first. And I'm under no illusion that I will be last. It isn't that I've successfully avoided it. I've been the only living person here for at least a day, so there is no doubt I am simply being toyed with.

I wonder if it would have killed Kennedy, were he here. Certainly, it must have held Kennedy in the same regard as matron, and yet she is dead.

I saw it.

Him.

I heard screams of pain and thought it was another survivor. It came from the training room that had been used to teach field medicine. By the time I got there the screaming had stopped. And it wasn't another survivor.

Instead, Stone sat up on a gurney, panting and covered in blood.

He had removed his own breast tissue, discarded slabs of meat on the floor. The remaining flesh was stitched together with a hand steadier than it had any right to be.

I stood there staring at him until he looked up and grinned at me. And in that moment, I realised the breadth of the mistakes we had made. That I had made.

We created a soldier and then made us its enemy.

I ran then, and have been waiting since. I've caught a glimpse of it in the corridors, barefoot, wearing just the grey sweatpants and bandaging around his bare chest. He might look like a regular male patient if not for the blood. Everywhere, caked in his hair, clothes drenched with it and then dried dark and hard.

He doesn't just wish to kill me; he wishes to terrorise me. And he is succeeding. I should open this door and shout 'I'm sorry Stone', but we would both know the words were only to save my own skin. So, I choose instead to keep what little of my dignity remains and say nothing at all.

L.R.

THE SIMULACRUM

Case Code Name: Simulacrum
File Summary: Case Closed.
Due to security measures, eight days passed between loss of contact and investigation.

All facility staff and General Smythe's unit were found dead.

The mutilated and burned remains of Doctor Rush were found posed at his desk in his office, his final note set before him.

Subject HAS14—self identified as 'Stone'—was not discovered amongst the remains. HAS14 is presumed at large.

All scientific files and genetic materials relating to the HAS experiments, including all remaining HAS embryos, were destroyed by fire.

Former employee, Doctor George Kennedy, has not been traced.

All materials relating to this investigation and the HAS experiments have henceforth been classified.

Investigation concluded: 17th October 1961.

[END]

THE ROOTS THEY PULL

Taylor J. Pitts

HALF-HIDDEN IN creeping wisteria, I whisper the name like a secret.

"Jo."

The rose hedge that stands like a locked door between our estates rustles as if disturbed by the wind. But there is no breeze here, deep in the secret glade. There never is.

"Boo," Johanna hisses, popping up behind the hedge. There are smudges of soil on Jo's light brown skin, leaves in their hair, stems growing from their head—silky black, enticing in the gentle brush against their shoulders. Some nights you can barely see the roots, obscured by the tuck of hair behind ears or a knit hat pulled tight. But tonight, they're on full display. I itch to tug on the fragile vines, to test how deep they go.

"You're a terror," I say instead.

"And you are a night-blooming flower." Johanna extends an arm across the hedge. In their hand is something soft, glowing pale pink in the twilight.

"Jo," I scold, lurching—instinct. I stop myself inches from the hedge. I can almost feel its surprise at being plucked, its indignity. Its rage. No one touches the rose hedge.

No one but Jo.

"They're just sitting here, growing aimlessly." There's enough light left to see the gleam of Jo's grin. I can read the unspoken rest of the statement on their face: *Just like us.*

"It's dangerous," I argue. But my own lips are already turned up in a smile. As always, Johanna is unharmed. They turn the outstretched flower between thumb and forefinger and let out a huge, dramatic sigh.

"If you don't accept my gift, I will have to assume you do not love me."

Blood fills my cheeks. Johanna has stolen roses before, but they've never given me one. I reach across the hedge—careful to avoid the prickly white thorns—and snatch the rose. Its scent intoxicates the air, poisons releasing from its petals as I draw it close, poised for malice. I can almost hear Aunt Rhoda's voice in my head, warning me of the bodies of countless careless children that lie beneath the rose hedge. Victims of curiosity or disobedience or unruliness—or perhaps a bit of each. A crucible of sins.

But I breathe with relief when nothing happens. Just as with Jo, the dangers the hedge cultivates don't seem to work on me. Petals smooth and pliant as butter set out all day slip between my fingers as I caress the rose. On its stem is one white thorn—a flag of surrender.

"Thank you," I tell the rose. "It's beautiful."

Johanna laughs, harsh and ugly. "It's hideous. Just like the rest of this thing. The rest of this *place*." They kick the hedge, and its leaves jostle with the movement. I freeze until the noise stops.

"Don't say that," I mutter. But what am I defending—the estates or the hedge? Is there a difference?

Johanna looks me over. "I promise not to say another word if you come over here."

The taunt is familiar; we both know crossing over is impossible. Even if the hedge has chosen to leave us unharmed, it's still impossibly dense. Whoever set themselves the task of wading through it would suffer the scorn of a thousand white pricks. The hedge stretches for miles in either direction, then veers sharply into each of our houses, growing into the cracks of the foundation. It may as well be made of stone.

Somewhere, a door slams. Birds take flight from nearby trees. The playful glint in Johanna's eyes vanishes.

"I should—"

"Yes," I finish, listening for the telltale rustle of cloth. Any moment, the arc of a lantern's swinging light will slice through the dusk-gloom like a scythe, and then Jo might not be able to come back next week. "Here," I say, thrusting the rose over the hedge.

THE ROOTS THEY PULL

So gently, Johanna says, "Keep it."

And then they disappear into the overgrown foxtails. Fuzzy heads wave goodbye at me, and I stay rooted to the spot until it's too dark to see them anymore. The lantern light never appears.

***

Three days later, the pink rose has lost most of its color, its petals flimsy. It barely looks like a rose anymore. I tuck it in my corset and wear it around the house, petals just peeking out from my breast, aware of my aunt's watchful eyes when we pass in the halls. I imagine her stopping me and demanding to know who my suitor is.

Jo, I would answer. She wouldn't know who I meant, not from the name. I would glow with the secret, writhe with the potential of giving it away. With all the words aching to burst from my chest. *Jo is short for Johanna. Jo is not who you think. Jo is . . .*

And if Aunt Rhoda dares to reach out—if she tries to take the rose from me—

But she doesn't. She doesn't demand a name for my suitor. She doesn't even give me a second glance. Over the course of the week, she keeps a distance from me that I've only ever dreamed of, paling whenever I'm near. There is only one word I hear her mutter when she brushes past me and catches a whiff of the flower, her nose wrinkling, features curling in on themselves like the pit of a sour fruit.

"Rotten."

***

A broken wisteria branch signals our spot. I turn left toward the hedge. The air is thick with cloying August humidity, and I work for a good breath. Each one feels thinner than the last, like broth strained too many times. But I'm at our spot, and it's our night, and Johanna will be here any moment. They'll smile at me like they always do, and I'll pretend it doesn't make my heart demand freedom from my chest, and everything else will fall away.

As I enter the scattering of trees that form the glade, I cup the rose carefully in my hand. It's brittle now. Fragile—like Johanna's hair. I wish they wouldn't hide their roots. I want to see them; I want the rose hedge to see them. Our families. The whole world, if Jo would allow it. When Johanna appears, I'll reach across the hedge as far as I can and grab a fistful of those roots—I want to pull them out and feel them, smell them, taste them.

193

Absently, I run my fingers through my own hair, nails dragging along my scalp, testing, searching. Could I grow them too?

Fireflies wink around me, keeping far from the hedge. Something feels off.—Normally, the glade is a haven, a place where Jo and I can be ourselves together even while we're apart. But this evening, it's weighed down by something I can't see. Is it the lack of rain? The way the clouds are filled to the brim and yet can't find it in themselves to have mercy on us? Twilight fades as the sun slips behind the trees. Cicadas wail while other unseen creatures murmur and twitch and consume.

The bones of my corset press in on me like fingers, my skin sticky with sweat that clings to the thick fabric. Fidgeting, I peer over the hedge in the direction of Johanna's house. Worry germinates inside me. Where's Johanna? They never arrive after sundown, and now even its orange afterglow has nearly bled itself dry.

Then, finally, I hear a rustle of cloth against foxtails.

"Jo," I breathe, a smile forming on my lips. "I thought—"

But the person breaking through the clearing is too tall to be Johanna. Too broad. The sudden flare of a lantern hurts my eyes, and I stumble over the hem of my skirt, falling to the ground.

"Who's that?" the man demands, raising his lantern above the hedge at a careful distance. It's Mr. Glasgow, Johanna's father. I can see him in the light: white skin, black stubble on his cheeks, sun-roughened skin, eyes that harden as they take me in. "You the reason my girl's been creeping around back here?"

I cringe at the word, at how wrong it is. Anger flares in my chest. But I can't speak; I can only shrink.

"She won't be coming around no more," he says. "You go on home. I'm sure your folks expect you back." He gestures with his lantern, but it's lazy, insincere. His gaze drags over my figure, lingering on all my soft parts. "Or maybe I'll just let them know you'll be late?" He grins, then begins to laugh. Halfway through, it seizes and becomes a horrible wet cough that disturbs the leaves of the hedge standing between us like a sentry.

A sudden thought grips me: If it weren't for the rose hedge, Mr. Glasgow would be on top of me by now, the whereabouts of the child he'd just scorned forgotten.

I scramble to my feet and run.

THE ROOTS THEY PULL

By the time I reach the stone steps, Johanna's father is far away, but I can still hear his laughter in my head. As I catch my breath, I unfold my clenched hand. Crumpled tufts of pink look back at me in the dark.

***

The next two evenings, I go to the secret glade and face an empty hedge. Johanna's father does not come back—but neither does Jo. I stay until the crickets begin to play their melancholy song and my ankles are bitten to shreds by bloodthirsty mites.

By evening of the third day, I'm desperate. The rose hedge mocks me. Every rose is Mr. Glasgow's laughing, gaping mouth. Each thorn is a white snarl of teeth grinning through shadows. I take a pair of shears and lift it to a twisted branch with shaking hands. But I can't bring myself to cut the hedge. It kept me away from Johanna—but it also kept Johanna's father away from me. I can't commit this act of violence against the one thing that protected me. And I can't force my way through it.

I'll just have to go around it.

My plan lurks in my head for the rest of the night. It stirs up rage I didn't know I had. I get little sleep as I begin to understand what it will entail, as I start to see the shape of it—muddy at first, a silhouette in the dark, then lighter until it's so clear I can't stand to look at it straight on. With the rising sun comes a clarity that weighs on me like chains around my bones as I dress in the corset Johanna likes best. They've made it abundantly clear they would much rather see me without one at all, but this—my oldest, most worn corset, with embroidered green vines curling intricate designs across the chest—is the one they've disparaged the least.

But not even Johanna's favorite corset can keep the anxiety at bay. What I'm about to do is unacceptable. A breach of etiquette, Aunt Rhoda would say. We never go next door—haven't in all the years we've lived here. No one visits their neighbors. It simply isn't done. And because it simply isn't done, I'm as discreet as possible when twilight finally falls and I snatch Aunt Rhoda's moldy green coat off its iron hook, then slip out the front door.

I'm sweating by the time I climb the decrepit wooden steps to the Glasgow Estate. When Mr. Glasgow answers the door, I flinch. Ridiculous. I've only ever had one interaction with the man, and he didn't—couldn't—come anywhere near me. But my body seems to understand something I don't as I'm hit with a damp, bitter smell that turns my stomach.

"Hello," I manage. "I'm here to borrow a pair of shears."

Mr. Glasgow's glassy eyes sweep over me again, the same way they did before, indulgent. He seems to hear the words slowly or not at all. The way he looks at me makes me feel small yet too large at the same time—unworthy of the attention and unable to escape it.

"Shears. For the . . . garden," I stutter, then rush to cover my uncertainty. "Our pair is rusted, and the wisteria needs trimming."

I barely hear what I'm saying. My thoughts are consumed with the darkness behind Mr. Glasgow, the off-putting smell. The quiet. Something is wrong. Where is Johanna?

Mr. Glasgow opens the door wide, and I step in. As soon as the door closes, I know I've made a mistake. I should not have come here alone. The foyer leads into a cluttered room whose only saving grace is a sliding glass door that leads out to the field of foxtails. Here, the damp, not-right smell is at home, and I realize what it is: mold. Water drips from a crack in the ceiling. It hasn't rained in a month.

"Over there," Glasgow says, nodding at a low table near a blackened fireplace. He hovers at a distance, watching me.

I drift to the table in a haze. Already I know what will happen, and the knowing is a poison—one that seeps through my skin and turns my blood to vinegar. Wet, like the smell of the mold that I can't see but I know is there. Sour, like the breath over my shoulder. His hands are on me before I reach the table. They clamp hard around my arms; tomorrow, I will have bruises.

"Don't fight," he grunts in my ear. The command is like a spell. My limbs go rigid, terror seizing me as the older man's hands creep toward my chest. He opens my coat—my aunt's coat, Aunt Rhoda's coat, not mine—and yanks it from my shoulders. Pulling, tugging, ripping, as if I am soil and he is tilling me. Everything happens too fast. Velvet falls around me like a moss shroud, clattering on the hardwood floor. The shears I had stashed in the pocket of Aunt Rhoda's coat are out of reach, and suddenly, I'm shivering. Mr. Glasgow tears open my corset, and my breasts spill out, along with bruised-pink petals.

"The hell," Glasgow mutters, distracted by the soft petals

grazing his fingers. The rose Johanna plucked, tucked away between me moments earlier, has crumbled to ash on Glasgow's skin. I smell something acidic, and then—burning flesh. The man wrenches away from me.

"You . . . " Slack-jawed, he points one festering finger at me.

Red in my peripheral vision. I glance down to find blood running in a thin line to my navel, originating from the smallest puncture wound between my breasts. The single white thorn had nicked me. I wonder how long I've been bleeding. Since the moment I pressed Johanna's bud to my skin? Since before then? I'm no longer shivering as I dig the shears from the burial moss.

Glasgow is on his knees now, staring at the flesh no longer on his hands. White bones shine through exposed tendon. His face is pale, too shocked even to scream. I can't speak either, but if I could, I know what I would say.

For Jo. I plunge the shears into his neck, turning away at the last second. A gurgling sound fills the room. It seems to go on forever. Then there's a thump, and I stay still for a long time, unable to move. Unable to look.

A familiar flicker through the glass door tugs me from my temporary paralysis. Twilight has painted the field of foxtails a battered purple. My heart pounds. My tongue is stuck to the roof of my mouth. I start to shake again. And then—there—near the hedge—

An arc of light.

I scramble to the door, tripping over something soft and fleshy on the way. Clamping a hand over my mouth doesn't keep the vomit from sliding up my throat as I wrench the door open, leaving rainbow stains of sweat and blood on the glass. I stumble out into the field. *Jo. Jo.* Jo is there, waiting for me. They're okay.

My dress becomes an obstacle as I run, and I tear it the rest of the way off, shedding it like too much skin. Foxtails brush my bare hips, graze my bloody navel as I spot the opening to the secret glade. It's different over here from Johanna's side, but I would know it anywhere, wisteria hanging sorrowful over the hedge.

From here, I can see into the well-kept field of my family's estate. Looking around, I search for the light. But the only glow comes from insects floating in the air around me, drifting like bodies on water.

"Jo," I mutter. My voice is hoarse. How long has it been since I used it?

An answering rustle disturbs the hedge. I fall to my hands and knees. Numb, eyes closed, I climb into the green that was once a dense, impenetrable wall. It seems to welcome me, and I crawl over branches that crunch like bones and vines that slide like veins. The familiar warning blares through my head. *No one touches the rose hedge. No one but Jo.* But I'm inside, and the earth is wet in my hands. *Why—It hasn't rained—*

I wade in farther. Thorns pull me back or push me on—I can no longer tell. The hedge kisses my skin with its sharp teeth, accepts my blood as sacrifice, and I give it—I give it all. I can't feel the sweet sting of brambles or taste the copper in my mouth or smell the rot settling in. Rot. *Rotten.*

Soil gives way to soft ribbons. Threads—so many of them. Hair. And something else that feels familiar between my fingers.

Wet on my face now. I dig my hands deeper into Johanna's roots. They're so soft. So fragile. Gently—so gently—I pull at them, the way I always longed to from the other side of the hedge.

The way I never could. Just to see. To feel. To *know*. At last.

***

I don't know how long it takes me to grow my own roots, there in the safety of the rose hedge. It cradles us like a secret. Like cupped hands around lips, holding in words until they're ready to be spoken. Like home. The earth dries and wets and dries again, and we grow roots, stems, petals, thorns. We remain. And someday, someone else comes to the hedge and gently—

—so gently—

—plucks a rose.

STENCH

Vincent Endwell

Therefore shall a man leave his father and his mother,
and shall cleave unto his wife: and they shall be one flesh.
~ Genesis 2:24, KJV

JESSICA BUTTONED THE ugly maternity jeans back up, tight once more against her bulging stomach. Every day lately, something was more uncomfortable, ill-fitting. There were moments—like here, in the rectory behind the meeting hall, with Caleb inside her, where the cumbersomeness of her stomach briefly became a fun kink, but the pleasure of that swiftly sank back into sickly discomfort.

At least she was sure the child wasn't Caleb's. She had only cheated physically after she already knew she was pregnant, though there had been tension between her and Caleb almost as soon as she took over altar duties. That *had* been part of the reason why she volunteered to be the candle minister—not so premeditated as to plan out the affair, but she'd just felt drawn to Caleb, watching him at the front of the church with his hardscrabble words and bust-a-rib sermons. He was so much younger than Darrel, too, not even a line of gray in his hair; and you know, she tried to be a good Christian woman. She knew that her husband was supposed to be enough for her. But she forgot how much she needed excitement, and then she'd seen Caleb looking at her across the finished basement at their game-day party, and somewhere in there her subconscious was making plans she couldn't control.

Jessica busied herself opening up the cabinets of felt drapery and half-burned candles, fat and multicolored, trying to ignore the flutter of her heart. A rain started outside and beat down heavily on the aluminum roof of the converted agricultural supply.

"What are we setting up for this afternoon?" she asked, voice raised above the hammering.

"A funeral," Caleb answered, and she had to strain to hear him over the pounding water. "Actually, you probably know of the woman, have you ever heard of—"

Jessica knew who it was as soon as the question left his lips. Her fingers curled in the dull purple felt with swaying comprehension.

"Oh god, Marylyn?" she said, and Caleb's mildly raised eyebrows told her she was right. "Caleb, I didn't know she was part of the congregation, are you serious?"

"Her family was," Caleb said, peering over a ledger on his desk, where just a moment ago the papers had been disarrayed from where her ass rifled them. The unsteadiness only worsened, until the spray of lace in the cabinet filled her vision, dancing and weaving and cutting across her eyes like writing to the illiterate. "They wanted to have it here. I actually tried to discourage them, given how she died, but I'm not really one to give a grieving family a hard no."

Jessica had loved Marylyn Doyle. Not personally, of course—Marylyn was an influencer, someone whose posts she'd followed and commented on but never met. Marylyn was The Miniskirt Wife, happily married and mother to five sons who she was raising in the ways of the Lord. What was she known for? Her huge hair sprayed bouncy blonde, her dark blue eyeshadow, and of course her clothing that wasn't quite what the modern, modest wife should wear, but Jessica would be lying if she said she didn't envy how much fun she seemed to have with skirts a little short and shirts a little low, low enough that her shiny gold cross sat right between her big spray-tanned—

Well, there was no need to say much more about that. Marylyn was devout, though, no one could challenge her on that. They could call her a slut all day if they wished, but she knew her scripture and she went to service with her family daily, and how many Christians could truly claim to do better? Honestly, part of why Jessica loved her is that she could put all those catty women in the church to shame: both with her knowledge of God's word and by being a hot little thing.

As for what she posted, it was everything from recipes to fashion for mothers and wives, to pictures of her and her sons. Some posts were light-hearted or instructional, and some were more personal.

And then she'd died.

Her death had been plastered all over the internet, on Facebook and Instagram, everywhere but her own accounts. Brooke had forwarded Jessica eulogy after eulogy until Jess told her to stop. As a regular guest on the evening show *The Grand Old Tyme*, the host Lorelai Trentham had eulogized her beside the smiling picture from Marylyn's blog, the Miniskirt Wife's grin wide and white in front of the hazy suggestion of trees, grass and sun. Jessica had been glued to the stream through surging tears as Lorelai declared, "We should all take her as an inspiration to live more truly in ourselves and in our love of Jesus Christ the Lord."

"I thought it was really weird," Jessica remarked, studying Caleb's expression, "that none of them would say how she died. It wasn't anywhere I could find."

Caleb glanced back at her. His face could have been the still of compassion or the calm of hidden mischief, but of course he didn't have a bone of mischief in him. "The body is in the front room," he said. "Let's take the flowers out and look."

And Jessica crossed her arms over herself, a chill coursing through her body.

Lights were half-off in the sanctuary as they passed through, and rain pounded against the windows. In the windowless foyer, the electric lights felt like a circle of known territory against the dark.

"When I talked to the family," Caleb said, "they said it was a medication interaction. Evidently she had just tried a new herbal remedy, and as best they can tell, that caused something to go wrong with some other prescription she was taking."

Marylyn's second-to-last post had actually been about a new oil—a naturally-derived skin treatment from a tree resin the name of which Jessica hadn't recognized. Marylyn had advertised it as a way to effectively stop aging, smooth out wrinkles, and make your skin soft and lush. It smelled like lily-of-the-valley, her favorite scent. The oil hadn't done much for Jessica, but it smelled nice and she'd used it for a few days before forgetting about it.

The fact that she'd worn it, that she'd tried it, twisted up in her stomach like sour milk. Nothing bad had happened to her. But maybe she'd got lucky. Or Marylyn hadn't.

"God, really?" she said. "So what happened? Did they just find her? Was it at least . . . quick?"

Caleb walked over to the side door and glanced back at her. "I don't really know, Jessie," he said, and a weird little thrill went through her, mixing with guilt like soap in the bath. Only Darrel called her that. "I don't think so, though."

"Why do you say that?" she asked, but as he opened the door, a smell hit her like the hot breath of a dead beast. She had a sudden vision of the only biology class she had been allowed to take, where they had dissected a dead cat in the name of anatomy.

It had come in a plastic bag filled with formaldehyde, and when they had pulled it out like a sick birth, it reeked like chemicals and preserved, gamey flesh. The students spent a freak hot week in March scalpelling apart this cat, pulling hard, lumpy organs from within the cavity of its body and pinning back the skin to see the structure underneath. The cat had been pregnant; in its womb— barely recognizable as anything of the sort, not that Jessica had really known what she was looking for—each wrapped in its own little sac, lay the tiny half-formed bodies of kittens. What had been strange, Jessica recalled, was that it wasn't disgusting because it was dead and preserved. What had been disgusting was all the things latched inside of it as it died, growing stronger as it weakened.

Caleb stepped into the dark room, and the foul scent followed. It clawed up into her sinuses and lodged there, breeding and fermenting. Lights flickered on like a concession, and the nausea turned to a pounding inside her stomach, a foot pressing against her organs, making space for itself by shoving her out.

"Oh, God, Caleb," she said. "That's not . . . *her*, is it?" The coffin sat up in the little viewing room, surrounded by fake plants. White with silver handles, it captured the dull light from the drop ceiling in a way that made it glow brighter than the rest of the room, like sunlight off a knife. "They wouldn't bring her here if she were rotting, would they? Caleb?"

He didn't answer. As Caleb opened the lid, Jessica saw the face of Marylyn Doyle. It was still, plastic and smiling, and Jessica realized that something was wrong. Her face was actually a cut out, a cardboard printing of that smiling picture on her blog. The grin was white and warm with projected sunlight. Just the eyes were cut out, showing open orbs beneath.

The longer Jessica stared, the more she understood. Marylyn wore a white dress, a white blazer and a thin white blouse, but her skin . . . Jessica climbed the step next to the coffin, not wanting to look, but needing to, in the same way she had needed to see what was in the cat.

The body of Marylyn Doyle had no skin. It was as if she had been peeled apart for autopsy and not put together again, or perhaps it had all sloughed off in some chemical reaction. All that was left beneath her clean white clothing were gray muscle and veins and yellow fat, sallow and preserved.

In the entry hall, Jessica heaved against the wall. Her eyes felt like pinpoints in white paper, light barely bleeding through. The door shut softly as Caleb came to her, the hand he placed on her back too hot and close.

"I thought you'd like to know what happened," he said, something which sounded almost true.

"Why would you think that?" Jessica blurted, though of course she had gone with him, and of course she was to blame for looking. The baby in her stomach kicked and squirmed as if it, too, wanted to rub its nose in the dirt until the rotting stench of flesh and chemical and varnish was gone.

"I didn't think it would upset you so much." His pastor's voice was calm and measured, a man of the community. "It's unpleasant, but in the church, we know that death is not the end."

***

After Kelsie was tucked into bed, Jessica scrolled through the last post again. Her finger hovered over the phone's lock button, ready to turn it off at a moment's notice. She had always wanted kids, just like Marylyn had. When she had been younger, she had wanted as many as seven, though after she had Kelsie that number had been revised to maybe four or something. Now in the middle of pregnancy number two, she didn't think about it at all.

"My husband knew I had cheated on him before I said anything at all," read Marylyn's last post. It was written in her usual dramatic style, but there was a sick self-loathing behind it. "I had been carrying all this weight with me, but when he came up to me with disappointment and compassion in his eyes, it all spilled out at his feet. Isn't the purpose of a wife to love her husband, body and soul, and hadn't I failed in that purpose? And for what, excitement?"

It felt like she should have been crying, but her eyes were dry as paper. It was rich, Jessica thought, for Marylyn to turn against excitement, the thing she was always talking about being good and important, just before kicking it. This felt like such a pivot from the woman who encouraged other women to *liven things up* in the name of better honoring their husbands. There was infinite joy in following one's purpose as a wife, Marylyn said many times—but you weren't to be blamed for wanting some *fun* sometimes, girlie!

"Paul sets the record straight for all who seek to be saved through their own righteousness, by reminding us we are weak through the flesh," Marylyn wrote.

It was strange that there was no photograph or video accompanying the post. Usually, Marylyn posted an image as well, but this was all text, nothing else. What if whatever had been happening to her had started taking effect, and her skin had hung loose and damaged around her eyes, peeling away from the muscle and tissue? What if she was too ashamed to look at her own face?

She wondered if Marylyn had been pregnant when she died. Inside her own stomach, Jessica imagined the bones of the child, that tangle of white sticks that would grow larger like tree branches, extending through her meat until they reached her bones themselves, looking for something just like them.

"Jessie?"

Darrel stood in the doorway. She didn't know how long he had been watching her, but there he was, the middle-aged enigma himself, in his pale blue button-down as exciting as a water cracker, with his boring brown eyes and fading brown hair the color of an animal. They locked eyes, the way a dog spots a frog on the edge of the water, and it comes down to who can lunge or leap the quickest. He didn't look angry. He didn't look like anything.

She asked him, *what's going on, honey*, and when his response dragged, that pressure on her lungs got heavier and thicker until it was like breathing in oatmeal.

He asked her to join him in the living room. She followed him like a scolded child, waiting for the question as he sat across from her, his face still and cold. Her stomach felt fatter than ever against her jeans, and she felt suddenly so vulnerable. There was a reason that animals protected their belly, and it was because it was a soft, easy place to tear into, just like she had with that cat. Darrel could fall on top of her right now, and she would have no defense, because why would she have a defense against her own husband, her protector?

When he spoke, it cut through her like a scalpel. "Are you having an affair?"

"No, of course not." The lie fell out easily, ready to be born. "Why would you even ask that?"

"Please don't lie to me, Jessie," he said. As he continued to question her, heat rose to her face, her hands trembled, and her mouth dried as if with the heat of the lie. Her body was weak, betraying her. "Are you cheating on me?"

***

"I didn't deserve Henry's love and forgiveness," Marylyn had written. "I didn't deserve a second chance."

Jessica's foot slipped off the accelerator, but then found it again. The porch lights at Brooke's shone like an eye in the dark, so bright that she almost missed the other cars in the drive. Tears streaked salt down her face like finger lines as Brooke came outside. A day had passed, and it had gotten no easier to speak to Darrel, no easier to remain in the house. She had stayed with her mother in her old child's bed, paralysis seizing her brain.

"Honey, are you okay?" Brooke asked as Jessica staggered toward her, feeling like a puppet holding itself up. "What happened?"

Brooke was an old high school friend. Jessica hadn't been close with her at first, but then they'd fallen in together, the way you sometimes do when other friends leave town or turn out to be two-faced. Jessica stared, mouth flapping open, no idea where to begin. There was too much to confess, and tears shook loose and imminent behind her eyes.

"Are you having a party?" she asked.

"It's a gender reveal," said Brooke, and wrapped an arm around her. "Honey, is this about Caleb?"

Something heavy and thick inside her pressed up. Her child was growing at an unnatural rate, she was sure, and reaching for room.

"How did you know about that?" she said hoarsely.

Brooke led her toward the door. "Jess, you told me."

Marylyn had written that her husband had her down on the couch, then sat beside her with his hand on her knee. *Do you want to stay?* he had asked after the horrible truth had been extracted. He had been giving her the chance to try again, to do better. Jessica had read her words with a judgment that came from somewhere deep and rotten within her. As if to say *yes* was cowardly. She was relieved that Marylyn's husband had taken her back, allowed her to redeem herself. She was scornful that Marylyn had accepted.

But that was days before it had been Jessica's turn. Darrel had sounded so much like Marylyn's husband, it was as if he had followed a script.

Do you want to stay? he had asked.

Brooke's house was hot as that dead-cat classroom, and the women sweltered as they circled around the living room; sweat beaded under a pink ball cap, along the modest neckline of a maternity dress, through the back of a t-shirt. Children played on the floor, ages one to four, as if it weren't long past their bedtimes, voices high and chattering. Some of the women looked up, but continued talking, the conversation rolling along like a boil.

Jessica hadn't told Brooke about Caleb. She wouldn't have. So how did she know?

"Whose gender reveal is this?" Jessica asked as Brooke positioned her on a sofa.

Brooke laughed, and the other women laughed and talked, and Brooke put some orange juice in her hand as if it were midmorning, not after dark. The black outside the windows was suffocating, and the lights inside were dim and electric-coil hot.

"Yours, Jess," Brooke said, and stretched out her hand to Jessica. "I may have lied a little. I actually knew you'd be coming.

Jessica took the hand before she knew what it meant. A familiar woman took her other hand, and the orange juice was now balanced between her knees, and there was seven months of pregnancy in the way, her center of mass all wrong. A little girl squirmed around her feet, laughing and laughing, as the women all joined hands, lowering their heads. The conversation stilled.

"But how do you know what it is?" Jessica asked inanely.

Brooke spoke, but didn't answer. "Lord, please be with us here. We gather here today to say a prayer for our friend Jessica, for you to bless her marriage to Darrel, and to ask for guidance. Before we learn the gender of her soon-to-be-born baby, we turn to you to bless her, and her husband, and her marriage, and to grant her your grace and forgiveness."

Heart thumping, Jessica stared into Brooke's face for signs of cruelty or coldness, something that would explain this mind game, but all she got was the clammy slop of disappointment.

A panic seized her like a hand around her spine, tugging on her bones. She wrenched her hands away and pushed herself up with a sudden motion, quicker than she thought she could. Orange juice splashed and soaked into the carpet. The room fell dead silent, tens of eyes drifting wide and unblinking.

I don't even want the kid!

"Bathroom," she said aloud. "I have to pee. Sorry."

The door latched behind her, not as firmly as she would like. She tested the handle, and it jiggled weakly. She stared into the mirror above the sink, then splashed water on her face. This was insane, what Brooke and the girls were doing. This was fucked up. She guessed it didn't matter how Brooke knew about Caleb. Maybe this was punishment for not coming clean. Maybe this was punishment for being an evil mother.

The porcelain sink was bone beneath her hands. The water was too hot on her face. Something in the room smelled like lily-of-the-valley, and the smell clung to her like a child that wouldn't let go.

Did she want to stay? Jessica couldn't imagine leaving. Where would she go, what would she do, with Kelsie at home, and seven months pregnant with a child that barely felt like hers? It wasn't like she hadn't *thought* before getting involved with Caleb. It wasn't like she didn't know the risk, and it had been worth it, and it hadn't, and even her friends weren't to be trusted.

Was there some reason Marylyn's skin had to be removed? Was there a reason it wasn't needed?

A knock came at the door. Jessica called out for a minute, please, just a minute.

The lily-of-the-valley was overpowering now. The shower curtain hung closed, and Jessica stared at it, and at the line of dry red-brown that stained it. The knocking grew more insistent, as did Brooke's sweet voice.

"Jess, open up. It's just me. Jessie, open up."

Something bony and sharp scraped inside her esophagus. She swallowed, trying to rid herself of it, but it just bobbed in her throat, *bob-bob-bob* like an Adam's apple, like a caught fishbone. She reached for the curtain, her hand shaking, terrified of what was behind it.

The curtain scraped back, and Jessica fell to her knees in sudden pain.

The Wife floated in the tub. Her bouncy blond hair was now soaked bloody spikes, the water the red and tan of blood and resin. Her eyes were gone, her mouth open to nothing. It was only her skin. All she was, was her empty skin.

Then Jessica doubled over as the bones pressed up. Her skeleton was broken. No; her skeleton was alive. There was another skeleton within her, and fingers wriggled in her throat, felt and reached around her mouth. She let out a strangled cry as she reached in between her teeth and the hand grasped at her, tried to grab her.

Bone clacked on teeth, then ribs, then clavicle and tibia and humerus. She felt her jaw crack, and then crack again, and then crack even wider still until she screamed and panted and choked.

Her skeleton pushed out, and then women's hands were all around her, holding her stomach, pulling at her mouth, at her arms, at her skin. "It's nearly ready, it's already loose," they said. Jessica felt her organs shoved away, and her hands felt too large, as if something was pulled from inside of them. Her head slid back from the skull, sliding down, and her eyes pointed up at the ceiling, then the wall, then up at all the women who helped, who helped so efficiently and with female wisdom. Bones snarled, knotted, wove together until Jessica lay, exhausted and helpless and thin against the floor.

"The gender is bones!" cried the many women, stained with blood and fat and viscera. "Everyone gather around, it's going to be bones!"

Their celebration carried the body and muscle from the bathroom, away from Jessica. The sounds swelled and dimmed and faded. With the last of her strength, she pulled herself over the white porcelain lip, and down into the tub. Marylyn's face, her true face, turned toward her. Skin caressed the back of her arm, and loose fingers tilted her chin toward the mouth, gaping and black, of the woman she loved. When it kissed her, she tasted meat and formaldehyde and lily-of-the-valley, sickening and loving.

Skin fit into skin fit into skin, their empty bodies entangled, and Jessica felt a warmth and love like she had never known before.

THE PEARL DIVER

Bri Crozier

THE TANG OF iron hit the buzzard's nostrils as he soared over the highway, bringing him to lazy circles in the sky. It wasn't long before he saw it: a car in reverse with blood on its hood and a sizable dent in its bumper. The buzzard watched with near apathy as the car sped away, leaving a mangled corpse in its wake. Blood trailed across the asphalt like an arrow, leading his eye from the lane to the shoulder where the corpse had come to rest. The buzzard circled down towards it, slowly. He was in no rush. He would not go hungry tonight.

His talons clicked sharp against the asphalt as he landed, already looking over his dinner. It was a buck, young enough that his neck and shoulders were slender, a few white spots still fading out of his hide, now stained a deep, dripping red. His belly had burst in the impact, still-warm blood oozing out from the wound. The hint of pink innards peeked from the unnatural window. Just big enough for a beak, and the skin easy enough to tear away for easy pickings.

What luck, thought the buzzard, *to stumble upon such a fresh meal.* With that, he ducked his head to eat.

"Wait!" came a breathy cry, "I'm not dead yet!"

The buzzard leapt back, his wings spread and feathers on end in momentary surprise. The buck had opened his eyes, wild and glazed with the shock and pain of his injuries. He had lifted his head to look at the buzzard, and that was obviously an immense amount of work, his chest heaving, every breath noticeably labored. The buzzard had been so focused on his meal; he hadn't noticed how fresh it truly was. He calmed himself, stepping closer. Dinner had never yelled at him before, but he didn't see a reason to change his plans. The buck would die soon, that was certain.

"I see," he said, his voice monotone. "I suppose I will wait, then."

The buck laughed bitterly as his neck gave out and his head hit the asphalt, blood dribbling from his nose and mouth.

"So, what, you're just going to sit there? What a funeral."

The buzzard wished the buck was quieter, like every other dinner he had ever had. He didn't have patience for the living. "What do you want me to do, sing you a dirge?"

"Yeah, that'd be nice." The buck sighed, eyes fluttering closed for a moment at the idea. "You're a bird, aren't you? Don't birds sing?"

"I beg your pardon!" The buzzard's feathers ruffled at that. "Presumptuous little . . . Not all birds sing, I'll have you know."

"Well then, tell me a story or something. I don't wanna die in shit company."

"What does it matter?" the buzzard scoffed. "Why should I bother? You are going to die and I—"

"And then you're going to eat me, right?"

The buck had lifted his head again, his breaths coming in quick huffs—of pain or anger, the buzzard couldn't tell, but the buck's eyes were full of something the buzzard had never seen. Call it desperation, or hate, or passion, whatever it may be, it was a feeling the buzzard had never experienced himself, but it wafted off the dying buck in waves. The buzzard stood quietly as he took it in, only the passing cars on the highway filling the silence.

"Is that really too much to ask? Just tell me a fucking story. Then you can eat." His voice was still full of scorn as he spoke, frustrated by the buzzard's noncompliance, and maybe something else, too. "By then I won't care."

Yet again, the passing cars filled the silence, so thick the buzzard wasn't sure he could break it. He swallowed, then finally, whispered, "All right,. I will tell you a story."

Once, there was a fox who fell in love with a silver vixen. Every night, he watched her as she danced on the ripples of the lake, begging him to join her. Every night, he would refuse, afraid of the water's edge, but dreaming of dancing with her. Eventually, his longing became too strong and overwhelmed him. He leapt into the water without a second thought.

But alas, the silver vixen was not there. She had gone down, deep into the lake. Once again, she begged him to follow, only the glint of her perfectly white tail to guide him. Down he swam, deeper and deeper until it was nearly pitch black, save for the glowing light of a pearl, perfectly round and perfectly white.

'I will take this as a gift for my love,' he thought, as he took the pearl in his mouth.

He began to rise back to the surface, only to realize with shock and terror, he had been down too deep for too long. His vision blackened as he struggled to return to the surface, the silver vixen dancing once again on the waves, and he realized with a bitter ache what she had been all along. He had fallen in love with the moon on the lake.

Too late now to break the surface, he drowned, wondering how he could have been such a fool to fall in love with something that never was.

The buzzard finished his tale and looked to the buck, who remained silent. The buzzard was about to take him for dead, when finally, he spoke.

"What was that? Some kind of sick joke? That's the story you tell me?" The buck spit the words with the blood from his mouth, nearly choking on them. "This is the best you could pay me for what I'm about to give you? Fuck you."

The buzzard was once again taken aback. *Pay him?* What was he paying him for? He was about to die. And hadn't the buzzard done what was asked of him? His confusion quickly turned to annoyance.

"You wanted a story, did you not? Well, there, I've done it. You've had your story! You're welcome!"

The buzzard waited for a response, waited for the buck to thank him, to apologize, to explain what he meant and why he was so bitter about his request. He waited for anything, but nothing ever came.

The buck was dead.

The buzzard felt a pang of remorse in that moment, a sense of loss. He had never wondered before about the dead he ate. They had never been vocal or real to him, all just dead and gone and rotting. Nothing more than a meal. But now, he wondered about the life of the buck. What he had been through. What he had been chasing that left him in such a sorry state. The buck had understood what the buzzard would do the minute he arrived. He understood what it meant for him. He had accepted it, however angrily. All he had asked for was a thank you in return. The promise of a small comfort, to sell him the idea that maybe this was not the end.

But the buzzard wasn't a salesman, simply a lucky passerby. Even he understood that, in time, something else would grow from his flesh when he had no more use of it. It was the natural order of things.

The buck had been presumptuous, rude, even. He was not owed anything. *None of us are at the end. None of us,* the buzzard thought, struggling to convince himself of this simple truth. But the buck's last words took root, drowning his mind with a single question: Will the flora that grow from the buzzard's remains know the gift they have been given?

He swallowed down the mirror feeling, the question an unanswered dinner prayer as he ducked his head to eat.

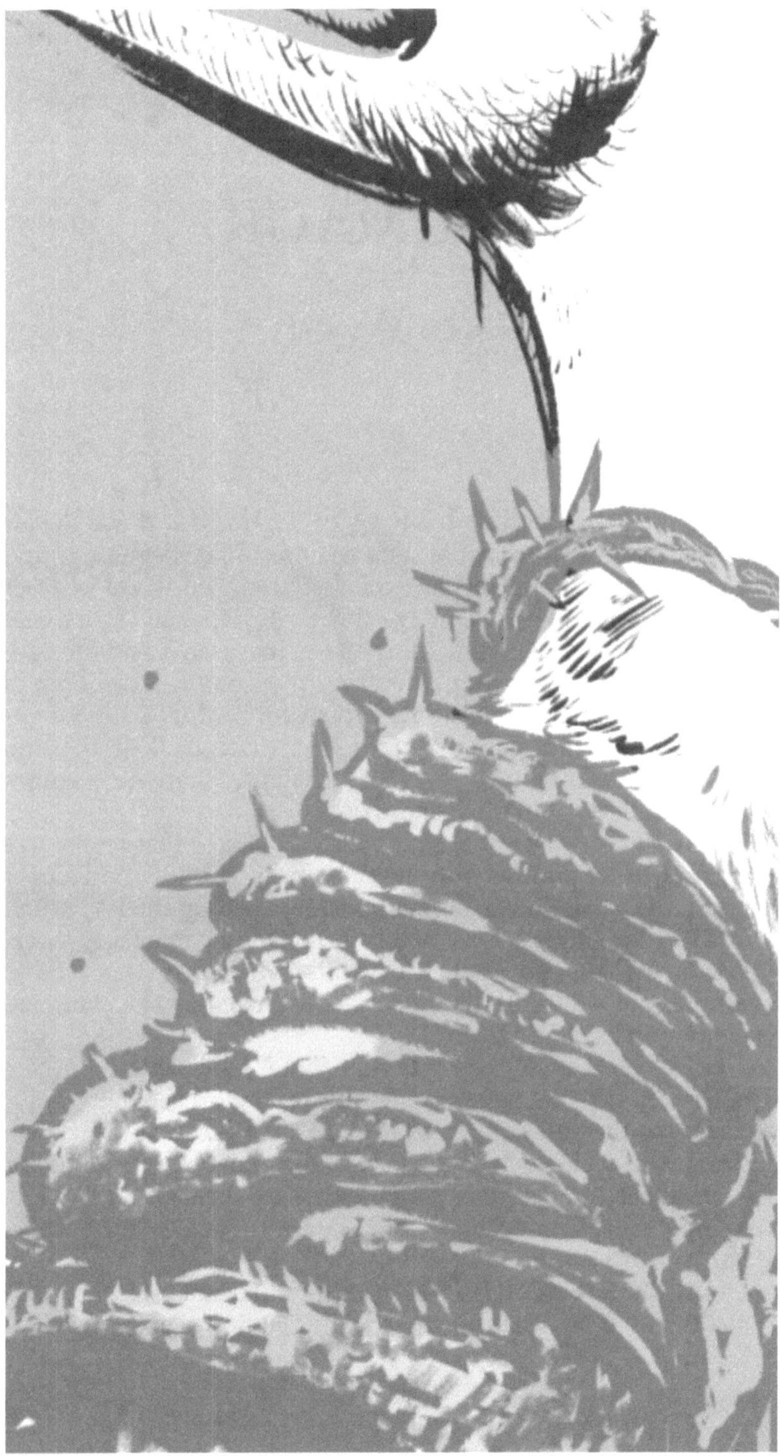

TINY MAGIC

G.E. Woods

THE VIOLENCE STARTED YOUNG. It was the air
they breathed. In the midst of such an unfortunate beginning, and
always curious, they liked to explore the known world of their
apartment. And so it was, at age three, they opened the cabinet
beneath the sink. It led into a tiny space, like a cave, and the cave
was *just* their size. Within the cave, they found a rainbow of
potions, and dragged and hefted them up in thin, pale dough-
skinned arms, each elixir *thwumping* to the kitchen floor, the kind
with those repeating tiles perfect for making square little homes
for each and every smashed-faced doll.

Every three-year-old knew beyond a shadow that magic was
real. And these potions bore helpful spray nozzles—perfect for
dousing the world in enchantment. They lined up their treasure,
and **THE MOTHER** careened into the room, smacking them.
"That is *poison*, you idiot. Chemicals. Don't ever touch them
again." From a careful distance, they watched as she slammed
every potion back into the cave.

When **THE BOYFRIEND** first came to live with them, the
adults were ribbons twisting together in the breeze. Aged four,
slightly less tiny, they observed from corners of rooms or through
narrow cracks between doors how bodies might blossom under
fists into such plum shades. And they passed through the kitchen,
remembering their potions, and they returned to their dolls.
Until.

Until **THE BOYFRIEND** took their hand and placed it on his
twitching stick, all that peculiar feeling hair disappearing their

fingers. There might be much they did not know at age five, but they knew they hated that twitching stick.

Two steaming brown drinks on the counter. "Momma's morning juice," **THE MOTHER** would rasp. They were bigger now. The potion did not *thwump* so loudly on the ground as they lifted it from the cave.

The magic worked. The monster died. When those people came, the ones with shiny symbols on their shirts, they put silver rings on **THE MOTHER'S** wrists and put **THE BOYFRIEND** on a bed of spider legs and lowered a pale sheet over his bubble bath-filled mouth.

Things changed quickly. Their bright eyes ate it all, the wooden halls with old men in black robes banging toy hammers. Grey rooms with soggy donuts and juice boxes and dizzying cartoons for hours. Car rides smelling of pee. A new home with other kids and **OTHER ADULTS**. The house, too, smelled of pee.

On their first night, they snuck from their bed and sock-walked to the kitchen, opening the child-locked cave beneath the sink to find familiar potions. It was a relief of sorts to know their magic was nearby.

Things were fine—for a time. Life went on—for a while. Some years passed, and it happened again, **A MAN** waving about his twitching stick like it was a gleaming, hirsute trophy.

Out came the potions.

Silver bracelets cinched *their* wrists this time, and the words of others trailed behind them. "Like their mother." It had only ever been like themself, the magic so happy to be used as they needed. The two following years did not matter, so they did not bother to remember them. Until.

Until the transfer came. "Cutbacks." "State budgets." "In the red." Guards muttered those enchantments down juvie halls, and thirteen-year-old them listened. Day after day, shackled children waited at exits. Their own transfer went differently.

The van carried only them. Unshackled, for they had not shown violence in two years, their hands grasped at lumpy seats and scratched walls as the van careened from the road. "*Idiots*," they heard in their head, the smoky voice a rasp. But she was not there. Had not been there in many years.

And they were alive.

The guards, not so much.

They picked through the guard supplies, shouldering a bag with first aid, crispy chips, two half-drunk water bottles, cash. A knife. Some other treasured items. Wrapped themself in a guard's heavy coat. The guns they left behind.

The forest curled its skeletal arms around them, and they disappeared down softly soiled hills beneath a green, green wood. Second Home had housed a kid obsessed with apocalypses, and he'd roped them into building shelters and disinfecting water, making bow drills and encouraging fire with gentle, kind breaths. They went deep in the woods now. They covered their tracks. They slathered mud over their pale clothes and trudged miles and miles into the forest, and night after night, they slept wrapped in an emergency blanket inside a log or beneath a pine bough or in any sliver of camouflage they found.

No one else ever seemed to believe in magic. Even though they knew magic to be real, they did not see **THE WITCH** coming. Fourteen now, their forest home had already provided for them for several months. Over time, they had worked themself further into untamed lands, until.

Until **THE WITCH** tripped them up, tied their legs, and cut their hair, putting it into a bag, and said, pinching at their skin, "My, what are you? Fourteen? Not much meat, but enough. Boy or girl?" She jutted her smooth, spray-tanned face, expecting an answer that would never come. "Well, if you've nothing to say, I'll bash your head in now and get started on dinner. Night comes early these days."

In a life-flashing second, they thought about tiny caves, potions, and about learning the true magic of the world. With a bit of desperation, they said, "I have killed two men with poison. I would learn, instead, if you would have me. I would sweep your home. Collect wood. Do your laundry. Boil your water."

The witch stared at them down a long, beautiful nose—only a hint of orange tanner caked in the creases—like she saw them in a light that perhaps no one else ever had. "Two men, is it? Did they deserve it?"

They nodded in silence.

The witch bobbled her head, her face appraising. "I suppose I do have a rather dirty cave, what with the floor being stone and dribbly with water." She raised her chin, her eyes glacial. "You show me you're willing to work, first, then maybe I'll teach you. Or, maybe I'll eat you."

They shrugged in the guard's too-big coat. There had been worse things.

The witch's cave was a spacious affair. It glistened from the dribbly water, and the stone ran their voice back into endless depths. It was cold, but it became a sort of home, and they did not mind terribly the cold, or the dribbling water, or the work the witch had them do. Until.

Until the witch began teaching her trade in earnest, and they learned about the sort of magic the witch performed, all those babies; their bloody entrails.

The witch cleaned only with a broom and an MLM-purchased essential oil she bought in bulk from a suburban mom. And while the witch brewed many poisons, she also practiced mithridatism. They would need a *different* sort of poison. An old potion, one they first met years ago.

"Witch," they said (they called her *witch*, for she had never given another name, but she had become a sort of guiding mentor and therefore the name carried less stifling weight), "I'd like to go with you to town next time. I'm craving iced cream something awful."

"Augh." The witch spoke through a disgusted face of clenched front teeth. She hadn't menstruated in a few centuries, so she claimed. "It's about that time of the month, isn't it?"

They flopped their shoulders about.

The witch sighed and settled her needlework on the table nearby, the one made of baby femurs. They had thought it animal bones when they first arrived. How pure they were back then. "Tomorrow won't be raining," the witch said thoughtfully. She sniffed as if she were about to relay terribly important information. "The rain messes with my dealer's blowout." The dealer was the MLM essential oil-selling suburb mom who wore a quarter inch of makeup and a stiff white smile.

They picked up the broom and swept to cover their excitement. The cave was atrociously dirty. No wonder the witch did not eat them. Plus, she seemed to prefer the doughy arms of small children. *A delicacy,* she said after one particularly slurping bite before using the viscera in her spells.

As promised, it did not rain the next day. The forest was forever gracious to them.

The witch dropped them in the town center and ordered them to return in a few hours. After getting her essential oils, she needed to check out a new daycare, and it took time to pretend to be a prospective parent and tour the facility and sneak out with a baby instead.

The hardware store sat next to the iced cream shop. With the money the witch gave them, they would say they got a milkshake— a more expensive purchase, meaning less change to return. When they entered the hardware store, a young woman wrapped in a lavender shawl, with arched brows, sleek black hair, and medium brown skin, leaned casually on a stool, reading a book. She smiled at them and easily dropped her eyes back to her book, concern for the world falling away.

The potions were in the back. Size mattered for concealment, but that was why they had stuffed an envelope down their pants. The young woman rang them up, gave them a quirked smile, and disappeared into the book's embrace.

Outside, they poured the powder into the envelope, dumping the rest of the box in a garbage can. And they waited. Later, the witch's rusted truck pulled down the road, so they went into the iced cream shop and purchased a child-sized cone for her. She loved tiny things.

"Change," asked the witch once they climbed into the truck. One of those smooth hands reached out, the nails all done up for her daycare performance. On the seat between them was an unmoving black bag. The witch smiled into the wind of the open window. "Dinner will be a roast tonight, I think. I picked up some fresh tarragon at the market. You *know* how I love tarragon and how poorly it grows for me. And yes, before you ask, I got you tempeh. You really should try the roast. Anyway, best head out before the sirens start."

It was not odd for them to make the witch her evening tea. The trouble was that tea came *after* dinner. They had planned for this, too.

Sticking their face down the old mine shaft might take a few years off their life, their throat seizing horribly in gasps and choking coughs, but it got the witch heating a kettle. While the witch poked through her herbs to find the appropriate ones for her *idiot charge*, they walked past the witch's mug and dumped the poison in with a tea bag. They stirred in copious amounts of sugar on their next pass. Then they cast all their hope into the powers of sweetener.

Mewling came from the shifting bag on the ground. The witch never made a kill until she started dinner. Wanted them fresh, but she drugged them for the getaway. This one was waking. They tried to ignore it. At present, they could do nothing more than they already had.

The witch plopped several handfuls of herbs into the kettle, let the fragrance grow, and poured it over a strainer into their mug, the one with a winky face half chipped away. They smiled plainly at the witch and inhaled the bitter scent. They were used to such things by now.

Easing herself into a rickety chair, the witch gave them a once over. "You're really coming into your own. Soon, I should think, I'll be revealing all the lore of my lineage." In a distantly sad sort of voice, she said, "Then you might leave me and go off on your own. Perhaps you'll even find your own protégé."

"Perhaps," they said and did not look at the black bag, but sipped the scalding tea to soothe the poisoned air burning in their throat.

The witch sipped her own tea for a while, grimacing at the extra sugar, but drinking it all the same. When she finished, she crossed to her shelves to gather cooking twine and seasoning, oil and knives of various pedigrees and sat to arrange each item with care. Light from the cave entrance shaded to black, night wandering in at the corners, curious about this room glowing in its dark embrace.

"Oh, my stomach." The witch clutched her belly and grunted. "Right. Time to prepare the meat."

A sheen of sweat broke out on the witch's face. She waddled to the black bag and awkwardly carried it to the table. A nasty belch escaped her mouth. Blinking several times, the witch sniffed harshly and gripped the bag's zipper before moaning and bending over, her hands at her stomach again.

She groaned out her words. "Those suburb moms. New lesson: never accept the food they offer. It's always undercooked." With that, the witch heaved herself to the washbasin, a bowl-shaped impression in a small boulder, and vomited globs of melted tissue, splattering crimson across the cave walls.

Setting down their tea, they checked the witch's pulse. Silent.

The bag unzipped slowly, and they lifted from within the would-be dinner. The infant balled its tiny beige fists and mewled again. "You'll find, I think, that many people, and especially adults, believe they can do as they please simply because they are something called *aged*. But that's not the case at all."

Wrapping the infant in a ragged shawl they had knitted, they spared the dead witch a glance. The body should be buried far from here and salted, and her eyes covered, and perhaps a few other things, so her ghost would not return, but the cave would go on making quite the home for two children lost no longer.

The baby bellowed its first true thoughts. For lack of anything better, they put a finger into the infant's mouth. "There's a cache of goat's milk in the river. We'll start there, and when you're older, I'll teach you all about the monsters that walk around wearing people suits and the magic to kill them."

Your Body
Is Not Your Body

ANATOMICAL CHART

Viktor Athelstan (he/him) writes historical fiction, dark comedies, and of course, body horror. He's fascinated with medieval monks and their relationship with gender and the supernatural. He's very excited to start grad school in the fall.

Cosmin-Mihai Bîrsan (he/him/any): Nonbinary horror nut. Real life vampire. Cosmic entity that casually dabbles in a myriad of artforms.

Matt Blairstone (he/him) is a writer, artist and indie comics creator, and the founder and publisher of **Tenebrous Press.** He lives in Portland OR with his wife and son.

Avi Burton (he/they) is an undergraduate student at the University of Toronto, where he's studying theater and classic literature. They enjoy writing about religion, revenants, and—on occasion—laser swords. His short fiction can also be found in Escape Pod and PodCastle magazine.

Catulla, (she/they) pronounced with a short "u" due to her horrifying accent, is a Brooklyn based artist who is fascinated by science fiction, the occult, and abstract art. They began writing at a young age, composing Dungeons & Dragons campaigns for their friends.

S. A. Chant (they/them) is a prize-winning pie baker and sci-fi/fantasy writer. Their debut novel, *Peter Darling*, was longlisted for the Otherwise Award (2018). They live in Seattle with a cat who was recently described as a 'gooey cryptid'.

Rain Corbyn (they/them) is a queer, nonbinary, autistic voice actor and writer. This is their horror writing debut. Their narration work includes audiobooks for *The Mud Ballad* by Jo Quenell, *Nightmare Yearnings* by Eric Raglin, and lots of pseudonymous smut. They live in sin and New York.

Bri 'Pi' Crozier (he/they) is a writer and illustrator with passion for the natural cycle of decay and death, finding beauty in how it relates to their experiences as a queer and disabled person. When not writing or painting, Bri can be found looking for dead things in Kansas City.

Vincent Endwell (they/them) is a third gender/androgyne writer, composer, neuroscience graduate student, and white settler located in Lenapehoking (New York City). Their work has been previously featured in *As it Ought to Be* Magazine and *The Apothecary*.

M. Lopes da Silva (she/they) is a non-binary and bisexual author, artist & poet from Los Angeles. Their horror fiction has appeared in *In Somnio, Neon Horror*, and *Nightscript Vol. IV* and *V*. Unnerving Books recently published their novella *Hooker:* a pro-queer, pro-sex work, feminist retrowave pulp thriller.

W. N. Derring-Judith (xe/it) was born and raised in Texas, and barely escaped with its life. You can contact xer at wnderringjudith@gmail.com.

Devaki Devay (they/them) is a writer & journalist previously published in *Okay Donkey* and *Entropy* Magazine. They are forthcoming in Barren and the Lumiere Review.

Lillian Hochwender (they/them) is a genderfluid artist and writer. In recent months, they've made art for the charity AbleGamers and written for publications like Polygon and *PanelxPanel*. Their first credit as a comics writer is in an upcoming anthology: *The Color of Always: An LGBTQIA+ Love Anthology*.

Meagan Hotz (any) is a Canadian writer and graduate of the Vancouver Film School's Writing for Film & Television program. Her short films have been screened internationally, and she received Best Short at the Screamfest Horror Film Festival. She lives in Vancouver with her pets and a potentially haunted couch.

Dayna Ingram (he/him) is a trans+queer genre fiction writer from Ohio. His book *All Good Children* was chosen by both Publishers Weekly and Kirkus Reviews Indie as one of the best Science Fiction titles of 2016, and was a finalist for the 2017 Lambda Literary Awards. More info at www.daynaingram.com.

Ori Jay (he/they) is a nonbinary Latinx writer, artist, and activist from Portland, Oregon. Their visual art has appeared in exhibitions in Chicago, Denver, and Portland. He is currently working on the book *The Life and Times of Trans People* for Microcosm Publishing.

Bitter Karella (he/him or she/her) is the writer and horror aficionado behind the microfiction comedy account @Midnight_pals, which asks what if all your favorite horror writers gathered around the campfire to tell scary stories. When not writing twitter jokes, she also dabbles in cartooning and text game design.

Joe Koch (he/they) writes literary horror and surrealist trash. Joe is a Shirley Jackson Award finalist and the author of *The Wingspan of Severed Hands, The Couvade*, and *Convulsive*. Find Joe online at horrorsong.blog and on Twitter @horrorsong.

Lex (they/them) is a nonbinary Viet American who loves creatures and is a fan of all the forms monsters can take. More of their art at scribbledeck.tumblr.com.

Jei D. Marcade (they/them) is a Korean-American writer whose interactive and traditional fiction has been released into the wild by Choice of Games, *Uncanny Magazine,* and *Escape Pod*. Jei can be found haunting jeidmarcade.com.

Hailey Piper (she/her) is the twice-Stoker nominated author of *The Worm and His Kings, Queen of Teeth, Unfortunate Elements of My Anatomy,* and more. A trans woman hailing from the haunted woods of New York, she now lives with her wife in Maryland, where their paranormal research is classified.

Taylor Jordan Pitts (she/they) works in the publishing industry on projects ranging from multi-volume manga series to picture books to bestselling middle grade and YA novels. An MFA candidate at the Vermont College of Fine Arts, Taylor is currently working on their debut novel.

Rhiannon Rasmussen (they/them/none) is a horror author and illustrator interested in monstrosity and the persistence of hope. Rhiannon's fiction has appeared in publications including *Lightspeed* Magazine, *Evil in Technicolor*, and *Magic: the Gathering*. Visit rhiannonrs.com for more.

Rieroo (they/he) is a trans/NB artist and illustrator who enjoys working with surreal and fantastical themes. They are fueled by a constant need to create.

Mx Morgan G Robles (they/them, he/him) is an artist and illustrator from Seattle, Washington. Their work is best known for utilizing animals and nature with surreal macabre, violent, and somber themes.

Rose Sable (she/her) is a California-based horror/SFF author and experimental musician. You can follow her on Twitter @anxietygothic.

Ziggy Schutz (she/him/he/her) is a queer, disabled writer always looking for ways to make his favourite fairytales and horror stories reflect people who look a little more like her. He finds gender euphoria in disruption and excess, and she hopes that folks reading this can borrow a bit of that when they need it.

Becca Snow (any) is an illustrator and bookbinder based in Arizona with a BFA in Drawing from Arizona State University. They enjoy designing book covers and posters with dramatic lighting, colors, and atmosphere, as well as illustrating scenes from their favorite books, shows, and podcasts.

Will Taylor (he/they) is a trans man who makes Weird Horror art about his experiences with gender, neurodivergence, and chronic pain. He is excited to express who he has discovered himself to be, and sincerely hopes that all of his trans and GNC siblings are able to experience living how they want to.

Charles Maria Tor (ze/hir/hirs) is an insane transexual butch from Warrang (Sydney) in so-called Australia. Charles Maria hopes to one day earn the title "A Queer Usurper to Vonnegut and Lovecraft's Thrones."

Max Turner (he/him) is a gay transgender man based in the UK. He is also a parent, nerd, intersectional feminist and coffee addict. Max writes science fiction, urban fantasy, furry fiction, horror, & LGBTQ+ romance and erotica. More often than not, he writes combinations thereof. www.maxturneruk.com

Gabriel Valentine (they/them) is a poet, amateur bog witch, and library-dwelling raccoon based in Albany, NY. "Gender Envy" is their first published poem, and their other writing similarly centers on themes of queerness, drag, and total absurdism. They can be found shitposting on Twitter at @lasagnajpg.

LC von Hessen (they/them) is a writer of horror, weird fiction, and various unpleasantness, as well as a noise musician, occasional actor, and former Morbid Anatomy Museum docent. An ex-Midwesterner, von Hessen lives in Brooklyn with a talkative orange cat.

Cori Walters (they/them) is a nonbinary lesbian cartoonist and illustrator from Florida. They like drawing plants and robots and body horror.

Harrison Webb (he/him/they/them) is a geeky, queer, horror-loving illustrator based in Portland, OR, and the face behind Fiendish Thingy Art. His art balances creepy and cute and often touches on the mythical in the process. He recently received his MFA in Visual Development.

Alex Woodroe is a Romanian writer and editor; member of the SFWA and HWA; Red Right Hand for **Tenebrous Press**; and has been published by Dark Matter Magazine, the NoSleep Podcast & more. She's passionate about infusing her country's culture and folklore into her work, and loves talking shop @AlexWoodroe.

G.E. Woods (she/her/they/them) ran into the arms of horror as a 5-year-old working in haunted houses. Queer, NB and disabled, she writes fantastical novels where marginalized identities are normalized. She's a parent of goblin twins, dances under full moons, and talks to the trees near her home outside Chicago.

ACKNOWLEDGEMENT OF COPYRIGHT

CONTENT WARNINGS

Your Body is Not Your Body contains scenes that may be triggering to some audiences.

This being a collection of mature Horror, **some degree of violence, gore, sex and/or death is present in most of these stories.** For more specific concerns, please check the list of stories below for specific potential triggers suggested by the publisher and by the authors themselves:

Tonsilstonespunksplatter666!: violent transmisogyny, partner emotional abuse, ableism, rape

High Maintenance: domestic abuse

Brother Maternitas: sexual assault, miscarriage

The Same Thing That Happened to Sam: child abuse

Playing House: domestic abuse

Hybrid: animal death

We We Keep Exploding: bullying and abuse

We've Been Trying to Reach You: suicide, ableism

Fencing Chestplate: transphobia, homophobia

The Simulacrum: transphobia

The Roots They Pull: homophobia, sexual assault

The Pearl Diver: animal death

Tiny Magic: domestic abuse, sexual abuse, child abuse, cannibalism

ABOUT TENEBROUS PRESS

Tenebrous Press was conceived in the Plague Year 2020 and unleashed, howling and feral, in spring 2021 to deliver the finest in transgressive, progressive Horror from diverse and unsung voices around the world.

We welcome the esoteric; the unorthodox; the finest in New Weird Horror.

FIND OUT MORE:
www.tenebrouspress.com
Twitter: @TenebrousPress

NEW WEIRD HORROR

1

"Dad, you should probably slow down a bit." Turning to look at him, I catch the broad smile on his face that makes him look like a little kid excited to go to a candy store. "We left early for this very reason. We have plenty of time."

"Sorry, sweetheart." He lets off the gas—slightly—and resumes his history lesson. "The second day of the Battle at Gettysburg was so intense. This reenactment won't be to scale by any means, but there will be fighting all along the Peach Orchard, the Wheatfield, Rose Farm, Little Round Top, and the Devil's Den. The Union had 2,400 men in that position compared to the Confederacy's 3,100, who effectively slammed into them...."

I try to listen as he continues since I know what an avid history buff he is, especially when it comes to the Civil War, and he's been waiting to attend this reenactment for months. But my mind can't help but wander to next week when I start my new job.

"That's when Ward's men had to pull back and—" He pauses,

turning his head quickly to catch a glimpse of me before looking back at the road. "And I'm boring you to tears."

I give him a chuckle. "No, Dad. You're never boring."

"But you don't want to hear all this war stuff," he insists. "You're busy thinking of your new job at the hospital on Monday."

He knows me well. "I am. I have to admit, I'm a little nervous. It's a lot different being an attending physician than a resident. It's such a huge responsibility. But that doesn't mean I'm not interested in your reenactment. You've been waiting for this for so long."

"Not nearly as long as you've been working on becoming a doctor." A different kind of smile lights up his face. "I know I don't say it enough, but I'm so proud of you."

"You say it every day, Dad, and thank you."

"Well, that's because I mean it." He blinks a couple of times, and I see the light glistening in his eyes. "Your mother would be so proud." A little quieter, he adds, "I sure do miss Audrey."

"I just wish she was here." Every time he mentions her, I remember the day they sat me down to tell me she had cancer. At eleven years old, I barely understood, and I definitely didn't comprehend the fact that she'd soon be gone forever. "I only went into oncology because I wanted to save at least one family from going through the same heartache."

"I know, sweetheart." He pats me on the knee. "I know. But she would be proud, graduating from high school so early and winning all those scholarships."

I shake my head. "Let's just talk about today, okay?"

"Deal. And you'll do fine on Monday. Try not to worry about it."

"I'm mostly worried about this dress choking me," I complain, running my finger along the neckline. It's a pretty dress in a light plum color that looks good against my blonde hair, with long sleeves and a button-down front that goes all the way up to my neck, hence the scratchiness. "I'm not sure why I need to be in costume. It's not like women were there on the battlefield."

"Well, actually, there were nurses and some civilians in the medical tents. And five women actually fought there."

"Disguised as soldiers," I add with a smirk. "I'm pretty sure they would have blown their cover in bright purple dresses."

He lets out a chuckle. "Probably. But I thought it might help get into the spirit of things if we're both wearing period clothes."

"You do look pretty sharp in your Civil War-era get-up." I'm not lying. Though lines of worry age him somewhat, it's not hard to imagine him as a young, energetic man of that era, especially with the hat, which he's kept on in the car.

"Thanks, sweetie." His eyes go a little wide as he looks at the sign ahead. "And we're here."

"Finally." Two and a half hours—three if I count rest stops—is more time than I like to spend in a car, though the trip from our house just outside Philadelphia really wasn't that bad.

He gives me a smirk as he pulls onto the road leading into Gettysburg National Military Park, where signs direct us to the main parking lot. "Oh, I guess we are early. Good. I want to get some pictures before everything starts."

"I wouldn't expect anything less." I giggle at him teasingly as he parks, and we step out of the car. "At least this dress has deep pockets." There's no way I'm going to carry around a purse, and one thing I'll never leave behind is my small medical kit, which thankfully fits easily in my left pocket. "I'm bringing some snacks, too."

He nods, walking around to my side of the car. "You should. They will have some food vendors here for the event, but I don't know if they're open the whole time."

"It's okay. For you, Dad, I really don't mind." I smile to reassure him. It's true I'm not into this the way he is—not even close. But I know how much it means to him to visit this place, and I try to be supportive. We're each other's only family, and we've gotten pretty tight over the years since Mom died. "I'm going to be pretty busy starting on Monday, so we might as well have some quality father-daughter time now."

"Thanks, sweetheart. Are you ready? I want to stop in the visitor's center to say hello, then we can take a look around."

"Sounds good." I slide my cell phone into the pocket with the snacks and head toward the building. It's a little strange walking in this long dress when I can't see my feet, so I lift it up a little to get up the steps and into the visitor's center.

"Oh, my...." Dad's voice trails off as he looks around when we step inside. "This gets to me every time I visit this place." If there's a heaven on earth for Civil War enthusiasts, this is definitely it. It's full of artifacts on display, and I can tell he wants to look at all of them, but he forces his way over to the front desk first.

"Wow, Mr. Little, you've gone all-out this time," a dark-haired woman behind the counter announces cheerfully. "I'm so glad to see you again! And what fantastic costumes! Do you want to sign our guest list?" She puts a folder on the counter and opens it to a practically empty sheet, handing Dad a pen.

"Now, Margaret, I've told you to just call me Martin," he says, and she chuckles lightly. Dad looks around. "I suppose we're a little early."

"Just a tad, but that's a good thing!" Margaret insists. "You'll have more time to enjoy the exhibits and tour the grounds."

"That's the plan."

I watch him sign his name, and my eyes wander to a collage of pictures in a nearby display. Some are simple portraits of soldiers, and a few are scenes around the military camp sites. But others are gruesome photos of deceased soldiers on the battlefield. It gives me a chill, imagining what it must have been like for the medics without the benefit of modern medicine, and most likely short on supplies.

I think about my hospital, where I'll have access to all the modern equipment and supplies I could possibly need. I'm even nervous about doing the best for my patients under those circumstances, let alone....

"You all right, sweetie?"

I turn to see my father right beside me. "Oh... yes. Sorry, I didn't realize you were finished."

His gaze looked past me to the photos. "Pretty intense, isn't it?"

"Yes." I nod, turning back to the pictures and trying not to look at the most troublesome ones. I catch sight of a group of soldiers. "They look so serious. Do you think they knew exactly what they were facing?"

"Most likely, yes," he says. "Most of these men were volunteers. They were committed to the cause and were ready to sacrifice themselves to make life better for their families."

"Very brave." The stoic eyes of a soldier with dark hair catches my attention. It's as though he's not just looking at the camera but right at me, as if he knows my gaze is on him. It gives me a strange sensation in my nerves, but it's not like a chill—more of a tingle.

Odd.

"Well, we'll be doing the tour tomorrow, so I think we can skip the exhibits in here for now and get out to see the battlefield." My father's voice takes me out of my thoughts.

"Oh... yeah. Okay, let's go."

I give one last look to the soldier and follow my dad out the back door of the visitor's center, which opens to a vast expanse of green, rocky landscape. A breeze kicks up as we stand on the overlook deck, and I fold my arms and shudder. I may not have felt a chill at all the photos I just saw, but to look at that quiet, now-peaceful land and know that a bloody war was fought here... it's indescribably intense.

"Incredible," my dad says.

"Yes," is all I can manage. This place gets to me every time we come here. I can see some of the same rock formations they showed in the aftermath pictures, both in the visitor's center and in all my dad's Civil War books, which I've seen a million times. The rocks are a bit smoother now, but they've stood firm for over a hundred and fifty years, though the grasses and shrubbery surrounding them have taken over quite a bit.

"Let's head down."

I nod and follow my father down the stairs and back toward the parking lot, pulling up on my dress again to see the steps. We follow the signs toward Devil's Den, which is a long way from the visitor's center, so we get back in the car and head out.

"Here it is," he says when we arrive and park near the Devil's Den. "Can you imagine all the Union soldiers up across here, and the Confederate soldiers swarming in for the attack from that direction?"

"I can," I say. It's almost like I can feel what happened here in the stillness. "It's so much different standing here than reading about it."

"I was hoping you'd say that." He smiles at me. "It'll be even more amazing when the reenactment takes place."

"Where do we sit and watch?"

"Those bleachers over there will be for us observers." He points to them off in the distance. It looks like a bit of a hike. "Meanwhile, let's get a few photos. Take one of me overlooking the place, will you?"

"All right." He hands me his camera—an actual camera with a long lens that he insists on using instead of his phone. It has so many buttons and adjustments to it, I'm pretty sure I'd need to take a class to fully understand it, but he's taught me enough to get the gist of it. "Got it."

"Did you take several?"

"Of course, Dad."

"Good," he says, gesturing for me to hand it back to him, which I gladly do. "I want to get a shot of you on the rocks over there. I think it'd be a perfect portrait in your dress."

I don't want to disappoint my dad, but there's some rough terrain between me and those rocks that I'd rather not cross in these shoes. "Won't all the people be arriving soon? I don't think we have time for this before the reenactors come."

But he gives me the famous 'dad' look. "Please, sweetheart? It'll only take a moment. This is our father-daughter time, and I—"

I hold up my hand to stop him. "Okay. Got it. Just give me a minute to get over there."

He lets out a chuckle. "Thanks. This is going to be great."

"Mmhmm." As I tiptoe across the grass, I can hear a bunch of people approaching—and a few loud gunshots—and quicken my steps to get to the rocks. "They're coming, Dad. I think they've already started the battle! Here, take it now."

"Just one more step back, sweetie!" he hollers from the path, holding up the camera.

"Fine," I whisper, backing up without looking. I realize too late that I've caught my dress under my shoe and feel myself falling back, tumbling completely over the edge of the large rock I'm standing on before I can even call out.

My arms flail as I try to stop myself, but it's too late. I'm falling. My head hits first, and my back slams up against another rock.

Before I can call out to my dad, everything goes black.

2

WHEN MY EYES OPEN, I PANIC FOR A MOMENT BECAUSE ALL I SEE IS darkness. My head feels fuzzy, and the world seems to be spinning around, but I'm not even moving. It takes me a moment to blink a few times, and I'm relieved when I see the twinkling stars above. At least I can see now.

But wait. Why is it so dark?

Seconds ago, I'd been avoiding looking into the evening sun as Dad snapped the picture… or at least he was going to snap the picture before I tripped over my dress. But now, it's pitch dark.

And where is Dad?

I want to shout for him, but my head is just pounding, and everything is so fuzzy, I can't even seem to get any words out. My back is killing me, too, and I remember hitting it on the rocky ground right along with my head. I hear crying from every direction, along with occasional gunfire that sometimes halts the whimpering. I don't remember the last reenactment being quite this detailed. And I just can't understand why my dad would leave me lying here until it was dark out.

Regardless, I need to get up and get out of here. Now that I see the rock overhead, It's apparent that I've fallen from a couple of huge boulders about six feet high. Despite my aching head and back, I fight the pain so I'm at least in an upright seated position.

"That is not a good idea."

I jump at the sound of the deep voice next to me. It's definitely not Dad. *Who is this guy?*

I turn to see a shadow of a man in what I make out to be a Union soldier's uniform. God, does he smell like a battlefield. I wonder what they used to recreate the scent of blood. I really don't think the reenactment needs that much authenticity.

"Are you one of the reenactors?" I ask.

"Shh, keep your voice down," he says. "The Rebs have sharp-shooters on both sides ready to pick you off when they get wind of you."

"What?" The reenactors shouldn't mistake me for one of them in this dress.

"Not just them, miss," he continues, his voice in a frantic whisper. "Even with the Rebs having a bad angle at a shot where we're lying, the whole lot of them out here will shoot anything that moves, so you might get hit by friendly fire."

"That's ridiculous." I don't know why he's so insistent on keeping up his role-playing, but I'm not about to lie here when I need to get my head looked at, not to mention that he really does smell of blood, and I need to get away from him. Reenactments are done with fake ammunition anyway.

I think this guy has done a few too many of these things.

I manage to prop myself up on my elbows and push up. As my head clears a bit, I hear a gun fire, and the strange man wraps his arm around me and pulls me down just as something whizzes by... within inches of my head. It hits the rock behind me, and even in the dark, I see the mark it left on the boulder.

Oh, my God... that was a real bullet!

Terror fills my veins as I sink back down and lay as still as I can. I suddenly don't care what this guy smells like because I'm too scared to focus on more than one sense right now, and I'm trying to hear what's going on. *Why are they shooting at me? And why are these bullets real?*

"Stay down," he says firmly.

This time, I just nod, listening to the sound of young men crying. Most are just boys from the sound of it, their voices not as low-pitched and masculine as the man beside me.

"I need water!" I hear someone shout over the crying, and another round of gunfire explodes nearby.

I can feel my heart pounding in my chest. The reenactor hasn't taken his arm off me, and until I know what's going on, that's not really necessary since I have no intention of sitting up like that again. The man keeps looking around and staying low.

All I can think of is those shootings at malls and things. *Is that what's going on?* I suppose someone could be unstable enough to take advantage of the crowd at the reenactment and start shooting for real. "Is this a mass shooting or something?" I ask.

Now that my eyes have adjusted to the darkness a little, I can see the expression on his face, with one brow up and the other crinkled in confusion. "Er… that's one thing you could call it. How hard did you hit your head?"

"Hard." I rub the back of it and feel a little moisture. *Damn.* I'm bleeding, but not much. Must be just a scratch, which is probably lucky considering the height of my fall and the rocky ground I landed on.

"What in the blazes are you doing out here?" he asks.

"I'm sorry?" I have to speak above a whisper now because there's more gunfire. *But if it's a mass shooting, why are there so many guns?* "We meant to make it to the bleachers on time, but I slipped when my father was taking a picture of me on the rocks."

"What in the bloody—" He lowers his voice again as the gunfire slows. "What the hell are bleachers, and why is your father bringing you onto a field of battle?"

This guy really doesn't know when to drop the act. "Well, it's not like we expected live gunfire at a reenactment. I'll get out of your way as soon as the gunman leaves or the police get here or whatever."

He stares at me, his face still wrinkled in confusion. It's like I might as well be speaking a foreign language. "Perhaps you live around here?" he asks. "We can find your father later, but now you've got to stay low."

"No, I'm from Philadelphia."

"Then you have no idea what we've been through here in Gettysburg and how dangerous it is for you to be here." He leans in close, and I can smell the blood on him again. Maybe I'm getting used to it because it's not so repulsive now. I guess I don't have much choice but to breathe him in since I'm stuck here until whoever is shooting real bullets out there gets arrested.

But now that he's closer, there's something familiar about his face. I can't place it, but I think it's his eyes.

"The ball opened when the calvary got surprised by Lee's men," he begins. I realize that sentence wouldn't make any sense if I hadn't been reading all Dad's Civil War books. Back in the day, a 'ball opening' meant a battle began. "My regiment arrived early this morning. They'd had a rough go of it all day and night with their flank in the air, and General Howard had ordered a retreat to the Hill. Still, they fought with impetuosity. They're holding the fishhook formation up there, and we're ordered to hold this ground. Looks like we've lost it though, with all those Rebs in front of us."

I don't know why he's giving me a history lesson in the middle of whatever's going on here. My eyes are adjusting better to the starlight, and to the right and the left I see bodies strewn everywhere.

Is this the reenactment? But what about that bullet?

Are all these people really dead?

Whatever is going on, I need to get out of here. I'm just about to try to sit up again when gunfire erupts all around us, and the man by me ducks again. I don't know what's taking the police so long to get here and stop this, but I know better than to walk out in front of a live shooter. I need to find another way out of here.

Looking over at the man, I notice for the first time that there's something off about his movement. "What's your name?"

"Sam. Lieutenant Sam Walker of the 4th Maine regiment."

"Okay, Sam. I'm Neveah."

"Neveah? What kind of a name is that?" He gives me a frown.

I've heard that reaction before. "It's heaven spelled backward." I can't help but roll my eyes. He says nothing. "Anyway, are you hurt?"

He puts his hand on his calf the second I ask. "Got shot in the leg. But it's nothing major. I'll be able to fight again–if we can get out of here."

Now it's my turn to look at him with a furrowed brow. "Fight? You don't even have real bullets."

"What do you—"

"Look, I can help you with that. I'm a doctor."

A strange laugh escapes his lips. "A doctor? Well, huzzah for you."

I sense his tone, dripping with sarcasm, but I don't get it. "I'm a little young, yes, but I'm an attending physician now at Philadelphia Memorial. I don't have my credentials here with me, but your leg needs attention, so you're going to have to trust me."

"Miss, you've really hit your head hard." At least he stops laughing now, but I don't understand why he doesn't believe me. "Maybe you can nurse it up, but that will need to wait because we're pinned down."

He's not lying, but if his leg really is shot, it needs immediate attention. I look around and listen, trying to get a handle on where we are and which direction the shooting is coming from. At first, it seemed like it was all around me, but my head is clearer now, and it's definitely coming from in front of us.

I've spent enough time reading Dad's books full of maps and photos to get a handle on Gettysburg well enough, and with this reenactment coming up, he's been obsessed with Devil's Den. I'm suddenly glad I've had the time lately to pay attention.

Looking around, I realize where I'm at in relation to a place Dad had pointed out—a cave formed by a natural spring beneath several boulders at Devil's Den. If I can get Sam in there, at least we'd be free of the shooter enough that I can try to patch up his leg, or at least get the worst of the bleeding under control.

"Follow me," I tell him.

But he doesn't budge. "I won't leave my regiment. I'm no shirker. Besides, if I don't hold this position, I'm a dead man with those Rebs both in front and behind us."

"If we keep low, no one can shoot at us." I still don't get why he's sticking to the playacting when there's real danger out here. Maybe the injury to his leg is somehow affecting his mental state. If that's the case, it's even more critical that I treat him. I just hope I have enough supplies in my medical kit to take care of it until an ambulance gets here.

He looks around like he's trying to choose between me and the stupid rock he's supposed to stay by.

"Sam, this is a reenactment," I say firmly. Maybe he just needs to hear that several times. "But if that is a real bullet in your leg, and if you don't let me look at it, you're going to be in trouble. Just follow me. I know this area well. There's a cave just over this way."

His gaze follows my finger as I point left. "All right. But just keep down to the ground."

I have no intention of letting the shooter take off my head. "Of course."

Finally, I start crawling in that direction, though I wince at the pain in my back the whole way. Careful to keep my head low, it's a slow process. Occasionally, I check the back of my head, and I'm glad I don't feel any more wetness. Hopefully, my bleeding has stopped.

Sam drags himself after me, also keeping low and pulling his bad leg behind. It feels like ages before we finally make it to where we can see the cave in the dim starlight. I turn to him, and his eyes are wide in surprise. "See? There's a cave. We can duck in there and take a look at your leg."

He nods and follows me inside.

3

———

Neveah

Only a few feet into the cave, I'm relieved that it insulates us—slightly—from the sound of the gunfire. There is still a possibility of someone shooting straight into it if they were to crawl down here on their bellies like we did, but it feels a lot safer than being outside in the middle of it. I'm just starting to feel better about all this when I step into a foot of water.

"Hold up," I tell Sam. Damn. I remember talking to my dad about the cave but forgot it's part of an underground spring system. The further into the cave we go, the more water we'll find, and it could get to a point where there's no place to sit and tend to his gunshot wound. Still, dodging water is much better than dodging bullets. "We won't be able to get much further in with the water in here, but we can find a place to rest. Here's a good spot over here."

I gesture toward a wide area of dry dirt that will hold us both. He follows me, dragging his wounded leg along... at least, he follows me until I pull out my phone and turn on the flashlight.

15

It startles me the way he quickly backs away, his eyes wide and full of fear. "What kind of witchcraft is this?" he asks, his voice quivering.

"Witch—what?" I can't believe his reaction. The guy looks absolutely terrified. "It's just my cell."

"What on earth is a cell?"

He keeps backing away toward the cave entrance—where all the gunfire is—and if I don't stop him, he's going straight outside. I need to calm him down and remind him where we are, not to mention that I need to look at his leg, and the more blood that pumps through him, the more will escape through his untreated wound, which can take his condition from bad to life-threatening.

Now that I've shined the light on him, something in me shudders. His uniform looks authentic—too authentic, as though this guy hopped right out of the 1800s and landed here.

But that's impossible. *Right?*

My physician's training kicks in just as he's about to back all the way out of the cave entrance. Pain and fear can do some unbelievable things to the brain, not to mention people's emotions, causing them to act irrationally, even making their situation worse. I've worked with several patients experiencing this in my internship program, so I have an idea about how to calm him down. I'm not sure why he's freaking out at a cell phone, but maybe his mind is playing tricks on him.

"It's just a light, see?" I stop shining it on him and point it toward the wall. I can see I have zero bars of service for some reason, even though I just had plenty at the visitor's center, so a flashlight is really the only use for this phone right now anyway.

He stops in his tracks—thankfully—but stays where he's at.

"That's it, Sam." I try to speak softly and calmly. Using his first name should also keep him grounded. "I need to look at your leg right away. This is just a light that will help me see it in the dark." After hesitating for a beat, he moves a bit closer to me, and I can breathe again. One foot out that cave entrance, I might have watched him meet his end.

For some reason, he keeps looking at the phone like it's some sort of demon. This is all so strange, but I think of an idea. "It's a new type of medical device." Not exactly… but the idea seems to calm him down more.

"If you'd like to hold it and look it over, you can," I tell him. I hold it out for him, still keeping the flashlight trained on the cave wall.

He reaches out, gingerly touching it and holding it for a second. "It appears to be harmless," he says, but he still hands it back to me quickly as though he didn't really want to touch it at all.

"It is." I gesture toward the wide dirt area again. "Please try to settle down here, against the wall. You should rest while I take a look at your gunshot wound, okay?"

He nods lightly and moves toward the area, awkwardly dragging himself across the smaller rocks between us. Since his leg is so badly damaged, I have to help him get situated, and I can see in his eyes that he's getting weaker from the injury. He exhales slowly as he leans against the rocky cave wall, then winces at the pain from his position change.

"Okay, just try to relax." Shining the light on the wound, I can tell even with his pants in the way that it's bad. He's lost a lot of blood. His pant leg from his calf down is completely soaked through—explaining the strong smell of blood I've been noticing—mixed in with a lot of mud and tiny pebbles that cling to him.

It's amazing he's still alive, honestly.

"I'm fine," he insists, though I can see in his face that he knows he isn't. At least he's talking now and not so afraid of the flashlight.

Once again thankful for the deep pockets in this dress, I pull out my medical kit, though it's probably not enough to handle an injury this bad. Still, I have to do what I can, and I look through to take out everything I'll need. The pair of tweezers I have is larger than standard, but it's hardly sufficient for pulling a bullet out. I just hope it isn't in too deep, or that it just went all the way through.

Before I waste my disinfectant on the tweezers or anything else I'll use, I need to get a better look at his wound. "Okay, I need to cut your pants so I can see what we're dealing with here."

He nods, still wincing, and I dread having to add to his pain by putting disinfectant on him. I don't have any strong pain medications in my kit. But it can't be helped. I have to clean it up before he gets an infection, if he hasn't already. I get through the thick fabric of his pant leg with my tiny scissors, thankful I didn't put my sterile gloves on yet since his pants are so filthy with mud, rocks, and blood—so much blood.

The bullet hole is pretty easy to spot, though it's oozing with blood. At least it's in a good spot, all things considered. "Good. It missed your femoral artery and clearly missed the bone." He would already be dead if it had hit that artery. "But I'm going to have to see the back side to see if it went all the way through. Do you think you can switch positions?"

He nods, but the look in his eyes tells me he knows how much this is going to hurt. Gritting his teeth, he adjusts his position and moves his leg just far enough for me to see the other side.

"Okay, good. It went all the way through. Hold still right there." Quickly, I slip on the gloves. "I have to sterilize the wound. This will sting–badly."

He nods again and braces for it, and there's nothing I can do but make it quick. I need to work fast anyway because he's still losing blood until I can get this cleaned up and get a few quick stitches in it. He lets out a stifled cry as I pour on some disinfectant and clean around the wound, just enough to get a bandage on so I can get to the front wound. I don't want him to put it back on the dirty floor, so I use a piece of plastic I keep in the kit to lay beneath his leg.

"Okay, now I need to clean up the front, so move it back to how you were." He readjusts faster this time, and I get the front wound cleaned up as quickly as I can. He doesn't wince quite as bad at the disinfectant on the front, which worries me. "I'm going to stitch it up the best I can with this small suture kit." He barely nods. I get to work stitching up the entry wound before moving myself this time to stitch up the exit wound. It's not my best work, but it will help stop the bleeding. Once I'm done, I tell him the next step. "All right. I need you to move one more time, just enough so I can wrap a bandage around the whole thing. The bleeding should be stopped for the most part now, so you can rest. Okay?"

He nods weakly but manages to lift his leg enough for me to tie one of the CATs—Combat Application Tourniquets—from my kit around him, making sure it's not too tight since he has the stitches. Then, I wrap a bandage around it.

"Okay, you can relax now." I can see in his eyes that he's relieved it's over. "Do you want to stay sitting up or lie down?"

"I—" He starts to speak, but then he closes his eyes, and I can see him sink against the cave wall.

"And now you've passed out." I feel his pulse, which is strong, so I swing his legs around and get him in a reasonably more comfortable position on the cave floor, careful to keep his wound on the plastic, even though it's well cleaned and covered.

Looking at his pants, it's pretty clear he's lost enough blood that his life could be in danger. But there's no way I can lift the man, and even if I could, I have no idea what the hell is going on out there. Gunfire keeps erupting now and then, followed by cries–or worse–silence.

I turn the flashlight off and put my phone away, thinking I should save the battery. I also put what's left of my kit back together and shove that in my pocket. "Where are you, Dad?" I whisper, settling against the wall across from Sam. I know there's not much in this world that could keep him from coming to me if my life is in danger. As much as I try, I can't help thinking the worst, though I try to get it out of my mind as soon as it comes to me. *He had to duck, and I had fallen down the rock cliff, and there was no way he could get to me*, I tell myself. *He didn't call for me so the shooter wouldn't know I was there.*

The more I think about it, the more it doesn't make sense. My dad would move heaven and earth to get to me in a dangerous situation, especially since Mom died.

No, I won't let myself think something bad has happened to him.

But clearly, something strange is going on. Sam here has a real gunshot injury in something that's supposed to be a reenactment. Whatever this is, it seems like more than one person is causing the chaos. Maybe a group of gunmen decided to shoot up Gettysburg for real. It's far-fetched, but crazier things have happened.

Regardless, leaving the cave doesn't seem to be an option because I definitely don't want to get myself shot. I pull out my phone and check for a signal again. Nothing. Maybe they jammed the cell tower. Who are these people?

I can't stop myself from clicking on my photos and scrolling through a few of the most recent ones with Dad, especially the ones I took of him from the overlook. That seems like ages ago. I stop when I notice my phone battery is at eighty percent. "Better save that for later when the signal comes back… if it comes back." I turn it all the way off for now.

Sighing, I'm suddenly exhausted, so I move across the cave and settle into a spot next to Sam's head so I can keep an eye on his pulse and his breathing. I lean against the dirty cave wall, inhaling and exhaling slowly, the way I often had when I got a few minutes of a break in a crowded ER during my internship. Things had gotten better in my residency since I specialized in oncology, though the heartache of seeing families torn apart by cancer also led to more than a few moments when a good cry and some deep breathing exercises came in handy.

With every gunshot that rings out in the night, I tense up. Whatever is going on out there, this is going to be a long night.

I just hope Sam survives until morning.

4

SAM

A BARRAGE OF CANNON FIRE GREETS ME WHEN I AWAKEN, STARTLING ME into action. I'm lying on the ground, and I try to move, but the pain in my leg overwhelms me. I call out in agony.

"Shh. You need to be quiet."

A calm, melodic voice brings me to the present. I look up to see that strange woman again, her brightly colored gown a stark contrast against the sandy brown cave wall. Enough light is filtering in that I perceive it must be morning. I can see her face, soft and beautiful. I nod once and close my eyes again, the pain radiating up my leg over-whelming.

The whole battle replays in my mind almost as clearly as if it were happening again.

"Hold the line, men! We must hold this Devil's Den!"

Along with the others, I stand firm, firing into the crowd of Rebs across the field as commanded. My eyes train straight ahead as I feel the men around me dropping.

"Walker!"

It is the voice of Smith, the man I had just broken bread with in camp the night before. He had been going on about a woman he intended to marry as soon as the war was over. She had brown hair and bright, green eyes. Why I remember this detail at this moment, I do not know. Friend or not, I cannot stop to help him as I need to reload my Springfield to prevent the Rebs from advancing and overtaking our line.

It is only moments later that I feel the bullet in my leg, just a quick, biting sting at first, followed by weakness that leaves me unsteady on my feet. I try to brace myself against the fall, but my leg fails me, and I collapse to the ground several feet down, behind a boulder.

The pain hits with a vengeance, and it takes every breath in me not to holler out. I hear the screams and painful whimpering of other men in my division. I need to get back up and defend our position.

But my rifle is no longer in my hands. I feel around for it, but the pain overwhelms me, sharp and biting, and shortly after this, the world goes dark.

I awaken to a quieter battlefield, filled with stifled whimpers of pain that are quickly extinguished. I know the Rebs have sharpshooters killing off the wounded who remain. I am one of them, thankful for the large cliff of boulders between me and the miscreants. I wonder if any other members of my division are still alive.

As I look around, I have to blink in disbelief at what I see—a woman in a bright plum gown is lying next to me. She must have appeared while I was asleep, as she was not here before. Why is a woman on a battlefield?

She speaks in riddles I do not understand, but something leads me to follow her into this cave.

Now, she is sitting beside me, and I push myself up to see that my leg is bandaged tightly. She helps me settle against the cave floor next to her.

"What is happening out there?" I ask.

She checks my bandage as she answers. "It's July third, so this barrage of cannon fire must be the lead-up to Pickett's Charge. We need to stay put."

"I'm afraid I don't understand." *How does she know what is happening outside?*

"That's Colonel E. Porter Alexander's battery trying to blow the Union soldiers off Cemetery Ridge so Virginia General George E. Pickett can make his charge," she continues.

I raise a brow at the statement, still unsure how a woman knows so much about the war. Yet, she seems quite well informed.

"Pickett is about to walk a mile over open ground to attempt to take the Union position," she adds.

Maybe she's not as informed as I believe. In fact, the idea is preposterous. "No sane commander would order such a thing."

The ruffles of her dress almost meet her ears as she shrugs. "General Lee ordered it. He hoped this cannon fire would take out the Union artillery batteries ahead of the charge. Lieutenant General James Longstreet tried to object to it, but Lee moved forward with it."

"That's madness." I hear the cannon barrage, so it is possible that what she's saying might be happening, yet the idea is so foolish, I cannot believe Lee will move ahead with it. Besides, how would she have any idea precisely what's happening on the battlefield right now? And why is she speaking in past tense?

"Pickett and the other divisions that participate in the charge will lose about half their men," she continues. "After the charge, the Confederates will retreat. That will give me the chance to get you to a hospital." She takes the strange medical device with a light out of her gown pocket and taps on it several times, her mouth curled down in a frown. "I don't get it. I still don't have a signal."

I hope she doesn't ask that I hold the device again as the object feels... wrong, though I cannot explain how or why. I keep quiet about it for now.

Thankfully, she puts it back in her pocket, releasing a long, frustrated sigh. After a moment, she turns to me, frowning at my leg this time. "Tell me about your family, Sam. Where are you from?"

I'm a bit surprised at the sudden question. But it appears we will be in this cave for some time, so perhaps speaking of home will distract us for the time being. "I'm from Maine."

"It's beautiful country up there."

I nod, hitching a breath as a pain shoots up my leg, but the sharpness ends quickly. "It is. My father is Edward Walker. He's a banker. He was too old to enlist and help the war effort directly. My mother passed away from an illness several years ago."

"I'm sorry," she says.

I notice her eyes go distant, but I continue. "I've gotten used to it. My sister, Clara, held the house together until she married recently. Her husband George is in the twentieth Maine."

"Under Chamberlain?" she asks.

I furrow my brow, surprised again at her knowledge of the military. "Yes, but only for the last few days."

She nods as the cannon fire picks up outside. I wonder again whether any men in my division are still alive. But I shake my head. I cannot think about that right now.

"How about you?" I ask. "Tell me about your family."

"I'm from Pennsylvania," she says with a shrug.

"Yes, you said Philadelphia."

"Well, I'm moving to Philadelphia to work at the hospital, but I currently live in the suburbs," she adds.

"I see." I don't know what that word means, but I'm not going to ask. She hasn't spoken of her family yet. "What about your parents?"

"I'm close to my dad," she says. "I guess he and I are—" She quiets down as we hear voices outside.

"Water! Please!" someone calls out. I don't recognize the voice but hope it's one of the men in my division, still alive. I want to go out and help him, but my leg feels heavy as a rock and useless for walking. Besides, some of that gunfire sounds dangerously close still.

"I wish I could help them," she says. "We have all this spring water here. It should be good to drink." She looks at me. "I know it's too dangerous. I'm not going out there. I just wish I could help."

My lips press together as I nod. Pain radiates up my leg again, and I shiver.

"Are you hungry?" she asks. "When's the last time you ate?"

"Yesterday, long before we marched into position," I explain. I do feel pangs of hunger, but I've gotten used to ignoring them over the past months. Food is plentiful back in camp, with fresh meat and desiccated vegetables that are filling, though decidedly hard to chew. But marching rations are another story. My supply of hardtack and salt pork seldom lasts on the front lines, as has been the case these past two days.

She reaches into her pocket again, and I fear she will pull out the light device again or something more fearful. Instead, she pulls out a rectangular object in a colorful wrapper made of material I don't recognize. "It's a granola bar," she says. "You can have it."

I shake my head. I cannot take food from her, especially not something of this sort. "Please, keep it for yourself."

"I'm not hungry," she insists. "Please take it. You need your strength to deal with your injury. A few calories will help."

Reluctantly, I take it from her, but whatever a 'granola bar' is, it's completely wrapped in… something that seems to be metallic yet paper-like.

"Here." She reaches for it, and I hand it back, happy that she's keeping it for herself.

But instead, she simply pinches the edges of the wrapping together and pulls it apart, pushing out the bar that looks like some sort of marching rations, but it's nothing I've ever seen before. I sniff it, and it smells sweet.

"It's fresh, I promise," she says. "Take a bite."

I look at her and somehow trust her, taking a bite of the bar, which is surprisingly chewy… and delicious. "This is good," I tell her, and I take another bite. It's filled with nuts and oats and coated in chocolate, which is quite tasty. In the army, they usually reserve chocolate for the higher ranking officers–or the injured.

I suppose I am one of the latter right now. "This is really good."

She chuckles lightly. The contrast between her musical laughter and the harsh sounds on the battlefield is unsettling. I think of all the men from my division who are out on the field suffering. If only my leg would let me help them….

I finish the last of the bar and hand the strange wrapper back to the woman… I now remember her name is Nevaeh.

"If I had more supplies, I'd get you into a fresh bandage," she says. "But I think I should save what I have for now."

"Yes," I agree. "Someone else might need them."

She nods and leans up, stretching her arms and moving closer to the cave entrance.

"You shouldn't get too close to that," I warn her.

"I'm just listening." Her tone is a little sharper than it had been.

I nod, in no mood to argue. My eyelids feel heavy, and I shiver, though it should be warm outside. Pain radiates up my leg again, and I wince. It feels like my leg is on fire. I'm so tired suddenly, so I lean my head back against the wall.

"The cannon fire has been slowing down," she says, still looking out of the cave. "The charge should start soon. I can't remember how long it lasts, but I know Lee retreats after that. We just need to wait it out."

She turns to me then and quickly closes the distance between us, leaning down over me. "Stay with me," she says firmly.

"Yes, ma'am." But I don't know if I can do that. Nausea washes over me, and the chills make me shiver again.

"Hold on," she says with the same tone. "Let me get you something."

She pulls out her box again, full of medical supplies, most of which are strange and unfamiliar, and she pulls out an oddly shaped container, along with a disc that somehow unfolds into a cup. I watch as she puts it in the stream flowing through the cave, unsure how she'll manage to hold any water in something that was once as flat as a flapjack.

She moves back over to me, holding out a pill and the strange cup filled with water. "Swallow this," she says. "It will help with the infection."

I swallow it without much thought, much accustomed to the pills the army occasionally gives us.

She kneels beside me again and feels my forehead. "You've got a fever."

But there's something odd about her voice this time. It's faint, and it echoes strangely in my ears. Exhaustion washes over me, and I think I feel a sharp pain radiating again, but it's faint compared to my overwhelming desire to sleep.

It's not long after this when I drift off, the sound of gunshots ringing out from a distant place.

5

Neveah

It worries me that Sam has passed out, but at least he got down some antibiotics before doing so. He won't need another dose for several hours.

As the cannon fire calms, I hear the roar of Pickett's charge outside. Roar is the best word to describe it because the gunfire is so intense, it sounds like thunder, not to mention all the shouting that's accompanying it. I suppose war cries like these help summon the bravery it takes to charge into a death trap.

Even if Sam was awake, I wouldn't dare move outside. I won't until I'm sure the Confederates have retreated. Even then, we'll have to be careful not to get shot by stragglers or stuck in the crosshairs of some sharpshooters.

It's completely crazy, but I'm starting to think of them as actual Confederates now. This is all too real. Reenactments are never this loud or realistic. Someone is always saying something that gives it away, and besides, I should definitely have a cell signal here.

One thing is for certain. Something happened when I fell, and I had to have gone back in time to the real Battle of Gettysburg. I don't know how it happened, but it's the only thing that makes any sense. Not that it would sound sane or reasonable to anyone else.

Sam's injury is one hundred percent real. It can't be a live shooter situation or the police and ambulances would have been all over this place already. And he seems to be a genuine Union soldier. At first, I thought he suddenly appeared in the future. But now I know it's me who went back into the past.

A chill rushes over me as I remember one of the stories Dad told me the first time we ever attended a reenactment here. That time, we'd been watching from Cemetery Hill.

"The battle was so intense that some of those souls must have been stuck here."

"Dad, I'm training to be a doctor," I insist. "I don't believe in ghosts."

"Neither do I, in any normal circumstance," he insists. "But this place... it's different. So many lives were lost so quickly. There were thousands of bodies lying in these fields."

"All right. I agree, that's intense." Looking around, I can almost feel the bravery of battle, the fear of death, and the unimaginable pain of the wounded.

"There's a story about Devil's Den, which is over that way." He points toward off in the distance, though I can't see that part of the battlefield from here. "During one reenactment a while ago, a woman disappeared for several hours."

"Disappeared?"

The look in his eyes tells me he believes every word of this story, and that gives me a chill up my spine. "Yes. No one could find her for hours. They finally did, and she looked like she'd seen a ghost. Some say she went back in time and experienced the battle firsthand."

"Dad, that can't be true," I insist. "This is a huge place. I'm sure she was just lost."

He shrugs, shaking his head. "We will never really know what happened to her. She was spooked, that's for sure, and she wouldn't talk about what happened to anyone, not even her own family."

I shiver again as I remember the story, wondering if the same thing has happened to me.

"Dad, are you looking for me?" He must be so terrified if he is.

I shake my head, trying to get that story out of my mind while paying attention to what's happening in the battle. I haven't heard anyone calling out that the battle has turned, but I'm not sure I will over all the gunfire and screaming. I suppose I'll just have to wait for the battlefield to quiet down and take a chance when it does.

I'm thankful Dad is such a Civil War buff because now I have a lot of information about it locked in my mind. He probably gave me the locations of field hospitals, and I try to remember which one might be closest to me, but it's no use. I'm just not sure.

This is insane.

I slide back over to Sam and check his pulse. His breathing is labored but reasonably steady, considering the injury. "You're still fine. Hang in there, Sam."

He's not fine, and I know it. He's lost a lot of blood and needs a transfusion immediately, but it's going to have to wait. If I can get him to a hospital that has the equipment, I can do it, but I'm going to have to rely on luck since transfusions were rarely done during the Civil War. At least I can use my own blood since I'm Type O negative, so it's not like I'm going to have to wait for a blood delivery.

Of course, I'm a woman, so nobody is going to believe I'm a doctor in 1863. *Will they even let me try?* I'm going to have to make them, and I'll deal with that problem when I get to it.

Though a transfusion isn't likely to work at this point, and the chances it will are going down every minute we spend in this cave.

Right now, there's still a barrage of gunfire outside, and Sam is still passed out. I look at his face, which seems so calm now that he's not directly feeling pain. "Thanks for saving my life, Sam. I'll do what I can to pay you back."

I shudder to think of what would have happened if he hadn't pushed me back down when that bullet whizzed by my head. Placing a hand on his forehead, I feel that he's quite warm. Even the antibiotics may have been too late.

As I wait for the end of Pickett's charge, I also worry about what I'm going to see when we crawl out of this cave. I've seen pictures of the aftermath of this place, and I'm not looking forward to seeing it firsthand. It was horrendous, with about ten thousand casualties littering the ground–especially the area around us. I've been in the ER when a bad bus accident occurred, but that was only a couple of dozen injured people... and it was horrible enough. I can't even imagine the gravity of ten thousand wounded and dead.

There's nothing to do but wait, and it feels like forever as the gunfire continues nonstop. Even with these ancient rifles that require constant reloading, the sheer number of soldiers out there means the killing is endless.

Finally, I hear the call I've been waiting for. "Fredericksburg! Fredericksburg!"

I know the Union soldiers are winning, avenging their loss from that battle in December 1862. It's only a matter of minutes before the retreat is complete.

Once it's quieter, I peek my head out. Not hearing anything, I crawl back out of the narrow cave and look around the large boulders in front of me, instantly wishing I was back with my father in a harmless reenactment. Carnage is everywhere. I've intellectually prepared myself to see this, but that doesn't matter. My heart throbs, and a sickening feeling like a rock in my stomach makes me want to throw up. I swallow against it and force myself to step around the rocks.

Death is everywhere. Bodies and wounded men lay on the ground so densely I wouldn't even have to step on the ground to walk out of here. The earth is bloodied and full of shrapnel and pieces of metal.

"Help me, please! Water!"

I turn to the sound of the first man calling for help, and immediately, several more spot me and ask for the same.

"I'll get you some water!" There's a spring right here with fresh water, so the best I can do for them is get them a drink and see what I can do with my medical kit before going back to Sam, who is still passed out anyway.

I've only got one collapsible plastic cup, so I'm going to have to do this one at a time unless some of them have canteens I can fill for them. But there are so many.... My heart thumps in panic for a moment before my doctor training kicks in.

We do what we can for as many as we can, and that's all we can do.

I rush out with the first cup of water for the man who asked me for it first. "Here, drink some."

He only takes one sip before he winces in pain. Looking at his injury, I can see why. His foot is dangling from a leg that's mostly gone, and blood is pouring out. He didn't get nearly as lucky as Sam.

He won't make it.

I know I need to move on to the next man, but I make him as comfortable as possible. A field tourniquet won't do him any good at this point, so I reluctantly save them for the next man. I rip off a piece of his pant leg and tie it around him anyway, though that hardly stops the blood.

"Drink some more," I tell him. At least I can make him comfortable in his last moments. "What's your name?"

"Smith."

It's probably his last name, but he's so weak, it's all he can say. I lay his head gently on the ground and position him so he's a little more comfortable, holding his hand as he squeezes mine against the pain. I want to get to the next man, but I feel like I need to give Smith some last moments of peace. When he stops squeezing my hand only seconds later, I place it over his chest and close his eyes.

I still have water in the cup, so I go straight to the next man, whose injury is a shattered left arm. For this man, I use a tourniquet, knowing it will hold him until he gets to the field hospital.

He empties the cup of water and hands it back to me. "Thank you. Go take care of them." He waves over to others writhing on the ground.

"I'll get more water," I say with a nod.

Once my cup is full, I run to the next closest man. But as soon as I see him, I know he won't make it either, being shot directly in the chest. The pool of blood beneath him is even bigger than the man with the leg injury. He can't even sit up, so I kneel down and get underneath him a little so he can at least take a last sip of water. His blood pours over my skirt.

"Help, please!"

The man calling for me is next to him and looks to have a less serious gunshot wound. I know the one I'm holding is not going to make it, so I lay him down softly.

"Close your eyes and relax," I tell him, unable to think of anything more soothing at the moment. It's hard to calm a man so close to death when there is nothing I can do to ease his pain.

Stepping away from him, I give the next man some water, disinfecting his wound and wrapping it as quickly as I can so I can move on.

I do what I can for several more men in the immediate vicinity, but I know I need to go back and check on Sam. I fill the cup of water again as I head back inside the cave, setting it on the ground beside him so I can shake him awake.

"Sam, wake up." At first, there's no response, so I feel for his pulse, which is still surprisingly strong, considering his condition. "Sam, you need to wake up. We need to get you out of here."

"Mm." His eyes remain closed, but he lets out a moan, then he calls out in pain. When he opens his eyes, he notices me with a start as his eyes go wide.

"It's okay," I say calmly. "I'm Nevaeh, remember? You're in a cave, and I patched up your leg."

His eyes look weak, and I feel his head. He's still feverish, despite the double antibiotic dose I gave him. He definitely needs to get to the hospital right away. I'll do what I can for him there. Hopefully, he can walk.

"Sam, we need to get you to a hospital. Can you move?"

He looks up at me hopefully and gives me a nod.

Grateful, I put my hands under him to help him scoot out of the cave only to have him pass out again.

I have to get him out of here. *But how?*

6

Nevaeh

I settle Sam back on the ground since he passed out again. He wasn't nearly as heavy when he was assisting my efforts, but right now, there's no way I'm going to carry his dead weight out of this cave.

His fever is getting worse, though, and I know I need to get him some better medical attention. I decide to give him a few more minutes of rest before I try to wake him up again. Maybe he'll be more lucid if he has rested longer.

In the meantime, I get a few more cups of water to the men outside I've been helping. Those I knew wouldn't make it have passed away, but those with the tourniquets are in better shape now than they would have been without them. I'm hoping the medics come around soon and start collecting them because they all need proper sutures. Maybe then I'll have some help moving Sam.

I head back into the cave after a few minutes and notice Sam stirring. "Are you awake?"

He nods weakly. "Yes… I think."

"Can you walk now? I'll help you."

"I can try." I assist as he drags himself out of the cave. Then, he pushes himself up off the ground, using the large boulders as a brace as he stands. He has to stop midway across the Devil's Den, and I can tell he's dizzy from the sudden movement, so I help him hold there for a few minutes to become steadier.

"Okay now?"

He nods again and I position myself by his bad leg. He looks apologetic as he wraps his arm around my shoulders, but that's the only way we're going to get anywhere, so I give him a nod of encouragement.

We haven't made it far away from the large boulders when he first notices the other wounded soldiers littering the ground. He pauses for a moment, overcome by the sickening landscape in front of us.

"I've helped as many as I could," I say. "For some of the others, there was nothing I could do."

He lets out a weak sigh.

It takes some doing to get him moving again, and he winces in pain more than a few times. But he straightens up and we get back into the position where he can lean against me and hop, and we move away from the boulders onto the area of the battlefield where the 4th Maine was told to hold their ground.

"No!"

I jump slightly at his loud, sudden cry, and he slips away from me, collapsing awkwardly on the ground next to the man I'd helped who didn't make it... Smith.

He feels for a pulse, though the man is obviously gone, and pulls back slightly. I see tears glistening in Sam's eyes. "He was a good man. He was going to ask his lady to marry him."

I kneel beside him, an arm on his shoulder. "I managed to get him some water."

"He was still alive?" He pulls his eyes away from his friend and looks at me.

"Yes," I say with a nod. "But his injuries were too severe. He'd lost far too much blood. I held his hand at the end."

He lets out a long, soft breath. "Thank you."

I wait for a moment until it seems appropriate to ask him to leave, but I worry he'll meet the same fate if we don't move it along. "We need to keep going," I tell him quietly. "You need to get to a hospital."

He starts to stand again, and I help him, then he gets his arm back around my shoulders as we move on. I scan the area and see nothing but wounded and dead. "No one has come to help yet."

"They've probably sent word to the hospitals that the field is clear, but it takes time for anyone to get here," he explains, his voice slow and raspy.

"We'll keep going." But I have no idea which way to go. I rack my brain trying to remember where Dad said the field hospitals were located, but I can't remember. I consider climbing a rise in the ground to see if I can spot one in the distance, but I decide against it.

That's probably a good way to get shot.

But we only get a few more feet before Sam starts slipping from my grasp.

"I need to sit," he says weakly.

"Okay." I nod and try to help him to the ground without falling, where I barely get him seated before he passes out again. "I guess we'll try again in a few minutes." Carefully moving his legs around, I get him into a comfortable position and let him relax. He's clearly not going anywhere, so I might be able to go out and find some help.

Reluctantly, I leave him and head out across the battlefield, keeping a mental note of the tree nearest where I left him so I know how to get back to him. There has to be someone out here soon caring for all these wounded.

There's nothing but bodies, blood, and sticky muck as far as I can see, but I start walking, lifting my now bloody, filthy dress to try to move faster. But I get out in the middle of all of it and there's still no one to be seen.

Maybe it's better if I just wait by Sam for people to come. I can help a few men while I'm waiting.

So, I turn around, assessing the wounded I see as I pass and stopping if there's someone I can possibly help. I don't have any more sutures, but I do have a few field tourniquets, so I use them on those who look like they might survive long enough for whatever medics are coming to get them arrive. Some are so terribly wounded that there's nothing I can do but walk past them.

It's unbelievable, almost incomprehensible, just how many of them there are.

Eventually, I get back to the area of the battlefield where I left my new friend and find Sam still asleep, his pulse as strong as it ever was but his temperature climbing. I have some acetaminophen in my medical kit, but only a little, and I didn't give it to him before because I was hoping the antibiotics would kick in. Now, he's unable to swallow it. Hard to believe I could find that on any corner store in 2025. If I remember correctly, I'm still decades away from even the discovery of aspirin in 1863, so the hospital won't have anything for the fever. Hopefully, he'll wake up soon, and I can give it to him.

I just hope he can hold on long enough for the antibiotics to kick in. Thankfully, I'd thought to include those in my kit. They're nothing too horribly strong, but they should make some difference–I pray.

"Help."

The weak cry from behind me snaps me into the present. *I have what I have, and I'll make the most of it. I can help some of these suffering men, and that's what I'll do until help arrives.*

"I'll get you some water," I tell the man who called out, sprinting back toward the cave with my collapsible cup to get him some spring water. That rock in my stomach is still there, but I ignore it and try to focus on who needs me and what I can do about it.

I return to the man, bringing the cup to his lips. "Take a sip," I say. "Where are you hurt?" There's so much blood everywhere, his uniform is a mess, and it's hard to see what's wrong with him.

"Left arm by the elbow," he says weakly.

Rolling up his sleeve with a nod, I reach a point where the fabric sticks to him and don't go further. It's probably dried up and serving as a bandage. "This is going to hurt a little, but I have to clean up the wound."

He nods but calls out in pain when I take the fabric off and quickly apply the disinfectant. It needs sutures, but there's nothing I can do but get a clean bandage on and a tourniquet. "I hope those medics hurry."

"The doctors have a lot of men to serve," he says. "This is a right mess around here." He gives a laugh that's stifled by a wave of pain I can see in his eyes.

"I'm sure they'll be here soon." I can't possibly know that, but I want to give him some reassurance.

"Thank you, miss."

All I can do is nod and say a prayer that he makes it through.

I spend several more minutes doing what I can to help the men lying on the blooded ground near where I left Sam. Finally, some soldiers start arriving carrying litters, crude stretchers to carry off the wounded. There are so many men in horrible shape, I can't possibly ask them to get Sam yet with so many in worse condition on the field, but I run down to give them my assessment of the men I've treated so far.

The first soldier I run up to furrows his brow. "Miss? What in God's name are you doing out here?"

It's a good question, and I don't have an acceptable answer. Thankfully, I think fast when under pressure. "I'm from Gettysburg." I wave in a general direction, not sure where we are on the field in relation to the nearest town. "I wanted to help."

"This is no place for a woman, miss," he insists while he and another soldier load up a man I haven't treated who looks to be in bad condition.

"I can help with triage," I suggest.

"Miss, we have a lot of men to get to," he argues.

"I understand that. I can help."

"Are you crazy?" He's already walking away from me.

Another set of soldiers come up and start loading up a man I treated earlier. I guess I need to prove I know what I'm doing, or they won't let me help. "He has a bullet lodged near the upper ulna," I explain. "I didn't have the equipment to pull it out here. I applied the tourniquet and did a rudimentary disinfection and applied dressing. I'm afraid I'm almost out of supplies."

They both stare at me with wide eyes. "Miss, are you a nurse or something?" one of them asks.

I nod, knowing that's a lot more believable in this time than trying to convince them I'm a doctor. I don't have time to argue with them anyway. "Yes, please let me help."

He shrugs and hands me a bag of supplies he was carrying over his shoulder, which I happily take and start patching up whatever men I can around me while they carry that man away. I wonder if there's an ambulance wagon nearby, but I can't see through the trees to know exactly where they're taking these men. The ground here is too covered with dead and wounded for horses to get through.

As more soldiers arrive, they ask me similar questions about what the hell I'm doing here, but they really can't afford to turn down help at this point, so they just leave me to work and listen to my advice about who to take first.

I get into a pattern of triage, assessing each man as I come to him and directing soldiers over to the ones who need the most immediate help—and still have a chance to survive. So many are on the verge of death that they won't even make the trip wherever they're going with the litters.

The supplies are rudimentary and don't seem sterile at all, but I don't have any choice but to use them the best way I can.

After a while, I get the attention of one of the soldiers and point toward the tree where I left Sam. "I left a man who needs attention over there—when you can get to him. I need to check on him, so I'll go check on the wounded closer to him." I've already helped many of them, but unfortunately, there are plenty more who need help.

"It could be some time before we make it over there," the soldier says, looking around gravely.

I nod and turn to head back toward Sam, hoping it doesn't take too long for the men with the litters to make their way over there. I help a few other wounded men, and then see the litters start to come closer and closer until these men finally get their turn.

Thankfully, Sam is one of the first to get loaded up. He's still unconscious, his face pale and sweaty. It's difficult for me to watch them carry away. He did save my life, after all. Even though I hardly know the man, I feel connected to him in some way.

I want to go with him, but I'm still needed here to help with triage, especially since I've been handed more supplies as more men sent from the field hospitals arrive.

"Where are you taking him?" I ask. I want to go check on him later. That might be a while, judging by how many men here can still use my help.

"There's a farmhouse over that way we're using as a field hospital." He nods in a general direction, but from here, I can't see a farmhouse, so I have to hope I'm able to catch up with Sam later.

As he's carried away, I think I see Sam open his eyes slightly, but I'm not sure. I do my best to smile at him reassuringly, just in case he can see me.

I get back to the nearest man as another set of soldiers arrives with a fresh litter. Something tells me the hard work of saving lives is just beginning.

7

I AWAKEN TO A BLURRY WORLD, VAGUELY AWARE OF THE SHAPE OF THE woman in the plum dress, but I move away from her quickly before my vision clears. My eyes close again from exhaustion. It's strange, moving as though I'm floating in the air, and for a moment, I worry that I've met my demise.

But bits of clarity slowly return, and I see the men carrying the litter I must be lying on, and they're not very gentle. With each bump and stumble, my wound sends sharp pains radiating up my thigh and into my back. Wincing doesn't make a dent in the pain, but I do it, nonetheless.

As my senses sharpen, I become aware that I'm being carried across the massive battlefield. The hot July sun beats down on me, making me feel even warmer than my fever has caused, though now I notice that fever is affecting me slightly less than before. I'm still woozy, but some of my body aches, save for the pain in my leg, have lessened. My parched throat demands water, but it's all these fellas can do to carry me, so I don't dare ask them to stop and get me a drink. In fact, their faces are trained dead ahead, and I begin to wonder, despite their Union uniforms, if they are friend or enemy. Perhaps the Rebs are forcing our own soldiers to capture us.

No, that's ridiculous. I must still be more feverish than I thought. Maybe Nevaeh is just a figment of my imagination as well.

The trek across the battlefield is excruciatingly endless, and now I become aware that those bumps and jolts are simply the soldiers avoiding all the bodies strewn across it. I can only hope there are more Rebs that met their demise than our men.

"That one's full! We're filling this one over here!"

The soldiers carrying me abruptly change direction, which causes another spasm of pain to pulse through me, and this time, I can't help but let out a groan. They sprint now, and in my position looking straight up at the sky, I have no idea where they are taking me.

They stop again once we reach some sort of wagon where I'm unceremoniously dumped inside, thankfully landing on the side of my good leg yet hitting my injured leg roughly in the process, and again, I groan in pain.

"They aren't too gentle."

I hear the voice beside me, his tone sympathetic, but my eyes are so heavy now, I can't even turn to him and answer. I'm vaguely aware that the wagon is full of other men, and many are whimpering or even crying out in pain. I smell the strong metallic odor of blood coming from every direction. I don't doubt many of these men are in worse shape than myself.

When my eyes open again, it's because a sudden jolt has me nearly up in the air and hitting the side of the wagon. It's moving now, and the ground isn't any easier for a wagon than the men who carried me to it. Once again, I wonder whether I'm being taken prisoner, having no idea whether our forces won or lost the battle, though I vaguely remember Nevaeh saying the Rebs would be retreating. But at that time, she was speaking of events that had not occurred. *How could she know about them?* It's hard to say.

"It's a rough ride, I'm afraid."

It's the same man as before, and now I'm lucid enough to turn to him. He gives me a smile. At least, as much of a smile as a man could have when his arm is bleeding as much as his is. I look around quietly at the many other men in the wagon and realize that my initial assessment was correct. Many of these men are injured much worse than I am.

I'm about to ask the man beside me if we're in a prisoner's wagon when I see the colors of the Stars and Stripes billowing in the air above me. I am on friendly territory, and whatever fears I had of being taken prisoner must have come from my feverish state. Relief washes over me as I push myself into a seated position. Ahead of us, I see groups of tents that must be a field hospital.

"It is a rough ride." I finally answer the man beside me.

My hopes that my leg will be examined sink a little as I see how many men are here waiting for treatment. It seems that hundreds of them are lying on the ground just outside the hospital tent. So many of our men are wounded, and I wonder how many can be treated here and how many are already inside receiving care.

We get as close as we can, considering that there are so many men scattered everywhere, and the wagon stops as several men come over and start sliding us out onto liters again. I want none of that as they are likely to dump me on my injured leg again. It's fine when it's not moved, and I'm not looking forward to another sharp pain.

When they reach for me, I hold up my hand. "I can get out on my own," I insist.

As I scoot slowly toward the back of the wagon, a woman walks up wearing a white apron. I take her to be a nurse, given her quick appraisal of the men as they're brought out of the wagon. She seems to be sorting us by level of injury. She directs the soldiers to carry the man next to me, the one who'd spoken, over to a tree, then turns to me. "Where were you hit?" she asks.

"In my leg."

She nods, looking at my leg and frowning with thin lips, her brow crinkled tightly. "What's this?"

"Someone patched me up a bit on the battlefield," I explain, though she still looks puzzled.

"What an odd tourniquet," she says. "I don't know who did this, but it's like nothing I have ever seen before." She looks at my eyes then shouts at a man near her. "Take him over there by that tree with the others."

She moves on to the next man while a soldier comes up to me as I'm painfully sliding myself off the wagon. "Can you walk?" he asks.

"With some assistance," I say with a nod. He helps me limp over to the tree and sets me down. "Why over here?" I ask.

"This is for those fellas not so badly injured," he explains. "I'm afraid there's quite a long wait to see a doctor."

Looking around, I can see that. I can't even count the number of wounded gathered here, so I simply nod, and the man walks away.

"So, you also win the not-so-bad award," a man beside me says. He sounds familiar, and it takes a beat before I recognize it's the same man who was beside me in the wagon. "Looks like we're bunkmates again."

"It appears that way," I agree, balancing to hold out my hand. "Sam Walker, 4th Maine."

"I'm afraid I'll have to give you a verbal handshake, Walker," he explains, nodding toward his arm. It's wrapped tightly in what looks like a torn shirt. "I've only one arm to hold me steady right now. But I'm Joe Corbitt, 140th New York."

"Good to meet you, Corbitt. I guess we'll wait here for a bit."

"Walker?"

The voice is very familiar, and I turn to see a friend from my division. "Harris! Happy to see you."

"Told you that was him," Harris says before hopping over and sitting next to me. Two others join us, one limping and another holding his arm. My eyes widen.

"Brown, Wilson… so glad you made it," I tell them, then turn to Corbitt. "These men are from my division."

After more formal introductions, Brown turns to me. "I haven't found Smith yet. Think he's run off and hid somewhere." All three of them start chuckling, but I shake my head. I can tell by the look in his eyes, though, he's trying to lighten the mood.

"He didn't make it," I say quietly.

All of them are silent for a moment, even Corbitt.

"It was a rough fight," Wilson says after a while. "The sounds of all those men falling around us… that was horrific."

All I can do is nod in response. I've been in several battles, and they are always horrible, but none I've been involved in so far seem nearly as devastating as this.

"It's something we'll never forget," Harris admits.

Wilson exhales slowly. "We can be proud of what we did here. We fought with honor, and we managed to reclaim the ground. They've retreated for now."

"We showed those Rebs," Brown agrees quietly, picking at the grass next to him. "I just can't believe they were foolish enough to make that charge."

"No doubt about that," Corbitt agrees. "The fools came over a wide open battlefield."

"They thought that barrage of cannon fire would overwhelm us," another man I haven't met yet says. "But what a grave error. It was poorly executed. Those men didn't stand a chance."

"We didn't." We all turn to a man lying on the ground under our tree… wearing a Reb uniform. I'm surprised none of us even noticed him before considering we've just been battling one another for the death. But a closer look tells me he's very young, perhaps too young to be in the army at all. And despite the fact that he's under the tree with the rest of us whose injuries are not as severe, his leg is almost severed, and he appears weak and near death. It's obvious he's been placed here to be ignored, and I'm surprised he was brought here at all.

I nod, not sure what to say, and turn away from him. There's nothing any of us here can do for him, even if he were a Union soldier, and no matter what his age.

"I'm afraid I missed that part of the battle," I tell the others. "How did it unfold?" Curiosity piques my interest. I think about what Nevaeh told me while we were hiding in the cave. She claimed to know a lot of details. I want to know if she was right.

Corbitt takes a deep breath. "They laid out a barrage of cannon fire on our formation, no doubt with the intent to overwhelm us. Then several divisions ran through the open battlefield toward our position, completely unprotected. It was hard to watch even from our end, and we were winning."

"They'd clearly been ordered to charge," another man says.

"Who would order that disaster, I have no idea," Corbitt continues. "I'm certain they lost at least half of their troops."

I stare at him wide-eyed, unable to believe that every detail is matching Nevaeh's account exactly. But I don't understand how she could possibly know these things. She was even aware of the commanders' names. I gasp and look at Corbitt. "What was the name of the general leading the charge?" I ask.

He crinkles his forehead, bending half his mouth in a crooked frown. "Of the Rebs?"

I nod. "Yes. Which one of Lee's generals got chosen for such a horrible task?"

Corbitt lets out an annoyed chuckle, and the other man looks at me with the same confused expression. "How in God's name would any of us know that? Why would you ask such a thing?"

Before I can explain, which I quickly realize I can't, we turn to a faint voice behind us. The Rebel soldier coughs a few times and turns his head weakly. "General George Picket led the charge. Alexander's the name of the man in charge of the cannon barrage."

My heart thumps in my chest, and every nerve in my body stands on end as a chill runs through me. It's impossible that Nevaeh could have known those names.

How does a beautiful woman who claims to be a doctor—and clearly understands medical treatments—suddenly appear on a battlefield knowing every detail of both sides as if she has read about the battle in a book?

I have absolutely no idea.

A part of me can't help but wonder if I'll ever see that woman again.

8

Neveah

No triage shift in the ER has ever been this intense. Injured men cover the ground as far as I can see, and I'm grateful for the setting sun, which will at least keep me from seeing how futile my efforts are every time I look up.

"Take this man," I tell the soldiers with the next liter. They've gone past questioning me by now and just bend down and lift him onto the cot, carrying him away. I don't even have time to wish him well before the next man calls out to me, this one with a leg injury that makes me think about Sam again.

But I need to keep going, so I shake the thought out of my head. I just have to hope he's okay, and I can find him later. So, I keep up the triage.

Nighttime arrives, and I can barely keep my eyes open. That changes as thunder roars above me and the rain starts falling.

I'd forgotten about this. I'd read that after the battle, heavy rains flooded some of the area. I keep working anyway, doing my best to help the injured men shelter themselves from the storm using their jackets until the soldiers show up with litters to move them. I'm not sure how much time has passed until a man taps me on the shoulder while I'm dressing a wound.

"You've been out here all day, miss." I turn to see one of the soldiers who has been carrying the liters. I hadn't even realized he'd noticed me, he's been so busy himself. "It's pouring rain. Why don't you head in? We've got a wagon that's not quite full."

Inhaling, I try not to think about what a half-empty wagon means —more of these men have died. "Have all these men been taken to the same field hospital?"

"Mostly," he confirms.

Maybe I can find Sam there. "All right. Take this last man here."

He gets the injured soldier loaded onto the liter, and I walk beside them. It's even harder to trample through the battlefield than it was earlier. The pouring rain has thickened the top layer of muck, mixing it with the blood of battle. My shoes sink with each step. It takes both hands just to get my skirt up so I can move.

Eventually, we reach the wagon where they dump the injured man in rather roughly, and I climb in after him, repositioning his wounded arm so it doesn't undo the rudimentary tourniquet I'd put on him. I'd run out of tourniquets from my medical kit long ago and have been using any piece of cloth I can find, including torn-off fabric from the uniforms of soldiers in the field who didn't make it.

The tragedy of this war is unimaginable.

There aren't many men in the wagon, but their conditions are much worse than others I've seen since they've been lying in the field all day untreated. It's amazing some of them are even still alive, and in fact, I know several won't even make the wagon trip.

I've been given a tin canteen wrapped in cloth to provide water. Even in the pouring rain, the wagon's movement makes it impossible for any of the wounded to get a satisfying drink, though they try to catch as much rain in their mouths as they can. I put away my plastic accordion cup long ago as it tended to confuse people unfamiliar with plastic, and I wasn't near the stream to refill it anyway. I pull the cork and hand the canteen to the man next to me, who weakly takes a sip.

His shoulder injury isn't that severe, but as with the others, he's been lying there untreated for so long that he's weak with fever.

He looks up at me, his eyes tired, and I pat him on the leg reassuringly, though there's nothing to reassure him about at this point. It's simply all I can do for him.

"Water," another man says weakly, and I scoot over toward him, which isn't easy the way the wagon is bumping and jerking every which way. I finally settle in next to him and offer him the canteen. He looks like he might make it, despite a bad foot injury. With everything I've read about the Civil War, I'm pretty sure he will lose that foot when the doctor gets to him. It's a shame because it could have been saved in 2025.

But I'm not there now, and I don't have the equipment to help him.

Finally, the bumping and jerking comes to a halt as we pull up to the field hospital, which looks to be a farmhouse behind a lot of tents. The lanterns' light from tree branches show there are injured men everywhere, lying in much the same way I'd seen on the battlefield, exposed to the rain as it pours down, though there are some soldiers trying to erect makeshift shelters over them. Here there are mostly injured men… though many have clearly passed away waiting for help and have yet to be moved.

Climbing out of the wagon, I turn to help them unload the few men we've brought. I want to tell them which men need treatment first, but that's clearly futile given how many are already lying on the grass waiting. So instead, I just shake my head nearly imperceptibly about the ones who can't be helped at all, which are at least half of them in this load. They set them on the grass anyway, over to the side, and I give them each a little more water to make them as comfortable as possible. I nod toward two soldiers who erect a sheet of canvas over them, thankful these men won't die out in the pouring rain.

In the dim light of the lanterns that barely flicker in the rain, there's really no way to find Sam. The soldiers who brought me are already gone, taking the wagon back to the battlefield. Eventually, I know they will run out of wounded to bring in.

Heading into the first tent, I inhale sharply seeing how many men are already inside, lying on cots. Moans, whimpering, and cries of pain come from every direction, and it takes a beat to re-summon my professionalism to stay focused. Several women go from bed to bed caring for the men, so many that I'm sure they're not all professionally trained nurses.

I squeeze the excess water out of my dress in the doorway before heading in to help.

A young woman who looks to be a teenager sits with one man, dabbing his head with a wet cloth. I sit on the edge of the cot on the other side of him, looking him over. "Where's his injury?" I ask.

"It's gone now," she says quietly.

"Gone?" He still looks to be in a lot of pain.

"It was on his arm, but the doc took it."

Inhaling, I uncover his shoulder and see the bandage over what's left of his right arm. The amputation is above the elbow, and I know the doctor sealed the arteries, but the bandage is soaked with blood. "We need to change his dressing."

The girl looks at me, her eyes tired. "I asked for some, but there's not enough."

My lips purse together in frustration. Despite the war lasting as long as it has, the doctors weren't prepared for thousands of casualties. How could they expect all of this?

"I'll see what I can do," I tell her. "Is there a nurse in charge?"

"I don't know," she says with a shrug. "I just ask whoever I see how I can help. I ended up here when I was running from the soldiers, and they asked me to stay and help–so I did."

I nod, a bit shocked at her story. Looking down at the soldier, whose eyes are closed now, I hope he makes it. "I'll see if I can find some spare dressing. And I've been looking for a soldier, Sam Walker. Have you seen him? He has an injured leg."

"No, sorry," she says, turning back to the man and wiping his forehead again.

I step away and try to find an older woman who might be a trained nurse and stop one as she's walking past. "The man over there needs a dressing change," I tell her.

She sighs, her expression sympathetic. "We're short on supplies. If I can find something, I'll bring it."

"Thank you." I understand her frustration. "Have you seen a patient named Sam Walker?"

"No, but then, we haven't exactly had time to ask names," she says, shaking her head. "I'm needed elsewhere."

"Of course." Walking away, I hope the man gets his bandage changed, though I doubt it will happen. He's probably lucky to have any dressing at all.

I hitch a breath when two little girls pass carrying buckets of water. I can't even imagine what this scene must feel like to a little kid. It's too much for any adult, let alone a child.

I pass another woman and wave her down. "Excuse me, have you seen a patient named Sam Walker?"

She shakes her head and moves on, and the pattern continues. No one knows where he is. So, I keep going and just start checking every cot, even though there are so many of them. He's not in the first tent, so I move to the next. The farmhouse itself seems to be where they're taking patients once they've been treated, so I avoid that for now. It's been hours since he was sent here, so it's possible he's received treatment by now, but his injury wasn't that bad compared to others, so it's possible he's still waiting.

As I pass some supplies and equipment, the stench of death and blood overwhelms me. I turn to see a pile of… discarded limbs. There are dozens of them—legs, arms—and I have to cover my mouth to keep from vomiting. Even with all my physician training, I almost lose it.

And those little girls have probably seen this, too.

Walking faster, I get to the next tent full of patients. I scan quickly first but don't see Sam, so I go from cot to cot. Finally, I see a familiar patch on a man's jacket with the insignia for the 4th Maine division. I hurry over to his cot and sit by him. It seems he also got injured in the leg. "Hello. I'm looking for Sam Walker."

"Walker?" He's clearly out of it, but I'm hoping he's lucid enough to point me in the right direction. "Walker didn't make it."

My pulse quickens, and my heart pounds in my chest. "Are you sure?"

But the man has closed his eyes again. I wait a moment until he opens them and looks at me. "I'm sorry for your loss. How did you know Walker?"

"He was my brother's friend." It's the only excuse I can think of.

"I'm sorry," he says. "He was a good man and...." He closes his eyes again, and I walk away, feeling a hard lump forming in my throat.

Sam saved me... but I couldn't save him.

I stand there for a moment trying to figure out how I feel about this news, but someone calls out to me, jolting me out of my thoughts.

"Water."

"Of course." I take off the canteen holder that was strapped to my shoulder, popping the cork and rushing over to the man who'd asked. He takes a grateful sip.

From there, I decide to help as many people as I can before I pass out from exhaustion and can do no more. Robotically I go from one man to the next, and thankfully a woman comes by who hands me some supplies, though it's not much, and they're clearly dirty.

So many of the men have had amputations, it horrifies me, and that image of the pile of limbs is something I can never unsee. But I keep working, trying to keep Sam off my mind even though it's impossible. Hadn't I done everything I could to help him? If I thought he was going to die, I never would've left him.

Shaking my head, I clear my thoughts and get back to work. Everything is dirty, and all the supplies the other women hand me are rudimentary at best. There's nowhere to wash my hands, so sanitation is out of the question. I've used all the disinfectant in my kit, so all I can do is try to avoid touching wounds directly as I re-wrap bandages.

"Miss, you need to get some rest." I turn to see an older woman smiling sympathetically at me. "A man told me you were out in the field, and you've been here for hours."

I nod, so overcome with exhaustion at that moment, I can't even argue. I make my way outside away from the stench and find a tree where some of the other women are lying with their eyes closed on the grass. It's wet from the rain, but it's on a hill so it's not too bad, and I'm too tired to care. I collapse under it and don't even remember the seconds that pass before I'm asleep.

But Sam's face haunts my dreams. I relive the way he pulled me down as the bullet passed over me and the few moments we'd had to talk when he was lucid.

My body jerks as I awaken just as the sun begins to rise. Any other day, I would see beauty in the way the pink and orange rays spread across the sky, meeting the deep green of the farmland beyond. The rain has subsided for now, but I feel moisture on my face and reach up to discover a tear. I hadn't even noticed any emotions, but they come to the surface like wildfire.

Hiding my face from the other women around me, I finally let myself cry. I can't believe Sam is gone. I should have followed him from the start and made sure he was treated right away. I should have done that blood transfusion.

But it's too late for that.

After several minutes, I wipe away what's left of my tears and decide to look for his body. I can't undo my choices from yesterday, but the least I can do is be sure he's buried with respect.

9

evaeh*

"Can you tell me where they put the deceased soldiers?" It's such a horrible question, but that's what I need to know right now.

The woman I'm asking doesn't even blink. "They're preparing a graveyard out back," she explains. "I don't think it's ready yet, so I think you'll find the bodies are back there, too."

"Thank you." This gives me time to look for Sam's body, though I wish I didn't have to.

I head toward the farmhouse, intending to go straight around back and start looking, but a familiar young woman runs up to me. I worked with her before. "I hope you got some rest. Please head in right away."

Taking one glance toward the back of the farmhouse, I abandon my plan and head inside with her. I'll find a way to look for Sam later. Since I can't really help him anyway, I like to think that he'd want me to help others. I'm pretty sure I'm right about that.

It's my first time inside the farmhouse, and my heart thumps as I

57

step in. The smell of rotting flesh and blood hits me straight-on, and I need a minute to refocus.

"Here." I turn to see the woman I'd walked in with handing me a piece of cloth. "It's from a tablecloth we found. Only helps a little, but it does help." She ties hers around her head as a makeshift mask, and I do the same.

"Thank you." She has already left, running to help a soldier limping out of a room. Looking around, I see a man who must be the doctor. The bags under his eyes are pronounced, and he closes those eyes occasionally before he forces them open again. I wish I could tell him I'm a doctor, and he'd believe me, but I know there's no way that will happen.

I scoot in beside him and look at the patient. "I'm a nurse," I say quickly. "How can I help?"

He regards me with thankful eyes. "A suturing will do for this one… bullet is out. Can you do that?"

"I can," I assure him. Thankfully, that's enough for him as he moves on to the next patient. I'm happy to have useful supplies again, though I question how sterile the thread is in this environment. Still, it's better than nothing, so I do what I can to sew the soldier's leg injury together without allowing too many germs into the wound. After the stitches, I bandage him up. "Try to rest," I tell the man, whose teeth look permanently gritted from the pain, but he nods.

I can't even imagine what these men are going through without anesthesia.

I don't have any more time with the soldier before another one comes in, bleeding profusely. Glancing at the doctor across the room, I see he's elbow deep in blood. "Let me take a look."

"He needs a bullet removed," the woman who brought him in tells me. She helps him onto a cot.

"Then I'd better look fast." I don't bother to give any more information, just pull up his pant leg until I can see the wound. The bullet is still in there, but it's thankfully not far from the surface. It must have ricochet off something to lose momentum. He's lucky it didn't shatter his bone like so many other men have suffered. Glancing at the tray of instruments, my heart sinks. They're filthy and have probably been used to pull bullets out of dozens of different soldiers.

"Do we have any iodine?" I ask the woman beside me. I don't think she's a nurse, probably just someone from town who came to help.

She shakes her head hopelessly. "I heard the doc say he used the last of it."

"Is there any alcohol in the house?"

"What?" She wrinkles her forehead.

"Check the kitchen and see if there's any rum or whiskey… anything." She's still staring blankly at me. "Hurry!"

She nods and runs out, and I hope she's doing what I asked. I can only wait for a couple of minutes before I'm going to be forced to use the dirty instruments. The doctor is still busy with the man on the other side of the room, and from the looks at the instrument tray beside him, it's pretty obvious he doesn't have any iodine either. It was the most common disinfectant at the time, as far as I know.

I start counting the seconds in my head, deciding I'll dive in after two minutes if she's not back. For all I know, she ran away and hid or got called over by someone else. I'm on a minute and a half when she reappears, out of breath.

"I found this." She holds a small bottle in front of me that looks like whiskey.

"Perfect." Pulling the cork, I pour some over the bullet worm, a term for the instrument I'd learned about in my dad's books. A twinge of longing pierces me, but I don't have time to think about Dad right now when this bullet needs to come out.

I look at the man, who is really more like a boy, probably barely old enough to enlist if that, and hand him the bottle. "You'd better take a sip."

"Me?" His eyes go wide.

"Yes, and make it a quick one," I add. "We'll need this for sterilization purposes."

He nods and takes a quick sip, groaning like he's probably never had any before. "Grab the bottle," I tell the woman, hoping she will so

I can take advantage of the man's distraction to pull the bullet out quickly. I don't want him to spill what little we have.

It's out in seconds, and he shouts loud as it exits.

"What's going on?" the doctor yells from across the room.

"Nothing." I don't have time to explain as I suture the wound while the soldier is still at the height of pain. It's done quickly, and I bandage him up. "You'll be fine. Just go rest." I tell the woman to take him to a cot elsewhere in the house, where it's quieter, and get ready for the next soldier to come in, feeling so thankful for the whiskey and the home's residents who'd stocked a little liquor in their cabinet.

I'm helping another man when we hear the sound of horses pulling in another wagon.

"No!" the doctor calls firmly from across the room. "Somebody go tell them we're full. Send them to the other farmhouse down the road."

I perk up at his words. "There's another field hospital?"

"Yes," a nurse nearby says. "Just north of here, about two miles down the road.

Is it possible Sam is there? Maybe the soldier who told me he is dead was delusional.

I finish up the soldier I'm working on. "I need to check on something." Running out into the tent, I look for the cot where the man from Sam's company had been lying. But it's empty.

"Where is the man who was here?" I ask the nearest woman.

"He didn't make it."

That man was feverish and must have been near death when I asked him about Sam. Maybe he didn't even hear me, or maybe he was thinking of someone else. A spark of hope rises in me. I have to go see if Sam is at the other hospital.

"I need to run home for a bit," I tell the woman.

She frowns, furrowing her brow. "You live in town? That's odd. I thought I knew everyone who lives there."

But I don't have time to explain, and I couldn't anyway even if I wanted to, so I rush out of the tent and try to catch up with the ambulance wagon.

It turns out the road is as rudimentary as everything else in 1863, full of ruts and jagged rocks that take some doing to avoid, not to mention the muck from the rain, but at least it's easier to walk through than the mucky battlefield. Even so, there's no way I can keep up with the wagon, even though it's not very fast.

At least it stays in my line of sight, so I keep going, holding up my skirt and feeling thankful I wore good shoes under this costume, knowing I'd be walking around Gettysburg all day.

Of course, when I put these on, I didn't quite imagine this much walking—or that I'd be walking in a completely different century.

Being covered from head to toe in this gown is rough in the summer, and I start feeling the heat and humidity the further I walk. Thankfully, I still have the canteen, though it's almost empty. I stop for a second under a shady tree to take a quick sip.

It's funny how beautiful I thought this place was in 2025. I wasn't wrong. The oak trees tower above me, and a few wildflowers grow along the side of the dry dirt road—Virginia bluebells, I think they're called. The beauty seems so out of place in the middle of such a horrifying reality. I close my eyes for a moment to ground myself, then put away the canteen and start walking again.

By now, I can't really see the wagon, but I'm sure I'm going in the right direction. This is confirmed when I see the Union flag billowing in the distance, as it was at the previous field hospital.

It's so odd to see the American flag with so few stars. They form a different pattern than I'm used to against the dark blue background.

I walk a little faster knowing I'm getting somewhere. There's a long, tree-lined driveway leading to the house, and, like the other field hospital, its massive yard has also been taken over by large military tents. All I can think of is finding Sam now, and I'm practically running.

People are everywhere, and also like the first hospital, rows and rows of men are waiting to be seen on the grass outside. There seem to be fewer of them than at the other hospital, so I walk along the rows looking for that familiar face.

"Water." A weak voice calls out to me, and I go to the soldier, offering a sip from my canteen. I'm going to have to refill it soon, and I hope there's a reliable water source that's not contaminated by the muck of battle.

It takes time, but I get through all the men and don't see Sam.

Be encouraged, I tell myself. If he were still waiting out here on the grass, he probably wouldn't have made it.

It's been over a day since his injury, after all. The dose of antibiotics might have kicked in and given him a chance. He should have taken the next dose by now, but it's still waiting for him in my pocket. I haven't had the heart to give them to anyone else until I am sure he is dead. Less than a full dose wouldn't have helped anyone much anyway.

I head inside the first tent, hoping he's among one of the men who have been treated and are resting. They seem to be even shorter on supplies in this hospital because many of the men are on blankets on the floor rather than in cots, so it takes some time to look through all of them. Row by row, I check for his familiar face and kind brown eyes.

But I don't see him.

"Here."

I'm startled by the voice of the woman beside me, but she's clearly looking right at me. "I need to get these supplies that just arrived to the doctor, but I've got my hands full out here. He's inside, past the main hall." She drops a basket into my arms and walks away, leaving me standing there, stunned.

Looking down, I see it's full of bandages, though none of them look very clean. There are also a few instruments scattered throughout. It's all nowhere near sterile, but it's probably the best they have. I'm finished looking here anyway, so I turn around and head toward the home's main entrance, which is open.

Rounding the corner with the basket, I hear a familiar voice that makes my heart soar—until I hear what he's saying.

"You're not taking my leg, and that's that!" he says firmly.

I rush inside clutching the basket. Clearly, I need to get to him right now.

10

Sam

I DIDN'T FIGHT HARD AND HOLD THE LINE, SURVIVE A NIGHT IN A CAVE, and survive another night waiting for a doctor on the grass under a tree just to have this man say he's going to take my leg. I won't have it.

"Soldier, we don't have a choice," he insists. "It's been two days with this gunshot wound now. Even if it missed the bone, it's bound to be infected!"

"You haven't even looked at it properly," I argue. The man is clearly exhausted, and I don't blame him for making rash decisions since he has so many other men to patch up, but this is my leg he's talking about.

He makes a sound somewhere between a grunt and a sigh. "Unwrap it," he tells the nurse.

She starts on it, but then her eyes go wide. "Doctor?"

"What is it?" He lets out another long sigh.

"That's what I would like to know," she says, holding up the tourniquet she just unhooked. I have to admit it's strange looking, made of an odd material. But I didn't pay attention to it on the field, I was in so much pain. It's something Nevaeh put on, and I loosened it substantially once the bleeding had stopped.

"Hm," he grunts. "Must be some sort of belt. I've seen some strange items used to patch men up these past few days."

The nurse shrugs and unwraps my leg as the doctor leans forward to take a look. "Odd," he says. "Who bandaged you?"

"A triage nurse on the battlefield," I explain.

He furrows his brow. "A nurse on the field? I didn't know we had such a thing."

"She was there, and this is what she did," I insist with a shrug.

"Well, it's a fine job for a nurse." He keeps examining the wound, and the nurse who is standing next to him rolls her eyes in frustration, but he doesn't notice. He straightens and shakes his head. "Still, I can't be sure the bullet didn't do any damage inside, especially since it passed clean through. I'm going to have to take the leg."

"No, you're not!" I argue again.

"I have no choice," he insists. "Nurse, get the chloroform."

The nurse pauses for a moment. "Doctor, are you—"

"I said get the chloroform!"

"Yes, Doctor." She shakes her head and steps over to a cabinet where she takes out a bottle and some cloth.

"With all due respect, I'm positive the bullet didn't do any damage," I insist. "I can bear weight on it, after all. Isn't that proof the leg can be saved?"

"Son, it's safer and faster to just cut it off before it rots more of your body," he insists, pouring some of the chloroform into the cloth. "You won't feel it. Just try to relax."

"I will not!" I insist.

"What's going on here?"

My heart leaps at the sound of the familiar voice. I look up to see Nevaeh holding a basket of supplies, dropping it on a table and hurrying over to me. "Sam, are you all right?" she asks.

I'm so stunned to see her again, I can't answer for a moment. Other than the physical evidence in the bandage and tourniquet, I'd been wondering if I'd just imagined her in my delirium. Yet, here she is, as real as anyone else around me.

"Miss, please go tend to whoever needs help," the doctor says. "This is none of your concern."

"It is my concern because Sam is… my brother." She says it with such conviction, it surprises me.

"Your brother?" He regards her incredulously. "This man is from the 4th Maine. Am I to believe you came all the way from Maine to find him here?"

"We have family in Gettysburg," she says quickly. "I was visiting."

He stares at her for a moment as if he's trying to figure out exactly how likely her story is. "Ugh, I'm too tired to deal with this," the doctor finally says. "This man needs an amputation to save his life."

"He does not," she insists. "His injury is already healing."

His annoyance turns to anger. "I'm the doctor at this hospital, and I'll decide on the correct treatment! This soldier has a bullet wound that may have caused internal damage. I'm removing the appendage, and that's final."

She shakes her head. "No. My father is also a physician, and I studied medicine under him. I can see by this wound that it couldn't have possibly hit the bone or caused other internal damage, and therefore, it does not need to be removed."

"I don't need you telling me—"

"This is my brother's leg we are talking about," Nevaeh says, interrupting him, her hands on her hips. "I won't let you do it."

"Your brother could die," he argues, "and that would be all your fault."

"He won't. He will live, and he will keep his leg." Her eyes are narrowed to cat-like slits.

My heart thumps at the way she holds her ground. I'm thankful she came along because I was becoming too tired to fight with him. She seems to have enough strength for both of us.

"Fine." The doctor drops the chloroform cloth on the table. "I have other patients to serve. You deal with him, and whatever comes of it is your responsibility."

"Gladly." Nevaeh smiles as the doctor walks away. I climb off the table, and she puts her arms around me. The feeling is warm and welcome after so much pain.

She pulls back. "I thought you were dead. A soldier from your company said you'd passed away."

My brow furrows. "Who was that?"

"I'm sorry. I don't know his name." She shakes her head. "He didn't make it," she adds softly.

A twinge of grief washes over me, even without knowing who it was. No doubt, I have lost many good friends in this battle. Just like all the others....

I look into Nevaeh's eyes, and I can see the exhaustion mixed with relief and what might be a tinge of happiness. I'm so grateful to her. "Thank you for your help, *sister*," I say, emphasizing the word.

She laughs lightly. "My pleasure. Let's get you somewhere else so I can take a look at your leg."

I nod enthusiastically as she turns to stand beside me, but she grabs the strange tourniquet and my old dressings off the table before leading me away. "This might be cleaner than what they have to offer," she explains. "Everything in that basket I brought looks questionable."

Wrapping my arm around her shoulder, she does the same as she leads me to another room of the farmhouse where some of the other soldiers are being taken after treatment. She helps me sit down in a chair. "First, you need to take another one of these." She looks around as if to be sure no one else is watching, then takes the strange bottle out of her pocket and pours two pills into her palm. "You should have taken another dose hours ago, but I think this will be better than nothing." She hands me the pills, along with the canteen around her neck. "Here. I'm almost out of water, but there should be enough for you to swallow these."

I certainly trust her more than the doctor in the other room, so I swallow them. "What is this for?" I ask.

"It fights the infection," she explains. "I know that probably doesn't make any sense to you, but you need to trust me."

"I do," I say. "You've helped me so far."

"I've done my best." She kneels down and pulls up what's left of the bottom of my pant leg. "Let's have a look. I couldn't see much with that doctor yelling at me." She lets out a soft giggle, and it sends a pleasant tingle up my spine, causing me to chuckle as well. Laughter is the last thing I expected in a place like this, but perhaps it is a helpful thing for healing… "A merry heart does good, like medicine, but a broken spirit dries up the bones," or so Proverbs says, though I'm not quite sure what's amusing.

"I need to see if I can find a clean bandage," she says, wrapping a bit of my old bandage around my leg. "He took this one off too aggressively and ripped it. Hold this until I get back."

I nod as she looks around the room. Finding an unused small table, she carries it over. I try to stand to help her, realizing with the sharp pain that it's something I cannot do right now.

She sets the table in front of me and puts a cushion over it. "Put your leg up here," she says. "We need to keep it elevated. I'll be right back."

"Thank you." The words seem hollow given everything Nevaeh has done for me. I don't know that I would still be alive if not for her. I'm certain I would be without a leg. I can't possibly repay her.

My eyes flitter around the room until I catch sight of a man who was not as lucky as I've been, his hands running over his thigh, the only thing left of his leg. A nurse comes by, accompanied by a couple of men. "There's a cot available now," she says. "These men will help you to it."

A cot available? There's so much meaning in those words. I wonder if the bed became available because another man died. I see the sadness in the soldier's eyes as he's carried past me, holding onto his bloody stump as he's carried toward an uncertain future. A lump forms in my throat as I recall how close I came to the same fate.

"Here we are."

I turn to see Nevaeh with a cheerful smile on her face, something I struggle to return after the encounter with the wounded soldier. But once I try, I find it comes naturally in her presence.

"These aren't as clean as they should be, but they're better than putting on the same bloody, ripped dressing," she explains, kneeling to look at my leg again. "I lucked out with some disinfectant as well."

I tilt my head at the expression 'lucked out.' I wonder how someone from Pennsylvania has such an unusual vocabulary. The men I'd spoken to from there didn't speak the same way. There are so many things about Nevaeh that seem a mystery, yet I find myself trusting her completely.

"This will sting," she warns me, holding a cloth with the disinfecting liquid applied.

I nod, and she applies it, but the sting isn't as bad as it was before. Quickly, she gets the bandages wrapped around my leg and tied off. "You do that well."

She smiles and leans in, whispering. "I told you I'm a doctor."

I'm beginning to believe her. I have heard of a few women who have done such a thing. I suppose it could be true.

"I'm glad to have my tourniquet back, but I hope you didn't leave it on tight," she says.

I shake my head. "I loosened it while waiting for the doctor. The wound didn't seem to be bleeding anymore."

"That's good because it could have cost you that leg to keep it on too long," she says. "I'm sorry I didn't find you sooner."

I smile reassuringly. "All's well now."

"Glad to hear it." I take that as an agreement. "Are you hungry? I saw they have some food I can get for you."

"I am, but I insist you eat as well."

"I'll grab something for both of us," she says, pushing up off the floor and heading into another room.

I close my eyes for a moment and try to relax. My leg is beginning to feel better already somehow, and the fever seems to be gone. I wonder if it's the pills she gave me, though I know of no medicine that will do such a thing so quickly.

She comes back with a bowl of soup and two biscuits, one of which she eats quickly. "I'd like to stay with you longer, but the medical team is short-handed. I can help, so I probably should."

"You should eat more," I insist.

"I'm fine."

I frown, wishing she would pay attention to her own needs. "Please do so later, but I will not keep you," I say. "So long as that doctor stays away from me, I'll be fine here."

She snickers. "I doubt he'll want anything to do with 'my brother' anymore. He's got a lot to do. Are you comfortable?"

"Yes, I'm as good as can be," I insist.

"Don't let them take you anywhere without having someone find me," she says. "I'll come check on you when I can."

"I'll look forward to that." I watch her walk away holding the tourniquet, no doubt off to save many more lives.

I've never been so impressed with a woman in my life.

11

"LET'S GET THIS DRESSING CHANGED." MY WORDS SOUND ROBOTIC EVEN to me, but that's the mode I've been in for a while now. I don't even know how many days have passed. I've been working with as many wounded soldiers as I can until I'm so exhausted that I have no choice but to sleep.

Sometimes that's at night. Sometimes it's during the day. Time doesn't really mean anything right now.

"This looks good," I tell the soldier to reassure him, though I doubt it's very reassuring to be missing a limb that probably could have been saved if we'd had more supplies. Even food is running scarce now. Though supply wagons keep arriving, they hardly make a dent given how many wounded soldiers we have here.

I've been checking in on Sam as much as I can, though he's been moved outside onto the grass along with some of the others who are stable. I'm happy about that since being around all this filth in the farmhouse and under the tents only exacerbates the risk of infection. At least it's stopped raining now, so the grass under the trees is dry.

71

I move onto another soldier and re-dress his wound, encouraged that this man seems to have made it through the worst. "Let's get you out with the men who are out of the woods."

I wrap my arm around him on the side without a leg and help him hobble out the front door and past the tents, which are still full of men who are in the worst shape. Several have been dying as the hours pass, and there are only a few able soldiers to carry them back to bury them. The stench of rot and blood permeates everywhere.

Inhaling deeply, the fresh air outside gives me just enough energy to make it over to the grass where Sam is situated. I help the soldier I'm escorting lay down and make sure he's comfortable. A nurse who has been looking over these men walks up to me.

"We're moving all these men today," she explains.

My ears perk up at the news. "To where?"

"They're being transferred to a hospital in Philadelphia."

"Do you think I could go with them?" I ask.

She shrugs. "Ask the doctor."

I smile at her but kind of doubt the doctor will let me. I'm not exactly on his good side after that scene with Sam… and a few other similar incidents over the past few days. He's a little too quick to get out the saw, and it's not always needed.

I find Sam and discreetly hand him a dose of antibiotics. I wish I had more with me for the other men because they seem to have helped Sam a lot, but I only have enough for him to finish the recommended dosage. "How are you feeling?"

"I should be asking that of you," he says. "I've been resting. You've been working nonstop. You need to slow down a bit."

"I can't," I argue. "There are too many men here who need me."

"You won't be of help to any of them when you can't keep your eyes open."

Frowning, I turn away, not wanting to admit that he's right. "They're transferring you to a hospital in Philadelphia."

"That's your home," he says. "Are you coming with me?"

Turning to him, I see that his eyes look hopeful, but all I can do is shrug. "I don't know. I have to get permission from the doctor, and he's not exactly my biggest fan."

He nods but doesn't say anything.

"Have you eaten?" I ask.

"Yes," he says. "Be sure you do as well."

"I'd better get back inside," I say. "I'll check on you again shortly."

It's easy to find the doctor, who has been in the same farmhouse room for days, and now he's getting ready to remove another leg. One look at the wounded man—and a whiff of the smell—and I don't argue with him about this one.

"I'd like to go to Philadelphia with the soldiers who are being transferred," I tell the doctor.

His exasperated sigh is louder than usual. "We do have quite a few wounded here who still need care."

"And the soldiers being transferred need care as well," I argue.

He regards me for a moment, and I can see the bags under his eyes have grown darker. "You've been a pain in my ass since the moment I first saw you, woman," he says. "But you've proven very useful." I open my mouth to say something, but he raises his hand to stop me. "You've worked hard for these men," he continues. "Go somewhere where you can get proper food and rest. We have more help coming here soon anyway."

I can't stop the smile that spreads on my face. "Thank you, Doctor. You've done well, too."

He gives me the first smile I've ever seen from him, though it's barely a raise of his lips. I've questioned his methods more than once. But considering the overwhelming situation, and the fact that he's dealing with 1863 medicine, I'm sincere about the compliment.

I spend the next several minutes preparing what I'll need on the wagon ride. I find a small basket and collect a bit of bandage cloth that doesn't look dirty as well as another small bottle of alcohol. Since my first day with Sam, the nurses have been searching the house for it and handing it out to nurses and the doctor in small bottles. At least it's something to wash off the wounds. I also boil some water on the cooking fire outside to refill my canteen. After the creek flooded following the battle, I haven't trusted any water I didn't boil, though it's been hard to convince anyone else to follow this basic precaution.

Once everything is secure, I set it all in a cabinet and turn back to my work to help a few more men, remaining vigilant about the sounds outside so I'll know when the wagon has arrived for Sam and the others. I've re-wrapped several more wounds when I hear the unmistakable sound of horses.

Finishing up quickly, I give the soldier in front of me a pat on the shoulder. "You should be fine." Finally, I could say it and mean it. "I think you should get transferred to the hospital. Come with me."

After I retrieve my basket from the cupboard, the soldier happily follows me out to the grassy area by Sam, keeping up easily since his injury was to his arm.

"Wait here," I tell him while gesturing to a spot on the lawn. They are already loading Sam into the wagon. "I'm coming with you to help the wounded," I explain to the wagon drivers. The man nearest me holds out his hand to help me aboard, and I set the basket up on the wagon ahead of me before hopping up.

Once on, I take a spot near Sam but help the others get more comfortable since most of them are either missing limbs or have injuries that make it difficult to move around. When the last man who will fit is on board, we start moving, making room for the next wagon that will hold the rest of the men, including the soldier I just brought outside.

It's been a few days since the torrential rain stopped. The roads have dried, leaving hard, crusty ruts where horses and wagons had passed when it was muddy, bumping and jolting the wagon relentlessly, at least until we get away from the battlefield area and onto the wider dirt roads leading to Gettysburg. Even those are full of ruts, and I have a new appreciation for pavement. It wouldn't be so bad if it were just me, but the men with injuries suffer greatly with each jolt of the wagon.

I notice a man across from me wincing in pain. Blood seeps into his bandage. I have to hold onto the front of the wagon to work my way over to him with all the bumps.

"We need to change that," I explain to him. "Let's have a look."

He nods passively, looking exhausted, his eyes heavily hooded. Even for the stable patients, this has not been easy. I'm more than thankful that I brought some alcohol because his wound looks like a mess again. I wish I had gloves to keep things sterile, but I work with what I have and get him rebandaged for the rest of the ride to Philadelphia.

The wagons come to a halt near an ornate building I recognize as the Gettysburg Lincoln Railway Station. I remember that some of the railroad was damaged when the Confederate soldiers made it to Gettysburg, and I wonder if they are certain we can even make it to Philadelphia. I soon get my answer when a giant steam engine makes its way down the tracks, slowing to a stop almost right in front of us. I don't have much time to marvel at it because the men driving the wagon hop off and start unloading the wounded.

"We need to work quickly to get everyone loaded so the train stays on time," one of the soldiers explains.

I nod and jump down, pulling my basket with me, then helping the rest of the men get off and onto the train.

"Get the others first," Sam insists when I reach my hand toward him.

That just makes me work faster, and soon all the other men from the wagon are safely on the train, so I assist Sam as he limps over to it. He seems to be getting stronger, and I'm feeling hopeful about his recovery.

An entire train car is dedicated to the wounded, so the soldiers can stretch out on the bench seats, though there's not enough room to lie down. Still, it's more comfortable than the bouncy wagon. I make the rounds to be sure none of the soldiers need anything. They're hungry, but I don't think we'll have food until we get to Philadelphia. The trip shouldn't take too long.

"Are the tracks clear ahead?" I ask one of the wagon drivers before he steps off.

"Yes, ma'am." He nods, wiping sweat from his brow. "They've worked day and night to do repairs on this route. It wasn't damaged much. Mostly, the Rebs made a mess of the line headed due south."

"Thank you." I head back over to Sam as the train starts to move. His leg is spread out on the bench seat, so I sit behind him. "Try to get some rest," I tell him. "Things will get better when we get to the real hospital." At least, I hope they will. I have no idea what kind of conditions await us there.

"Thank you, Nevaeh—for everything."

"Of course," I say, then I crack a little smile. "You saved my life, 'brother.'"

He chuckles, closing his eyes, and even in his somewhat uncomfortable position on the hard bench, he falls asleep quickly.

I look out the window and watch the fields and shrubbery pass by. The scent of the coal fire is new to me, and the locomotive loudly announces itself as it snakes through the landscape.

It occurs to me that I'm leaving Gettysburg far behind, and I wonder if that's wise. *Am I doing the right thing?* It's hard to tell. I don't know if it's something about that particular spot that made me go back in time. If it is, I could be ruining my chances of ever getting back to Dad by traveling away from the battlefield. I can't imagine what he's thinking right now.

I have a million questions of my own.

Have I disappeared from 2025 like that woman Dad talked about in the story? Why was I sent back in time? Am I supposed to do something here to change things? And why does Sam seem so familiar?

A sudden realization hits me. "Oh, my God," I say it out loud, but the locomotive is so loud I don't think anyone hears me. I couldn't help it. I've finally figured out why he looks so familiar! Sam is the man from the picture in the visitor's center! A chill runs up my spine as I think of the way his eyes seemed to meet mine across time itself.

Am I supposed to help Sam? What does all of this mean?

Maybe I'm in a coma, and this is all a crazy dream. It's possible, yet this all seems so real. I've worked myself to exhaustion helping all the men, and I've felt every moment of this. So, maybe all of this is real. And maybe by leaving Gettysburg, I'll never get home.

Regardless, I won't stop caring for these men, especially Sam. These wounded soldiers deserve my very best work, and that's what they're going to get.

12

SAM

I'M AWARE OF THE TRAIN SLOWING DOWN AS THE LOCOMOTIVE LOUDLY bellows black smoke into the sky, the Philadelphia station visible in the distance. Blinking, I gather my wits and sit up straighter, only to wince at the pain in my leg from the change of position.

I'm not looking forward to a wagon ride again, but that's what pulls up near the train to take us into the city to the hospital. We load up and depart, and at least it's not as bumpy this time since the roads are in better shape. As usual, Nevaeh busies herself with caring for the men along the way.

I wish she'd just relax for once and get some food and rest. I have no idea how she's kept going for this long in these conditions.

Once at the hospital, I lose sight of her as the staff begins to take us inside.

"I'm fine," I try to insist to the woman helping me limp in. "I should be able to go home soon."

"That's impossible," she argues. "Gunshot wounds take weeks to heal, assuming they don't get infected, which most do. We're keeping you here until we're sure you won't lose your leg."

"My leg is fine," I insist, but she ignores me, leading me to a room full of cots. Apparently, our wagon was just one of many to arrive, as this large room is crowded with beds and injured men. There's barely enough room for the staff members to move between them to take care of the men who really need them.

The stench is powerful, mostly coming from the bed pans I reckon. Though the nurses hurry around trying to keep them cleaned, there are too many bedridden men here to keep up.

The nurse escorting me hands me a pan.

"That won't be necessary," I tell her. "I can get up and relieve myself in the proper facilities."

"You shouldn't move your leg," she insists. "It might get infected. Just use this, and I'll come along and clean it when it's needed."

She looks at me as though there's no room for argument, so I sigh and take it from her. I lie on the cot as she's instructed, which has been haphazardly filled with straw and is therefore lumpy, especially in the one place I need to place my leg comfortably. It's still less painful than the train seat or the rough wagon ride, so I attempt to close my eyes.

But then I hear the moans and whimpers of the men around me more profoundly, so I open them seconds later. I doubt I'll get much rest here.

Looking around, I seem to be in a lot better shape than the vast majority of these men. I wonder whether the pills Nevaeh has given me are the reason why. She mentioned she only had enough for me, yet she keeps giving me more. I wonder why she doesn't spread them out among a few men at least. I have no idea how they work, though.

Hours pass, and neither the smell nor the loud cries and moans have calmed. Lying down is no longer comfortable at all, so I attempt to sit up and lean against the wall. I regret it immediately because now I can see everyone's suffering as well as hear their cries. A stern nurse barks orders at the other women located around the room who are clearly already doing their best. I can nearly feel their collective relief when she finally leaves the space.

I long for the fresh air and soft grass beneath me I'm akin to, as well as Nevaeh's reassuring voice. She's been gone for quite some time, no doubt working tirelessly to help others. I reckon there's no way she's sleeping or finally getting some food in her empty belly.

I'm about to lie back down when I spot her entering the room with the stern nurse, who marches straight for my bed and throws both of her arms on her hips. "I'm head nurse Catherine Strawn. This woman… is she your sister?"

I know better than to say no. "Yes, she is."

"Well, she's being a complete nuisance and is entirely in the way." She stands there with her authoritative pose, as if I have the power to tell Nevaeh what to do. I haven't known the woman for more than a few days, but I know enough to be sure no one's gonna tell her anything.

I decide to stick with the story Nevaeh had told the doctor back in the field hospital. "Well, our father is a physician, and she's his assistant. She's very skilled and could be of use to you."

"I'm not interested in your father or her help." Nurse Strawn eyes Nevaeh with contempt as she continues. "The nurses in my outfit must be at least thirty, unmarried, and homely."

Nevaeh certainly isn't the latter.

"She told me she doesn't have a husband, but she's too young and far from unattractive." Nurse Strawn rattles on. "Regardless of her unmarried status, the other two requirements are quite stringent. I won't tolerate anything less in this outfit. Your sister cannot be a nurse here."

"I can be useful," Nevaeh argues, and I'm surprised she hasn't interrupted in protest. "You clearly need the help. These women are working nonstop, and it's still dirty and reeks of urine in here. None of these men stand a chance of properly healing in these unsanitary conditions"

The nurse's eyes narrow in a vicious squint, and I can see Nevaeh is pushing her buttons. "Young lady, you can be of use to your brother–and that's it." She takes her hands off her hips and folds them beneath her massive bosom with a huff. "If I see you trying to treat any of these other soldiers, you'll be forced to leave." She storms off before Nevaeh can get another word out.

I can't help but let out a chuckle at the way Nevaeh is staring after her with her mouth agape.

Once she recovers from the shock, she looks at me almost as intently as the head nurse was looking at her. "I don't see what's so funny," she protests as she takes a seat next to me on the cot. There isn't much room, but there's nowhere else to sit. I don't see any empty chairs nearby for her to drag over. I scoot over a little to give her some room, which makes my leg hurt again and stops my laughing.

After a moment, I change my tone to something a bit more understanding and try to be more sympathetic. "What's funny is that she told you what I've been trying to say, albeit not quite in the same way." I get my leg straightened and slightly more comfortable, and the pain subsides a bit. "You need to stop taking care of everyone else and give some attention to yourself."

"I can't do that when there are so many patients who need me," she argues. "It's not fair that her stupid rules are preventing that. Why on earth do I need to be homely to care for people?"

"These are soldiers," I remind her.

"That doesn't matter."

Rather than trying to explain how some of the men can get, I let it be. "Try to relax for once," I tell her. "She won't let you work here, so there's no need to pout about it."

"I'm not pouting," she argues, her eyes narrowing again.

But her mouth is clearly turned down in a pout, and it makes me chuckle again. "You most definitely are pouting." She looks at me with an angry frown, and I decide it's time to change the subject. "Your dress is different."

She looks down at the pale blue gown she's wearing, free of all the blood and muck of the battlefield. "One of the nurses gave me this."

"It suits you," I say. It doesn't hide the fact that she is far from demure, but I decide not to tell her that. "You never finished telling me about your family. What is your father like?" I hope it gets her mind off her inability to help the wounded.

"He's really into history, but it's hard to explain." She looks around, and I can tell she still wants to jump up and help wherever she can.

I don't want her to be ejected from the hospital altogether, so I try to distract her again. "Try to relax, Nevaeh. You're only going to be allowed to help me, and I'm feeling much better, other than a little pain when I move."

"That reminds me," she says, reaching into her pocket. She looks around before pulling out the strange bottle again and pouring two more pills into her hand. "You need to take the last dose."

I take them from her, but I don't have any water to drink them down with. She realizes that, too and jumps to her feet. "I'll get you a drink. I hope they'll at least let me do that."

I chuckle lightly at the exasperated look on her face as she walks away. She's back soon with the water, and I swallow the pills. "What's in these pills anyhow? I seem to be feeling a lot better than these other men, and some have less serious wounds than I do."

She looks around again, but this time it seems she's making sure no one is paying attention. The men who aren't sleeping are all focused on their own pain, and the nurses are too busy to care. She scoots in a little closer. "I have something to tell you, and it's going to seem unbelievable."

"With what I've been through these past few weeks, I doubt you'll shock me." I can't imagine what she's going to tell me.

She looks around again before turning back to me. "I'm from 2025."

My eyebrows shoot up as I try to understand what that means. But I don't follow. "Excuse me?"

I feel her warm breath fan against my cheek as she looks me in the eye and whispers, "I'm from the year 2025–in the future."

I can't help but burst out laughing at the serious look on her face, as if she believes what she's telling me, but that's ludicrous. She can't possibly think I'd believe that–can she?

"I'm not kidding!" She looks around again and continues when she sees no one is paying us any mind. "That's why the pills work. They're antibiotics, and they haven't even been invented yet in 1863. But as you can see, you're feeling better than anyone around you."

I scan the room and can't say she's wrong about that. "You're from the future then?" I'm only half serious, but she certainly seems to be. I wonder whether she's gone mad from all the days and nights of solid work. Or maybe she hit her head harder than I thought she had.

"I can prove it." She scoots in closer and looks around. "Do you remember the light I showed you in the cave, the one I said was a medical device?"

"Yes." I'll never forget how strange I felt holding that thing.

She pulls it out of her pocket, hiding it somewhat in the blanket from my lap so no one else can see it. "It's a telephone, my cell phone, not that it works in this day and time."

"What?" I'm confused. "What in the hell is a telephone?" It sounds sort of like a telegram, but it can't be related to that at all.

"In the future, we use these to communicate." She wiggles it back and forth in front of me. Then, she turns it toward herself and moves her finger across the front of it. When she turns it back around, I see some weird writing in green and gray shapes. "We use them to text more than to actually call and talk. I was texting my dad here. You can read it if you want to. We weren't even in the same town when we sent these messages to one another."

I take a look, but it's making my head hurt. "I don't understand what that is." Some of the words don't even make sense, just several letters strung together. I consider myself a literate man thanks to my father, but I cannot read this.

"There's more," she says, looking around again. She turns it around facing her again and taps on it a few times. "These are my photos." She turns it back to face me. "This is my father at Gettys-burg—in the future. It's a memorial park now. Right there, those are the rocks I slipped off right before you found me."

I hitch a breath when I see the man standing there, clear as if he were standing before me, yet he's on this small device. No photography in the world is that good.

The rocks behind him do look like those I fell next to when I was shot, yet they cannot be. These are covered in greenery with trees nearby, not full of mud and muck. "I don't...."

"This is the apartment I'm moving to—was about to move to–in Philadelphia," she continues, moving the pictures with her finger. "These are cars, and the street is paved, see? I was going to live on the third floor." She taps the device again, and other images appear before she stops on one. "This is me, wearing my doctor's coat from 2025."

My heart thumps as I lose all ability to speak. Before me is an exact replica of Nevaeh in full color, wearing something that looks like pants along with a white jacket. She makes more movements with her fingers, and the image gets closer, focused on something pinned to the jacket. It's her name, followed by some letters, with 'Oncology Physician' written beneath it. I don't know what oncology means, but I know that second word.

She's really a doctor from the future? It can't be.

She looks right into my eyes. "Do you believe me now?"

13

Nᴇᴠᴀᴇʜ

Iᴛ sᴇᴇᴍs ᴛʜᴀᴛ sʜᴏᴡɪɴɢ Sᴀᴍ ᴛʜᴇ ᴘɪᴄᴛᴜʀᴇs ᴏɴ ᴍʏ ᴘʜᴏɴᴇ ʜᴇʟᴘᴇᴅ alleviate some of Sam's doubts, but this is so impossible to believe, I'm not sure what he thinks. I decide to show some more photos so I can convince him completely.

"This is a hospital in Philadelphia from my time," I tell him, showing him the picture I took the day I went to tour the hospital after I landed my job. The parking lot is full of cars, and there's even an ambulance rushing by in the foreground. The hospital is huge and modern, nothing like the buildings Sam has seen so far. I'm sure it's a lot to take in for someone who only knows life in 1863..

Finally, he says something. "I-I'm shocked." His eyes meet mine, and I see realization setting in. "But... how else could you explain it?"

"It took me a while to believe it myself, but you're right. There is no other explanation." He continues to stare at me with a furrowed brow, so I explain. "Those bullets were real. The battle was real, not the reenactment I'd gone to see."

He's still clearly shocked.

"I'll explain from the beginning," I say. "In the future, we have reenactments of the war."

He pulls away from me in disgust. "What? Why would you do such a thing?"

"It's a way for history buffs like my dad to get a visual of what happened there—here." I look around, making sure no one else is listening to us. The nurses are so busy, they don't have a spare second to stop and pay attention to us, so I'm not worried about them. Most of the wounded soldiers are either sleeping or in so much pain I doubt they care what I'm talking about anyway, so I continue. "Every year, they hold reenactments at Civil War battlefields around the country, but my father's favorite battle to study has always been Gettysburg. It's close to home and the most important battle of the war. Now, there's a... museum there, as well as a lot of monuments and memorials. Here." I show him another picture. "This is the visitor's center where people come to learn the history of the battles."

I wonder whether I should tell him about the photo of him on display there, but I decide against it for now. This is already a lot to take in. "I've gone to lots of reenactments with my dad. He's really into them, and I just go with him because I like spending time with him." I flip back to the photo of him standing at Devil's Den. "We were both in costume, which is why my dad is dressed this way. We don't dress like that in 2025. He had a Civil War era suit, and I was wearing that plum colored dress. Dad wanted to get a shot of me up on the rocks wearing it. We were running out of time before the reenactors got there, but he asked me to go pose, so I did. That's when I stepped back too far and slipped off the rocks."

Blinking a few times, I fight back tears, remembering how much fun we had on the drive to Gettysburg. It was supposed to be a perfect day for us.

"I miss him so much," I continue. "And I'm worried about what he's thinking right now, now that I'm missing." Finally, I just stop fighting and let the tears fall. I know Dad must be in a panic. But that other woman came back... if what happened to her is the same as what I'm experiencing. If it is, maybe I can get back, too. I just don't know how to do it.

Sam reaches out and places his hand gently on my shoulder. Blinking back tears, I stare at him in surprise. When I look into his deep brown eyes, I don't see any of the irritation or pain I often see there. Instead, he looks sympathetic. I take a deep breath, noticing how chiseled his jawline is, how perfectly straight his nose is. I exhale with a slight shiver and pull away from him. He looks away, and the moment is lost.

It's just as well. I can't stay here. I need to get back to Dad. I'm all he's got.

I clear my throat and lean further away, discreetly tucking my phone back into my dress pocket. I don't think anyone else saw it. "My dad must be so scared that he can't find me. I would have been right in front of him, then I fell back and from his perspective, I disappeared. He might think someone kidnapped me or something. I don't know what to do."

"I'm sure he's frightened, but I'm guessing he would be proud to find out how well you've handled the situation," Sam says softly, wiping a stray tear off my cheek. The touch of his fingers sends a shiver through me I wasn't anticipating. I try to ignore it. "You've been completely selfless since you first got here, only looking after others nonstop for days. I'm sure you'll find your way back to him, and when you do, he will be unbelievably proud of you."

Looking in Sam's eyes again, I realize that right now, I'm not being that selfless person he's describing. It's hardly the time for me to bother him with my problems. He's been shot, almost lost his leg, and these other men have actually lost limbs and nearly their lives fighting a real war. They didn't come here to just watch playacting as my father and I had the luxury to do. They risked their lives to serve their country when its leaders asked them to.

"You're probably right." I inhale deeply again, pushing my emotions aside the same way I would in a medical emergency. "That's enough about me," I add, wiping away the rest of my tears. "You're the one who's hurt. I'll make sure you're taken care of. What do you need?"

"To go back to my company," he says without hesitation.

"Go back?" Startled, I tip my face down and stare up at him in disbelief.

"Yes," he affirms. "I need to go help everyone who's left. We've got the upper hand. We need to continue the work."

I let out a long sigh. "Well, you're not going back anytime soon, if at all."

That irritated look is back in full force. "But I want to go back," he insists. "I can help my company."

"When is your enlistment up?" I ask him.

"At the end of August."

"Well, that's just a couple of months." I straighten out the blanket I'd messed up trying to hide my cell phone while I was showing it to him. "They'll probably just keep you out till your term ends."

He shakes his head emphatically. "No. I want to go back."

"Why, Sam?" I shake my head right back at him. It's ridiculous for him to go back with an injured leg. He won't be as effective as he was before, which will be aggravating to him. I don't understand what he thinks he's going to do. "You've already served and gotten shot in the line of duty."

He seems to ignore the truth, but he furrows his brow even deeper than before. "Tell me what happens next."

I let out a light gasp, a little taken aback by his direct demand. I haven't even thought about what to say if he asked me about the war's outcome, or anything else that's going to happen between 1863 and my time. *Can I do that? Isn't that messing with the space-time continuum, or is that just something they made up for the movies?*

I really don't know, and I spend a few moments going back and forth over this in my mind. Sam is just one man. *What harm could telling him do?* He can't just go up to someone and say, "Hey, I know a woman from the future, and she says blah blah blah will happen." They'd think he was crazy, and no one would listen to him. The only reason I have proof of the future is because of my phone, which will go dead with no hope of charging it if I keep turning it on.

On the other hand, he could try to do something that changes history without talking to anyone. What if someone dies who shouldn't have, or someone lives who should have died? That would affect entire families who would or wouldn't exist based on whether they make it past the war.

It's so much to think about. And I've probably already done something to save someone who wasn't supposed to live. What will that change?

"Tell me," he says again, his voice firm.

I nod softly and lower my voice. "Gettysburg will be the turning point," I explain. "Throughout the next couple of years, there are so many battles I can't remember them all. Some of the major ones include the Battle of Chickamauga in September. The Confederates win that one. Then there are two big battles in November—Lookout Mountain and Missionary Ridge. The Union wins both of those. They're all in the Western Theater. Here, there will be a huge battle at Petersburg, including a siege."

Scanning the room again, I see there's still no one paying attention. I'm not sure how much I can tell him, but there are so many battles I can't be precise anyway. "There will be some major battles in Virginia next year that are inconclusive. There are several more in Georgia, Tennessee, the Carolinas, and Virginia throughout the next year. Some the Union wins, some the Confederates win. The Union does win the war in the end. It will finally be over in April 1865 when Lee surrenders to Grant, though there is still some fighting through June in other parts of the country."

I can see the weariness in his eyes as he realizes how much longer these battles will go on. After experiencing the field hospitals at Gettysburg, I can understand why two more years feels like an eternity to him. I wish I could change everything and just end this whole war, but there's nothing any one person can do.

After a few seconds, his eyes brighten. "Thank God we prevail," he says. "And that means there is still time for me to reenlist and be a part of the victory."

I don't understand why he still insists on going back to fight. Granted, his leg will recover faster than others due to the antibiotics, but I can't believe he wants to put himself in harm's way again. Maybe I shouldn't have told him about the Union victory. "You need to let your leg heal. Why would you go stand in front of bullets again when you know how it feels to be injured? If I weren't there, you would have lost your leg. Is that what you want?"

"What I want is to fight for my country with honor." He says this with such conviction in his eyes that I don't know how to respond.

This man is impossible.

"I can't wait to see what Lincoln does in his second term."

His words stop me cold, and I can feel my eyes widen in alarm.

"What is it?" he asks.

I can't tell him about Lincoln. Can I? While I wish I could do something to save Lincoln while I'm here, the ramifications would be beyond comprehension. While I truly have no idea why I'm here, I'm almost certain it's not to save Abraham Lincoln.

"Nevaeh? What is it you are not telling me?" Sam insists.

I can see the impatience mixed with worry in his eyes, but I'm still not sure I should tell him. He certainly couldn't end an entire war single handedly, as much as I would like that to happen. But the Lincoln assassination is an isolated event. He might be able to show up at Ford's Theater and warn the president, changing history forever. *How would that change the future of our country?*

"Nevaeh...?"

"Okay," I say quietly, leaning in more, though we're already pretty close. I definitely don't want anyone else to hear this. "Lincoln will be assassinated."

"What?" His reaction is loud, but he quiets down and whispers, "When?"

"Lee surrenders on April 9, 1865," I explain. "Lincoln will be shot on April 15 that same year."

He shakes his head, his eyes filling with anger. "That cannot happen."

"I don't think we can stop it," I argue. "I don't want it to happen, either." *How can I explain to him that everything I do here might change the future?*

"That is something that must be stopped," he insists. "Nevaeh, you need to tell me every detail of the event so we can stop it from happening."

14

Sᴀᴍ

I ᴍᴜsᴛ ʙᴇ ᴏᴜᴛ ᴏꜰ ᴍʏ ᴍɪɴᴅ ᴛᴏ ʙᴇʟɪᴇᴠᴇ ᴛʜᴀᴛ Nᴇᴠᴀᴇʜ ɪs ꜰʀᴏᴍ ᴛʜᴇ future, but these pictures on her device that she calls a phone are unmistakable. They're so clear, in full color, it's as though the people are right there in front of me, just on a smaller scale. I've never seen anything like it.

I cannot wrap my mind around the strange wagons they have in these images, and the buildings look as though they're from another world. I can't think of a way these images could be created other than being true pictures from the future, and the idea is unsettling, to say the least.

But what she has told me about the war—that concerns me more than any strange images. Though I feel joy knowing the Union will prevail in this war, my heart froze when Nevaeh said Lincoln will be killed. His leadership means everything to the fighting men of the Union, and I can't imagine what will happen without him. She did say that Lee surrenders before that happens, but rebuilding the country after this is over won't be the same without Lincoln here.

Still, Nevaeh shakes her head when I ask her to stop it from happening. "But Sam, we can't stop it."

"I don't understand," I tell her. I lower my voice, though no one seems to be paying particular attention to us. Still, if they overheard us, they'd think us insane... or perhaps traitors to speak of Lincoln's death. "To lose him would be devastating to our country."

"I agree," she says, looking around. She's as concerned about others overhearing as I am. "But whatever I do here could have catastrophic implications for the future. One change can mean that a person living in the future might not be there, or someone could be there who isn't meant to be, and those differences could change the future forever. This could affect whole families... so many lives."

"But in this case, only one man lives," I argue. "Why would that be a problem?"

She shrugs, her eyes weary. "I don't know if it is or not. That's the risk. It's impossible to predict how one thing will change the course of the future. But with him, there is potential for lots of outcomes to change. He is revered as one of the most influential presidents in history, in my time, and him living instead of dying at the hand of an assassin will most certainly have ramifications we can't predict. As much as I'd like to save his life, I'm afraid it's too much of a risk."

She doesn't seem to understand what I'm telling her. "Lincoln holds the perfect vision for our nation's future. How could saving him possibly make the situation worse?'

Nevaeh lets out a soft sigh of frustration. "Sam, I want him to live too. The Civil War is one of the most important events in American history., It's true that Lincoln could implement many changes that will improve the future of our country.. But we don't know that for sure. The future could also turn out much worse. Just one pivotal moment, one person who lives or dies when they weren't supposed to could change everything."

I consider this for a moment. It's logical, yet still, Lincoln's death is impossible to accept. "Yet you are here. What purpose does that serve? Is there something you must do here?"

Shrugging, she admits, "I don't know. I've been trying to figure that out since I realized what happened."

"Perhaps you are here to save President Lincoln," I suggest, hoping it's true.

"I don't think so." She looks around again. Still, nobody seems to care about our discussion. Most of the injured men are asleep or in the throes of pain. Leaning in closer, she lowers her voice. "I saw a photograph of you before I fell. I think I'm here because of you."

My heart flutters, surprising me. I pause for a moment and then ask, "My photograph?"

"Yes." She continues to whisper. "Well, as I explained, Gettysburg is a memorial park now. It has a visitor's center building there with photos and artifacts. I saw you in one of those photos."

I shake my head. "But I haven't been photographed, certainly not on the battlefield, and that battle is over."

"I know," she says. "I've been wondering about that myself. I'm not sure what it means, but I think I'm supposed to be here for you for some reason."

Another pleasant ripple murmurs in my heart. What is it I'm feeling for this feisty woman from the future? I try to dismiss the thought. "You did save my life."

She shrugs. "Maybe that was it.

"Or, perhaps it was one of the others you helped," I suggest. "Perhaps it's all of us. You worked tirelessly for days."

"I don't know," she admits, biting her lower lip.

Headstrong as she is, Nevaeh is kind and caring, and she puts herself before others without anyone asking her to help. In fact, from what I witnessed of her confrontation with the head nurse here, she has fought to continue to stay here and help the wounded however she can when she could've walked away.

"Still, I just can't help but believe that seeing your picture was important," she adds.

I chuckle lightly. "I hardly think I'm worthy of a trip back in time."

"You most definitely are."

Our eyes meet for a moment, and a pleasant tingle runs up my spine. Her blue eyes, though weary from days without proper sleep and food, soften and sparkle, and I soak in her beauty for a moment. Every contour of her face is soft and lovely, her blonde hair the color of butter, with delicate tendrils that have fallen out of her high bun now framing her face.

I clear my throat and break the gaze before I make a fool of myself. As I look around the room trying to collect my thoughts before I dare look at Nevaeh again, I catch sight of a woman sitting with another wounded soldier. He's dictating a letter to her. This is an opportunity to change the subject and give Nevaeh something to do.

"I'd like to inform my family about my whereabouts," I say. "They're no doubt concerned if they've received news of the battle."

Her eyes are wide when I meet them again. "Of course." She puts her hand on the pocket that holds her device but then pulls it away, giggling. "I guess my habits are stuck in the twenty-first century. Obviously, I can't call them on my phone. I suppose you'd need to write a letter, right?"

"Yes," I confirm, smiling at the pleasant tinkle of her laughter. It's a sound I haven't heard much of since we met, but I like it.

"There must be some paper and a writing utensil here somewhere." She looks around. "I'll be right back."

"Thank you." I watch the flow of her skirt as she walks away. I've never met a woman quite like her, which I suppose is why I believe that she came from the future. Women are commonly doctors there, apparently, and Nevaeh certainly shows that authority in her actions and speech. It's quite unexpected, but I like it. She truly cares about people and doesn't miss an opportunity to help when she can.

Perhaps the reaction I'm having is just a natural reaction. She saved my life and the lives of many others. She's a beautiful and impressive woman. I push away those thoughts as she approaches again with paper, pen, and an inkwell in hand.

"I didn't think about this," she says with a smile as she sits on the edge of my cot again. "I've never written with an inkwell or this kind of pen, so I might need some practice to make it legible."

"You have no pens in the future?" I whisper.

She chuckles, and the smile meets her eyes. "Of course we do. But the ink is inside of them, and it rolls on a little ball." She looks at me and no doubt catches the confusion on my face. "I guess it's surprisingly hard to explain. But we don't have to dip the nub in ink. Anyway, I'll start with the envelope. What is your father's name again? How do I address this?"

"Simply write Mr. Edward Walker, Augusta, Maine."

She nods as she gently dips the pen into the inkwell and begins writing on the envelope, and it's obvious she doesn't need any practice. "This is fun," she says, smiling. "The ink flows beautifully. Okay, that's the envelope. Let's start the letter."

I nod. "Dear Father," I begin, and she writes as I speak slowly. "I am writing to let you know I am well. I was wounded in the battle at Gettysburg, Pennsylvania, but I've been receiving the best of care."

Nevaeh looks up and smiles, finishing the sentence before I continue. "I am in the hospital in Philadelphia. I miss you and the rest of the family." I pause for a moment. "Hmm. I haven't considered what else I should say to him."

She looks up, her lips pressed together, her eyes lifted slightly to the ceiling, trying to help me come up with another sentence or two. "Should you tell him where you were wounded?"

"I suppose I could. Just say, 'I was wounded in the leg, but I'm recovering nicely.'"

She nods and writes that down before adding, "Maybe ask him something about home?" She asks, "Your father is a banker, right?"

"He is," I confirm. "All right, please add this. 'I hope things are going well with the bank. I know the Union appreciated the financial donation you made to the war effort. No doubt it contributed to our victory in battle at Gettysburg.'"

Nevaeh continues writing, that pleasant smile back on her face, and I wait a moment until she has caught up before I continue again. "'Have you hired the new housekeeper you mentioned in your last letter yet? I hope all is well at home. Please give my love to Clara. I pray she won't worry long before hearing from George.'" I give Nevaeh a moment to catch up again. "'Please tell her his division was quite heroic in battle. I have heard from others that we would have been flanked had they not held the line. Is Clara still making quilts with the other ladies? I know the soldiers will kindly appreciate such comforts. My love and regards, Samuel.'"

Nevaeh looks up when she has finished. "That's a sweet letter," she says. "I'm sure your family has been very worried."

"I do hope it brings them comfort." I pause for a moment, wondering if there is anything else I want to tell my father, but I don't believe there is more to say. "Oh, and mark it as a soldier's letter," I suggest. "That won't require postage. Include my name, rank, and division."

She nods. "Got it. The nurse who gave me the paper said there's a post office a few blocks down the street. Before I leave, can I get you anything? Are you hungry?"

"You've done so much," I say. "I can hardly ask for more."

"But your water is almost empty." She picks up the glass the nurse left on the table earlier. "I'll refill this at least."

I chuckle lightly as she hurries away with the glass, knowing there is no use in arguing with her. I'm not surprised when she returns with not only the full glass but an apple.

"I'm not sure how long this will take, so I don't want you to be hungry while I'm gone." She sets them on the small table next to me.

"Thank you," I say. "I'm sure I'll be fine until you return."

"All right." Her eyes hold mine for a second before they drift down my body. I know she's just looking to make sure I'm well, but it makes that tingle shoot back down my spine. When she's looking at my face again, satisfied I'm not bleeding or on the verge of death again, she adds, "I'll be back soon."

I nod as she walks off, once again watching the flow of her skirt as she leaves the room. I don't know what it is about this woman from the future, but that light flutter returns to my heart as she disappears from sight.

15

NEVAEH

IT'S SO SURREAL, WALKING THROUGH PHILADELPHIA IN 1863. I'VE BEEN on this street before in my time, but not often. This hospital no longer exists in 2025. In fact, it was shut down after the Civil War. But still, I've been in this area enough in my time that I think I recognize a couple of these buildings nearby. They look similar to their appearance in the future, though it's clear they've been remodeled at some point.

Though there are many people out and about, the lack of cars and trucks make it relatively quiet here, so much so, it doesn't seem like a big city. Instead, horse-drawn wagons meander down the dirt road, and a few people ride in on horses. Most others stroll down the wooden sidewalks. Women wear gowns like the one I have on in a rainbow of somewhat muted colors, though a few of them are a rich burgundy or royal blue. Men are primarily dressed in black or brown. Some people look worried and care-worn from the war, while others are carefree. I can't imagine what it must feel like to live in a country that is half torn apart by civil war.

The irony of all of this is so strange. I was supposed to be reporting to a Philadelphia hospital. This just isn't quite what I had in mind.

After several blocks, I reach the post office, which I wasn't expecting to be so big in 1863. It's a large square building with ornate windows and edge trim at the top. I can't remember whether it's still standing in 2025, or if it's still a post office, but I hope it is. If I ever get back, it would be interesting to visit it someday.

Stepping inside, I see several people mulling around, including many soldiers. I'm not sure whether I'm supposed to put the letter in a slot or hand it to someone, so I step up to the counter. After a few other people are helped, it's my turn.

"Can I help you, miss?" The middle-aged man behind the counter is dressed very well, his slick black suit perfectly tailored to fit.

"Yes, I need to mail this for a soldier who is in the hospital," I explain.

"He's recovering well, I hope." His mouth turns up at one corner in a sympathetic smile.

"Yes, he is" I assure him.

"Good. That battle took too many of our young men." He takes the letter from me, and I thank him before turning to leave, pausing to scan the intricate architectural details of this beautiful building.

As I step out onto the street, it occurs to me that I can take a picture on my phone if I turn it on and off quickly and somehow keep it hidden. It's tempting. Will I ever be back home to show it to anyone? Who would I show it to even if I did make it back? Shaking my head, I decide against it. This street is full of people who may notice if I took out a sleek, futuristic item and started waving it around.

Yeah, that's a horrible idea.

So, I keep it in my pocket and try to burn all these images into memory as I head back to the hospital. It's an amazing opportunity, experiencing such an important time in history. My dad will be jealous when I get back... if I ever do.

I hear the shouts echoing through the hospital before I even get back inside. When I do, I realize it's a doctor barking orders at somebody in an exam room. Despite my need to avoid Nurse Strawn, who will kick me out of here if I don't keep my nose out of the hospital's business, I head straight toward the yelling.

It's a gory scene. The wounded man lies on a table, bleeding profusely from his hip while nurses frantically hand the doctor whatever device he screams for them to give him. I can see the stitches from here, so I know he's already removed the bullet, but the blood keeps pouring out regardless. Since there hasn't been a battle nearby, I have to imagine this patient has arrived here recently and either took a turn for the worse or the doctor has decided further surgery is required—and it's not going well.

"Give me the sutures so I can sew him up!" the doctor shouts. "It won't stop gushing blood until I sew the wound closed!"

I can't just stand here. "That's not the problem," I call out as I weave my way through the nurses.

"What the—" The doctor turns and fixes me with a glare. "Who the hell are you?"

"It doesn't matter who I am at the moment," I assure him, rising up on my tiptoes a bit so I can look him in the eyes as I use my strictest physician's voice. "You clearly missed closing a vein in this man's hip, and if you don't close it, he'll die of internal bleeding regardless of whether or not you close the exterior wound!"

He continues to look at me, his mouth moving, but I'm not listening. Turning to the nurse holding the thread for suturing, I hold out my palm. "Give them to me. Now!"

She blinks twice, and then looks up at the doctor. I rip the materials I need out of her hand and turn back toward the injured soldier. Thankfully, he's unconscious.

"Just what the hell do you think you're doing?" The doctor presses in against me as I begin to dig in the wound for the vein the blood is pouring from. "Get the hell out of my operating room!"

I ignore him since he's not yet physically trying to push me aside. He's clearly exhausted, which may be why he missed the vein to begin with. "I need a sterile rag," I say to the nurse, "and disinfectant, stat!"

Her eyebrows raise, and I realize she probably doesn't know the term "stat," but I say it with enough authority that she knows what I mean and hurries to hand me what I've requested.

Using the rag to clear away blood, and still ignoring the doctor yelling at me, I finally catch sight of the damaged blood vessel. It's small, but it's ripped bad enough that it needs to be cauterized. "Here it is. I need the hot iron." At this, the doctor quiets down, and the nurse quickly hands me the tool. It's not a very precise instrument, but I manage to use the tip of it to seal up the rupture. I get it stitched up in seconds, and the repair holds.

Satisfied with my work, I take a step back, wishing I had gloves to take off to remove all the blood coating my fingernails. Instead, I'll have to scrub the stains away–again.

"Who are you, and what the hell do you think you're doing here?" the doctor demands.

I turn to face him, not backing down. I've done enough to get myself kicked out now anyway. "I'm Dr. Little, and just saved your patient's life!"

His eyes widen, and an even more arrogant air settles on his face. A deep chuckle emanates from his throat. His reaction doesn't surprise me. Male doctors in 2025 hardly know how to react to being bested by female doctors, let alone in 1863. Belittling is usually their first tactic. "Doctor?" he asks sarcastically. "You expect me to believe that you're a doctor?"

I glance back at the patient before meeting his eye again. "How else would I have been able to do what I just did?" His eyes narrow into slits, and I know I'm not helping my situation, but I'm too invested now. Before he can yell again, I ask, "Haven't you heard of Dr. Elizabeth Blackwell or Dr. Rebecca Lee Crumpler?"

He folds his arms across his chest. "I have, but women doctors are rare, Dr. Little." His tone is dripping with sarcasm, "I'm Dr. Benjamin Lynn, and I'm in charge here. If you ever interfere with my patients again, I'll throw you right out of here!"

"She won't be bothering you again, Doctor." The stern, familiar voice rings out behind me, and I feel the tight squeeze of Nurse

Strawn's hand wrapped around my arm as she drags me out of the room. She says nothing until we're two rooms away, when she spins me around and lays into me. "That is our best surgeon! He's the head doctor in charge of this entire hospital! Where do you get off telling him what to do?"

Looking her directly in the eyes, I reply, "I saved that man's life."

"You interfered! I have no doubt, Dr. Lynn had the situation fully under his control," she insists. "You have no right interfering with the doctor's work. Either you remain by your brother's side and don't move, or I'll throw you out of her personally with a swift kick!"

I decide it's best not to say anything else so Sam doesn't end up getting the brunt of her anger, and she pulls me back down the hall and over to Sam's bedside. "I'll thank you to keep your sister in check!" she shouts at him before storming out of the room.

"Um… Nevaeh?" he asks, his eyes wide. "Are you all right?" He glances down at the blood coating my hands.

I'm so angry, I don't know how to answer. My hands are steady as always, but I feel the tingles of frustration in my nerves, and I'm about one second away from letting tears fall, but I hold them back.

"What happened?" he asks, his voice softening.

I take a deep breath. "There was a man bleeding out on the table. I knew what was wrong with him, and I had to step in. I saved his life. Apparently, that was the head surgeon, and he's… not happy with me."

"I see," he says. I think I see a hint of humor in the way his mouth lifts at one corner. "I suppose you shouldn't have done that."

I close my eyes for a second and inhale, trying to calm the frustration. When I open them again, Sam is fully smiling.

"And I'm so proud of you."

"What?" I stare at him for a moment, not sure what he means.

His grin grows wider, and I'm about to say something when I feel a sheepish tap on my shoulder. Turning around, I see one of the nurses who has been going back and forth with patients all day. "Miss?"

"Yes?"

"I saw what you did in there, and I'm wondering—" She pauses, looking around, then lowers her voice to a whisper. "Can you follow me please?"

I look at Sam, whose grin has melted, his brow furrowed. "I'll be right back," I tell him.

The woman leads me back to another room where a wounded soldier is holding his leg and moaning in pain. "I can't get the bleeding to stop," she explains quietly. "The doctor is too busy, and since you helped...."

She trails off because I'm already examining the soldier. "This is rushed," I say, "much like with the other man. He's probably left something open." I turn to the nurse. "Can you get me supplies without anyone noticing?"

"I-I think so." I can tell she's equally worried about her job and this man's condition.

"I'll need to cauterize it," I add. "Is a hot iron something you can get me?"

She nods. "Yes, we have several of those. I can sneak one away for a few minutes and pretend I misplaced it."

"Good." I hold the man's wound firmly as he continues to moan. "I'll need disinfectant, clean cloths, some anesthesia if you can manage it, and sutures as well."

"Right away, Doctor." She says the last word almost imperceptibly before she runs off. While she's away, I go to the nearest sink to wash my hands so as not to contaminate this man with the other soldier's blood.

She's back quickly, and I get the man's wound cleaned, properly cauterized, and restitched. The bleeding stops.

"Can you get it bandaged up?" I ask.

She nods enthusiastically. "Yes, of course. Thank you so much."

"You're very welcome, and he should heal well now," I tell her. "Be sure not to touch the wound. Keep it sterile. There are germs we can't see with the human eye that cause infection." I know that sterilization practices aren't standard yet in 1863, so I've had to explain this to many of the nurses in the field hospital. I imagine most of these women never got proper medical training since they're just expected to do whatever the doctor tells them to. They'd have no reason to understand germs either.

"Yes, Doctor," she answers, getting started on the bandage.

"And you'll want to wash your hands as often as possible," I add, "especially between patients. That way, you're not spreading the germs around."

She's barely finished when another nurse comes up to me. "Can you take a look at someone else for me, please?" Petite with bright blonde hair, this woman is almost "too pretty" to be a nurse, so I wonder if she happens to be married.

"Of course." I glance around for Nurse Strawn. Not seeing her anywhere, I wash my hands and then make my way out of that room and down the hall with the nurse. She leads me to where another man is struggling in much the same way as the others.

I think I've discovered how I'm going to help these people, and to do that, I need to stop acting like I'm an attending oncology physician in 2025 and just do the work under the radar.

"All right, let's take a look." I manage a smile for the poor man who's grimacing against the pain. I unwrap the bandage and take a look at my next challenge, determined to keep helping all these wounded soldiers as best as I can—in secret.

16

"WALKER!" SMITH CALLS FOR ME AS THE REBS ADVANCE.

The gunfire is relentless, and everything in front of me is a blur. "Reloading!" I tell him, hoping he hears me. It's a struggle to get the cartridge in with shaky fingers as bullets fly all around me. Finally, I get it loaded and pound the ramrod as fast as I can so I can get another shot off at the advancing Rebs.

Suddenly, Smith is right beside me. "The Goddamn Rebs are trying to flank us. See the ones crawling up the rocks over there?"

I look, but it's impossible for me to see anything from this angle. My nerves rattle as cannon fire erupts, adding to the uproar that seems to be coming from all around me.

"There, Walker!" He's close enough that I can follow where he's pointing, but all I see is dust and smoke. I shoot into it anyway, emptying my cartridge and fumbling to find another to reload and do it again.

"You got one!" he hollers. "I hit the one next to him. We're holding them back!"

We're both frantically reloading as the gun and cannon fire continues relentlessly. This time, I can see where I'm firing because the Rebs are uncomfortably close. If we don't continue to pour shot into them, they're going to overtake us. Smith and I reload and fire again, continuing to keep up the pace the best we can.

I turn to him in the middle of reloading and see him doing the same. "We've got this, Walker!" he cries, that wicked grin he often gets in the heat of battle twisting his face into a fearsome grimace. Smith always gets excited when he has a chance to kill some Rebs.

I nod, feeling the same energy, but the second I do, Smith is hit with a barrage of gunfire as though he is the only target on the battlefield. His body explodes before my eyes, and what's left of him flies off several yards, landing in a splatter of blood and muck.

As my mind reels from the sight, gunfire rains all around me from every direction. I can't even stand to finish reloading my rifle, so I kneel to the ground, holding, searching fervently for what's left of Smith's body and praying that he's still alive—somehow.

"Sam!"

The voice echoes from miles away. I look around, but all I see is a line of Rebs barreling for me. I'm a goner, too.

"Sam, wake up."

My eyes fly open, my heart pounding against my rib cage. I'm not on the battlefield anymore, and Nevaeh's warm blue eyes gaze at me in concern. "You had a bad dream," she says softly.

I nod and swipe a hand over my sweaty brow. My heart continues to pound violently. Instinctively, I clutch a hand to my chest.

"Take some deep breaths," she says, her voice still calm and soothing. "Like this. Inhale… one, two, three, four. Now hold it. Okay, now exhale slowly… one, two, three… that's it. Do it again. Inhale…."

She talks me through this strange type of breathing, and I truly feel my heart calming, though it's still beating harder and faster than normal. Nevaeh comes into focus as my eyes adjust to the light. She's sitting in the chair beside my cot, her face practically glowing in the dim light.

Suddenly, I'm embarrassed. "Did I say anything?" I look around, not wanting any of the other men to know I'd called out in fear.

"No," she assures me. "You were just tossing back and forth. No one saw you or heard you. They're all asleep as well."

This is a tone I've rarely heard from her. She sounds nothing like the tough, assertive doctor who has been storming into exam rooms pushing incompetent doctors aside. Now, she's relaxed and tranquil, and it's easy to feel the same, though the images still race through my mind—the Rebs approaching quickly, the bullets flying over my head, Smith's body exploding before my eyes. I shake my head, but none of it clears.

"It was so real," I say. "Smith was blown to smithereens right in front of me. The bullets were everywhere. The cannon fire was so loud."

She nods, patting me softly on my good leg as soothing tingles of warmth wash over me. This nurturing side of her I have only had a glimpse of before. I understand why she must be brash and matter-of-fact when handling emergency situations. But this is a much different Navaeh, and I quite like the feel of her hand on my leg.

"You've been through some serious trauma," she whispers. "You will continue to have reactions like this one, but there are techniques we can use to lessen those feelings. For now, just try to relax and breathe. It was just a dream. You're no longer in danger."

I swallow hard, getting lost in those bright eyes of hers. I try to blink the feelings I'm suddenly aware of away, but it's difficult. Nevaeh is a beautiful woman. She saved my life. She believes she may have come back to 1863 solely for me. Is it possible that, when she looks at me, her heart beats erratically, too?

No, that's ridiculous.

This is a woman from the future, and I need to help her get back there, back to her father where she belongs. I can't act like a schoolboy and fall for her now.

Nevaeh timidly slides from her chair onto my cot, sitting next to my hip. Through the thin blanket, I feel her warmth. I take a deep breath as the familiar tingling sensation races through my veins. I can't pull my eyes away from hers, and as her hand grazes my cheek, I lean into her touch.

Fingertips brush the hair off my forehead, and as she leans closer to me, the intoxicating scent of wildflowers washes over me. Her lips press against my forehead in a kiss I can't define. I know she cares for me. She wouldn't have gone to so much trouble to be here with me if that weren't the case. But is it possible that lingering kiss means more than I could hope for?

A gentleman would back away. I should protest, tell her she shouldn't be sitting so close to me, that she shouldn't be stroking my cheek or caressing my cheek. Bound to my cot, I have no means of retreat, and when I open my mouth to protest, nothing comes out but a longing sigh.

Her angelic face hovers over mine, so close I can feel her warm breath, catch the scent of mint with each exhale. I bite down on my bottom lip as I can't help but debate whether or not she'd welcome me pressing my mouth to hers.

But that's absurd. She's from the future. She doesn't belong here—she doesn't belong with me. And it's insane for me to even consider the possibility of trying to hold onto her. It would be just as viable for me to attempt to catch the wind in the palm of my hand.

Navaeh straightens a bit and withdraws her hand, hesitating slightly before she places it in her lap. I wonder if she's regretting her actions or simply overthinking them.

"I think I should try to go back to sleep," I manage to whisper. "I'm still very tired."

"Okay," she says, nodding lightly. "Try to get some rest. You need that to heal. I'm going to go check on a few other patients, but I'll be back soon. If you have another bad dream, I'll wake you."

"Thank you," is all I can say.

Giving me another smile, she stands and walks away, but before she's two cots away, she's looking at me over her shoulder. Then, she glides gracefully through the narrow walkway lined with cots toward the exit. The moment she disappears from sight, my heart drops, and a longing settles into my chest like nothing I've ever experienced before.

It's preposterous for me to think about her this way.

Closing my eyes tightly, I call to mind all of the things she's told me about the future. I still feel uneasy about that device she uses, and my mind can't wrap around how vivid the photographs are that she's shown me. I think about the hospital where she's supposed to work. When she talks about her assignment there, I see energy and excitement in her eyes. Staying here would take that away from her, and that is something I cannot do. I can't ask her to stay here with me when she has a life with her father in the future.

Why am I thinking this way? She has nothing but platonic feelings for me. I need to stop letting myself imagine a possibility of the two of us developing romantic intentions for one another.

I believe her parents named her properly, though. Nevaeh is Heaven spelled backward–and that's what I'm beginning to feel whenever I'm in her presence. Her angelic smile, the warmth of her touch, her calming scent, all of it seems to be sent from up above.

No matter how hard I try to think about another topic, I can't seem to stop thinking about her.

Squeezing my eyes closed even tighter, I reach for sleep. My body and mind are exhausted. I should easily be able to slip off into bliss again. The soldiers all around me are deeply engrossed in their own dreams… or nightmares, as the case may be.

Images from my dream return, and my eyes fly open again. Do I dare to drift off again? I picture Smith's grinning face in my mind– and then see the blood and gore as his body explodes right before my eyes.

But, I realize, that wasn't real. I didn't see Smith get shot, and he didn't explode in a hail of gunfire as I pictured in my dream. I saw him lying there in the pool of blood, but it was just a single shot that killed him. My imagination has taken control, even in my dreams, making a gruesome experience even more revolting.

I shake it off and close my eyes again, and all I see is Nevaeh's pleasant smile, her soft blue eyes gazing at me warmly, beautiful golden ringlets framing her beautiful face.

Smiling, I drift off, still feeling her warmth and comfort.

I'm on the battlefield again, and my muscles tighten. Smith isn't around. He must be somewhere on the other side of our line. The Rebs are far away. I'm back at the beginning of the battle.

"Men, their approach has begun!" my commander shouts. "We fight here for the future of our country, for our families, for the families we will have when this war is over. The Rebels think they can claim our land, but they cannot! We must show them here and now that their time of resistance is over, and that the rule of law in our Union is strong!"

"Union strong!" I shout back along with all the other men in my company.

I think I hear Smith's voice in the distance, but it's muted by the shouts of the others. The commander continues his speech, stirring us into a fever of excitement and bravery.

Yet, underneath my enthusiastic cries, fear rears its ugly head. I see Smith's body exploding into nothing beside me. I stiffen as the explosion of gunfire begins, though it is still far away and seems aimless. Cannon fire follows, loud and frightening, and it's clear the devil himself has arrived in Gettysburg in the form of a Rebel soldier.

The Rebs come closer, chewing up the ground between us. Like the others, I raise my rifle and shot as quickly as I can. Smoke and dust fills the air, making it difficult to see. They're getting closer, and we can't seem to hold them off. I duck behind a large boulder, but even here, I won't be safe. I know in my bones I'm about to be shot.

Aiming another round at the closest Reb, I catch sight of something else out of the corner of my eye. Though I know I shouldn't look away from the enemy, I turn my head a fraction anyway.

A silver mist hovers in the center of the battlefield. It's nothing but a cloudy form at first, but then, as I watch, it takes shape. A woman's body comes into view. Dressed all in glistening white, a halo of golden light surrounds her blonde hair. She glides across the battlefield, cutting through the violence untouched—like an angel in flight.

"Nevaeh." My mouth forms her name effortlessly, like she's always been tucked away inside my heart.

As she grows closer, I see the warm smile on her face, and all the fear I've been experiencing since the battle began—since the war broke out—melts away. Even from this distance I can see her soft blue eyes, soothing and relaxed. The battlefield is nothing but another empty field of wildflowers. The Rebs are a kaleidoscope of butterflies.

Sounds of battle disappear. The battlefield fades from view as I am enveloped by her glowing white light. Nevaeh reaches for me, her hand cupping my cheek, and when her soft lips grace my forehead, I know what Heaven truly is.

17

Nevaeh

I wait for Louise, one of the nurses I've been working with to secretly see patients, to give me the signal that Nurse Strawn is busy, then I sneak into the room with the wounded soldier who needs help.

"Let's take a look."

He tries to smile, but I can see he's in too much pain. His wound is swollen, covered in white pus, with streaks of black around the edges. Unfortunately, this is just one of several I've seen in the same condition. I try to give him a reassuring look, but it's difficult. I can help, but without antibiotics, it'll be up to his body to fight this off–and that's not likely in his weekend state.

"Am I going to be all right, miss?" he asks, his voice weak.

I conjure a reassuring smile I hope doesn't look as fake as it feels. "Of course you are." I pat his hand. "We're just going to clean this up a bit. You'll be feeling better soon."

As I clean the wound properly with disinfectant, I whisper to Lois and a few other nurses that have congregated nearby about the importance of what I'm doing. "I know it's difficult to imagine, but there are all sorts of germs crawling on everything we touch. We have to do our best to kill them off to keep them from causing infections like this one." I use the strongest astringent I can to clean the wound and tidy up the stitches before rewrapping his injured leg.

As I work, my mind returns to Sam. Pressing my lips to his forehead earlier may have been a mistake, but in the moment, it felt... right. When I pulled back, I thought I saw something in his eyes. The two of us have been at one another's throats off and on since I got here, but we have also saved one another's lives. Could it be that we are beginning to develop other feelings toward one another? Deeper feelings?

"I think it's good now, miss."

"What?" I look up to see the soldier I've been treating smiling at me, then glance at his leg. "Oh. Sorry." I'd kept unrolling the bandage mindlessly, and it's a bit overdone. I snip it off and tie it closed. "This should heal well now," I tell him, and I hope it's the truth.

"Thank you." His smile is weak, his eyes glassy with fever. "You know, there are so many of us here, we don't all get to see the doc much."

I want to assure him that he just saw a real doctor, but I don't want to stir up trouble again. "I do what I can to help. You just get some rest and let your body heal."

"Yes, ma'am."

I pat his hand and stand, stretching my arms up over my head. The only sleep I've gotten recently was interrupted by Sam's nightmare. I'd dozed off in the chair next to his bed only a few minutes before he started to thrash around. I need sleep–but there's just so much to do.

The least I can do is pour myself a drink of water. The pitcher kept in one corner of the room is warm, but it'll do. I drink it down and then refill, swallowing that down, too, before I turn and survey the room. Right now, everyone seems to be doing all right.

My mind drifts back to Sam–again. He'll be reliving the horrors of war for many years, no doubt. PTSD is not a condition recognized in 1863. Normally, it takes years of therapy just to learn to cope with those emotions and even longer to heal. I'm not a therapist or a psychiatrist, but I know a few coping skills I can teach him. I'll do my best to help him with those intense emotions.

While I'm here.

If only he could come back with me. But that's ridiculous. I don't even know how I got here in the first place. There's no way I could figure out a way to take him with me–if I ever get home myself. Besides, he has a family. Why would he choose me over everything he knows, everyone he loves?

"You should get some sleep."

The kind, blonde nurse startles me out of my thoughts. "Does anyone else need me?"

"They all do," she admits. "But you need to take care of yourself as well."

"That's good advice." I've been beyond exhausted for so many days, it's hard to keep track of how long we've been here, in Philadelphia. "I'll check on my brother then go to the nurse's resting room."

Sam is sleeping when I stop by to check on him, and he's even smiling a bit. Hopefully, he's dreaming of his family and other pleasant things. He really needs the rest.

I make my way down the long hall to the room where the nurses take their breaks. It's set up with several cots, and lots of the women are already asleep here. The room is cast in shadows, the moonlight filtering through thick curtains, but there's enough light to find my way around, and I manage to find an empty cot and quietly slip into it.

It's only now that I realize how sore my muscles are from all the days of rushing around. The cot has a few lumps, but the pillow is surprisingly soft and comfortable. My head sinks into it gently as I curl up on my side, and it takes only a single breath before I drift away into dreamland.

"Amazing day, Dr. Little."

I give an exhausted smile to my colleague as I grab my coat and purse. "It has been, Dr. Ashford. It's wonderful to see so many patients in remission."

"Thanks to your early diagnosis and targeted treatments." She gives me a smile, admiration beaming from her blue eyes, as we head to the elevators.

I let out a light chuckle. The door slides open and we step inside. "I can hardly take credit for that. The amazing researchers are the ones who found new ways to treat types of cancer we thought were untreatable."

"Granted," she agrees. "But without you to put them into practice, lots of patients would suffer. It's not often that doctors are so invested in individualized treatments."

"I seem to recall you doing the same." I laugh again as she shrugs. "Anyway, let's just say it's a team effort."

"Agreed." We step out into the lobby. "Enjoy your night! I'll see you bright and early tomorrow."

"See you, Andrea." The automatic door opens in front of us, and the fresh air caresses my face as we head toward our cars. Being mid-summer, it's still light out, even though it's long past my normal dinnertime. Pressing the key fob to my new light blue sedan, I hurry to my car, excited to get home after a long day. Though it's always tiring, my job is so emotionally satisfying I don't mind it at all, but it's always wonderful to see the sparkle in the kind brown eyes that await me.

Pulling into the driveway at home, I see the upturned earth along the front path that tells me he has planted yet another row of flower bulbs. It makes me smile. Gardening has been an important part of his therapy. He tells me that it's a way of creating something beautiful to wash away all the pain and ugliness of war, and I couldn't agree more. Not only has he taken to lining every spare inch of planter space with flowers, but the huge vegetable garden in the back has given us an abundance of fresh produce this year.

Pulling into the garage, I park and step through the door that leads to the mudroom where I slip out of my hospital shoes and put on the fuzzy slippers a certain someone has left there for me.

A wide smile, as well as the scent of toasted garlic and herbs, greets me as I step into the kitchen. "How was your day?" Sam has me in his arms before I can even answer, pulling me into a warm, romantic kiss.

"Much better now," I say with a giggle as he pulls back, joining me in laughter. "Seriously though, it was wonderful. My favorite patient is in remission."

His eyes go wide with excitement. "Betty?"

I nod enthusiastically, turning my gaze away from him to peek at the thick sauce bubbling on the stove.

"That's fantastic," he says. "She's such a sweet old lady."

I giggle. "I think she'd object to you calling her old."

He gives the sauce a stir and shrugs. "True. I don't look one hundred and eighty-four though. And I'd say eighty-two is up there."

"It is, but she still doesn't want to be called old." I steal a spoon from the drawer and grab a quick taste of the sauce. "Oh, my God. This is incredible."

I can see the pride in his smile. "Thanks. It's my own creation that I put to—"

"Mommy!" The melodic sound of two of my favorite voices ring out together, and we both turn to watch our two little angels run into the room.

Audrey, named for my mother, reaches me first as usual, and I squat down to receive my kiss on the cheek. She's inherited my tenacity, as well as my interest in all things medical. Yet she has the distinctive dark hair and deep, brown eyes of her father.

"Hello!" I greet them both as Eddie, named for Sam's father, wraps his little arms around my neck, his blond hair neatly combed. His light blue eyes look up at me, beaming with joy. In his hand he carries a toy soldier, like usual. Thanks to my dad, he has a keen interest in all things military. Sam and I have often wondered if we will ever tell him that his father is a real-life Civil War soldier. I can't help but think about that as I look at him and run my hand over his smooth cheek.

"Can we eat now?" Audrey asks impatiently, a wide grin on her pretty face.

"We sure can," Sam tells her. I turn to help him with the food as the kids set the table.

As we all head to the dining room table, I think about how truly lucky I am to have such a wonderful family and a home full of love.

A crashing sound startles me out of my dream. Looking around, I see several of the other nurses in the room sitting up in alarm. We hear a male voice shouting at a nurse to be more careful. It sounds like someone's simply dropped a tray of medical tools. We all settle back into our pillows.

Letting out a deep breath, I let my mind wander back to the

dream. An ache reverberates in my heart, which seems silly. How can I miss children I've never had? It was a dream. That's all.

Nevertheless, my mind wanders back over the short, sweet dream. It felt so real.

If I leave here alone, Audrey and Ed will never exist. If I stay here, and it turns out Sam and I truly do have feelings for one another, I'd have the chance to meet those children. But I'd lose the career I love, and I'll never get the chance to see all the latest medical innovations helping my patients. I'll be stuck here, where it's all I can do to convince a few nurses to wash their hands more often. Not only that, but my father will be left alone in 2025, having lost both me and my mother. I'll never see him again, and I'll always know how devastated he must be wondering what happened to me.

But staying here also means I can stay with Sam.

The entire train of thought is ridiculous. I don't even know if I can get home–and perhaps more importantly, I don't know if Sam and I even want to have children together. He did save my life, and the more time I spend with him, the more I realize I do have feelings for him. But I'm making a huge assumption on both of our parts.

The idea that life was more romantic in 1863 does come to mind. If Sam truly does have feelings for me, I don't suppose he'd hesitate to let me know. I swallow hard, wondering if the secrets I see behind those brown eyes will ever be revealed to me.

My breath staggers in my throat and comes out in a sob. I cover my face with both hands, my mind lost in turmoil. A gentle hand on my shoulder has me turning to see Alice, one of the nurses who has been helping me care for patients in secret, standing next to my cot. Even in the dim light, her bright red hair shimmers.

"Poor dear," she says softly. "You've done a lot for these men. You should get more rest."

"Thank you." I know she couldn't possibly understand my true situation, but her sentiment only serves to remind me that going back to 2025 also means that many of these soldiers will suffer even more than they already are. They'll have no one to suggest other treatments besides the unsophisticated medical practices of 1863.

"I think I should go check on my brother," I tell her. Alice nods, and I swing my legs off the cot, wiping my eyes on the back of my hand. Alice follows me out, but before we get to Sam, Lois waves me down, leading me toward a wounded soldier I'd helped before.

"Can you take another look at his wound, Navaeh?" she asks, and I can see how tired she is in the way she's struggling to keep her eyes open.

"Let me see." I give him a reassuring smile and approach his bed.

"It's been feeling a lot better." His smile is finally free of the pain he'd been in the first time I checked him, a few days ago, when his wound was infected.

"That's good to hear." I gently unwrap the bandages to see that his wound is, in fact, healing well. I turn to Lois. "Do you have some disinfectant?"

She nods as she hands me the small glass bottle and some cotton that I use to clean it up. "We'll get this rebandaged, and you'll be good as new in no time," I tell the soldier confidently.

But despite the smile plastered on my face as I help him, I can't stop thinking about my predicament. I miss my father and want to go back to him, sparing him the pain I experienced when I woke up from my dream.

On the other hand, the more I think about it, the more I realize I also want to be with Sam. The thought of leaving him, of never seeing those warm brown eyes again, never hearing his laugh, makes my heart ache in a way I've never experienced–not even in my dream.

If only I could have it both ways.

18

Morning light suddenly blinds me as the nurses pull back the curtains. I blink into the sharp rays, lifting my hand to block the glare, and slowly come back to reality. The world comes crashing in on me as I hear the sound of whimpering men, nurses doing their best to soothe them, and the constant footsteps of staff bustling around the hospital doing what they can to help the wounded.

I focus on the empty chair next to me. Nevaeh's not here. I take a deep breath and swallow down the disappointment. Of course, she's not here. Knowing her, she's out there helping an unfortunate soul who's been crippled by this blight of a war. Despite my initial reaction, I can't help but smile. Nevaeh will never be still so long as there's someone around that needs her help.

A gruff voice nearby has me turning my head. I can't help but scowl as Dr. Lynn comes into view making his rounds. He is exactly what I expect from a wartime doctor, gruff and short with everyone, particularly the nurses. Granted, he's overworked. More men than cots occupy every room of the overflowing hospital, from what I can surmise. Nevertheless, he could work on his bedside manner. I suppose I've been spoiled by the exceptionally kind treatment Nevaeh provides her patients. Luckily, he doesn't come to check on me much since he's been sparring with Neveah.

After looking over several more men, he reaches my bedside, his lips pulled tightly together in an expression I can't quite read. He's not happy, that's for damn sure. But I'm not certain he's angry either. Saying nothing, he flips through the notes the nurse hands him. "Unwrap the bandage," he orders. The nurse, a petite blonde woman, kind but homely, quickly does as instructed, giving me a friendly smile. I find it within me to muster a small smile in return.

The doctor bends over and looks at the wound, raising his eyebrows before gesturing toward the nurse to leave it and follow him. Her mouth twists into a half-smile, half-frown in apology. She wants to rebandage it, but the doctor has been moving from patient to patient so quickly, expecting her to follow, so she doesn't have time. I give her a light nod, knowing Nevaeh will take care of it when she returns.

"You'll be going home soon, soldier."

Somewhat startled that he's actually talking to me, I look up at the doctor to see that he's already moved on to the next man. Frankly, I'm relieved to have him gone. Of course, Nevaeh has already told me I'm healing well and will likely be sent home soon, so the news is not unexpected.

What is unexpected, however, is the voice I hear from across the room. "Sam!"

Turning my head, I catch a pair of familiar eyes, and my mouth falls open in disbelief. A low chuckle rumbles from the back of my throat as my father rushes across the room, arms open wide. My step-mother follows, her cheerful smile lightening some of the load I've been burdened with these past several months.

He stoops to hug me, and I sit up as straight as I can in bed. "Father! You're here."

"Of course, we are, son." He squeezes me so hard, I'm glad I don't have any injuries to my torso or else I'd be in severe pain right now. "We came as soon as we got your letter."

Father steps away, and Rosemary glides in to hug me in a much more controlled fashion. "It's so good to see you well, Samuel." She's impeccably dressed in a full-skirted, cream-colored gown with ornate buttons down the front.

My father pulls aside Nevaeh's chair, offering it to Rosemary, who waves it off in refusal, adjusting her substantial skirt with nervous fingers. She looks around, her lips drawn to one side as she takes everything in. I can't blame her for being uneasy in here.

Dropping down into the chair, Father tucks his banker's suit coat-tails behind him. "It looks like you're recovering well, son."

I nod in agreement. "I'm glad you came," Tears threaten to dampen my cheeks, but I fight them, not wanting him to see me emotional. It's difficult; I haven't seen my folks in so long. Now, here they are. If I can't handle not seeing them for a few months, how in tarnation could I possibly go to 2025 with Nevaeh?

"How is Clara?" I ask to refocus my mind.

"Your sister is doing well," he says. "She's feeling so relieved having heard from you and George."

"George is well?" My eyebrows raise, happy to hear that my brother-in-law made it through the battle.

"Quite well, I'd say," my father explains. "He was uninjured at Gettysburg and has moved on with his regiment. Clara still worries for him, naturally. She's excited at the thought of having you back at home, though."

"Well, I'm not home yet." Even if I can't go with Nevaeh, I intend to reenlist, though I see no reason to spring that on my father just yet.

"No, not yet, but soon," Father continues.

Whatever he says next falls on deaf ears. Across the room, Nevaeh comes into view. She freezes about ten feet away from us, clearly noticing my father and stepmother. It's clear she doesn't want to intrude, but I gesture for her to come over. "Father, Rosemary, I have someone I'd like for you to meet."

Nevaeh hesitates for a moment longer before walking over to us. The tightness in her smile reveals how uncomfortable she truly is.

"This is the woman who saved my life, Miss Nevaeh Little." I smile at her and see her mouth relax a bit. "Nevaeh, I'd like you to meet my father, Mr. Edward Walker, and my stepmother, Rosemary."

My father stands and removes his hat as Nevaeh offers her hand assertively. She pulls back slightly, second guessing the appropriateness given our current year, but my father doesn't notice. He takes her hand in his and puts his other one on top in a friendly gesture.

"Well, I owe a debt of gratitude to anyone who saves my son's life," Father says. "Seeing that you're a lovely young woman, I'm even more intrigued." He chuckles under his breath, a mischievous twinkle in his eye as he glances at me. My cheeks warm at the insinuation.

Nevaeh smiles in return, a slight hint of blush rising in her cheeks. "It's wonderful to meet you." Turning to my stepmother, she extends her hand, this time more gently. "Rosemary, it's a pleasure to meet you as well."

My stepmother's eyes light up as she performs a proper ladies' handshake. She's always been more comfortable around other women, which is no doubt why she's so stiff in this room full of soldiers. I hate that I've caused this uncomfortable situation for her. "It's lovely to meet you," she says. "What a unique and beautiful name, Nevaeh."

"It's heaven spelled backward," I explain before Nevaeh has a chance.

"Well, how wonderful." My father offers her the chair. "You sure do look like an angel!"

"Thank you," Nevaeh says, her eyes widening slightly at my father's compliment. "I think your son is exaggerating a bit with the lifesaving." Noticing my unwrapped leg, she immediately begins to properly secure the bandages.

"Nevaeh, you know I am not," I insist. I open my mouth to explain but then realize I can't. She shouldn't have been on the battlefield, only showing up there when she'd been dropped from the future. She gave me pills that I've come to realize most definitely assisted in my healing, yet those don't exist yet. And I certainly can't tell my folks she's a doctor.

Thankfully, Nevaeh understands completely. Looking at my father, she explains. "I helped direct the medical soldiers to get him off the field."

He raises a brow at even this small revelation. "I wasn't aware they had nurses on the battlefield."

"Nevaeh happened to be nearby and assisted in the medical wagons," I add quickly. Though not untrue, it is not the complete story.

"Where are you from, Nevaeh?" Rosemary asks.

Nevaeh looks relieved at the change of subject. "Originally, just outside of Philadelphia. But on the day of the battle, I happened to be in Gettysburg."

My father smiles. "Oh, how wonderful. Perhaps I know your father? I do business here occasionally. I'd love to pay him a visit while I'm here if that's the case."

Nevaeh adjusts her position uncomfortably before answering. "His name is Mr. Martin Little, though I doubt you know him."

"I'm afraid I don't." Father sighs in disappointment. "I'd love to make his acquaintance."

Nevaeh inhales lightly, so I interrupt. "I'm afraid her father is away at the moment."

"Away on business?" my father asks.

"Not exactly." I know she's struggling for an answer that's not a lie, and thankfully, Dr. Lynn walks over and interrupts us. She looks relieved to be in the doctor's company, probably for the first time ever.

"I see we have visitors." The doctor's jovial tone catches me by surprise, until I realize how well dressed my parents are. No doubt, he enjoys a life in high society. Truthfully, my father is very down to earth, unlike most bankers, yet he's currently dressed the part.

"I'm Mr. Edward Walker, Samuel's father." He extends his hand. "And this is my wife, Rosemary."

"An honor to meet you both," the doctor says. "Your son is doing quite well, and he will be discharged in two days' time."

"That's fantastic!" my father exclaims, looking back at me. "Well, then. You can travel home with us."

I smile but don't answer. A glance at Nevaeh tells me I am not the only one to hesitate. Her plump pink lips are slightly parted, frozen in an inhale that tells me she is equally caught off guard. Her eyes flicker to me for a moment, and I attempt to calm her with a gentle smile, but she looks away.

Could it be that she wants to continue in my company longer? Why do I dare hope that is the case?

Dr. Lynn excuses himself, stepping away to assess another soldier, his gruff countenance returning, though he at least speaks kindly to the men in my parents' presence.

"It was lovely to meet you both," Nevaeh says once the doctor is out of the room, standing and stepping back. "I do need to see to the other patients."

"I hope to see you again soon," Rosemary says quickly, flashing a friendly smile. It makes me wish Nevaeh could spend more time with my parents.

"Likewise," Nevaeh says sweetly. Her eyes meet mine again as she turns to look over her shoulder. "I'll be back to check on you later, Sam."

I nod, holding her gaze for as long as I can until she turns to walk away.

Rosemary takes her place in the chair, apparently feeling more comfortable now that she's met Nevaeh. We begin to chat about my father's work, Rosemary's flower garden, and my sister's activities as we continue the visit.

Yet, I'm not focused on the conversation enough to follow completely. Every few moments, I find myself staring at the figure making her way from cot to cot, checking on the other men. Try as I may to keep my attention on my visitors, I unconsciously seek her out, watching her flitter around the room with a commanding grace and beauty unmatched by any woman I've ever met.

"Well, we'd better get back to the hotel," my father announces after a time, assisting my stepmother as she rises from the chair. "We'll remain in town and await your release. Have a good night, son."

"We'll see you soon, Samuel," Rosemary offers.

Father bends to hug me again, and I pat his shoulder. "Thank you for coming. See you soon." As they walk away, a flood of relief washes over me, followed by immediate guilt. I should want to see them, but I'm glad they're leaving. Now, I can give the angel across the room my undivided attention.

Several minutes pass as I watch her tend to the others. She doesn't so much as glance in my direction. A heaviness settles in my chest as I try to surmise what's changed. When she finally steps over, her tone is cold, like she's just another nurse coming to tend a patient she hardly knows. "It's time to change your bandages."

I say nothing, only nod, and she goes about the work, keeping her eyes down.

She's almost finished when I decide I can't take this any longer. "What's wrong, Nevaeh?" I whisper.

Her eyes widen as if my question has caught her off-guard. "Nothing," she insists.

"Nevaeh?" The knowing lilt to my voice leaves her little room to argue.

Letting out a sigh, she continues with the bandage replacement, holding her silence for a long pause. "It's really nothing." The frigidity of her voice cools, and I pick up a note of melancholy. "Your parents are very nice. I'm sure you've missed them."

"They are lovely, and yes, I have." I watch her finish her work. "Is this because of what the doc said? That I'm leaving soon?"

Finally, she looks up at me, her bottom lip quivering slightly. Shrugging, she says, "I suppose… I'm going to miss you."

I let that settle between us for a moment, staring at her until she lifts her eyes, catching mine through her lashes. Clearing my throat, I fight the lump forming there, ignoring the way my heart begins to beat out of time. "I'll miss you, too."

Her mouth moves, but no sound comes out. Instead, all I get is a solemn nod.

My voice cracks a bit as I manage to eke out, "You could… come with me."

Again, she's silent, but this time, her eyes never leave mine. Eventually, she clarifies, "To Maine?"

All I can manage is a slight movement of my head, back and forth.

A gentle laugh like a tinkling bell meets my ears as she begins to shake her head. "I think your parents would find that strange. Besides, I have soldiers here to help."

Finding a bit of courage I was afraid I left on the battlefield, I plow ahead. "You've already done so much. Many of them are making quick recoveries because of your work." She blinks once, twice. "You could stay at my sister's house, which is near my father's home. She has plenty of room, and she'd love having another woman around to talk to." Desperation ebbs from every word flowing from my mouth. I can't let her go–not yet.

Nevaeh's eyes shift slightly as she weighs my plea. When she looks at me again, conviction has settled in. With a deep breath, she says, "I need to stay in Pennsylvania so I can go home, Sam."

Another argument pops into my head, but how can I argue with that? She wants to go back to the future, to her father, to the life she's worked so hard to build for herself. What does 1863 have to offer to an ambitious woman like Nevaeh? Not much. What do I have to offer her? Not enough.

We continue to stare at one another for an eternity wrapped in a moment. My forehead burns from the touch of her lips left engraved there the night she woke me from my nightmare. How can I continue to dream without her by my side?

"I… I don't want to… say goodbye. Not yet." Her voice catches, and tears begin to form in her eyes.

Instinctively, I extend my hand to her, and she slips her slender fingers into my palm. I hold her there as long as I can, attempting to reason through a breadth of feelings and thoughts I've never navigated before and failing to put the jumble of words floating through my brain into any sort of logical order.

But she knows. I can tell by the look in her eyes. She feels the same way I do.

Confused. Bewildered. Entranced. Hopeless.

The next instant, she pulls her hand away, and my hand turns to ice in her absence. If I can't withstand the loss of her grasp, how can I possibly live the rest of my life without her by my side?

Across the room, one of the nurses calls to her. Nevaeh lifts her head, breaking the trance. "I… I've got to go, Sam. I can't stay."

I nod, but she continues to hold my gaze until my head rocks back and forth again. She walks away, and I understand. She's not talking about now. She's talking about forever.

19

———

Nevaeh

Letting go of Sam's hand was one of the hardest things I've ever done. I can feel his eyes on me as I walk out of the room, and it pulls at my heartstrings. I want to turn around and run back to him, telling him yes, I'll go to Maine with him. Yes, I'll stay with him. If I did that, at least some of my dreams would come true—being with the man I love, raising our children together. We would have a beautiful wedding. And in a couple of years, little Ed and Audrey would be running happily around our home without a care in the world as we showered our devotion on them.

But my dad would still be back in 2025, wondering whatever happened to the only family he had left in the world. He'd never get to see his grandchildren or laugh and play with them in the soft, green grass. And the hospital would move on without me, with no Dr. Nevaeh Little, Resident Oncologist, having ever stepped foot inside. Here, I'd be expected to be a full-time mother, and though I admire any woman who chooses that life, I know I would always regret that one missed opportunity.

So, my legs pull me forward, out of the main patient room and toward the next wounded soldier who needs my care, despite the ache in my heart.

"Your hand is healing very well." I force a smile toward the young man who looks at me with hope in his blue eyes, worried he'll never be able to use his hand again. I can't say he won't have any trouble with it, but he's quite lucky the bullet passed through between the upper and deep palmar arches. "You should be able to go home soon. When you do, be sure you change your bandage often, and keep it clean. That's the important thing."

I go on to explain how to do just that, which I've done so many times I've lost count. When I'm finished with him, I turn to walk away, Sam's face resurfacing in my mind. He's leaving the hospital tomorrow.

I don't know how I'm ever going to tell him goodbye.

"MISS LITTLE, I'M SO HAPPY TO SEE YOU AGAIN."

It's late afternoon the next day, and I turn to see Sam's dad, his grin so wide it lights up the room. "Mr. Walker, it's good to see you. Mrs. Walker, I hope you're enjoying Philadelphia."

"I am, thank you, Nevaeh," Sam's stepmother says, her smile broad and genuine.

"I'm glad to hear it." I try to hide the ache in the pit of my stomach as I think about what their presence means—Sam is leaving. For good. "Sam is in the main room as usual."

"We'll see you soon," Edward tells me.

I manage a wide smile back at him and turn to the patient I'm working with, vowing to keep myself busy and try to ignore the ache in my heart.

Several patients later, Alice comes up behind me. "Can you help in the main room?" she asks. "Two of our nurses are sick, and I can't keep up with the bandages. I even asked Nurse Strawn if I could ask you, and she approved it."

The last place I want to be is in the main patients' room watching Sam leave, but I can't turn her down when she needs help. Besides, I have to say something to him. I can't just let him leave and never say goodbye, no matter how hard it's going to be. "Okay."

"I'll start from the left and work my way over," she tells me as we walk into the room. "You can start from the right."

I hitch a breath as I walk in, and all I can do in answer is nod. Sam stands near the center of the room, dressed in a tailored suit his father must have brought him. Even out of his uniform, he has such a strong, confident presence. He looks so handsome, despite the limp he still has from his injury. I can only see his profile, his jaw firm and defined, with a smile that doesn't quite meet his eyes.

When his gaze flits over to me, I look away and move toward the first wounded soldier to re-dress his wound. My heart practically thumps out of my chest, and that ache in my stomach has turned into a boulder. *How am I going to say goodbye to this man?* I don't think I have the words.

I busy myself as he shakes hands with the soldiers around the room, saying goodbye to his friends. I know he's been a beacon of light to them as they all struggle with various degrees of recovery. That's the kind of man he is, caring and thoughtful of others, and it's just one of the things that draws me to him and makes my choice to stay or go home impossible.

"Write to me, Campbell." Even his voice sends pleasant tingles up my spine from all the way across the room. "I expect an invitation to your wedding."

"You will have one, I assure you," the man answers. I know Campbell reminds Sam of Smith, who was also going to get married right after the war. At least this man will have that opportunity.

As he continues to move from cot to cot saying his goodbyes, I keep my eyes focused on the bandages in front of me, knowing that if I catch his gaze, I won't be able to hold back the tears.

But soon, I feel his presence behind me and his strong hand on my shoulder. "Nevaeh?"

I inhale sharply, trying to prepare myself for what's about to happen, but when I stand and turn around, all my anguish nearly bubbles to the surface. To avoid meeting his eyes, I pull him in for a hug, but that's no better since feeling his strong arms around me and knowing I'll never hold him again is unbearable. My eyes burn with unshed tears, but I refuse to let them fall.

He pulls back gently, and I know we've embraced too long to be acceptable in public in the 1800s. Not everyone thinks he is my brother. Now, I have no choice but to look into those kind brown eyes. "We'll be staying at the hotel tonight," he tells me, his tone softer than normal. "We aren't leaving Philadelphia until tomorrow." His brow raises almost imperceptibly, and he meets my gaze directly as if trying to tell me something, but I don't understand.

"Have a good trip home." They are the only words I can say without letting the tears loose.

His smile fades instantly, but his eyes linger for a moment.

"Are you ready, my boy?"

His father's voice breaks our silence, and without another word, he turns and follows him out the door. My heart rips into shreds, and I have to turn away before I see him take his final step away from me... forever.

Summoning my physician's training, I manage to put my feelings on hold—just barely—and tend to the next patient. But a harsh voice rings out behind me.

"Aren't you leaving with your family?"

When I turn around, Nurse Strawn is giving me the most intense stink eye I've ever seen, and that's saying something since a good third of the male doctors in my program thought they deserved the attending position before me. "I have work to do," I explain. "You're short two nurses, and these men need tending to."

Her brows knit together as she realizes I'm right, but she clearly doesn't like it. She doesn't say another word as she sticks her chin in the air and struts away, and I go back to my patient.

"It hurts more," the soldier tells me.

Unfortunately, his wound is infected. I wish I had more antibiotics, but those are long gone. I do have a little antibiotic ointment left, though, but I need to get it out of my kit. "I'll be right back," I tell him.

Slipping around the corner, I pull the case out of my pocket and grab what's left of the ointment, which is probably only enough for this one soldier since I've been using it when I needed it most, which has been far too often. I head back into the room, happy that Nurse Strawn has her back to me as I clean the wound, apply the ointment, and bandage the man up. "This should help," I assure him, though an actual course of antibiotics would be much better.

"Thank you, Nurse."

I smile at him then move on to tend several other patients, still trying to hold back my thoughts of Sam. A while later, I notice Dr. Lynn talking to Nurse Strawn. Both of them gaze at me with tightly knitted brows. My breath catches in my throat as the doctor approaches.

"Miss Little?" he says firmly. I don't want to look at the man, but his tone commands attention. "I've been inquiring to my colleagues. No one has ever heard of a Dr. Little, certainly not a female Dr. Little. Not to mention, Mr. Walker just left, and he's not a physician. You said Sam was your brother."

"He is. We have different fathers." I shrug and turn around to tend the next soldier, praying Dr. Lynn walks away, which he does. For now.

But I know that's not the end of it. It's not safe to stay here anymore with people asking about me. I'm unable to explain anything to them and running out of excuses. I need to try to get back to Gettysburg and hope I find my way home to 2025.

"Be sure you keep this clean," I tell another soldier, finishing up his bandage. A few more men need my attention, but knowing Dr. Lynn and Nurse Strawn are on to me, I don't dare linger any longer.

I hurry for the door, practically crashing into Dr. Lynn as he steps into my path. "I need to speak with you, Miss Little," he says, his tone gruff and impatient.

"Sorry, I need to go see my family at the hotel," I say quickly. "I'll be back."

He's obviously not thrilled, but at least he steps aside. I hurry out, wishing I could have said goodbye to Alice and some of the other nurses, but it's too late for that.

Out on the street, I realize I have no money and no way to get back to Gettysburg, and it's getting dark out. The only one who can help me is Sam, and we've already said our goodbyes… well, sort of.

But I have no choice, so I walk the few blocks to the hotel and slip inside. "Can you please tell me which room my brother is staying in?" I ask the front desk clerk. "His name is Samuel Walker."

"Of course." The middle-aged man smiles pleasantly. "Your brother has been expecting you. He's in room fourteen. It's right down that hall to your left."

My pulse quickens as I thank him and walk down the hallway. *What the hell are you doing?* I ask myself, my nerves heightened as I approach Sam's room. I've already been through a last goodbye. *How can I face him again, especially in private where I'll need to actually say the words I really mean?* I won't be able to hold back the tears this time.

But I have no choice. Tapping lightly on the door, I jump when it opens almost instantly. Those brown eyes meet mine again, but now, there's something else in them I can't quite read. He steps aside to let me in without a word, leaning his head into the hallway and looking both ways before closing and locking it behind me.

My heart races as he turns to face me. I'm as ready as I'll ever be to say goodbye, to tell him I'm ending it before we even have a chance to start and going back to my father and my career in the future. But as I struggle to find the words, I see something new in his eyes, a burning hunger that demands to be satiated.

In an instant it becomes clear—why he invited me here, why he stayed another day—and my breath catches in my throat as he closes the distance between us.

"Nevaeh."

His voice is gravelly with want as I move toward him too, wrapping my arms around him as our lips meet. His strong hands stroke my back as he pulls me in tighter, and I part my lips so I can savor the taste of this man I cannot live without.

20

Nevaeh

He pulls away from our kiss, and my heartbeat quickens as he lifts his hand, caressing my cheek with his palm while his eyes bore straight into my soul. My breath catches in my throat when he pulls me back in and our lips meet again. I close my eyes and inhale the scent of citrus with a hint of musk. He smells so intoxicating, especially after so many days on the battlefield and in the hospital.

He has prepared for this moment.

Pleasant tingles echo down my back as his strong hands explore me, and heat ignites in my core. I deepen the kiss, letting loose all the restraint I've forced deep down inside me since the day I recognized my feelings for Sam... the glint in his eye I couldn't explain, the desire to stay with him despite knowing I don't belong here.

The pain of the choice I must make still looms in the back of my mind, but for right now, this instant is all that matters.

In the next moment, I can feel his hesitation as he pulls his hands up higher on my back. "Are you... sure?" he asks me, and I understand why. He's attempting to protect my chastity, but all I can think about is how completely my body responds to his.

"It's okay," I reassure him softly, guiding his hand back to where it had been, low on my back. Hesitation keeps him from moving, his eyes still locked on mine. With a gentle smile, I tell him, "All I care about right now, in this moment, is you, Sam."

At that, his face softens, all the restraint draining from him as he pulls me in tighter ,and his fingers begin to unfasten my dress. I reach for his jacket buttons, my fingers awkward with unfamiliarity as I try to find my way inside this unfamiliar type of suit. Finally, he assists, making quick work of the outer layers as I struggle with my dress, aching for his touch and wanting the layers between us to melt away.

Eventually, our clothes are piled on the floor around our feet, and we're staring at one another as if seeing each other for the first time. His eyes wander over my body, drinking me in. My heart rate quickens as I admire his physique, his rippling biceps and washboard abs.

Sam moves toward me, his lips warm and inviting. He kisses me like he needs me in order to breathe. My tongue tangles with his, a swirl of mint and whiskey, and I simply can't get enough of him.

In one fluid motion, Sam lifts me off the ground and moves us to the small bed a few steps away in the narrow room. With him hovering over me, placing sweet kisses on my flushed skin, I feel safe, and nothing else matters in this moment except for him and me.

He pauses a moment, breaking the kiss. His gaze locks with mine. "You are so beautiful." His gravelly tone elicits a light moan from me, and I quiver with pleasure as he touches me again.

He trails kisses along my skin on the same path his eyes have just worshipped, leaving a trail of tingling goosebumps behind. I close my eyes to focus on each place where his lips touch me. My heart flutters when he gently cradles my breast with one hand. He pauses, tasting me, and my breath catches in my throat.

He raises his hand to brush against my cheek, gently fingering a stray curl and pulling it away from my face. Taking a deep breath, I inhale his scent and close my eyes for a moment. When I open them again, he's staring at me. With no words, he tells me a thousand ways he loves me, and there's no question left in my mind that I love him, too.

I have to find a way to be with Sam, and the date on the calendar makes no difference in the world… not right now.

Softly, he takes my inner thigh in his hand, caressing it gently and softly spreading my legs. I don't wait for him. I lift up off the bed, longing for him. He looks at me again then as if asking permission, inquiring whether I am sure.

My hips answer for me, grinding gently against the bedsheet. I nod, letting him know I've completely surrendered to him.

His hungry gaze lingers on mine as he moves over me, his eyes clouded over with desire.

He enters me slowly, and I instinctively squeeze against him to pull him in, but he's still hesitant. "I'm okay," I whisper, and he nods.

I let out a gasp as he pushes in, stretching against me and hitting me in all of the right places. Fireworks explode behind my eyes as he reaches the perfect spot and sends rumbles of bliss across every nerve.

The depth of connection is so intense, I almost look away, but I keep my gaze locked on him as moans of contentment escape me. I've never felt so much a part of another person. Our love across time is so perfect, so complete, so undeniable.

He leans into me, wrapping his arms around me and rolling us over. Until now, I haven't realized how hard my heart was pounding, but as his chest rests against mine, I feel our rhythms are matched. He doesn't loosen his arms, just holds me tight against him as we make love.

And that's exactly what this is, for the first time in my life—true lovemaking.

When he pulls back and kisses me again, I let loose, exploding into him, seeing those sparks of silver erupt in my field of vision again as I tighten against him and purse my lips to avoid screaming out his name for the whole hotel to hear. It's only seconds before he joins me, and I feel him spill himself inside me.

Heat rises up my neck and into my face, the sweet blush of satisfaction as he holds me tightly again, my face pressed to his chest. "Sam...."

"Shh," he whispers softly. "Words can come tomorrow. Let's let tonight be ours."

I nod against his body, listening to his heartbeat beating as erratically as mine. He stays inside me, caressing my hair and running his hands softly across my back. The stark difference between the heat of his touch and the cool air against my back sends tingles across my spine, and it's not long before I feel the heat in my core again.

Rocking against him needfully, Sam responds and begins to meet my rhythm again, and he soon rolls us back over softly so I'm lying under him. This time, it's slower, more intentional, his eyes telling me he never wants to end this night, wishes he could stop the clock and make time nonexistent. It's just us, it's just now, it's just our love as we can connect with each other, freezing this moment in time.

Sam reaches up to caress my cheek. Tracing the lines of my lips, he smiles. "You are perfection."

I try to answer, to tell him he's perfect, too, but my words catch in my throat as another wave of ecstasy washes over me. This time, I have to turn my head to the pillow to catch the cries of pleasure that escape my lips. He joins me, and our final moans are caught between our lips as he kisses me again.

Exhausted with gratification, he rolls gently off me onto the sheets, pulling me with him to snuggle up in his chest again. It takes a moment to regain my ability to breathe, and my heart slows to a steady pace as I trail my fingers along his well-defined chest.

There's so much I want to tell Sam, and I don't know where to start. I can't leave him, and I can't stay here and leave my father alone in the future. But I can't ask him to come with me, even if that is a possibility. He has his own family here, a father who truly loves him and a stepmother who is kind and loving. He has a sister I've never met who is scared for her own husband off at war. What would happen if she lost both of them?

I can't even imagine the pain of kissing Sam goodbye knowing he was going to face the trials of battle, especially after having seen it for myself.

If he doesn't come with me, he'll likely go straight back to the battlefield, this time feeling he has nothing to lose. He'll be a man with an impossible love to satiate, throwing all his energy into his love for his country.

His chest rises and falls slowly as his breath grows steady, and he reaches over to grab the blanket and pulls it over us, tucking it around me protectively as though that will keep me here with him forever.

I open my mouth, intending to express all these thoughts, but I close it again, realizing Sam is right. Tomorrow, we'll have time to talk about what I've chosen to do and how I can't ask him to come with me because he has a life here. He will ask me to stay, and my heart will wrestle with the impossible choice.

But that's a conversation for tomorrow.

Tonight, we have this moment for each other, and I'm going to savor every moment of it. We'll hold each other for as long as we can, burning that feeling into our souls so when we do separate, we will never forget the timeless love we experienced, a love born on a battlefield in a distant memory.

Tonight, I'll hold him in my arms and in my heart as his strong, steady heartbeat lures me into a blissful, yet uneasy, sleep.

21

I INHALE HER SWEET SCENT BEFORE I EVEN OPEN MY EYES, AND MY LIPS rise into a pleasant smile. My arms still encircle her warm, soft body, her skin smooth like the purest silk. Instinctively, I pull her in closer, her breath altering slightly before it settles back into a light, steady rhythm.

But as my eyes open to the orange sun rays filtering through the gingham curtains, consciousness hits with our grim reality—Nevaeh is leaving soon, and parting from her is a thought I cannot bear. I simply can't stand idle while she travels back to her life in the future, not now, not after the love we expressed last night. It isn't possible for me to survive without her, no matter what happens to me next.

My decision is easy, especially as she lets out a soft moan and changes position. Even in this light murmuring, her voice is a symphony. It's my next act that shall be difficult—facing my father.

Cautiously, I slide my arm from underneath her, hoping not to stir her awake. I replace my touch with a gentle tuck of the bedsheet, slowly rising until I'm standing beside her, watching her turn gracefully and fall back into steady slumber. My body shivers at the loss of her warm touch, and I hurry to the closet to get dressed for the task ahead.

As I head for the door, I feel a blush of heat rise in my cheeks at the sight of our clothes cast aside on the floor. My heart flutters as I recall the moment… and those that followed. Though joy had overcome me when she appeared at my door, I recall how apprehension washed over me until she assured me our feelings about the encounter were mutual. After that moment, I let go of all inhibitions in a way I had never done before. I know my heart will never allow me to touch another woman in such a way ever again.

I hang my suit back in the closet without a thought but linger when I hold her dress, inhaling her sweet scent once again before I lay it out carefully on a nearby chair, straightening it in an attempt to remove any wrinkles. After doing the same with her undergarments, I gaze back over my shoulder to find her still sleeping peacefully, her hair flowing in graceful curls over the pillow as the morning light shines above her, casting her in an ethereal glow. My hand freezes on the doorknob for a quiet moment as her stunning beauty leaves me breathless. Knowing I must complete my task, I reluctantly turn away from her as I step outside and carefully lock the door behind me.

A flush rises in my cheeks again as I pass my neighbor's door, wondering whether our efforts to muffle our expressions of love last night were sufficient. Regardless, I'm fortunate the rooms between me and my parents were already booked for the night so I don't have to worry about them having overheard. We weren't that loud….

After pausing a moment outside the door to let the blush drain from my face, I lightly tap to announce my presence.

My father's smile is as wide as the doorway when he greets me. "My boy!" he exclaims, his eyes lifting as he catches his error at making such a loud greeting so early in the morning. Quieter, he adds, "Come in, come in."

"Good morning, Father, Rosemary."

My stepmother nods with a kind smile as I tip my hat to her. "Good morning, Samuel."

"Sam," my father continues, "the coach will be here to take us to the railroad station shortly. Your sister is going to be thrilled when you—"

"Father?" I don't wish to interrupt him, but this must be said.

His forehead wrinkles as he regards me. "Sam, what's the matter?"

"I won't be traveling back to Maine with you." My words tumble out despite the knot in my throat.

His eyes widen, and Rosemary's arms freeze, the shirt she was about to place in the steamer trunk unfolding itself as she faces us. "Pardon me?" my father asks.

"Respectfully, I'm afraid I cannot return home with you," I repeat. "I have decided to reenlist. We're at the crossroads in this war, and our country needs me."

Rosemary turns back to her task of packing garments, trying not to interfere, as my father steps closer to me. "This cannot be," he argues. "Your sister is expecting you. Will you have her wait in fear for another year or more?"

I clear my throat, fighting the knot forming there, and stand straighter. "Every soldier has a sister awaiting him, or a mother, or wife. I am not unique. Fear is the price we must pay to ensure the Union survives this challenge."

He shakes his head, backing up into a lounge chair, where he sits and places a palm on his forehead. "No," he says firmly. "You're coming with us."

My nerves steel against his refusal, and I'm bitterly aware of the great sacrifice I'm asking of him. Knowing I truly don't intend to return to battle makes the argument all the more difficult. "I must do this." I speak of my need to follow Nevaeh, so I know these words, at least, are true.

"This is absurd," he continues, pain evident in his eyes. "Your leg, Sam! You're still injured. Surely, you've given what you could to the cause of our nation."

"But I haven't," I insist. "My leg is healing well, and there is yet more I can do to be of service."

"How can this be?" My father stands again and approaches me, his eyes searching mine until sorrow reflects what he finds there. "Your decision is final?"

"It is," I confirm. Putting my hand on his shoulder, I soften my voice. "Is this not the choice you would make in my position? I believe it would be."

Defeat clouds his eyes as he nods softly. "Most likely, yes, son."

A tap at the door draws our attention. Father calls, "Yes?"

Sticking his head in, the hotel clerk says, "Sir, your coach has arrived." He accepts a nod from my father as acknowledgement and steps away, closing the door behind him.

Father's eyes find mine again. "Is there no way to convince you to come with us?"

"There is not," I confirm.

He lets out a light chuckle despite the pain in his eyes. "Then I bid you farewell." He pulls me in for a strong embrace, lingering a moment as he whispers, "I am proud of you, Sam. Remember that always."

"I will," I say quietly as he pulls back. Rosemary steps forward with a polite smile. She has always taken pains not to intrude since she is not my real mother, though we do share a fondness for one another. Still, she did not dare add to my father's arguments. "Farewell, Samuel," she says softly.

"Farewell, Rosemary." She pats me lightly on the arm, and I lean in to give her a light kiss on her cheek. "Take care of him for me."

"Always." Her smile fades. My father wraps his arm around her. With one last glance through tear-filled eyes and a nod to me, he leads her out the door, and I step aside as the coachmen come in to collect their luggage.

I watch as they disappear around the turn of the hallway, knowing this will be the last time I lay eyes on them if events go as I have planned. The fact that they will assume I'm dead and not even have a body to bury vexes me, but it cannot be helped.

Once the hallway is clear of the coachmen, I return to my room and slowly open the door. Nevaeh turns around as I enter, her arms over her chest, and her dress not yet fastened. "My apologies," I say as I move to swiftly close the door.

She glides over to me, and I take her in my arms, holding her dress up for her. "Nevaeh, all is well." She begins to pull halfheartedly from my embrace, but soon relents, relaxing into my chest. "I want to be with you, Nevaeh, no matter what happens."

She pulls back slightly and looks into my eyes, a silent question in those bright orbs. "What do you mean?"

"I will be coming back with you to your life in the future, if that is something that can be done," I explain.

Her mouth opens with no sound at first, her lips turning down. "You can't do that," she says finally. "Your family will be worried about you. Your father is ready to take you home."

"My father has already left for the railway station."

"How? Why would he leave without you?" Her eyebrows knit together.

"I told them I was reenlisting," I explain softly. "My family will go on without me."

"Reenlisting? But—"

I take a step forward to close the distance she's put between us, taking her hand in mine. I absently stroke her soft skin with my thumb as I look into her eyes. "I was willing to give up my life for my country regardless. My family knows that. I don't know whether it's possible to go back with you, but I don't see a reason not to try."

A short exhale escapes her throat, but she says nothing.

"Let me help you with this," I suggest.

She narrows her eyes in confusion before I gesture toward her gown, which she's still holding up to her chest. Stepping behind her, I reach down to awkwardly fasten the buttons leading up to her neck. Her skin is covered with her undergarment, yet being so close to her causes a warm tingle to radiate through me.

For a moment, I consider unfastening all the buttons.

She finds her voice again. "What about your sister? She's home waiting for you, too. You'll never see her again. You won't be able to say goodbye."

I finish the last button and turn her gently to face me. Her soft blue eyes betray she's not fully invested in this argument. "I've already said my goodbyes when I first enlisted," I explain. "She knows the risks involved in going off to war as much as anyone. The only place I wish to be is in your arms forever. This cannot be unless I go with you. Though I don't know if it is possible, I must endeavor to try."

She exhales, her fingers fumbling with the edges of my suit, working the material needlessly. "I'm not going to talk you out of this, am I?"

I chuckle lightly, smiling as my head sways side to side. "You are not."

"Well, then, I guess I don't have a choice." Her eyes twinkle as she attempts to hold back a smile. "I don't even know how I got here, so I sure the hell don't know if you can follow me back."

"We must have hope that I can," I tell her. "Providence could not be so cruel as to bring us together only to force us apart."

"I hope not, but I'm not even sure what we need to do." She lets out a sigh, breaking her gaze with me as she collects her thoughts. "I guess we need to go back to that rock on the battlefield at Devil's Den. I hope I don't have to fall again."

"That would not be ideal," I agree.

Her eyes meet mine once more as she regards me firmly. "But you have to promise me that if we try, and it doesn't work, and I go back, but you can't go with me that you're not going to reenlist."

My brows raise at her request.

"You have to promise me, or we won't try it," she insists before I can answer. "If you go off to fight again and get killed this time, my coming here will have been in vain, assuming I was sent to the past to save your life–and I truly believe that's why I'm here."

I chuckle lightly at her insistence. "For you, Nevaeh, I will make that promise."

"You'd better," she adds, her eyes narrowing before she finally allows herself to smile.

The sparkle in her eyes is so beautiful, I cannot resist the pull of my lips toward hers. When they meet mine, that now-familiar warmth and softness sends a quiver to my heart. My arms wrap around hers joyfully as her hands explore my back, and I deepen the kiss, relishing her sweet taste while praying I will forever feel the Heaven of being in this woman's arms.

"I love you, Nevaeh, so very much," I tell her as we part to catch our breath.

"I love you, too, Sam… more than anything."

I pull her even closer, my heart pounding in equal rhythm with hers. But beneath my blissful smile, fear that I will be pulled from her grasp when she falls through time has my lungs struggling for breath.

22

Nevaeh

I gaze out the window at the last few buildings in Philadelphia before they give way to the Pennsylvania countryside. Seeing this world in 1863, maybe for the last time, it almost seems dreamlike. Even with the dust of the dirt roads billowing around them, many of the grand brick buildings are so new, even their mortar shines brightly. I can recall a few of them that still stand in 2025. Their facades have faded by then, wear and tear taking a toll on them, the bricks lackluster from the weight of age.

Warm sparks of electric energy flush over me as I feel Sam squeezing my hand, pulling my attention away from the window. I can't hold back my smile. He looks so handsome in his civilian suit. His long jacket is stylish and elegant, with his pocket watch chain dangling across the silk vest. I inhale the scent of his musky cologne, scooting a bit closer to him. He holds his Union jacket folded in his lap, all that's left of his uniform after the pants were so bloodied and torn. I can see in his eyes the same mix of excitement and worry that has my heart beating fast.

"Are you sure my jacket will go through?" he asks.

"I hope so," I say, lifting my shoulders in a shrug. "I don't know the mechanics of how I traveled here, but my phone came along, and that was in my pocket. Maybe it's only the things you're actually wearing. You should probably put it on when we get there in case you can't just carry it through."

"I hope it will," he says, tracing the 4th Maine patch with the tip of his finger. "I should like to keep it as a memento. These cufflinks here were given to me by my father the Christmas before I enlisted."

"I'm certain they'll go through," I assure him, though I really can't say for sure, but they're more a part of what he's wearing than my phone was. "What else did you bring?"

"I have my sister's lapel pin and this." Fumbling through his pocket, he slides out a crisp, clean envelope with only a slight tear from opening it previously.

He hands it to me, and I open it carefully. "Lieutenant Samuel Kent Walker, 4th Maine regiment of John Henry Hobert Ward's brigade under the Union III Corp under Major General David B. Birney. Your middle name is Kent?"

"For my grandfather."

"It suits you." I return my gaze to his letter and notice a second sheet. "We commend you for your brave commitment to the service of the Union.... This is your enlistment certificate."

He nods, folding and stuffing the paper back into the envelope tenderly when I hand them back. There's a gleam of pride in his eyes, but he changes the subject. "I am glad that my final pay was more than enough to purchase our train tickets."

"I'm glad, too. I was a little worried about how we'd get back to Gettysburg."

"You needn't have worried," he insists, tilting his head slightly as he looks into my eyes. Recognition rises in them. "You're nervous about the trip."

"Of course, I am." A light giggle escapes my lips involuntarily, releasing a slight bit of tension.

He smiles, his brown eyes glistening in the sunlight shining through the window. "May I ask you about what the world is like in the future?"

Looking around, I see the men in the seat in front of us hunched over a stack of papers. Across the way, a mother holds her child as he points excitedly out the window. Clearly, they're too engrossed in their own business to bother with our conversation. "What do you want to know?"

"I am curious about the strange wagons."

"Wagons?"

"In the picture you showed me," he adds.

"Oh, you must mean the cars in the parking lot." I reach for my phone, but the battery is dead. My breath catches in my throat. My last connection to the future is gone. *What if I don't make it back?* I force an exhale and focus on his question. "They each have engines, like this train but more sophisticated, and of course, much smaller, so we don't need horses."

"Fascinating. And your device—" He nods toward my phone, which I still hold in my lap. "Can you describe how it works?"

I chuckle lightly. "I don't think I can. The technology is way more complicated than I can explain. But I can tell you what it does. It's a phone, and I can talk to people, but it does a lot more. I guess we don't have a lot of time for me to explain the Internet. But basically, it's a place where you can share information from all over the world."

His quizzical eyes widen with interest. "That sounds quite wonderful."

"It can be." *Should I hold back or tell him more of what I know?* If he doesn't come with me, it might change the future if he mentions some of these things to anyone. But I have to believe he will follow me through the portal–or whatever it is that will take me back–so I describe a bit more about what Philadelphia is like in 2025, telling him what he needs to know in order to prepare while also trying not to overwhelm him.

Eventually, I get around to my job at the hospital, and I can hear the excitement in my voice.

"If women can be doctors in the future…" he begins thoughtfully.

"Yes?"

"Would it be permissible for me to raise the children?"

My heart flutters, and visions of our little Ed and Audrey from my dream flow back to my mind. My heart fills with hope that I'll one day hold them in my arms. "Of course you can. Is that what you want to do?"

"I have seen so much of war," he explains, "bullets, blood, and death. I believe I would like to enjoy life for a change, to relax and find happiness with our children when they are young, should we be blessed to have any."

I squeeze his hand. "Then that's what we'll do."

The steam engine whistle blares as we pull into the Gettysburg station, and my heart thumps in my chest. I have no idea if I'll be able to get back to my father or not. And we won't know whether Sam will pass through to 2025 with me until we try. If I go through and he doesn't, I'll never see him again, and I'm not ready for that possibility.

"Maybe we should wait a bit before going to the battlefield," I suggest.

He turns to me, his brown eyes searching mine until they soften with realization. "We can get a room at the inn. Perhaps it is best we wait for morning." He squeezes my hand, and I exhale with relief.

We exit the train and are nearly overcome with the stench of death, even at this distance from the battlefield. I hitch a breath as wagon loads of wounded men pull up to the station. It doesn't seem possible there can be so many left. I get the attention of a nurse tending a limping man. "Are these the last of the wounded soldiers?"

Her grim expression deepens as she shakes her head. "Thousands are left," she explains. "I accompany several wagons a day, and other nurses do the same."

"I'm so sorry to hear that," I say as she walks away. "Thank you for your work." She nods as my eyes flit to the wagon where several of the men have poorly bandaged wounds and many are clearly in pain.

"You cannot help them all, Nevaeh," Sam whispers into my ear.

Pursing my lips together, I give him a firm nod and start walking alongside Sam. He stops to ask which direction the inn is, and a passerby points us in the right direction. It's just a few blocks down the street. I let him lean on me slightly so his leg doesn't bother him as much. He steps up to the front desk confidently when we arrive.

"We'd like a room for the night, please," he tells the clerk.

"Name?"

"Mr. and Mrs. Sam Walker." My heart flutters as he winks at me.

The clerk smiles knowingly. "Newlyweds, huh?"

My eyes widen as Sam answers for us with the story we'd concocted this morning. "We were married just last year. We're here to locate my wife's brother, who fought in the battle. We're hoping to find him well."

"I see," the clerk says. "Room fifteen is available. One dollar a night."

Sam hands over the money and takes the key, turning to me. "Perhaps we should go to dinner?"

"The tavern next door is your best choice," the clerk explains, and we turn back to him. "It's simple fare but quite good, I assure you."

"Thank you." Sam offers his arm, which I gladly accept.

"Godspeed on finding your brother, ma'am," he calls after us as we exit.

"Thank you."

With no luggage to put away, we head straight to the tavern for dinner. I'm not surprised to find it so full of people. They still have a lot of mouths to feed in this small town. My nerves rattle as I look around, hoping I won't recognize anyone. I made myself fairly well known at the field hospital, and I can't help but wonder whether news of a woman claiming to be a doctor made its way back to the nurses of Gettysburg. I don't need any more trouble before trying to get home.

We find a table by a middle-aged couple and Sam pulls out my chair.

"Did you serve?" the man next to us asks, eyeing Sam's jacket.

"Yes, I was in the 4th Maine," Sam explains.

"Well, congratulations on your victory!" he exclaims. "Allow me to buy you a round."

Sam looks at me, and I give him a nod. He deserves to have people appreciate his bravery. He's asked the same question more than a few times before we finish our simple, but tasty, meal of meat and potatoes, and I'm glad the attention is on him instead of me.

That doesn't last long because a familiar blonde nurse walks up to me as we're strolling back to the hotel. Elizabeth, I think her name is. "Navaeh? Is that you? Are you back to help at the field hospital?" she asks.

"Um… no. Just visiting family" I reply, hoping for a short conversation. My eyes flicker down the sidewalk, hoping I don't find more familiar faces in the crowd.

"That's too bad because we could use the help," she says. "We still have quite a few tents full of wounded men to tend to." She eyes Sam. "You're her brother, right?"

"Yes," I answer for him. My heartbeat quickens as I look around the crowd again and come up with the first excuse I can think of. "I'm sorry, but we need to go. We're meeting someone."

"Oh, then perhaps I'll see you in town before you leave," she says with a friendly smile.

"Perhaps." I quicken my pace, but not so much that Sam can't keep up.

"We'll go straight back to the inn," he whispers, patting my hand with his free arm.

"Good idea." The sooner I'm off the street, the better. I liked that nurse and she's a nice person, but I need to put some space between me and the people of this time. I don't know why I'm here, but I hope I've accomplished whatever it was I was supposed to do.

I can only hope that my task was to find Sam and bring him home with me.

Relief washes over me once we're inside the hotel room, and Sam locks the door. "Perhaps we'll find our way to the battlefield early in the morning so as to avoid any crowds," he suggests.

I nod as I wrap my arms around him, leaning my head against his muscular chest. "I kind of want to go now, but I'm just not ready. I'm scared."

Pleasant tingles radiate up my spine as his strong hands rub my back. "As am I. Yet, we must have faith."

"I'm trying," I whisper as his hand ghosts over my neck and gently traces the line of my jaw. He lifts my chin lightly, and I look up to see his brown eyes gazing longingly at me. He pulls me in for a kiss, slowly at first, then deepening it as I close my eyes and savor his taste.

All thoughts of a portal to another time disappear as my heartbeat quickens, and I pull him impossibly closer. But he soon moves back, lingering on my lips before we part. "If all the time I have in this world with you is this very night, then I shall replay it every moment until my final breath," he whispers.

A chill runs up my spine at the stark reminder of our situation, but my core melts with his gravelly tone. Silently, I reach for his lapel buttons, my fingers working through them as quickly as possible.

We have tonight; it could be our last, or it could be the beginning of forever. Either way, I'm going to savor every second of his touch and burn it into my memory… just in case.

23

My eyes open as Nevaeh adjusts her body to sink her head onto my chest. "Good morning," I whisper.

Her troubled eyes lift to meet mine. "Did I wake you?" she asks.

"Yes, but not much earlier than I would have awoken myself." The light filtering under curtains is too faint to ascertain the time. Holding her with one arm, I stretch with the other to retrieve my pocket watch from the night table. "The hour is early yet, but perhaps it's prudent we be on our way."

She squeezes me in response, her hands softly caressing my shoulder. "I don't want to get up yet."

Familiar electric tingles play with my nerves at her touch. "We can take a moment, but I believe it would be best to get ahead of the crowds on the streets."

A groan escapes her lips, and it lingers so long I can't hold back a chuckle. "All right," she says, sitting up and flashing me a sideways grin. Her hair flows like a silken waterfall over her bare shoulder, and I am breathless in the presence of her beauty.

The moment passes, and our eyes meet again. I see her hesitation. "This is going to work, Nevaeh," I assure her.

"I wish I had your confidence," she whispers, exhaling with frustration. Her eyes narrow as she looks into mine in search of reassurance. "You really don't have any doubt about this, do you?"

"I cannot afford to." I run my hand through her hair, marveling at its silliness. "I have no life without you, and therefore I must believe we will fall through time together."

She nods with another long sigh. "Okay. I'll try to stay positive. Let's get on with it."

It pains me to separate from her long enough to dress, but she approaches me as I reach for my vest buttons.

"Let me do that." Her smile broadens as she fastens the buttons, carefully looping my pocket watch chain through the top one. "This is such a classic look. In 2025, most men wear wristwatches, but for some more formal occasions, a man might wear a pocket watch instead"

"Those are quite elegant." I recall one of my father's clients wore one, having purchased it in Europe.

"They can be." She pats my pocket as she tucks the watch inside. "They get cheaper with more functions, though there are some that act like my phone now."

My brows rise. "With pictures?"

"Yes, sometimes. I'll show you when we get back."

"I am looking forward to it." I gently stroke her soft cheek before gesturing for her to turn around. "My turn to assist."

A musical giggle escapes her lips as she turns around so I can fasten her dress. A shiver of desire rushes over me as my fingers glide along her back. After struggling on the final button, I pull her close, brushing her hair aside to kiss her neck from behind.

"We're never going to leave if you start that," she whispers, adding a tender smile.

"Then I shall wait until we're on the other side." Despite her laughter, her posture stiffens, and she fingers the decorative buttons on her dress nervously. I know the tension will not dissipate for either of us until we have passed through.

I slide my hand around her waist, and she catches it in hers, pressing it firmly against her and grasping my arm with her other hand. Silence surrounds us as I close my eyes, inhaling her floral scent in what could be our last moment alone together.

Inhaling, I steady my resolve. I can only pray we will have many years of intimate time together once the hurdle is crossed. "Are you ready?"

She turns to face me with a decisive nod. "I am."

Rays of orange and yellow dance across the horizon as we step out into the street. Though there aren't nearly as many people now as there were yesterday afternoon, Nevaeh still glances around nervously. "The best way to get to the battlefield is to take one of the returning hospital wagons, but what if we run into someone we know?"

I pause for a moment to consider it. "They believe us to be brother and sister, so we may need to devise a purpose for our journey."

"Let's say we're looking for someone from your division," she suggests.

"I believe that will be suitable."

"There's a man I don't recognize." She points to a driver mounting his empty wagon, and I take her hand and hurry over.

"Sir." The driver turns at my urgent call. "May we ride with you?"

"This is an army wagon," he argues.

I hold up my jacket to show the badge. "I'm 4th Maine under Brigadier General Ward."

His eyes lighten. "Then you saw combat here. You were wounded?" He gestures toward my weaker leg.

"I was."

"Then why would you wish to return there?"

"I've been unsuccessful in finding some of the men in my unit," I explain. "I would like to find out if they're still in the field hospital." When he looks at Nevaeh, I add, "This is my sister. She's betrothed to one of the men I'm looking for."

Nevaeh's eyes narrow, her jaw clenched as the soldier regards her with sympathy. "I can't guarantee you'll find your man out there, miss."

"I would like to try," she says, her tone strained.

"Climb aboard. I'm afraid the ride will be a bit uncomfortable."

"That's quite all right," she insists. I offer my hand to help her climb into the wagon, and we settle toward the front where the ride might be smoother.

My breath catches in my lungs as we approach the battlefield. Though it's quiet now, the sounds of gun and cannon fire echo in my mind, and my heart pounds. The stench of death permeates the air so profusely, my stomach roils.

Nevaeh, who is looking a bit green from the smell, holds my hand tightly, her worried eyes meeting mine. "Are you okay?"

I nod reassuringly and force a smile, though it's difficult to speak with the knot forming in my stomach. "I will be fine."

Her eyes narrow. "You'd tell me if you weren't, right?"

"I will go wherever I need to in order to be with you."

She nods, but I see the concern in her eyes. The field is soon blocked by a row of trees along the road to the hospital. Having no logical reason to ask to step off the wagon here, we ride with the man to the field hospital.

"There's still just as many tents here." Nevaeh exhales as her lips turn downward. "I thought it would be almost empty."

"As did I." I wonder how many of the men in my unit are still alive, how many will live with a missing limb, and how many will continue to awaken to the nightmare of battle in their dreams each night. I step out of the wagon and turn to thank our driver, who is already assisting a nurse in loading a man into it. Thinking it best not to engage in more conversation, I gesture for Nevaeh to follow me behind some thick bushes where we can make our way back down the road.

The pain in my chest grows stronger when we finally approach the battlefield, where scores of bodies still lie about. My lungs choke at the unbearable stench. I pass my handkerchief to Nevaeh, who places it over her nose and mouth while I use a portion of my jacket to attempt to block the smell, but nothing can hold off the odor of rot and decay.

Nevaeh puts a hand to her chest. "This is… horrifying."

I nod, unable to speak any words that might do any measure of justice to the scene before us. Men lay in the crusted muck like rag dolls, their faces frozen in anguish, swollen almost unrecognizable with maggots crawling over them, their bodies twisted and half-enveloped by the rugged earth beneath them. Recovery soldiers thrust shovels into the earth to extricate them one by one, but they litter the field as far as I can see in the distance, making their task seem futile. And that's to say nothing of the huge amount of dead horses.

"There were so many more men than this that night," she continues, "though many of them were still alive then." She turns to me, and I realize how stiff I've become. Flashes of what we all went through here overcome me. We are almost to the Devil's Den, and I have to brace myself. "Are you going to be able to go back there?"

I do not hesitate to answer. "I must do, and I will. It's that way, isn't it?" The vast fields before us are nearly unrecognizable from when my unit first arrived to secure our position, its vegetation merely trampled at the time. Now, not a blade of grass survives in the uneven dried muck stained in blood.

She nods, pointing off into the distance. "There's a tree on a hill over there, just under the formation of rocks where I fell. We'll have to walk across this field. Can you do that?"

I give her a nod in answer.

Soldiers continue to work along vast sections of the battlefield securing the dead, so I offer my arm in a brotherly way in case we encounter a familiar face. She locks her elbow around mine with understanding in her eyes as we slowly make our way over the challenging terrain, the sun having dried the muck into steep crevices.

As we continue, we pass men with camera equipment taking

photographs of different areas of the battlefield. When we near the large boulders, we see a group of four soldiers gathering near a small mound less troubled by uneven ground. One man turns to me, his smile growing wide.

"Walker?" Recognition brightens his eyes. "It is you! Take a gander, boys. It's Sam Walker!"

Relief washes over me as I recognize some men I'd feared dead. "Collins, you're alive!"

"I am.!" He steps forward, patting me hard on the back. "Wounded, but still on my own two feet."

I recognize more men from the 4th Maine. "Baker, Calvert, Roberts! Good to see you all well."

I accept another slap on the back from Roberts. "Walker, we'd lost track of you. Looks like you took one in the leg?"

"I did," I confirm.

"And who is this lovely lady?" Calvert asks.

Though I wish to tell him the truth, I keep to the account Nevaeh and I arranged. "This is my sister, Nevaeh. Nevaeh, these are men from my unit."

"What a beautiful and unusual name," Baker says, tipping his hat to her. "I hope you're not spoken for."

"She is," I answer louder and faster than necessary, and Nevaeh laughs in response. Calmer, I add, "I'm afraid she is engaged to be married soon." I avoid her eyes, knowing my gaze will be less than brotherly at this moment.

"Well, he's a lucky lad," Calvert says, turning to face me. His countenance is much more solemn now that the thrill of seeing one another has dissipated. "We came back to pay our respects to the fallen before going back to the unit. The boys and I were just remembering our formation. You were on our left flank, if I remember correctly."

"I was," I confirm, though I feel a twitch in my injured leg at the thought of the battle. I shift my weight to try to disguise the tremble

"That was a rough advance," Baker chimes in. "I could scarcely reload before another band of Rebs approached."

Ghostly gunfire returns to my mind, and my vision clouds with a dizzying sensation. I take a deep breath to clear it and feel Nevaeh's arm squeeze mine for support.

"I was sorry to hear about Smith," Roberts adds. "What a fine man he was."

My breath catches in my throat for a moment as I remember the way my friend lay dead in the mud. My eyes well up with tears, but I hold them in and find my voice. "Yes, he was a good 'fella."

"May I photograph you men?"

We turn to see a photographer, his eyes eager.

"I suppose so," I answer, seeing nods from the other men.

"Excellent," the man says. "Please stand close together as a group. Give me a moment to set up."

"I'll let you be in the shot together," Nevaeh says, dropping my arm with one last glance into my eyes. I nod to assure her I am well, though I still hear some of the sounds of battle in the back of my mind.

She moves aside while we stand still for the photographer to finish his work. It takes several moments, and the entire time, I'm fighting the urge to turn and run away from this field of death as quickly as possible. Finally, he is finished. "Thank you, gentlemen. Congratulations on your well-earned victory."

We all nod to thank him, and I turn to rejoin Navaeh who takes my arm again.

"Well, boys, we'd better get back to the unit," Calvert says, gesturing to my leg. "I assume you've been discharged, Walker?"

"I have," I say, though I may never receive my official discharge certificate. If I get my way, I'll be gone soon anyway… and in the arms of Nevaeh forever.

We bid one another goodbye, and I wish them well, praying all of them survive this horrendous ordeal.

With fewer people nearby in this section of the field now, I slide my fingers down to take Nevaeh's hand in mine as we watch the men walk away, her warm, soft skin clearing my mind of the gunfire for the moment.

"Are you okay?" she asks softly.

I nod, turning to gaze into her beautiful blue eyes, a salve against the horrors that echo in my memories. "I am, so long as I am by your side. Now, let's fall into the future together."

24

Nevaeh

"It's just over here, isn't it?" Sam asks, pointing to a large boulder just ahead of us.

"Um…." I turn to look at him and get lost in his eyes. I don't want to break our gaze, his soft brown eyes are so full of love. He seems so confident that he'll come with me back to 2025, but I just can't be so sure. "Yes, it was right over there." I recognize the spot because I know where the cave with the spring is located, thanks to Dad drilling it into my head over the years.

He nods and holds my hand as we make the slow journey over, avoiding all the ruts in the ground and saying quick, silent prayers as we pass dead soldiers along the way. My sense of smell has become almost numb by now, but I have a feeling that even after I leave here, phantom scents of the stench will remain burned into my mind.

Sam squeezes my hand reassuringly as we walk closer to the large boulders by the gully where I first woke up, but doubts cloud my every thought.

I'm a physician, a scientist. The whole idea of traveling through time stands in stark contrast to everything I have ever believed about the world, yet here I am. This isn't a dream. My mind couldn't possibly invent the intense sound of the battle that night, the pouring rain that fell on my face as I assessed all the injured men on the field, my exhaustion from all the work I've done repairing wounds for so many days I lost track of it all… or the sweet taste of Sam's kisses, his musky, manly scent, or the fully satisfying feel of his skin against mine.

Whatever means brought me here, I made it through once. I can't help but imagine the impossible odds of not only making it back to 2025 but taking Sam with me as well.

Stopping short of the boulders, I admit my darkest fear. "Sam, I don't think this will work." Saying the words takes a very slight edge off my worries, but they persist.

He wraps his arm around me and interlocks our fingers, squeezing tightly. "It will work," he insists. "You and I both feel that our love was clearly meant to be. It cannot be possible that you return, and I do not follow."

"I want to believe that, but I can't help but have second thoughts."

He turns to me. "Your fear is reasonable and valid, but we must try regardless."

I let out a chuckle despite my pounding heartbeat. "I think that's almost a famous quote, but I don't remember who said it. 'Courage is being afraid and doing it anyway,' or something like that."

A warm smile lights up his eyes. "Then whoever said that is quite wise."

"Is that how you faced things here on the battlefield?" A chill runs up my spine as I think about him standing in a line of soldiers as the Confederates advanced. Few men fought from foxholes in this war, though some had the natural lay of the land to shield them as they fired. But mostly the soldiers, Sam included, stood their ground and walked forward, shooting every time they could reload their rifle while the enemy shot at them with nothing to protect them from the flying bullets.

I quickly set those thoughts aside when I notice his smile fade. I shouldn't have said anything to trigger his PTSD, not right now. I can't even imagine how much pain he's in, standing in the actual spot where it all happened.

But his expression softens as he squeezes my hand. "I used my love of country," he explains. "It's what caused me to enlist, and it's why I could stand on the line to fight back against those who would rip this nation in two."

I nod softly, knowing the way he holds fast to his convictions is just one of the things I love about him.

"And now," he continues, "it is so much easier to use my love for you to believe we will come through this together. I feel our love so much stronger in my heart than even my love for this great nation."

Tears well up in my eyes as I look into his for a moment before I find my words. "I'll try to do that," I say softly. "It's just so hard not to think about the worst-case scenario."

"Then I'll attempt to take your mind off it," he says. His expression molds into a smirk as he continues. "Nevaeh, when we reach the rock before you jump, I will kiss you with all the love I have. And when we reach the other side, I will kiss you again and never stop."

I giggle despite my worries. "Deal. Okay, I guess we'd better keep going."

We continue trudging along toward the spot where I fell, but it's slower going now since the ruts in the mud are deeper here from all the soldiers trampling it on battle day. I notice Sam's limp is more pronounced the further we go.

"Is your leg all right?"

He nods firmly. "I can continue. We should get there as soon as we can."

I feel a little sense of relief knowing he'll have modern treatment for his healing wound in 2025, with physical therapy to help him recover his range of motion—if he makes it through.

"I feel like I was supposed to do something in this time," I admit as we get closer to the rocks. "I don't know if I even did it. What if I can't leave because it isn't done?"

"You've done so much here, Nevaeh," he assures me. "Just your care for me alone is something I would have done without had you not appeared. Perhaps, saving my life is the task you were meant to do."

"Maybe," I agree. "I did see your picture in the visitor's center. It was like you were gazing right at me. Maybe we're meant to be together."

"I fully believe we are."

His tone is firm and confident, and I wish I felt the same conviction. I inhale, trying to take a deep breath to calm my racing heart, forgetting the stench for a moment until it's burning my nostrils. Of course, it's no use, so I go back to my shallow breathing.

"I don't know," I say finally, shaking my head. "I hope that's it."

"Providing me with assistance is just one small part of what you've accomplished here,," he continues. "You saved many lives. Perhaps your task was to help the wounded at Gettysburg. You are a compassionate doctor, after all. What better person to send than you?"

My shoulders rise in an exaggerated shrug. "I'm not sure I did much at all."

"Nevaeh, you spent many days and nights healing the wounded," he says. "How many hundreds, or perhaps even thousands, of men did you treat?"

"I have no idea. It would've been impossible to keep count."

"Precisely." He pulls me closer as we step around another rut. "You explained before that you had to be careful not to change the future. Perhaps there was a man among the many there who needed to live for the future of the country, one who could not be treated properly by the care available in this time."

"I guess that's possible."

"It's possible that man was me." I hitch a breath at his words and turn to him as he continues. "Nevaeh, I can never express how grateful I am that you saved me."

"You might have lived anyway," I insist.

He shakes his head. "I strongly believe I would have left this world had you not been here to help me. Your love and your expert medical treatment saved my life."

"I don't know—"

"Nevaeh, have you ever considered that our children might be the ones who will make all the difference in the world?"

Once again, his insight has me shaking, and I don't know what to say.

"We had better move forward," he adds. "I believe we are near the cave."

"Oh." I turn to face the rocks I'd climbed what seems like ages ago —in the future. They seem to be waiting for us, unchanged from where they'd been when Dad tried to take my picture. "Yes, that's the spot."

It takes some doing to climb up the rocks with his limp, but we make our way up to the top, to the largest boulder in this section of the Devil's Den and stand on its flat surface.

Sam drapes his arm across my shoulders as we stare down to the ground far beneath us. "It's further down than I remember," he says softly, pulling me closer protectively. "But I suppose I was viewing it from a different perspective."

All I can do is nod as all the air seems to freeze in my lungs. I don't want to go, not if there's a chance Sam won't follow me to the other side. *And what if I don't even go home? What if I end up in some other time without either my father or Sam with me? What if I crush my skull this time and die in front of Sam's eyes?*

My heartbeat quickens as panicked thoughts race through my mind.

All this time, I've been thinking I have a purpose here—maybe I'm wrong and all this was just random. Maybe if I jump, I'll just travel forever into different times aimlessly, having only the memory of a few nights with Sam to take me through eternity. *What if I have to live without him?*

My palms begin to sweat as I knead my hands together.

What if our children never come into this world? The ache in my heart at the thought seems bigger than the boulder I'm standing on.

I have to try.

But he's right. It's a long way down. Maybe I got lucky last time. *If*

I damage my brain in the fall and live with permanent brain damage. I might turn mid-air and slam myself into the rocks below, hitting my head in the wrong way and damaging my hippocampus. That might erase any memories of my time with Sam, and possibly my entire life with my parents.

I'll lose all the love I've ever had in my life.

I struggle to catch my breath, but it's quick and shallow, matching the furious pounding of my heart inside my chest.

I have to try this. I'll never see my father again if I don't. I have to believe that Sam will follow me and that in a few years, I'll hold both our children in my arms.

My foot slides toward the edge of the rock, but I pull back as uncertainty fills my mind, flashing pictures of my life before my eyes like a slideshow—a random birthday party as a kid, the last time I saw my mother, my graduation, the first day of my internship, the day I sat in the hospital administrator's office and received my invitation to be a resident, my dad's face when we pulled into the parking lot at Gettysburg… and those few precious nights with Sam.

From the day I admitted my feelings for him, I wanted to stay with him always. He made me feel so safe in his arms, yet there was always that nagging tug of uneasiness, the fear that we'd be ripped apart.

And now, that might just happen… or Sam might be right, and everything will work out perfectly.

I won't know unless I jump.

I start to feel dizzy, vertigo hitting me as my legs sway unsteadily on the hard rock below my feet. I clamp my free hand to the side of my head, trying to keep from spinning out of control.

I have to do this, but it's impossible….

"Hey, you two!"

Inhaling sharply, I spin around at the sound of the unfamiliar voice, feeling Sam's arm release my shoulder. *Are we in trouble for being here?* Visions of the battle come back to me, and for a moment, I fear getting shot at again.

But there's no gunfire, no rebel soldiers, no time for a last kiss… just the realization that my foot is slipping off the smooth rock below me. My body swaying as I try to steady myself, and a scream—*is it my voice or Sam's?*—that echoes across the battlefield.

I stretch my hand toward Sam, but it's too late. Once again, I'm falling.

I see Sam above me, his eyes wide with terror as he extends his arm to me.

But I can't reach him, and before I can tell him I love him, that he is the one man I can't live without, that I need him to follow me or my whole world will fall apart, the bitter darkness envelops me.

25

Someone's voice echoes in my mind, but I don't understand the word until it's called again.

"Nevaeh!"

My name... *but whose voice is that?* My head throbs as I try to remember. In fact, the pain runs all down my back. Groaning, I struggle to open my eyes. Sky-blue orbs greet me, filled with a mix of relief and concern.

"Dad?"

"Nevaeh... oh, my God. I found you!" he says. A tear escapes his eye. "But you're hurt. Don't move. I'll get help..."

"I'm fine," I insist, though the harsh pain throbs in my head. I try to push up to prop onto my elbows, but my dad grabs my shoulders.

"Don't get up," he says firmly. "I think we need to get you to a doctor."

"Dad, I am a doctor." But I don't move. Instead, I try to work through the pain to figure out what happened. *Where am I?*

"Maybe you should get up slowly then," he suggests.

179

I nod and hold onto his arm, pulling myself up and looking around, hitching a breath when I see dead soldiers lying around. *I'm still in the war! Why is Dad here?*

My dad keeps talking quickly, as if he can't stop. "What on earth happened to you? I've been looking for a couple of hours, and here you are, right where you fell. When you first went over, I didn't see you down there. I kept looking everywhere, and when I'd come back here, you weren't here. I'm certain of it. I've been trying to find you, but with the reenactment underway.... Nevaeh, are you okay?"

Memories flood back into my mind. This isn't the war. This is the reenactment, and these soldiers are only pretending to be dead and wounded. My dad is here, and he says I've been gone for a couple of hours. Nothing makes sense right now.

Then it hits me.

I'm in 2025. Without Sam.

My vision blurs the moment I think of him, and I erupt into violent sobs as the tears flow down my cheeks, my heart aching like it's turned into a lump of stone in my chest.

How am I going to live without Sam?

Dad bends down and slips his arm around my shoulders. "It's okay, sweetheart. I know your back hurts. It'll be okay."

I shake my head but can't choke out any words. Visions of Sam's loving brown eyes fill my mind. We didn't even get our last kiss....

"Maybe you need some water," Dad suggests, straightening up. "You stay here, and I'll go get you some. Don't go anywhere, okay?"

I nod through the sobs and watch him walk away, imagining Sam standing on the rock above, holding out his hand hopelessly. "You were so certain it would work," I whisper out loud.

"And I was right, of course."

My breath catches in my throat at the familiar voice, and I turn around, looking up to see Sam, still in his suit with his army jacket over it, standing behind me. My heart pounds as he reaches down to me, and I take his hand.

Sam....

"You're here!" Leaping up, I spin around as if I haven't just fallen from the top of a boulder–again.. "Are you real?"

He nods, chuckling, his eyes welling up with glistening tears. "I'm here. I'm real. God, you look beautiful in every century, Navaeh."

A sound halfway between a scream and a squeal escapes my lips as I throw myself into his arms, squeezing tight and inhaling his musky scent. He pulls back slightly and places a palm on my cheek, stroking it softly before pressing his lips to mine.

He starts off gently, but I can't hold back and deepen the kiss, savoring him, his minty taste intermingling with my salty tears. The feel of his strong hands rubbing up and down my back has me leaning into him. As our kiss lingers, my heart races, excitement and relief warring as my body lights on fire.

Eventually, we separate, well aware now that we're standing in the middle of a reenactment with dozens, if not hundreds, of eyes on us. A shy smile lights my face, but then, I don't think I'll ever stop smiling now that Sam is here beside me.

"I told you I would kiss you when we came through," he says, and we both laugh joyously.

"And you kept your promise well," I tell him. "What happened?"

His shoulders rise as he gives a shrug. "I was horrified when you slipped, but I couldn't catch you. Seeing that you disappeared, I was sure it worked. I simply jumped after you."

I nod, still feeling tears slipping from my eyes, but these are tears of happiness. "I'm so glad you did."

"Nevaeh?"

I inhale at the sound of my dad's voice and turn around, trying to assess whether he saw this kiss, but we are standing between two large boulders, so I don't think he did. "Dad?"

Sam straightens up beside me, dropping my hand as my father comes closer, and I immediately miss his touch.

My father's brow furrows in confusion. "Hello," he says, cautiously. "Who might this be?"

"This is Sam, Sam Walker. He's... I know him from college. He's here for... the reenactment."

"Oh?" Dad's countenance brightens. "Are you in town for a while?"

"For... a while," I answer on Sam's behalf. It's the understatement of the year. He'll be here forever.

Dad hands me the water bottle he'd found me and extends his hand. "Sam, good to meet you."

"The pleasure is all mine, Mr. Little," Sam says with a firm shake.

"Oh, please," Dad complains. "Mr. Little sounds too formal. Call me Martin."

"Martin it is, then." Sam smiles wide while I try to figure out what to say next.

"You're a Civil War buff?" My dad's eyes are hopeful, and I can barely hold back a chuckle.

"I have some knowledge of it, yes," Sam answers.

I have to look away to keep from laughing out loud. I'll say he knows about it... firsthand. And now, so do I. I can't wait to have another moment alone with Sam so we can talk about everything.

"Well, you and I have a lot to discuss then, Sam." Dad chuckles. "It's a shame we didn't run into you earlier. Anyway, Nevaeh just took quite a fall." His fatherly gaze turns my way. "Maybe we'd better head inside the visitor's center for a few minutes so you can cool off before the rest of the reenactment. Are you sure you're okay?"

"I'm fine, Dad, but I would like to go inside for a few minutes." It's quiet now, so I'm guessing the reenactors have moved on to another part of the expansive battlefield. But I'm not sure how Sam will react once the fake bullets fly again.

My dad nods. "Let's get inside then. Sam, I hope you'll join us."

"I would love to." Sam offers his arm as he always does, and I slide my hand around his elbow, his warmth settling into me. I catch my dad's eyes as they flit toward Sam's gesture, and his smile tells me he approves. It's too formal for 2025 yet appropriate for 1863, so I know he thinks Sam is just getting into the spirit of the reenactment, especially since he's dressed for it–and so am I, though this is not the gown I had on before. I wonder if Dad will notice.

We start toward the path we'd been walking along before Dad

decided he wanted a photo of me at Devil's Den, and Sam leans into me every other step.

"You're limping, Sam," my dad says. "Are you injured?"

I open my mouth to answer, but Sam speaks first. "Yes, I twisted my ankle during the reenactment earlier. Tore a hole in my Union uniform pants and had to borrow these from a friend."

I'm impressed at how quickly Sam has come up with the fib. I see the twinkle of mischief in his eyes and realize we'd better get used to lying–unfortunately.

"Well, I suppose that's the hazard in reenacting such a dangerous event. At least no one was really shooting at you." Dad laughs and pats Sam on the shoulder as he passes us.

With Dad in front of us, I catch Sam's eye–and he winks at me. I hide a smile. Under less of a joyous situation, Dad's comment might've been difficult for Sam to hear, but we're too happy right now to think about all the horrible events we've both been through.

We make it a few more paces before my dad turns around and looks at me with a furrowed brow. Sam and I stop, and my heart thumps for a moment as I wonder what story I'll need to tell him next. I don't want to lie to my dad at all, but everything that just happened to us is crazy. Maybe someday I'll explain it, but it's way too soon.

"Is something wrong, Dad?"

"Wasn't your dress purple?"

I hitch a breath, realizing I'm still in the blue gown the nurse had given me a few days ago. "Um… no. I told you I found a blue one."

He holds my gaze for a while, his eyes narrowed. We'd been in the car together for almost three hours if we count rest stops, so there's no way he wouldn't have noticed my dress color. Not to mention, he took pictures…

But finally, he just says, "Hmm." We'll sort that out later. Dad turns around, continuing toward the visitor's center. It's a longer walk than before because we can't drive over, thanks to the reenactment going on, but it's nice to have a moment to breathe and try to calm my raging heart.

· · ·

We reach the visitor's center, and he opens the door and holds it for both of us as we pass through. "Maybe you should have a seat." He gestures toward a nearby bench. "I need to use the restroom."

Sam nods as my dad walks away, and I lead him over to the bench. A modern restroom sounds like heaven right now, but I don't want to leave my 1863-era boyfriend sitting alone when he's brand new to 2025. He's already gazing around as if in a daze. This has to be a lot for him to handle. "Are you all right?"

He turns to me with a warm smile that meets his brown eyes. "I am much more than all right, Nevaeh."

I want to hold his hand but know it will look awkward when my dad gets back. "That was a great story you came up with earlier. We'll just have to follow one another's lead with whatever we tell my dad."

"Most certainly," he assures me. A few moments later, Dad is back.

"Dad," I tell him as he sits by me. "Sam mentioned that he's visiting Pennsylvania after this, but he hasn't booked a hotel yet."

"You don't need a hotel," Dad says without hesitation. "We have a spare room in the house. Nevaeh will be working, of course, but with her apartment in Philly not quite ready yet, we can all spend some time together."

"I would enjoy that," Sam says. "I hope it's not an imposition."

"Of course not." Dad shakes his head. "When Nevaeh is at work, I can show you some of my Civil War memorabilia."

I hitch a breath for a moment, wondering if any of that will trigger Sam's PTSD.

But Sam answers without hesitation. "That would be wonderful."

"Well, it's settled then." Dad slaps his hands on his knees and stands. "I'd like to go grab a seat for the Pickett's Charge reenactment. Should be starting soon, and it'll take a while to get over there."

Sam and I get up, but I'm worried that it's too soon for him to watch the battle unfold. He can't exactly sit through the reenactment right now with all the gunfire. "Um... Dad? Would it bother you if

Sam and I took a break? You can enjoy the reenactment, but we'd like to catch up a bit."

Dad tilts his head, his brows knitted together, but after a while he says, "Sure. You should be able to take the car now. The reenactors have moved on from where we park." He digs into his pocket and hands me the keys. "Just don't forget to pick me up before you drive back home."

I give him a chuckle. "Of course not. Enjoy the reenactment. I'm sorry you missed the first part looking for me."

"I'm just glad you're all right, sweetheart." He turns to Sam and extends his hand. "Sam, good to meet you. I'll see you later."

"I'm looking forward to it," Sam says kindly.

As my dad walks off, I take Sam's hand and squeeze it tightly. I have no idea how I'm going to take this man from 1863 and make it so he can survive in 2025, but I'll definitely do whatever I can to help him. All that matters right now is that he's here, and we're together.

I lead him out to the parking lot, and his eyes are wide with amazement the whole time. "It's just like the picture with the strange wagons."

It takes me a moment, but I remember he's talking about the picture of the hospital parking lot. "Yes, it's just like that. Here's my dad's car."

I open the passenger door for him, and he slides in, touching the dashboard for a moment before pulling his hand back quickly. "It'll be okay," I assure him. "I'm just going to go around and sit there."

Hurrying around the car, I get into the driver's seat and show him how to buckle his seatbelt. When I push the button to start the car, he jumps a little.

"It's just the motor," I explain softly. "Do you trust me?"

"Nevaeh, my love, of course I do," he says, his brown eyes smiling despite his nervousness. "I trust you with my life."

I smile wide and put the car into reverse. We back out of the parking lot and then drive off into our future together.

EPILOGUE

Nᴇᴠᴀᴇʜ

"Wᴇ ᴍɪssᴇᴅ ᴍᴏsᴛ ᴏғ ᴛʜᴇ ᴀᴄᴛɪᴏɴ ᴀᴛ ᴛʜᴇ Pᴇᴀᴄʜ Oʀᴄʜᴀʀᴅ, ᴛʜᴇ Wheatfield, and Rose Farm last time, so I'd like to be sure we get there early." My father skims through his reenactment brochures excitedly. "Sam, I'm glad you didn't give away that jacket. It sure looks authentic."

"Thank you," Sam says politely from the back seat, and I can't help but let out a chuckle as his brows raise in the rearview mirror. Ever the gentleman, he'd insisted that my father ride up front.

I turn back to the road, but my heart flutters when the diamond on my ring catches a ray of bright summer sunshine as I hold the steering wheel. It's been a year since I fell through time and met the man of my dreams, a year full of memorable moments like that evening three months ago at the arboretum. I'll never forget the loving look in his eyes when Sam got down on one knee with a backdrop of cherry trees in full bloom and slid this ring on my finger. Of course, my dad was there snapping pictures, so I'll have plenty of tangible memories to show our future kids.

I just can't wait.

"We're here," I announce as I turn into the Gettysburg National Military Park. I catch Sam's eye again in the rearview mirror, and he gives me an approving nod to show he's all right. His PTSD treatment is going well, but a year isn't nearly enough time to heal the pain of being in the middle of such a gruesome, bloody war. Especially since he can't be completely honest with his therapist. They discuss the war he fought in–but no one knows it was the Civil War but the two of us.

"I'm supposed to meet the guys in the visitor's center," Dad says impatiently. "Just park in the nearest spot. I don't want to be late."

"Dad, I know." I pull into the first spot I find that's relatively near the visitor's center. "That's why we left so early."

"I'll see you inside!" Dad steps out and runs off to meet some friends almost before I put the car in park.

"He's quite enthusiastic," Sam says with a chuckle.

"That he is." I give him a smile in the mirror. "I'm glad he met that group of guys last time, though. At least he has someone else to talk to about the Civil War other than pestering you."

"I enjoy my discussions with your father," he insists.

"Yes, but I don't want all those memories to keep haunting you."

"We never lose our memories or the pain they cause," he says. "But I am beginning to learn how to grow around that pain."

"I know you are." I take a sip of water as he gets out of the car and comes around. The one thing that hasn't changed is his chivalry, and even with my successful career as an oncologist, I still enjoy the gentlemanly things he does for me.

With the door open, his strong hand grasps mine, and I step out into the warm afternoon sun. The air is fresh, and birds sing cheerfully in the bright green trees. Yet, I still remember the horrific stench of the place that lived in my nostrils for months after coming home.

I press my lips to Sam's softly, and I gaze into his eyes, but see no fear there. "I am well," he assures me. "This place is quite different from the days that I fought here."

"I know, but it's still the same place."

"I have my tools to use, and they are serving me well." His therapist is a wonderful man who's a veteran himself, and he's provided him with techniques to use whenever he is in a triggering situation.

"Good."

As we walk toward the visitor's center, he looks down at my ring on the hand he's holding. "I forgot to tell you that Richard has agreed to be my best man."

"Oh, that's great. He's such a nice guy."

"As are my other coworkers." Sam has made a lot of friends at his new job as a security officer at the hospital over the past few months. Unfortunately, there was no legal way to get him settled in 2025, so we did what we needed to do; there wasn't any other way to get a birth certificate, driver's license, and a college diploma for a man from 1863.

"They are all nice guys," I agree. "And I'm glad you have the option to go part time if you want once we have a family." My heart warms at the thought of seeing our little Ed and Agatha one day soon. We haven't tried for a baby yet because Sam wants to be married first, but with the ceremony just five months away, I've been secretly scrolling through to pick out baby items between patients.

"I may want to stay home with the children altogether while I attend classes to become a therapist," he says thoughtfully. "I haven't decided yet. In the meantime, I truly love the security job."

"You're going to help so many soldiers with PTSD." I stop walking and smile at him with pride.

"I just want to do my part," he says. "I didn't finish the war, but I can help those who have served recently."

"You're so kind and caring." He smiles, and we start walking again, his warm hand in mine. "You know anything you decide to do is fine by me. I make plenty of money, even with the new mortgage payments."

"I know," he says. "I am glad we purchased the home. I enjoyed living in the apartment for a few months, but I'm pleased we were able to buy a house with a big yard for the kids to play in someday."

"One look at that place, and I knew it was for us." I lean into his arm as we continue walking. "I love that it was built in 1850." It's almost as old as he is.

"As do I." When we reach the top of the visitor center stairs, he pauses and faces me for a moment. "I cannot wait to see you walk down the aisle, Nevaeh."

I feel like squealing with excitement at the thought, but there are too many people around, so I manage to stay dignified. "I'd do it tomorrow if we could, but my aunt really wants to come, and she can't get here until the holidays." It'll be a small ceremony, but I want as many family members as possible to be there.

"A Christmas wedding will be quite lovely."

"It will, but it feels like a long wait." Ever since he introduced us as Mr. and Mrs. Walker in the hotel in the past, I've been longing for it to be a reality.

"We have the rest of our lives together," he says softly, squeezing my hand before opening the door.

I don't have time to say anything more before my father sprints over to us. "What took you two so long? The guys have already left to go out to the battlefield. Don't worry, they're saving us seats."

A year ago, I would have wanted to roll my eyes at him, but since I thought I might've lost him forever, his enthusiasm is a source of delight. The whole time I was gone, I wondered if jumping back through time was possible and whether I'd ever see him again. Priorities change when we think we may have lost someone. "You didn't need to wait. We would have caught up with you."

My words almost catch in my throat as Sam's hand tightens around mine, and I see him looking around, his eyes wide. I should have been watching his reaction closer. It's a lot to take in, even for me, all the exhibits about soldiers who were wounded, all the photos of the battlefield with dead soldiers… I hope he's all right. But then I see his chest rise and fall with the slow, purposeful breaths his therapist has suggested, and his eyes soften.

I follow Sam's gaze across the visitor's center, and then we're slowly moving in that direction. I can't help but pause in front of the picture of Sam, his eyes staring straight into the camera like I remember them from before I fell into 1863. But this time, it's different. The composition is different, and it's clear that the original photo was taken before the battle began, probably by a different photographer. In this one, the battle is over, and instead of fear, I see only relief on the faces of the subjects

But something else is different, too. I take a step forward and squint at the photo. There's a woman in the background, standing to the side of the soldiers.

It's me.

Sam and I exchange a glance, and a light chuckle escapes both our lips. This attracts my dad's attention, and he turns around, his brow furrowed. "What's so funny?"

"Nothing, Dad." I hitch a breath when he turns to the picture and try to talk fast to stop him. "Um, we're just anxious to get out and see the reenactment. We'd better get going." I put a hand on his shoulder to push him along, but he just stands firm, his eyes on the photo of Sam.

"Well, would you look at that?"

"Um, what?" I try to push him again, but it's no use. His eyes are locked on the photo.

"That woman looks like you." He looks at me then back at the photo a few times. "She looks a lot like you, actually."

I lift my shoulders in an exaggerated shrug, still trying to move him away from it. At least he hasn't realized how much the man in the photo looks like Sam.

It's too late to move him along. "You know, I've looked at this photo at least a dozen times before and never once noticed the woman there."

"Hmm." I regret making any sound because my dad turns, and his narrowed eyes meet mine, his mouth pressed together to one side.

The guilt from keeping him in the dark has felt like a permanent rock in my belly ever since I came back. I still haven't told him what happened, though Sam has asked that we do so before the wedding. I suppose we should, though the look he's giving me now tells me he already suspects something is up.

He says nothing else and turns to head outside where golf carts are transporting spectators out to the reenactment area, something new this year. Sam and I sit in the back seats while Dad chats with the driver, his cheerfulness having returned. Hopefully, he's decided that I'll tell him when I'm ready. Maybe we can even do it on the ride home, provided I'm the one driving again.

"Do you have your noise-canceling earbuds?" I ask Sam. He'll still be able to hear the fake gunshots and cannon fire, but it should muffle them a bit. I know from experience that the reenactment sounds are nothing compared to the overwhelming cacophony he experienced during the real battle.

He pulls out the case to show me. "Yes, don't worry."

"I always worry," I whisper back.

He chuckles lightly and gives me a warm smile, taking my hand in his. Once again, my ring glistens in the sun. "Nevaeh, my love, I can do anything with you by my side."

I have to blink a few times to hold back the tears welling in my eyes, but our tender moment is interrupted by my dad's sudden shouting.

"Oh, there's Devil's Den, the same place we stopped last year," he says loudly. "How about we stop here, and the two of you climb up so I can take a picture?"

"No!" We both yell it at the same time, and I catch Sam's gaze again, his brown eyes glistening with laughter. I can't help but chuckle… until he leans over and steals a kiss.

As his lips meet mine, I close my eyes, savoring his sweet taste and inhaling his scent, a mix of musk and citrus and patchouli, a scent we'd recently found that was close to his 1863 cologne, though not exactly the same. He'll always smell like Sam to me..

Images of everything that's happened to us flash through my mind as I deepen the kiss—that moment I'd burst into the room in the farmhouse to stop them from cutting off his leg, the many nights I sat beside him in the hospital, the joy I felt when I turned around and saw him standing behind me in 2025, and that beautiful evening under the cherry trees where he asked me to be his wife... all the moments that represent how our love transcends time.

Some women fall in love with the guy next door. I had to go back over a hundred and sixty years to find the man of my dreams.

And I'm never letting him go.

THE END

Thank you for reading! *Back to Bunker Hill* will be out soon!

Celestial Springs

(psychological thriller/literary fiction/women's fiction)

<u>Beneath the Inconstant Moon</u>

<u>The First Mrs. Edwards</u>

<u>Leaving Ginny</u>

The Motherhood

(dystopian romance)

<u>Rain's Rebellion</u>

<u>Rain's Run</u>

<u>Rain's Return</u>

Ashes and Rose Petals

(contemporary romance/retelling of Romeo and Juliet and Cinderella)

<u>Girl in the Attic</u>

<u>Girl From the Tomb</u>

<u>Girl On the Beach</u>

Nashville Country Dreams

(contemporary romance)

<u>Meant to Marry Me</u>

<u>Lead Me Home</u>

<u>You Are the Reason</u>

Forever Love series

(clean romance/historical)

<u>Cordia's Will: A Civil War Story of Love and Loss</u>

<u>Cordia's Hope: A Story of Love on the Frontier</u>

The Clandestine Saga series

(paranormal romance)

<u>Transformation</u>

<u>Resurrection</u>

<u>Repercussion</u>

<u>Absolution</u>

<u>Illumination</u>

<u>Destruction</u>

<u>Annihilation</u>

<u>Obliteration</u>

<u>Termination</u>

A Vampire Hunter's Tale (based on The Clandestine Saga)

(paranormal/alternate history)

<u>Aaron</u>

<u>Jamie</u>

<u>Elliott</u>

<u>Christian</u>

The Chronicles of Cassidy (based on The Clandestine Saga)

(young adult paranormal)

<u>So You Think Your Sister's a Vampire Hunter?</u>

<u>Who Wants to Be a Vampire Hunter?</u>

<u>How Not to Be a Vampire Hunter</u>

<u>My Life As a Teenage Vampire Hunter</u>

<u>Vampire Hunting Isn't for Morons</u>

<u>Vampires Bite and Other Life Lessons</u>

<u>Gone Guardian</u>

<u>Death Does Not Become Her</u>

Blood of the Vampire Hunter (based on The Clandestine Saga)

(paranormal romance)

<u>Night Slayer</u>

Shadow Stalker

Queen Catcher

Mother Hunter

Father Finder

Ghosts of Southampton series

(historical romance)

Prelude

Titanic

Residuum

Lusitania

Heartwarming Holidays Sweet Romance series

(Christian/clean romance)

Melody's Christmas

Christmas Cocoa

Winter Woods

Waiting On Love

Shamrock Hearts

A Blossoming Spring Romance

Firecracker!

Falling in Love

Thankful for You

Melody's Christmas Wedding

The New Year's Date

Charles Town Brides (based on Heartwarming Holidays Sweet Romance)

(Christian/clean romance)

From This Moment

Can't Help Falling in Love

<u>It's Your Love</u>

<u>When You Say Nothing At All</u>

<u>My Girl</u>

<u>Unchained Melody</u>

<u>I Only Have Eyes For You</u>

<u>At Last</u>

<u>The Very Thought of You</u>

Reaper's Hollow

(paranormal/urban fantasy)

<u>Ruin's Lot</u>

<u>Ruin's Promise</u>

<u>Ruin's Legacy</u>

When Kings Collide

(steamy historical romance)

<u>Princess of Silence</u>

<u>Princess of Hearts</u>

Collections

<u>Ghosts of Southampton Books 0-2</u>

<u>Reaper's Hollow Books 1-3</u>

<u>The Clandestine Saga Books 1-3</u>

<u>The Chronicles of Cassidy Books 1-4</u>

<u>Celestial Springs Collection</u>

<u>Heartwarming Holidays Sweet Romance Books 1-3</u>

<u>Heartwarming Holidays Sweet Romance Books 4-7</u>

Websites: https://books2read.com/ap/xX7ZD8/ID-Johnson

For updates, visit www.authoridjohnson.blogspot.com

Follow on Twitter @authoridjohnson

Find me on Facebook at www.facebook.com/IDJohnsonAuthor

Instagram: @authoridjohnson

Follow me on Bookbub: https://www.bookbub.com/authors/id-johnson